TIME AND AGAIN

Evelyn Hood

LITTLE, BROWN AND COMPANY

A *Little, Brown* Book

First published in Great Britain in 1998
by Little, Brown and Company

Copyright © 1998 Evelyn Hood

The moral right of the author has been asserted.

A CIP catalogue record for this book
is available from the British Library.

ISBN 0 316 87921 5

Typeset in Times by
Palimpsest Book Production Limited,
Polmont, Stirlingshire
Printed and bound in Great Britain by
Creative Print and Design Wales, Ebbw Vale

Little, Brown and Company (UK)
Brettenham House
Lancaster Place
London WC2E 7EN

This book is dedicated to the Scar Club – Linda, Sophie, Margaret and Myrtle – who proved that hysterectomies can be enjoyable

Acknowledgements

My thanks to Esther McIlvenny, May Shovlin, Jim Devenay, Margaret Christie, Morag and Bob McLaughlin, Bobby Ross and Catherine O'Neill for their generous assistance with research on the history of Port Glasgow, Gourock Ropeworks and ship carvers.

I am also indebted to Mrs Lesley Couperwhite of the James Watt Library in Greenock, Eddie Monaghan and the staff of Rothesay Library, and the Scottish Maritime Museum at Irvine – home of the puffer *Spartan*.

And finally, but certainly not least, my thanks to Jenny and Jim Chaplin for their friendship and their warm hospitality during research trips to the beautiful island of Bute.

1

Lawrence Weir surged impatiently into his brother's house as though he owned it, divesting himself speedily of his bowler hat and handing it and his walking-stick to Morag.

'Good afternoon, Morag.'

'Good afternoon, Uncle Lawrence.' She had to edge round him in order to reach the coat-stand, which was right behind him, but it would never have occurred to him to hang up his own hat. He didn't look at her or move out of her way, too busy concentrating, as usual, on pulling his silver watch from his waistcoat pocket and consulting it with a frown to see how much time he could afford to spend in the house.

Since a weakening heart had forced his brother Sander to take to his bed, Lawrence had fallen into the habit of calling every Saturday and Sunday and on three weekdays during his mid-day break from the large grocer's shop where he had started years before as errand boy, and had worked his way up towards the exalted position of under-manager by way of the bacon counter.

The scented hair-oil he favoured wafted towards Morag from the hat. It was lined with silk, for Lawrence Weir set great store by appearances and always dressed smartly.

1

'So . . . how is the invalid today?' he asked.

'Much the same. The doctor says . . .' she began, but Lawrence was already striding up the handsome staircase on his way to Sander's room. As he reached the half-landing and moved out of sight, Morag hung his hat on a hook and put his stick into the stand with slightly more force than was needed, made a face at herself in the mirror and went to the kitchen to make tea.

Lawrence was pacing the bedroom when she took in the tea-tray. He moved restlessly from the large bed to the window, talking volubly, but falling silent as soon as she entered and moving to the window to stand with his back to the room, staring down at the River Clyde. Morag bit her lip as she looked at the tray lying on a small table by the bed and saw that the light lunch she had so carefully pre-pared had scarcely been touched. She opened her mouth to protest, but Sander Weir, propped against a mound of snowy pillows, raised a hand slightly, and Morag folded her lips over the forbidden words and replaced the tray with the one she had just brought up.

'Thank you, my dear,' Sander said. As she went out and closed the door, she heard Lawrence burst into speech again, as though he had been bottling up the words in her presence.

Back in the scullery, a small stone-floored room built on to the back of the house for use as a laundry room, she finished hauling wet clothes from the boiler and wrung them out by hand in the sink before putting them through the huge, unwieldy mangle, which squeezed the last possible drop of water from them. Then she folded them into a basket and carried them out to the back garden.

Lilybank Road had been built on a bluff above the Clyde shoreline, and the back gardens on this side of the road all sloped downwards. Below, hidden by the hedges which marked the garden boundaries, lay the railway line, and below that, on the other side of the shore road that led to the neighbouring town of Greenock, were the shipyards which fringed the river. Although the continuous clang and rattle of the yards could be heard throughout the town, the Lilybank houses and gardens were high enough to overlook them, except for the high cranes which made their own erratic pattern against the background of the river.

March winds had been blowing hard all through the previous week, but today there was only a breeze, just strong enough to make the sheets already hanging on the clothes-line stir restlessly most of the time, but tossing and stretching now and again like sails readying themselves to take a ship across the seas to foreign lands. The air was soft with the promise of spring, and crocuses and daffodils had brightened the dreary winter garden. Morag pegged her own and Sander's underclothes on to the line, automatically choosing an area behind the sheets so that nobody could see them. Not that anyone would, for their neighbours in this row of large houses were folk like themselves, intent always upon keeping their own counsel and minding their own business; certainly not the type to ogle other people's nether garments on a washing line. But Georgina Weir had instilled the niceties of life into Morag from the beginning, and habits learned in childhood were difficult to break.

When the basket was empty she picked it up and then paused, resting it against her hip as she took in the panorama spread before her. As it passed Port Glasgow,

3

the River Clyde, opening out into a firth on its way to the sea, was a broad stretch of water filled at almost any hour of the day with the bustle of cargo ships, passenger steamers, colliers and tug-boats as well as the small steam puffers which carried all manner of goods to the many islands studded throughout the Firth and further north, to the islands and coastal towns of the West of Scotland.

A passenger-carrying paddle steamer thrashing its way down-river from Glasgow slid past a cargo ship, low in the water, heading in the opposite direction to off-load at a Glasgow port. There were some puffers beetling along, and in the distance – tacking near to the residential town of Helensburgh on the opposite bank – she could see the snowy sails of two yachts.

Lawrence Weir called to her from the back door, and reluctantly she made her way back to the house. He was in the hall when she arrived, fussily consulting his watch while waiting for her to hand him his hat and stick.

'Leaving so soon, Uncle Lawrence?'

'Some of us,' he told her crisply, studying himself in the mirror and brushing an imaginary piece of fluff from his high, rounded white shirt-collar, 'have work to do. Sander had a mind to sit by the window, so I helped him into his chair before I left him. You're not going to the teashop today?'

'I'm due to start in an hour.'

'Your Aunt Margaret tells me that she called in there for a cup of tea the other day while she was shopping in Gourock,' he remarked, using the mirror to check that his hat had been set at its usual dandified angle. 'She was not impressed by the cashier on duty. Slow with the change, she said, *and* tried to keep back a halfpence for herself.'

4

'I'm sure she just made a mistake counting out the money.'

'Hmmm,' said Lawrence darkly, and departed.

'Fetch my telescope,' Sander ordered as soon as Morag went into the bedroom where he now sat in his large-wheeled bath-chair by the window. When his wife was alive they had shared one of the two large bedrooms at the front of the house, but almost immediately on being widowed Sander had moved into a back room where he had a view of the river.

'You scarcely ate a bite of your lunch,' Morag accused, doing as she was told.

'I wasn't hungry. I'll take it for my dinner tonight.'

'It'll not heat up again.'

He stared intently through the handsome old tele-scope at the river below. 'I thought so . . . there's the *Ailsa Craig* on her way up-river. Low in the water, too, so she's carrying a full cargo.' Pleased, he laid down the telescope as Morag came to look over his shoulder at the puffer, one of the five owned by Weir Shipping. 'If it won't heat up again, I'll have it cold.'

'You will not. If you didn't have the appetite to eat it hot, you'll never manage it cold,' she scolded, and Sander, who hated waste, especially at his own expense, looked vexed.

'You'd have been best not to give me anything at all, since I wasn't hungry anyway.'

'I'm supposed to be tempting your appetite. The doctor said—'

'Ach, doctors – what do they know? How can a man have an appetite when he's stuck indoors all day and every day with never a bit of exercise or a lungful of fresh air?'

'The weather's improving. By next week we'll mebbe be able to get you out into the back garden.'

He gave a gusty sigh. 'Aye – sittin' in a chair. God, Morag, I wish I could get out on to the water again!'

'It's been a good while since you were on the boats.' She tidied the empty bed with deft sweeps of her hands, and plumped up the pillows.

'I know, thanks to this!' Resentfully, he thumped his large fist on the chair just where the blanket in his lap lay flat instead of mounding over his left leg. 'That damned war has a lot to answer for!' Even though he had been housebound all winter, Sander's cheeriness and sense of humour had been to the fore. He very rarely complained about the loss of the limb during service in the Great War, which had put an end to his work as mate of one of the Clyde puffers. This sudden surge of bitterness was an indication as to just how low he felt.

'Would you like me to strap the leg on for you?' It was in the wardrobe, a thing of metal and cloth and leather straps which had terrified her the first time she had come across it when jumping into the wardrobe as a child to hide away from her mother.

'No point, since I can't walk about on it.' The fist which had thumped the emptiness beneath the blanket clenched until the knuckles whitened, and he sighed. Sander Weir was quite unlike his younger brother Lawrence; broad-shouldered instead of slim, weather-beaten instead of pale-skinned, for he had always been an active man with a strong dislike of being indoors. On his feet he stood a good head taller than Lawrence and, even now, his features drawn after an illness which had confined him to the house for the past three months, he was by far the better-looking of the brothers, with his head of thick grey hair and brown eyes crinkled at the corners with laughter-lines.

'You'll be walking again come the summer,' Morag reassured him now.

'Our Lawrence doesnae think so. He's been on at me those past few weeks to let him take control of the business . . . so's I don't have to worry about anything, he says.' His usual humour swept back as he gave a snort of laughter. 'I'd be more worried than ever, with a grocer tryin' to run my shipping business.'

'He's not a grocer now, he's an under-manager. And anyway, there's no need for anyone to take over,' Morag said firmly, furious with Lawrence. Pessimism was the last thing Sander needed . . . did his brother not realise that? 'You're managing fine, even though you can't be down at the harbour.'

She returned to join him at the window, leaning forward to look down at the busy river below. 'Mr Laird'll be along tonight with the books.'

'Aye, right enough.' Sander brightened at the thought of his clerk's visit. Going over the books with the man helped him to feel that he was still involved in the small shipping company he owned. 'I'll tell you what, lass, you put the kettle on and make another cup of tea. I couldn't enjoy the last one for listening to Lawrence fussing on about this and that. The man puts a sour taste in my mouth.' He shook his head. 'Being the under-manager of a grocer's shop seems an awful hard responsibility for him.'

'Uncle Lawrence takes his work seriously.'

'He does that. Even when he was on the bacon counter he took his work seriously. I mind Georgina saying that it fair made her skin itch, watching Lawrence work out the exact thickness of a slice of ham.' He paused, then said thoughtfully, 'He's ambitious too. He and that wife of his have high expectations.'

'Have they?' Morag collected the tray and made for

the door. She never quite knew what Sander really thought of his younger brother, and was always reluctant to pass any comment about Lawrence in case she said the wrong thing.

When she returned with fresh tea, it was to find that his mind was still on his brother. 'It's strange the way things have worked out,' he said as she set the tea-things out on a small table within his reach and poured the first cup for him. 'When the two of us were lads I asked for nothing else but to work on the puffers when I grew up, but Lawrence wanted much more – money, and a fine house, and to be important in other folks' eyes. I always thought that our mother, rest her soul, encouraged him too much in that direction. And how did it turn out? I end up with everything Lawrence would have wanted for himself, while he had to claw his way up to become an under-manager in a grocer's shop. It's soured him. He's resented me for it ever since – especially where Georgina was concerned.'

'Mother?' It made her uncomfortable to hear him criticise his younger brother; recently, following Lawrence's visits, he had been doing it more often, and she always tried to change the subject. But on this occasion her curiosity was aroused.

'He wanted her for himself – and why wouldn't he, since she was the bonniest lass in the area, and her father owned a fine stone quarry and some handsome property to boot? Marriage to Georgina would have suited Lawrence very nicely. But it was me she chose, for all that my brother looked more of a gentleman. It was the only time I ever won over Lawrence, and what a grand prize I got!' For a moment his eyes misted at the thought of his beloved wife, dead now for several years. Then he cleared his throat and blinked rapidly.

'Lawrence still resents me for that, though when he

8

comes fawning round me he thinks I'm too stupid to remember the past, or the things he said to me when he first heard that Georgina and I were to wed.' He glanced up at her from under bushy grey brows, his deep-set brown eyes suddenly alight with mischief.

She knew that look well; in her childhood it had usually meant that he was about to draw her into some ploy which would end with Georgina railing at the two of them and ordering her husband to grow up, for goodness' sake, and stop setting a bad example to the child. She waited to find out what torment he was planning for his unfortunate brother, but he merely said, 'It's strange how daft folk always seem to think that it's others that are daft, not them at all.'

'Uncle Lawrence means no harm,' Morag said uncomfortably. Then, aware of the way time was whirling past, 'Now . . . there's an exercise book and a pencil and your newspaper to hand. Are you sure you'll be all right until I get back from the teashop?'

'Of course I will,' he said with some surprise, as though he and not she had been the one to organise his comfort.

There was just enough time to change into the white blouse and black knitted skirt and jacket she wore while on duty at the teashop. These days, she thought as she ran a comb through her hair and smoothed the blouse collar into place, she seemed to do nothing but rush. She had to run down the road, and spent the tram journey to Gourock taking deep breaths and thinking calming thoughts. Miss Lamont, the teashop owner, liked her staff to appear serene and unflustered at all times.

Gourock was the last of the three towns snuggled shoulder to shoulder along that section of the Clyde

9

shoreline. While Port Glasgow and Greenock were industrial towns, Gourock was residential, catering for those who had made their money and wanted to settle in comfort on a picturesque part of the Clyde shoreline. It also catered for the river travellers, having a large railway station directly linked to the pier where passenger steamers could be found, particularly at weekends and during the summer, lying bow to stern along the length of the pier or waiting on the river for an empty berth.

The teashop where Morag worked as a cashier was situated at a short distance from the station and pier, in order to deter day-trippers and to encourage what Miss Lamont and her sister, joint owners, referred to as 'a better class of clientele'. Some ten years earlier the younger Miss Lamont had become the second wife of a manager in the Gourock Ropeworks and had retired from business to devote her time to looking after him, his growing family and his large, comfortable home, leaving her sister to run the establishment single-handed.

Morag had obtained her post there because she came from a good address, and because Miss Lamont and Georgina had liked the look of each other at the interview. Morag herself had been an onlooker, rather than the job applicant.

'Being a cashier in a teashop is respectable enough work for someone of your class, and you'll meet a nice type of people in Gourock,' Georgina had said when she tried to object.

'But I want to work with people of my own age. Everyone else in the teashop is much older than me.'

'Nonsense. Young ladies come in with their mothers . . . and young men, too. You'll get to know them. You'll make new friends,' Georgina said, with a gleam in her wide blue eyes. Morag well knew what the gleam meant.

'She's hoping that some rich young man will come with his mother and fall in love with me in the time it takes him to drink a cup of tea and eat an Empire biscuit,' she told her best friend Wilma gloomily.

'Mebbe he will.'

'Who sees me, stuck in a wee glass cashier's box in the corner?'

'The Prince found Snow White in a glass box,' said Wilma, ever the optimist.

'That was a coffin – and so's the thing I work in,' Morag said in despair. 'But I doubt if any young man, rich or otherwise, will ever notice me in it.'

She was right. After five years at the teashop, trapped behind the glass of the cashier's booth with little to do but check bills, take in money, give out change and watch the waitresses rush hither and thither at the whim of the bored, well-dressed women who came in for morning coffee and afternoon tea, she had not met anyone at all. Sometimes the women brought their adult children with them, both male and female, but they too were bored and, as far as Morag was concerned, extremely uninteresting.

Today was no different from any other day. Perched on her stool within the little glass box at one end of the room, she watched women sweep in and then out again, replete with tea and cakes and ready to get on with their lives.

She could, perhaps, have made a bid for freedom after Georgina's death from a stroke, but by then Sander's heart was giving him trouble and the shock of his wife's sudden death did not help. Morag was needed at home, but had suddenly panicked at the prospect of giving up her only scrap of independence.

Tedious though the work was, it allowed her to spend some time out of the house and to earn some money of her own. Her employer had agreed reluctantly to let her work for three afternoons a week instead of full-time, so that she could look after the house and her ailing father.

She would have aged before her time and become as dull and uninteresting as the customers, or the waitresses – most of whom talked about nothing else but their aching feet and their dislike of the customers – if it hadn't been for Wilma, who insisted that they spend at least one evening a week together and some time at weekends. Now that spring was on the way and Sander's health improving, Morag could look forward to the occasional short steamer trip with her friend to the Great Cumbrae, where they could hire cycles and spin round the island with the salt wind whipping colour into their faces.

Cheered by the thought, she beamed at the waitress passing her booth, and the girl smiled tentatively back and asked, 'Would you like a wee cup of tea?'

'I could do with one, Grace,' Morag said gratefully. Grace Hastie, a gentle, self-effacing girl, was younger than the other waitresses. Her slight figure and long slim neck always seemed to Morag to be too fragile to balance the mass of fair hair pinned at the back of her neat skull.

When Grace brought the tea, Morag said, 'I was just thinking, now that the better weather's coming in I'll be able to go across to the Cumbraes with my friend and cycle round the island. Do you ever go on trips on the steamers?'

'I've never got much time. There's always plenty to do at home.' It was quite a long speech for Grace, who never had much to say for herself. The other waitresses tended to think of her as stand-offish, putting on airs because her father was a foreman at Gourock Ropeworks and the family lived in one of the handsome flats the works rented out to its top and middle management, but Morag felt that there was more to it than that and would have liked to get to know the girl better.

'You should come with us some . . .' she began, but just then a fur-clad woman at a corner table flapped a hand in the air and called, 'Waitress!' in ringing tones. Grace was off at once, leaving Morag alone in her upright glass coffin.

2

John Laird, Sander's office manager, arrived on the doorstep at exactly 7.30 p.m., his frail-looking body pulled to one side by the large, battered case he always carried the ledgers and account books in. Once she had escorted him to the bedroom, Morag escaped from the house and hurried to Ardgowan Street where her friend, Wilma Beckett, lived in a tenement flat.

Ever since her earliest schooldays, when she and Wilma had shared a desk, Morag had loved her visits to the Beckett household. Even her mother's disapproval hadn't managed to break the firm bond formed on their first day at school when five-year-old Wilma had slipped two toffees from the pocket of her smock and pressed one into Morag's hand.

'Keep it tucked in your cheek,' she had instructed out of the side of her mouth, 'and mind that one' – she ducked her head in the teacher's direction – 'doesnae see you suckin'.'

Morag, her fear and homesickness calmed as much by the act of kindness as by the sticky, sugary sweet, had known from that moment that Wilma and she were fated to be best friends for ever.

Mr Beckett, a shipyard worker, had died in his mid-thirties of a chronic lung complaint, leaving his wife Mags to raise their three sons and three daughters single-handed. This she had done, taking on any kind of work that would bring in a few pennies to support her family.

The three oldest children – two sons who had followed their father into the shipyards, and a daughter – were married with homes of their own, but as Mags Beckett was still the living heart of her family they and their partners and children were usually to be found crowded into the flat in Ardgowan Street.

Morag was therefore not surprised to find the kitchen full when she arrived. The menfolk – sons and son-in-law – sat around the big table that filled most of the living-room-cum-kitchen. Mrs Beckett, her considerable bulk squeezed into a small space by the sink, was ironing a pile of clothes, while Wilma and her married sister sat at the fire, cheek by jowl with an elderly neighbour and both daughters-in-law, one heavily pregnant and the other suckling a small baby. The only Becketts missing were the two youngest, Daisy and Archie.

'Come on . . .' Wilma dragged Morag into one of the two small bedrooms. 'You can't hear yourself think in that kitchen. Anyway, I want to show you my new blouse. We'll have to use Archie's room, for Daisy's doing her homework in ours and she'll screech like a scalded cat if we disturb her. I'll just fetch it.'

Morag waited, perched on the edge of Archie's narrow bed. Although his brothers had gone to work in the shipyards, Archie, ever the adventurer, had opted to work on the puffers and was mate on the *Sanda*, one of the five boats owned by Sander Weir. The room, not much larger than a cupboard, smelled of tar and oil and grease from his working clothes, underlaid with the strong scent of the pomade he liked to put on his hair when he was off duty. All the Becketts were handsome but Archie, with his beguiling grin and sparkling deep blue eyes, his confident bearing and curly black hair, was undoubtedly the best looking. He strongly resembled the dashing gypsies and brigands featured in some romantic stories for women; there was even an air of danger about him which drew the girls to him like moths desperate to reach a flame that could easily destroy them. Archie was the apple of his mother's eye, because – as she often said – he was his father's spit and image.

Morag heard a murmur of protest from Daisy, then Wilma was back in the room with the new blouse tossed over one arm. 'She's as crabbit as an old hen when she gets interrupted at her books. It's a good thing she's leaving the school soon and coming into Birkmyre's with me.'

Like most of the women and girls in Port Glasgow, Wilma worked at the Gourock Ropeworks, known locally as 'The Gourock', and to the female workers as 'Birkmyre's', after the family which owned it. She stripped off her blouse to don the new one, displaying rounded arms and full breasts swelling above her lace-trimmed crêpe de Chine camiknickers. Wilma loved nice underwear and, her sisters claimed, spent more money on herself underneath than on top.

'What d'you think?' Her fingers nimbly slid each button into its allotted buttonhole, then she gave a little shrug and the blouse – orange-red, and of a silky texture – seemed to ripple and shift as it fell into place, giving the effect of moving flames or richly bronzed autumn leaves tossing in the wind.

'Oh, Wilma, it's beautiful.'

'I thought it would do for the Saturday-night dancing. Geordie Lewis is taking me.' Wilma stripped the blouse off. 'Here, you try it.'

16

The material was soft, and warm, and perfumed from contact with Wilma's skin. Morag loved the feel of it, but it didn't look nearly as well on her as it did on her friend. Its bold, dramatic shade suited Wilma's jet-black hair, whereas it clashed with her own auburn head.

'I don't suit it at all.'

'Try loosening your hair, you always have it pinned up like an animal penned in a cage . . .' Wilma yanked the ribbon from the nape of Morag's neck to let her long hair tumble free, and as she moved into the mirror's range the proximity of her smooth olive skin and black hair seemed to bring the blouse to flickering life again. When they were together, Morag thought despairingly, she herself was so clearly the less attractive of the two with her pale skin and uninteresting hair.

'You should get your hair cut, like mine.' Wilma's first act on leaving school and obtaining a place at the Gourock Ropeworks had been to have her hair bobbed so that it fitted about her head like a gleaming black cap. She had told Morag dreadful stories about machinists at the mill who had carelessly let their heads get too close to the huge, relentlessly throbbing machines they tended, and been horribly mutilated. The women who worked with the spinning and twisting machines had to wear one-piece boiler-suits, and they were all under orders to keep their hair tied back or covered with scarves. Many of them, like Wilma, had bobs.

'I don't think that would make much difference.' Morag had apparently inherited her straight reddish-brown locks from her maternal grandmother; Georgina, her own hair an indifferent brown, had spent hours during Morag's childhood brushing it and wrapping it up in rags every night; but to no avail, since it always hung limply in the morning when the rags were removed.

17

At school she had worn it in one long plait, and spent a good part of each day fending off the boys who loved to tug at it. Many a time, when her tormentors attacked in strength and there were too many for her to deal with on her own, she had had to be rescued by Wilma, a small tornado whirling her satchel by the strap like a hammer-throwing athlete. Wilma's own rebellious locks frequently escaped from the straggling bow that started each morning at the nape of her neck, then slid lower and lower until, by the time the afternoon bell freed them all from the classroom, it clung desperately to a solitary lock; but nobody ever dared to pull it, or to steal her ribbon, for retribution was swift and Wilma Beckett had no qualms about using teeth and nails on anyone who annoyed her.

'You just need something in a different colour,' she advised now. 'Green, mebbe . . . there was some nice deep green material in the shop. We could go there tomorrow.'

'I don't need a new blouse.'

'You do if you're coming dancing with me.'

'You're going with your young man.'

'He's not my young man,' Wilma said scathingly. 'He's just a lad who's taking me to the dancing. He'd be happy to take you as well.'

'No, he wouldn't.'

'Yes, he would, if I told him to.'

'I've got my father to see to. I couldn't go out two nights in a row.'

'You can't spend the whole of your life looking after an invalid, Morag. You're too young for that.'

'I don't mind.'

'I know you don't, but that's only because you're too nice altogether. What about your auntie . . . could she not take a turn of sitting with your father?'

18

Morag gave a snort of laughter at the idea. 'I can't see Aunt Margaret doing that! Anyway, she has Uncle Lawrence to look after, and Flora and Crawford.'

'My mam had six of us, and she always managed to look after sick folk as well – relatives and neighbours. It did us no harm to have to be without her for a few hours now and again.'

'I don't know how to dance.'

'It's time you learned, then. I'll teach you.' Wilma jumped to her feet. 'There's not much room here, but we can do our best.'

Humming a tune, she pulled Morag to her feet and began to dance her around the tiny piece of linoleum available between Archie's bed and the minute dresser. Helpless with laughter, tripping and tumbling on to the bed as often as not, they went through every dance that Wilma knew. It came as a shock when Morag heard a church clock chime nine o'clock. 'Is that the time? I'll have to go.'

'You've just come!'

She searched for the discarded ribbon, found it, and gathered her hair back in one large handful. 'I've been here for nearly two hours. John Laird'll be leaving in five minutes.'

'I'll walk half-way with you,' Wilma said as always, stripping off the blouse. While she pulled a jersey on over her dark head, Morag – her hair tamed – smoothed and folded the blouse, relishing the feel of the soft material beneath her fingers.

Daisy was in the kitchen now, and Archie and his girl-friend had arrived. There were two more neighbours in the room too, and the older of the babies, gurgling with pleasure, was being bounced into the air by his father. The air was thick with tobacco smoke from the men's cigarettes and pipes, the range had been stoked and the ironing-board had been put away. The family were clearly settling in for at least another hour of talking.

'Away already, hen?' Mrs Beckett asked from the stove, where she was making a batch of drop scones for her ever-hungry family. 'Daisy's just brewed a fresh pot of tea, could you no' stay and have a cup?'

'I have to go home – my father . . .' Morag said regretfully. Just then, in the sudden lull following a piercing scream of delight from the baby, one of the men was heard to say, 'So he says he'd be damned if he would, an' then the gaffer—'

'What did you say?' Mrs Beckett whirled round, the good-tempered smile on her face suddenly obliterated by a fearsome scowl. The men looked at each other apprehensively, shuffling their feet.

'It was nothin', Mam, just a bit of crack about the work . . .'

'It wasnae nothing at all, our Robbie! It was foul language!'

Robbie, a husky young man who could have given a good account of himself in any pub brawl, went crimson. 'It was just the one wee word and, anyway, it wasnae me that said it, it was this man at the work.'

'It was your mouth it tumbled out of, not his!' His mother gave him a hefty open-handed slap on the back of the head, 'You know fine that I'll not have foul language in my house!'

'But you never said a word last night when Archie said fu—' Robbie yelped again as he received another clout, this time on one ear.

'Will you take a tellin'! In front of your sisters . . . and Morag too!'

'It's different when it's Archie – he cannae do any wrong,' Robbie muttered sullenly, and Archie,

20

balancing his sweetheart on one knee with a casual arm slung about her waist to support her, grinned and winked at him.

'Are you goin' tae apologise, or d'ye want another slap for yer impertinence?'

'I'm sorry, Mam.' Robbie rubbed at his stinging head.

'I should think so too! How is your father, lassie?' Mrs Beckett turned back to Morag, as though their conversation had never been interrupted.

'Not too bad. Wearying for some good weather, so's he can get out to sit in the garden.'

'We could all do with a bit of sunshine,' Mrs Beckett agreed, adding, as always, 'Haste ye back, lassie, we're always pleased to see you.'

'I don't know what got into our Robbie,' Wilma said apologetically as they scurried down the stone staircase to the narrow close which led out on to the street. 'He knows fine that Mam'll not tolerate bad lang—'

She ended in a squeak of surprise as she bounced out of the close mouth ahead of Morag and almost collided with a man striding past. He steadied her and began to apologise, then his voice trailed away as she looked up, turning her face into the glow of the street lamp. 'It's yourself, Wilma.'

'Hello, Danny.' She stepped back, moving away from his steadying grasp. 'What're you doing in Ardgowan Street? Have you been courting?'

His empty hands, no longer needed, fell back to his sides. Because his back was to the lamp Morag didn't actually see colour flooding into his face, but somehow she knew – by the set of his shoulders and the tone of his voice when he said, 'I've been out running with the Harriers Club' – that the blush was there, hot and crimson.

'The Harriers? Now if you'd been out walking,' Wilma told him pertly, 'I'd mebbe have gone with you.'

'Would you?'

'You never know. This is my friend Morag.'

He whipped his cap off. 'Good evening.'

Morag returned the greeting and wished, as an awkward silence began to grow, that she could think of the right thing to say. Wilma always knew what to say – but maddeningly, on this occasion she chose to remain silent, watching Danny with eyes that sparkled with mischief in the lamplight.

'I'd best be getting home, then,' he said at last, cramming the cap back on to his tumbled fair hair.

'See you tomorrow,' Wilma said cheerfully and he raced off along the road, not quite running but walking swiftly.

'Who was that?' It seemed to Morag that the man's face and fair hair was vaguely familiar.

'Just one of the foremen at the mill.'

Morag had no idea why she thought she knew him. 'Would you have gone walking with him if he had asked?'

'Of course not.'

'That's a shame. He looks like a nice lad, and he's got a real fancy for you.'

'If I went out with every lad that takes a fancy for me, you and me'd never see each other. Danny's nice enough, and he's good to the women at the work, but he's too shy and quiet for my liking. His father's a right b . . . beggar! He's been a foreman for ever, and the women who work in his section hate him. Him and Danny are as different as chalk and cheese.'

She put a hand under Morag's arm in order to navigate her through a knot of youths lingering on the pavement outside a fish and chip shop, eating with their fingers from newspaper-wrapped bundles. They took up the entire pavement, their muscular, sweat-smelling bodies barring the girls' way, and for a moment Morag panicked, but Wilma merely pushed into the midst of the group and poked her fingers into one of the bundles, ordering, 'Give us a chip, then, Johnny Dunn.'

'As many as ye want.' Johnny held out the package, beaming round at his mates, pleased that she had singled him out.

'You can have one of mine.' The youth nearest to Morag pushed his bundle under her nose. She was about to refuse, but the smell of freshly cooked fish and chips was inviting. The strip of potato was delicious, crisply fried on the outside and soft and hot on the inside.

'Here, have the rest of my chips, Wilma, I've finished with them,' Johnny offered, then, eagerly, 'and we'll walk you home.'

'You'll do no such thing.' She took the crumpled paper from him and popped another chip into her mouth. 'We're on our way to meet our young men, and they'd not be pleased to find the likes of you tagging on behind us.'

'Who're you going to meet, then?' he challenged.

'That'd be telling'

'Is yours as good-looking as me?'

'His dog's better-looking than you, and it's got the mange. Ta for the chips.' She pushed him aside and swept on, Morag scurrying in her wake, as the rest of the youths sniggered noisily at poor Johnny's expense.

'A nice enough lad, but he's got too big a conceit of himself. Have another chip,' Wilma offered as the two girls rounded the corner into Chapelton Street. By the time they had finished the chips between them, they had reached the half-way point where they usually separated.

Wilma thrust a handkerchief into Morag's hand. 'Wipe the grease off your fingers with that,' she ordered and Morag obeyed, then returned the handkerchief and set off on the uphill walk home while Wilma skipped back to the crowded tenement kitchen.

3

As Danny Hastie walked home his mind was filled with
the memory of Wilma Beckett's vivacious little face,
washed by lamplight, and the feel of her shoulders
beneath his hands. He wondered if she had meant
it when she said that she would have gone walking
with him, and wished that some day he might find the
courage to ask her.

He was so busy thinking about her that he had
covered the length of Bouverie Street and was well past
his own close before he realised that he was home. The
street, half-way up the hill that rose from the shoreline,
consisted of a long row of sturdy four-storey sandstone
tenements built by the Birkmyre family and rented out
to lower and middle management in their Ropeworks.
As a senior foreman and a long-standing employee,
Bill Hastie, Danny's father, had been allotted a cosy
home consisting of two rooms and a large kitchen on
the third floor of one of the buildings.

Danny himself, recently promoted to foreman, stood
a good chance of getting a flat in the same street if he
should marry. Mounting the stairs, he thought with a
touch of bitterness alien to his placid nature that that
wasn't likely. He wanted only one girl, and he was
such a ham-fisted tongue-tied idiot that he would never

25

find the courage to woo her, not even if they were the only two people in the world with eternity before them. Wilma was popular, with the other girls as well as with every man who knew her, and he was too frightened of failure, of her laughing at him, either to his face or, even worse, behind his back with her friends. His father, a bare-knuckle boxer in his youth, had always told him that he was spineless, and his father was right.

In any case, now that he was a foreman he couldn't afford to be made a laughing-stock at the mill. 'Always remember, lad, that you must stand apart from the rest,' Bill Hastie had instructed when the appointment was announced. 'You are their superior, and you must always be their superior. It makes no difference if they hate you for it – in fact,' he added with relish, 'that can be all for the better.'

The living-room was silent and peaceful with only Grace in it, her head bent over her sewing. A pile of neatly darned and folded clothes lay on the table nearby, and her bare feet rested in a basin of water.

She looked up and smiled at him as he went in. 'Did you enjoy yourself?'

'It was grand,' he told her enthusiastically. It had been more than grand up on the hills with the lights of Port Glasgow, Greenock and Gourock spread out below him, the river shimmering palely beyond and the town of Helensburgh sprinkled like a handful of diamonds on the far bank. It had given him a rare, and precious, sense of freedom. It had made him feel that for once, he could breathe properly.

'You've brought in the smell of the hills with you.' She wrinkled her neat nose and sniffed appreciatively. 'I'll make us a cup of tea in a minute.'

'I'll see to it . . . and no argument,' he added as she began to protest. 'You need to rest your feet.' In the Hastie household the men were always looked on as the bread-winners and the women as the skivvies; secretly, Danny disagreed with this edict, and when his father wasn't around he often made tea or set the table or washed some dishes. After all, Grace went out to work too, as a waitress in a teashop. It seemed wrong to him that she was also expected to toil in the house in the evenings and at weekends while her father and brother were idle.

While waiting for the kettle to boil he stood at the window over the sink, looking down over the great bulk of the Gourock Ropeworks mill where he and his father worked, to the river beyond. It, too, gave him that wonderful sense of space and freedom. After making the tea, he tossed a towel over his shoulder and, when he had handed his sister her cup, he knelt down and lifted one foot from the basin, then began to dry it.

'Danny . . .' she protested, trying to push him away.

'Don't make such a fuss, woman. You drink your tea and leave me be,' he instructed, and after a further half-hearted protest she did as she was told, sipping gratefully at the hot drink and then resting her head, with its pinned-up mass of soft fair hair, against the high back of her chair and closing her eyes.

'I believe I could enjoy being a lady, with servants to obey my every whim,' she murmured.

'Mebbe one day you will be.'

'Aye, that'll be right.' A smile curved the corners of her mouth. 'And on that same day folk'll be able to walk across the Clyde instead of needing to go by boat.'

She had pretty feet, small and slim like the rest of her. Danny too was fair, but while he had inherited his maternal grandfather's sturdy body, Grace had taken

27

after their father's side of the family and was neatly built and pale-skinned.

'There, that's you done.' Looking up at her from below, he could see the violet shadows beneath her eyes and the weariness about her mouth. Their mother had been delicate all her life, and had died of heart trouble while Grace was still at school. Danny still suffered from the loss of her, and although Grace was fit enough he was secretly haunted by the fear that she too might die at an early age.

'You should go to bed,' he urged, handing her her stockings and getting to his feet, the basin in his big hands.

'I'll just wait until father comes in. He'll mebbe need fresh tea.'

A wave of irritation suddenly rose in Danny. 'For God's sake,' he wanted to cry out, 'why can't you do as you please for once, and not as he pleases? Why can't we both stop letting him rule every last fragment of our lives?' But he bit back the hot words, knowing that they would only distress his sister, as his frustration always did. Better to leave things be, he told himself as he emptied the basin and carefully dried it before putting it away.

He had been eight years old, and Grace five, when their father went off to fight in the Great War. Over the next five years they had only seen him sporadically as a noisy stranger who arrived suddenly and unexpectedly to turn their world upside down, taking over the neat little two-roomed flat they then lived in, demanding their mother's continuous attention, talking incessantly and frighteningly about war and killing and danger, his eyes gleaming and his large moustache almost bristling with enthusiasm.

Bill Hastie had loved the war, finding in it the male

camaraderie, the challenges, the discipline that suited his nature. He had survived without a scratch – what enemy soldier would ever have had the courage to harm a hair on the head of such a formidable man, Danny had thought at the time – and had come home, his medals for long service, loyalty and bravery pinned to the breast of his suit, to a hero's welcome. The neighbours had hung out banners and held a party for him, the Ropeworks management had given him instant promotion and, a few years later, the house in Bouverie Street, and he had settled down to rule his family and those under his charge in the mills with a rod of iron, using all the barrack-square discipline he had learned and absorbed like mothers' milk during his military service.

Danny often thought that his father's return had been the beginning of the end of his mother's life. Although she worshipped her husband, she was not strong enough to cope with his energy and drive. A few months after he was demobilised from the Army, she miscarried a child and almost died as a result. Within a year of the tragedy she was to all intents and purposes an invalid, with only another year left to live.

Bill Hastie had not married again. Neither, when her chance came along, did Grace, although Danny had always assumed – and, as she grew up, hoped – that she would marry and escape their father's tyranny as soon as possible. He had been delighted when she had fallen in love with a friend of his. He could still remember her radiance in those few short weeks, the glow that took Danny's breath away every time he looked at her.

But Bill Hastie, used to having his house well cared for and his meals on the table whenever it suited him, had found the young suitor wanting and not good enough for his daughter. Danny had tried to persuade Grace to marry the lad anyway, but while she hesitated, reluctant to defy her father for the first time in her life, her sweetheart left Port Glasgow for a good job in England, and she had never heard from him again. This, her father had lost no time in pointing out, proved that he had never loved her in the first place.

'What sort of man would let me come between him and the woman he loved?' he had demanded of his daughter. 'He was a coward, Grace – a snivelling coward. You can do better than the likes of him!'

There was still time for Grace, and for himself, but sometimes Danny looked into a frightening future where the two of them drifted along as they were, living their lives to please their father until he died. And by that time, he thought bleakly, they might well be too old and cowed to make much of the years left to them.

He started gathering the cups together. 'I'll just rinse them,' he began, but Grace, who had excellent hearing, pushed her stockinged feet into her slippers, sprang up and took the cups from him just as he heard his father's key in the lock and his heavy tread in the tiny hall. When Bill Hastie came into the room, she was at the sink and Danny by the window.

He grunted a greeting and sank down into the most comfortable chair. 'Where's the tea? I've got a right thirst on me.'

'Just coming. I'm making some fresh.' Grace filled the kettle and lit the gas stove. Bill reached out for the newspaper and snapped it open, making it crack with a sound like a rifle-shot, while Danny sat down at the table and concentrated on thinking about Wilma's bright, laughing, fearless face, and how quick and lithe and beautiful she could look even in the clumsy boiler-suits that all the machinists wore at work.

*　　*　　*

When Wilma's schooldays came to an end on her thirteenth birthday, Morag, who had celebrated her own birthday a month earlier, did her best to persuade her parents to let her leave school too and go into Birkmyre's Ropeworks with her friend. Apart from a fear of losing Wilma if their lives led in different directions, she wanted to taste the heady pleasure of being one of a crowd, leaving work at the end of the shift linked arm-in-arm with several other girls, taking up the entire width of the pavement and sharing private jokes. She wanted to go swinging jauntily along the streets at night on her way to or from the cinema or the dance-hall with her pals, eating hot, crisp fish and chips from newspaper and cheeking lads the way Wilma could.

Georgina had been horrified at the very idea. 'The Gourock's for those that can't do anything else but work machines. Women with no other talents.'

'What talent have I got?' Morag had wanted to know, baffled.

'You're good with figures, all your teachers have said so.'

'Then I'll try for work in Birkmyre's offices.'

'The very idea! You'll stay on at the school, and mebbe become a teacher,' Georgina had announced.

Morag had had no option but to do as her mother decreed, although as it turned out she did not have the ability to become a teacher. To her surprise and delight, Georgina, possibly at Sander's urging, had reluctantly accepted the strong friendship between her daughter and the girl from Ardgowan Street, though Wilma was never invited to Lilybank Road. But at least Morag had been able to go on sharing something of the excitement of Wilma's life, even if it was only as a bystander.

She arrived home to find that the clerk had helped

31

Sander into bed before leaving. He was propped up against his pillows, peering through a large magnifying glass at a sheet of paper. The entire bed was strewn with books and loose papers.

'I'm glad you're back, lass . . . John's handwriting's getting worse by the day. I'm beginning to wonder if he's getting too old for the work. Fetch the other set of books here, will you?'

'In the morning. You need your rest.' She began to tidy up the mess.

'I never do anything else but rest!'

'Well, I'm tired if you're not. I'd as soon start on the accounts in the morning, Father, when I feel more able for them.' She removed the books to the table, out of his reach. 'I'll fetch you a glass of warm milk and get you settled down for the night.'

Although he was in his mid-thirties when the Great War started, and could have stayed at home for a year or two before finally being called on to fight for his country, Sander Weir had enlisted in 1914, only to return home a year later having lost a leg at Ypres. The same fighting spirit which had sent him into war brought him, together with his wife Georgina's dedicated care, through months of pain and rehabilitation. But he had to give up all idea of working on a puffer again; when his wealthy father-in-law offered him a position as manager of his stone quarry, Sander had had no option but to accept.

He handled his new post with the same determination and attention to detail that he had once used to guide his boat through a rocky reef during a storm, and when Georgina's father died in 1917, leaving everything to his only child, Sander took over the running of his wife's many business interests. But he was still a seaman at heart and when Fergusson Tollin, the small shipping company he himself had once worked for, ran into financial difficulties, Sander, with Georgina's blessing, disposed of the quarry and her other assets and bought an equal partnership in the company.

In Sander's time, William Fergusson had owned and run the business and his son Samuel was captain of the puffer Sander crewed on. By the time Sander came in as a partner Samuel had taken over from his father, but had proved to be no hand at office matters. Sander, well versed by now in paperwork, undertook to run the office and warehouse on East Harbour, while Samuel returned to his old post as skipper of one of the puffers. From 1918 the business became known as Fergusson, Tollin and Weir.

Unfortunately, Samuel Fergusson's financial difficulties proved to be not so much a case of incompetence in the office as a matter of unwise bets on dog-racing, followed by Samuel consoling himself over his losses in one of the downtown bars frequented by the watermen. His self-indulgences, plus the cost of keeping a handsome home for his wife and young son, meant that Samuel had to dip more and more into the office funds. Finally, his debts became so serious that Sander, aware that the company couldn't stand such plundering for much longer, bought the man out, paying what he and others considered to be a fair sum.

Soon after Fergusson, Tollin and Weir became the Weir Shipping Company, Samuel Fergusson drowned one dark night in the East Harbour, close to where the boats which had once been his were berthed. At the inquest, it transpired that in an act of sheer stupidity he had tried to recoup his vast losses by gambling with the money he had received for his share of the business, and had lost it. His widow had been forced to sell their fine house in Gourock and buy something much smaller in Port Glasgow for herself and her schoolboy son. Whether her husband's death was an accident or the final act of a man made desperate by one failure after another, nobody ever knew, but Janet Fergusson had made no secret of her belief that Sander was to blame.

He had refused to let the woman trouble him, telling his wife and daughter that he had no reason to feel guilty as all his dealings with Samuel had been made fairly in the offices of a lawyer and with Samuel's full agreement, but Janet's venomous looks whenever they happened to meet had upset both Georgina and Morag. Even when Sander offered work to young Calum Fergusson, Janet had interpreted the move as a way to rub her nose in the fact that her son was working for another man in the very business he should have inherited. Georgina and Morag had both felt guiltily relieved when Janet died of pneumonia two years before Georgina's own death.

When Morag, in her final year at school, had shown him how to work out a ledger entry that was causing problems, Sander had almost burst with pride at her ability. After that she had been encouraged to help whenever he had occasion to work on the Weir Shipping Company books at home, and since his illness – when he was forced to do what work he could from his sickbed – he had come to rely heavily on her for assistance.

Morag had always enjoyed the book-work. The five Weir boats had been named after some of the smaller West Coast islands – *Pladda, Ailsa Craig, Sanda, Jura* and *Coll* – and it was a joy to her to trace their journeying in the account books as they carried

34

freight up and down the fragmented, craggy coastline, out to the Clyde islands and further afield, trading with the scattered mass of islands which made up the Inner and Outer Hebrides, or sailing inland through the Crinan Canal and the Forth and Clyde Canal.

She enjoyed looking through the old account books and ledgers too. Before Sander bought into the business John Laird had kept the books in pristine condition, the pages neatly covered with copperplate writing. But as age crept up on him and Samuel Fergusson's slapdash attitude corrupted the entire firm, Laird's handwriting, like his standards, had sagged, then lapsed. For a while Sander himself had taken over the books, filling the pages and columns with a strong, somewhat sprawling hand, but Laird had regained control of them since his employer's illness. Now, the pages of the account and order books looked as though a demented and possibly drunken spider had run amok over them.

Frustrated at having to make sense of the scrawls, Sander had appealed to Morag who had set to and learned, with the help of books borrowed from the local library, about bills of lading and balance sheets. Then she began to write out a second set of books, kept in a neat, clear hand that Sander found easy to follow.

When she had dealt with the breakfast dishes on the morning after Laird's visit, and seen to it that Sander was washed, shaved and comfortable, Morag spread out both sets of books on the dining-room table and began the task of interpreting Laird's latest figures and transferring them slowly, and with some difficulty, to the replica books. When she finally took both sets upstairs, Sander, who had been waiting impatiently, scanned her copy without any need to revert to his magnifying glass.

'I sometimes wonder if John's getting past doing the job, yet I don't like to turn the man off. I wish, though, that you could see to the accounts instead of him, Morag.'

'I've got enough to do, with this house and the teashop as well.'

'You could give up the teashop.'

'It would upset Mr Laird if I tried to take over from him.'

'So you think it best that he upsets me?' Sander asked sharply, then sighed and shifted slightly in the bed. 'Ach, I suppose you're right. The man's got no other life than that office – though it would almost be a relief if he was to come and tell me that he had decided to give up work. He must be all of seventy years of age. Sentiment has no place in commerce . . . and I just wish I'd learned that earlier. Never let an employee feel that he's got his feet under your table, Morag, for it doesn't do.'

'I'll bear it in mind, Father,' she told him dryly, but he was too busy poring over the figures she had spread before him to notice the tone of sarcasm in her voice.

'There should be a better return on the *Pladda* than that, surely? She's scarce paying her way!'

Morag took the book from him and cast an eye over the page in question.

'He took granite to Mallaig, then came back unladen. That's where you've lost your money. Surely he could have picked up a cargo to bring back?'

Sander snatched the book back from her and studied it closely. 'By God and you're right, lass. What's John Laird thinking of, letting a boat come back lightship, guzzling good coal for no return? This never happened when I was in charge. The sooner I'm out of this bed and back in the office the better! Morag, you take the

36

books back right after the mid-day meal and ask John Laird what's going on!'

'I have to go to work this afternoon.'

'Then you must go to the harbour first,' Sander ordered with the peevishness of an invalid. 'I'll not let the matter wait on until the morning!'

4

It meant preparing a hurried mid-day meal earlier than
usual in order to get the dishes washed and her father
settled before she set off, but Sander was insistent.
Morag loaded the heavy account books into a bag
which had begun to drag painfully at her elbow before
she had covered half the distance to the harbour, as well
as bumping against her thigh with every step she took. It
was a relief when she reached the shabby little building
owned by the Weir Shipping Company.

Before going in she paused as usual outside the door,
because the small office had the most interesting entry
she had ever seen. The door itself was made of timber,
supposedly from an old ship wrecked on the hidden
reefs off Port Glasgow. It was shabby, scored with
years of assault from the winds and the rain and even
– a rarity in that part of Scotland – bouts of hot sun.
To reach it, visitors walked up two steps on to a wide
stretch of concrete where, to one side of the door, a
handsome figurehead – a woman looking out towards
the harbour and the river beyond – was mounted on a
sturdy block of stone. She wore a long flowing dress
and a shawl held closed by one hand; the other hand
pointed towards the harbour and the river beyond.

As a child, Morag was often held up by Sander

to study the painted face with its broad cheekbones, high forehead and rounded cheeks. She had touched the strong straight nose and peered into the painted eyes which stared unwaveringly beyond her own small inquisitive face.

'She's looking for land, and pointing to it to guide the sailors,' Sander had told her. 'That's her task, to lead the ship safe to port.'

'What ship?' Morag had wanted to know, dangling without fear from his strong hands, her small booted feet swinging in mid-air.

'Her own ship, that she was made for. But it's long gone now, and she's had to become a landlubber, poor lass . . . like the rest of us,' he had always added sombrely, but she hadn't realised then what he meant.

Morag recalled twisting her bonneted head round to gaze at the harbour. There were plenty of boats there, including Sander's puffers, but none that looked as though it was right for the wooden lady. 'Mebbe she's looking for her own ship to come back for her.'

'Mebbe,' Sander had agreed. 'Give her face a wee stroke, lass, tae let her know that she's got friends here.'

Morag had obediently patted the cold wooden cheek, and she had always made a wish because Sander said that the wooden lady had the power to grant wishes. He spoke the truth for the wishes, usually for items such as a sugar mouse or a liquorice strap, were almost always granted on the way home.

After Morag had been set back down on the cobbles she had carefully fitted a small booted foot into the imprints of two feet in the concrete just before the figurehead, one small and neat, one large and deeper than its companion, both dwarfing Morag's own foot at that time. But for a good few years now her own foot had been too large to fit into the smaller depression. Whoever had made the original imprint had had daintier feet than hers.

As a child she wasn't allowed to visit the office on many occasions, because Georgina felt that the harbour was not a seemly place for a little girl, but whenever she went there Morag stopped to look at the figurehead and swiftly, with a glance to make sure that she wasn't being watched, she always patted whichever part of it that she could reach, just to let the wooden lady know that she had a friend. Sometimes, when storms lashed the river at night, she lay snug in her small bed, worrying about the figurehead out in the open and at the mercy of the winds and the rain.

'That's where she belongs, lass,' Sander explained when she suggested that the lady should be brought to Lilybank Road and put in a more sheltered spot in the garden. 'She needs to feel the salt spray on her face. She'd not be happy away from the water.'

Now, Morag noted the patches of bare wood showing through the figure's skirt and shawl and even her face. She put a hand against one of the patches, grieving for the figure, then jumped when a voice said by her shoulder, 'Poor old lass, she could do with a good coat of paint.'

She spun round, almost dropping the heavy bag in her embarrassment and confusion. Cal Fergusson, skipper of the *Pladda*, moved forward to rescue it, but the strap had become twisted round Morag's fingers, and the confusion of untangling herself and letting Cal take the bag from her gave her time to collect her wits. 'I was just thinking that myself,' she said calmly, turning back to look at the figurehead. 'I thought she was repainted once a year.'

'When your father was running the office, she was.

But old . . . Mr Laird,' he corrected himself smoothly, 'hasn't got round to it. Poor Isabella, it must be hard for such a lady to look so shabby in public.'

'You've given her a name?'

'Not me . . . it was the name of the clipper she was made for, the *Lady Isabella* out of Greenock on the tea run about a century ago. My great-grandfather carved her.' He was tall enough to reach up and pat the wooden face without effort, and he did so now, easily and affectionately, with no concern apparently about being seen and thought daft. 'Matthew Fergusson was one of the best wood-carvers in the trade. He worked for the Tollin family. They were ships' carvers.' He nodded at the building before them. 'The downstairs room that's used as a store now was their workshop. It was my grandfather who changed it to a shipping company when the demand for wood-carving and figureheads began to fall away.'

'It's a very handsome figure.'

'Aye. She was rescued when her ship was broken up, and brought back to the Port where she was born.'

'D'you know the story of the footprints too?'

'No.' He squinted down at them, reading out the initials scratched into the concrete above them. '"A M." I wonder which print belongs to AM. Mebbe he or she had the figurehead put here.'

'It seems a strange thing to do.'

Cal pushed back his peaked skipper's cap and raised an eyebrow at her. 'There's nothing strange about folk wanting to leave their mark. It's their way of telling those to come after them that they were once here.'

'I suppose so. It would be interesting,' Morag said, her eyes on the footprints, 'to know more about your grandfather and his work.'

'There are some old account books from those days

41

in the house somewhere. I've been thinking of looking them out. I'll let you have a look at them if you—'

'If you've got time to stand around and chatter you're not working hard enough,' John Laird said harshly from the shelter of the doorway. He stepped out, glaring at the seaman, then suddenly noticed Morag standing to one side. Colour rose to his cheekbones. 'Miss Weir . . . I didnae realise that it was you,' he said in some confusion.

'I was just going, Mr Laird,' Cal said unhurriedly. He held out the bag of books and Laird took them automatically, then sagged noticeably under the sudden weight on his arm. 'Miss Weir . . .' Cal touched the peak of his cap, then swung round and started across the cobbles towards the edge of the harbour.

'It was my fault, Mr Laird. I was asking Cal what he knew of the history of the figurehead.'

'It wasnae your fault at all, lassie, that one'd waste time if he was standin' in a burnin' house,' John Laird said peevishly. 'He's got altogether too much of an opinion of himself. He needs remindin' of his station in life. Are ye comin' up?'

'For a moment, just.' She followed him up the narrow stairs and into the office, so overflowing with paperwork that she wondered how he could possibly manage to find everything he needed to run the company efficiently. Sander Weir had had the ability to carry all the information he needed in his head: the whereabouts of each of his boats, the size, content and cost of the cargoes they carried, a foreknowledge of the weather they might expect to encounter and the time each would take to reach its destination, unload one cargo and load another, and make its way back to Port Glasgow. In his day the office had been tidy, with scarcely any paperwork to be seen.

42

Laird swept an armful of papers off a chair. 'Sit down, Miss Weir, sit down.' He was almost gushing now, with none of the harshness he had used towards Cal Fergusson before discovering that she was with the young skipper.

'My father wants to know why the *Pladda* came back from Mallaig empty. Surely a cargo could have been found for her?'

'Aye, and it should have been and all. But young Fergusson was altogether too eager to get back to dry land and his comfortable bed. He'd not wait for a cargo.' The clerk fussed with the papers on his desk, almost sending a pile crashing to the floor. 'The man's no use to us at all.'

'But I remember my father saying that Cal was doing well; that's why he was given the *Pladda* when Captain MacIndoo retired.'

'He's too young for such responsibility. If you ask me, Miss Weir, your father was too generous altogether when he offered work to that one. Fergusson's just taken advantage of the kindness shown to him. He's lazy and untrustworthy, like his father.'

'I don't see how you can think that . . .'

'It'll be in the blood,' John Laird said darkly.

The man's unwarranted venom angered Morag. As she gathered up her gloves, suddenly anxious to get out of the untidy, stuffy room and away from its occupant, she said with a sharpness not usually in her voice, 'My father has asked me to tell you that in future he wants the boats to carry cargoes both ways whenever possible. After all, Mr Laird, you're in charge of the office. Surely decisions about cargoes rest with you.'

He flushed. 'If I was you, Miss Weir,' he said as he followed her downstairs, 'I'd not give too much of my time to talking to the likes of young Fergusson.

He could be a bad influence on a young lassie such as yourself.'

The tide was high and the *Pladda* could be seen by the jetty, a stolid, bluff-bowed example of the hundreds of puffers that worked the Clyde and the Scottish coastal waters. As she began to walk away from the building Morag saw Cal Fergusson step down the two steps from the wheelhouse to the low bulwarks, then walk on to the harbour itself with the effortless ease of one used to being around boats. Like her, he was making for the street, and she dawdled so that he could catch up with her – more to annoy John Laird, if he was still watching, than from a wish for the young skipper's company.

'Miss Weir,' he greeted her cheerfully as he reached her. She had not seen all that much of him, but she was struck by the way he always seemed cheerful and at ease with the world, quick to smile and with a way of moving as though completely at home with himself. It was a strange way of putting it, but that, she realised as he fell into step with her, shortening his loose swinging stride to accommodate her smaller steps, was the way the man moved. 'I forgot to enquire after your father's health. It was remiss of me.'

'He's coming along, but fretting to be out again and back in the office.'

'I can understand that. He enjoys his work. I admire him greatly.'

'In spite of the fact that he bought your own father out and deprived you of your inheritance?' It was a cheeky question, and one that she regretted as soon as she had uttered the words. But he wasn't at all troubled.

'I'm still entitled, surely, to admire him as a business-man and an employer,' he said mildly, and she seized her chance.

44

'He was wondering about your trip to Mallaig . . .'

'Tell him it was a good run, and we made it in grand time. I was sorry, though, that we couldn't have waited another day for a return cargo. I don't like to travel lightship.'

'D'you mean that there was a cargo you could have brought back?'

'Aye, but it wouldn't have been ready until the next day, and when I telephoned Mr Laird to tell him he ordered us back at once. He was fussing about some furniture he had promised would go over to Rothesay, and there was no other boat to take it. It turned out that *Sanda* could have done it, for she was in the area and with enough deck space to take the extra cargo, but Mr Laird didn't realise that,' he said blithely. 'It was just a wee confusion. Well now, this is where I must leave you. Thank you for your company, Miss Weir.' And with a swift salute and a nod of the head, he was off.

Morag stared after him, then glanced back at the office. Sander would be looking for an answer to his question, and although it meant getting John Laird into trouble she was going to tell him the truth. Although she scarcely knew Cal Fergusson she liked him, and she was not going to stand by and let him be blamed for the older man's errors.

As the weeks slipped by and May arrived, bringing warmer weather and the promise of summer to come, Sander's health took a distinct turn for the better. With the help of Lawrence, John Laird or one or other of the men employed by the shipping business, Morag managed on several occasions to get him downstairs and out into the back garden, where she settled him in a comfortable chair padded about with cushions, and with a rug over his knees. The man who had looked after the Weirs' garden for many years was sometimes there to help, and while he worked about the place he and Sander gossiped contentedly in the warm sunlight.

John Laird continued to bring the books to the house every week, and Morag continued to convert the spidery scrawl which covered the pages into readable lists for Sander to study. She felt more and more as though she was trapped like a fly at a window behind the glass of her small cubicle in the teashop, and envied Daisy Beckett who left school in April and went to work in Birkmyre's.

'It's grand, earning my own keep and being in with all the other girls,' the girl told Morag, her pretty face shining. 'Much better than school. It'll be a while before I can be like our Wilma and run my own machines, but that'll come one day.'

Daisy might have been started off in the carding department, where the raw material was cleaned and prepared and the air was thick with dirty fibrous dust that got into the workers' eyes and hair and mouths; or in the winding flat, where the fibre, if it happened to be of a poor quality, broke time and again and had to be mended. When that happened, Wilma had told Morag, the work was delayed and the winders, who were paid on a piece-work basis, often went home in tears of despair after a hard week's work with almost no money in their pay packets. But Daisy was fortunate in being started in the twisting flat, where Wilma ran two of the huge noisy machines used to twist the threads already prepared in the carding and winding departments into strong cord.

'Our Daisy,' she told Morag with an affectionate shake of the head, 'could fall into a cesspit and come out smelling of roses. She was always the lucky one.'

46

Daisy's good fortune was largely due to her sunny nature, which won her friends wherever she went. Within two weeks she was well settled in at the mill; it was to be a further two weeks before she ran foul of Bill Hastie and discovered that life at Birkmyre's had its setbacks as well as its joys.

She and another girl had been given the task of taking a bogie – a high-sided trolley – filled with completed bobbins from the twisting department to a store-room. It was a job that needed two people, for bogies were clumsy contraptions and this one carried a full load of bobbins, each of them large and heavy. Between them, the girls managed well enough to pull it along one of the alleys between the long rows of noisy machines, then when they had almost reached the door Ellen suddenly stopped and gripped her stomach, a look of consternation on her face.

'What's amiss?' Daisy mouthed at her above the whirr and rattle of the machines on either side. Ellen, crimson with embarrassment, looked to either side, for all the world as though someone might hear her in all that din, then came close to put her mouth against her friend's ear.

'It's my monthlies started early, and it's a bad one. It's that damned bogie that's done it!' She kicked out at one of the wheels, then gasped in horror as several drops of bright red blood suddenly spattered over the floor between her boots.

For a moment both girls gaped at the spots, then Daisy took charge. 'D'you have any clean rags with you?' she demanded to know; then as Ellen shook her head, tears of mortification and fright glittering in her eyes, 'Go to the lavatory and stuff a handful of newspaper into your knickers, then. You'll just have to run home at dinner-time and get some rags, but newspaper'll do for now. Hurry up!' she added, as the other girl hesitated.

'What about . . .' Ellen motioned towards the bogie.

'I'll manage until you get back. You can't pull it just now, you'll leave a trail all the way to the store. Go on, the sooner you go the sooner you'll get back,' Daisy urged, and Ellen skittered off in an awkward run, knees pressed tightly together in an effort to prevent further accidents and heels kicking out to the sides. Hurriedly scuffing one foot over the telltale drops to disperse them and rub them into the floor, Daisy set to to haul the bogie as far as she could, thanking her lucky stars as she did so that she herself hadn't as yet been bothered by the monthly bleeding which was the curse and torment of her older sisters.

She had almost gained the door when Bill Hastie walked in on one of his rare visits to that particular part of the factory. He stopped, watching her struggle for a moment, then roared, 'What d'you think you're doing?'

Although he was a small man his voice could easily make itself heard above the roar of the machinery. Several heads turned, but as soon as the women saw the senior foreman they spun back to their work. They knew better than to call down his wrath on their heads too.

'I'm taking bobbins to the store.'

'And making a fine mess of it!' Bill Hastie rounded on his son as he came hurrying up, alerted by the sound of his father's voice and the sudden stir of interest among the workers nearest the door. 'This is a fine piece of time-wasting!'

'Daisy? Who told you to haul that bogie on your own?'

The girl's eyes were frightened as they fastened on

48

Danny's face. His father had that effect; most of the workers in the mill went in dread of the man who, they well knew, could and would dismiss them on the spot if he even suspected them of any wrong-doing.

'Ellen was with me, but she was . . .' she hesitated, then said in a rush, 'she was caught short and she'd to go to the lavatory. She'll be back in a minute.'

'And you tried to pull the thing on your own?' Danny was horrified. 'You should have come to me for help.'

'The daft lassie's either too stupid or too arrogant to do that,' his father sneered. Frightened as she was, Daisy drew herself up.

'I'm not stupid,' she told the senior foreman, stung by his contempt. 'And I happen to know what arrogant means, and I'm not that either. I just thought that I should try to manage on my own until Ellen came back.'

'I'll get one of the men to give you a—' Danny began, but his father stopped him with an upraised hand.

'No, no . . . the lassie thinks she can manage, so let her try. See how long she takes to get to the store.'

'For pity's sake!'

'It's the only way she'll learn,' Bill grated at his son. By now several women in the area were trying to see and hear what was going on while at the same time keeping the bobbins spinning on their machines. Wilma, down at the far end of the room, was still unaware of her sister's situation, which Danny felt was just as well.

'Go on, then, pull the thing!' Hastie ordered and Daisy, determined not to be bested by him, caught hold of the metal handle, hauled as hard as she could and found that a raised knot on the wooden floor just

49

in front of one of the rear wheels was acting as a brake. She gritted her teeth and pulled harder, knowing that once the great heavy trolley started to move its own momentum would keep it going. Pain began to run along her arms from the wrists and she felt her face swelling with the effort, but she wouldn't, couldn't, admit herself beaten.

Danny Hastie watched her struggles with helpless anger and saw the smirk on his father's face as Daisy strained every muscle, but couldn't get the wheels to budge even a fraction of an inch.

'Go on then, you stupid wee bugger! Get it moving!' the senior foreman roared at her, and all at once the mood of defiance snapped and Daisy, exhausted and defeated, burst into tears and fled past her tormentor, out of the twisting department, down the stairs and out of the mill, heading for home as fast as her feet could carry her.

'Give her her books when she comes back,' Bill Hastie told his son unemotionally. 'And get someone to shift that bogie.'

'Father . . .' Danny caught at the older man's sleeve as he went by. 'You can't treat the lassie like that. She's new, she was only doing what she thought was best—'

'It's no' her place to think, it's her place to ask for orders and obey them. She doesnae fit in here. Get rid of her. And learn your lesson – that's the sort of decision that makes for a good gaffer,' Bill told his son and moved further into the department, his eyes alert for any other misdemeanours in need of nipping in the bud.

5

Mags Beckett was home when her youngest daughter burst into the kitchen, her face tear-streaked, her story tumbling out as soon as she saw her mother. Mags listened with mounting outrage, then reached for her coat and hat. 'Wash your face, our Daisy, we're going to the mill.'

'I can't go back there, Mam, not ever! I'll have lost my job!'

Mags held a cloth under the cold tap, wrung it out and ran it over Daisy's face with the expertise of one who had spent most of a lifetime washing small, dirty faces. 'Whether you've been turned off or not, nob'dy swears at any of my bairns. Come on, now,' she commanded and Daisy, protesting and blubbering, was hauled down the stairs and out into the street.

When they reached the Ropeworks, Mags marched past the gatehouse without as much as glancing at the man on duty there and made for the twisting department. She had worked in the place before her marriage, and she knew every inch of the large red-brick building. When she reached the right floor she prowled the long alleys between the rows of machines until she spied Bill Hastie himself, conferring with his son. She bore down on him, prodding at his shoulder

51

with a stiff forefinger so that he spun round in surprise.

'I'm here tae right a wrong, Willie Hastie,' she told him in a voice that, while it didn't boom like his, could still be heard clearly despite the clamour of machinery about them. 'Nob'dy swears at any lassie of mine!'

'You've no right to be in here!'

'I've every right tae be wherever I want tae be,' Mags told him mercilessly. Although his bullying manner and upright carriage usually made the man seem larger than he really was, it didn't work with Mags, who loomed over him physically and in every other way. 'And you'll apologise tae my Daisy!'

Hastie, taken aback and totally unprepared for such an attack, floundered. 'I will not. I didnae swear at anyone.'

'Ye did. She says ye did, and she doesnae tell lies. I don't allow lies in my house – nor foul language, so my bairns arenae used tae it.'

'Danny, tell this woman that she's haverin'!'

Danny opened his mouth, then shut it again.

'Leave the laddie be, Willie, and fight your own battles,' Mags snapped, 'Anyway, there's no need for him to say a word, for I can see the truth of it in his face. You were aye a wee liar at the school, Willie Hastie,' she drove on, 'an' I'm not the only one in the town that still minds you well from those days. Just because ye're a foreman here it doesnae entitle ye tae abuse decent wee lassies like my Daisy. Now . . . she's comin' back home with me because she's too upset tae finish her shift, but she'll be back on Monday mornin' and no more'll be said tae her. D'ye understand me, Willie?'

She wheeled round without waiting for a reply and marched off towards the door, leaving the senior foreman crimson in the face and with his reputation in tatters. Already, he well knew, the sign language which generations of women had devised as a means of communicating in the noisy mill was fluttering and nodding and eyebrow-raising its way up and down the rows of twisting machines. By the time he reached the door every worker in the huge room would know what had happened. Before he went home that night, the entire place would know.

'You daft gommerel!' He turned on his son.

'I couldn't say that you didn't lie when you did.' Danny, sorry for his father but at the same time delighted to have seen the man bested for once, faced up to him. 'I take it that there'll be no sacking?'

'You'll never amount to anything in this place . . . or in this world,' Bill Hastie said witheringly and walked out, straight-backed, past rows of smirking, delighted twisters.

When Morag called briefly at Ardgowan Street on her way home from work she found Mags Beckett glowing like a fighter who had battled mightily and won, while Daisy was pale and wan in the aftermath of the ordeal she had gone through.

'I'll be too scared to go in on Monday,' she snivelled. 'The man'll be taking it out on me.'

'He'll not, hen, don't you worry about that,' her mother assured her, adding with a gleam in her eyes, 'an' even if he does, he'll have me tae answer tae again.'

'And me,' Wilma chimed in. 'If I'd known what was going on I'd have sorted him out for you, Daisy.'

'Then you'd both have been in danger of being turned off,' Morag pointed out, but Mags shook her head.

'No, they wouldnae, I'd have made sure of that.

Anyway, young Danny'll look out for you, pet. He knew fine that his father was in the wrong, and he was ready tae say it if he'd had to. Willie was aye a coward in the playground, and I've heard that wee men like him sometimes turn intae bullies tae make up for the lack of inches. Bein' in the Army durin' the war made him worse.' She shook her head. 'His poor wife didnae last long after he came home, and from what I've heard that lassie Grace doesnae have much of a life, out tae work all day then havin' tae run the house tae her father's orders the rest of the time.'

'Grace Hastie?' Suddenly Morag realised why something about Danny Hastie's bearing and manner and fair hair had seemed familiar when she met him with Wilma. 'She works in the teashop. She's a nice girl, but very quiet.'

'Timid, more like, livin' with a father like that,' Mags snorted.

'I'm going to the pictures tonight with some of the girls, Morag. It's Greta Garbo . . . come with us,' Wilma coaxed.

'I can't. I'll need to go now, for I've left my father in the garden and he'll be waiting for me. I just came to see if you wanted to go for a walk tomorrow afternoon, since the weather's so nice. Uncle Lawrence's visiting him, so I might as well keep out of the way.'

'We could take a turn along to Newark Castle if you like, to watch the lads rowing.'

Daisy peered up at her sister. 'Isn't Danny Hastie in the Newark Rowing Club?'

'I believe he is – but that's not why I'm suggesting it,' Wilma added hurriedly. 'I just wondered what it was like.'

'I'll come for you at two o'clock.' Morag began to

gather up her shopping bags. 'I'll have to go . . . my father'll be shouting for his tea.'

Sander wasn't shouting for his tea. Instead he was lying back in his chair, with a breeze riffling through his thick hair and bird-song all around him, and he was dead.

Morag thought at first that he was asleep, and was reluctant to wake him, but the breeze was cooling with evening's approach and she wanted to tuck another blanket over his shoulders while she waited for some-one to come up from the harbour to help him back to his room.

She began to put the blanket about him, trying not to disturb him; then, alerted by his complete stillness, she bent and peered into his face. His eyes were half-open, and blank like the windows of an empty house.

'Father?' she asked gently, tentatively, then louder in a voice harsh with fear, 'Father?' There was no reply, no movement, and although his cheek was cool rather than cold beneath her fingers, there was a strange absence of something – some vital essence of existence – that sent her reeling back and then stumbling to the corner of the house, not knowing what to do next or who to turn to. She ran along the side path towards the road and almost bumped into Cal Fergusson as he came swinging along from the front of the house on his way to help his employer upstairs to bed.

'It's Father, he's—' She caught at him, shaking him in her need for understanding. 'He'll not wake up . . .'

He set her aside without a word and hastened past her, disappearing round the corner. Afraid to be alone, she followed to find him stooping over the slumped figure. 'He's gone,' he said quietly as she arrived.

'No!' It was a wail of denial. Not now – not after Sander had survived the long winter and had begun to show signs of returning health. Not before he managed to get back to the harbour and his beloved river!

'There's no doubt of it.' Cal spoke crisply, with a sudden note of authority in his voice that jerked her out of her mounting panic. 'D'ye have a telephone? We must notify the doctor.'

'No . . .' His lack of sympathy helped to start her brain working properly again, as did just having him there, tall and sturdy and in control of the situation. 'But the doctor lives just two doors down, that way.'

'I'll fetch him. You go into the house and make yourself a cup of tea. I'll be back in no time at all.'

'Father—'

'He'll be fine on his lone,' he said impatiently. 'He's no need of you any more. Go on!' He waited until she had gone into the house before moving away from the chair and its still occupant.

True to his word, he was back before the kettle boiled, bringing with him not only the doctor but Mrs Kennedy as well. The woman scooped Morag up and swept her back to her own home, where she gave her tea with 'just a touch' of brandy, and telephoned the grocery store where Lawrence Weir worked.

Lawrence took over as soon as he arrived, and from then on Morag had nothing to do. At first, numbed by the suddenness of Sander's death, she was content to sit in a quiet corner and leave everything to her uncle and her aunt, but by the evening of the third day she felt as though the house, with its doors closed and windows curtained to indicate that there had been a death, was suffocating her. Fortunately Lawrence and Margaret

56

were too busy with their own concerns to object when she asked if she could go out.

She fled to Ardgowan Street and the noisy comfort of the Beckett household, so full of life compared with the house of death she had left. Mags Beckett, like the doctor's wife, insisted on lacing her tea with brandy.

'I'll become a drunkard at this rate,' Morag protested.

'Ach, it'd take more than a spoonful now and again tae dae that, hen,' the woman assured her, giving Wilma some and then half-filling her own cup with tea before topping it to the brim from the brandy bottle. 'It's good for you.'

'It grows hairs on your chest, I've heard,' Wilma giggled, then took an appreciative gulp. 'It's good.'

It was. It was warming, and comforting, like the Becketts themselves and their crammed kitchen smelling of cooking and ironing and washing soda, not to mention the scent of the fresh-baked scones, still hot from the oven, that Mrs Beckett buttered and handed to the girls.

'Fresh made by our Daisy. She's a rare wee baker, so she is. Now, hen . . .' She settled herself by the fire. 'What's to become of ye?'

'I don't know.' Morag hadn't given it a thought.

'But your father'll leave the house to you, and enough money to live on, surely.' Wilma bit into her scone, then scooped some escaping melted butter from her chin with the tip of a finger.

'The house will go to Uncle Lawrence, and the business.'

'That's not fair!' Wilma stared at her friend, shocked by the injustice of it. 'After all you've done, nursing your mam and then your father . . . what has your uncle done to deserve things that should go to you?'

57

'He's a man, hen,' her mother told her dryly. 'Men run businesses, lassies don't.'

'But you need food and clothing and a roof over your head just as much as your uncle does. And you're the daughter of the house!'

'It's not as simple as that – there are reasons . . .' Morag tried to explain clumsily.

'If the house goes to your uncle, where will you live?' Wilma asked.

'I'll probably go away from Port Glasgow to find work.'

'You've already got work here.'

'Being a cashier in a teashop won't bring in enough to keep me.'

'You can always come and stay with us if you find yourself with nowhere else to go,' Wilma said firmly. 'There's more room now that the older ones have left home, though it's still a bit crowded.'

'Aye, hen, we can always fit another one in – specially a wee skelf of a thing like yourself,' Mrs Beckett added heartily.

'Stay with us tonight. You can squeeze into my bed.'

The idea was tempting, but Morag had to shake her head. 'Aunt Margaret's staying every night just now, to keep me company. I'll have to go back.'

'If you do leave the Port,' Wilma said as they walked along the street together, 'I'll come with you.'

'What about your job, and your family?'

'If you can look for other work, so can I. As to Mam and the rest, there's enough of them to keep each other company. You're my best friend, Morag,' Wilma said earnestly.

*   *   *

Until then, Morag hadn't seen further than the funeral in two days' time, but later she began to give her future serious thought. She knew that her father would have left both house and business to his brother and nearest male relative – but surely, she fretted as she got ready for bed that night, he would have made adequate provision for her? All she required was enough money to start a new life. Even if for some reason he had neglected to make provision for her in his will, she was certain that Lawrence would be prepared to give her the money needed to make a new life for herself . . . as long as it was far from Port Glasgow, which would be her wish too. She knew she was an embarrassment to him.

As she put out the light and scrambled into bed, she found that the idea of becoming an independent person at last excited her. She might choose city life in Glasgow, or she could go across the river to Dunoon or Helensburgh, both fairly busy towns frequented by holiday-makers. She could surely find work there, either in a shop or as a domestic worker. The thought of cleaning someone else's house didn't trouble her – she was used to housework, and skilled enough at it. There could well be a suitable vacancy in an hotel or a boarding-house, she thought, then stopped, appalled by the realisation that she was excitedly planning for a future made possible because of a good man's death.

With a horrified gasp she bounced out of bed and kicked away the rug in order to increase her penance by kneeling on the cold linoleum. Folding her hands and squeezing her eyes shut, she said in a low gabble, 'Lord forgive me for these unworthy evil thoughts and bless Father's soul, Amen.' Then, crawling back into bed, she started reciting her multiplication tables, a ruse

Georgina had taught her in childhood to keep wicked thoughts from her mind.

Lawrence Weir cleared his throat loudly. 'Mr – er . . .'

'Grieve, sir,' the young lawyer said patiently, for the third time that day. 'Aidan Grieve.'

'I can't see why Mr Dalrymple couldn't have been here in person. After all, my brother was a good client of his for many years. He would have expected him to make the effort.'

Morag, her nerves rubbed raw in the week since her father's death, culminating in the funeral the day before, wanted to scream at the man, but she forced herself to be as quiet and as polite as possible. 'Mr Grieve told you, Uncle Lawrence, that Mr Dalrymple is indisposed. Would you like some tea?'

'I've had tea this week until I feel I'm awash with it.'

'Lawrence!' Now it was Margaret Weir's turn to chastise her husband, who shot her a huffy glance.

'I'm speaking no more than the truth.'

'D'you have to be so vulgar about it?'

'I am not,' Lawrence said evenly, 'being vulgar. I am never vulgar. I just want to get on with it! We've all had a difficult day.'

'Mr Laird?'

John Laird, perched uncomfortably on the edge of a chair, shook his head, but the lawyer said unexpectedly, 'I would welcome a cup of tea.' He smiled up at Morag, 'If it isn't putting you to too much trouble.'

'It'll waste more time,' Lawrence barked.

'I must get the papers into order before we can proceed with the reading of the will, Mr Weir.'

'I won't take a moment,' Morag said swiftly and

whisked out of the room. She too was tired of tea, both the making and the drinking of it. It seemed to be the solution to everything in Scotland, and the many people who had called at the house in the past week to express their condolences – neighbours, businessmen, shop-keepers – had all expected, and received, refreshment. But at least this particular tea-making ritual gave her the chance to be on her own for a moment.

Now that the funeral was over, she was allowed to open the curtains again and raise the blinds; it was a relief to be able to gaze out at the garden, even though it was being swept by the rain that all too often fell on the West Coast of Scotland, even in June. She took a moment to go to the back door, where she stretched her arms high above her head, breathing the fresh moist air in deeply and revelling in the luxury of some time to herself.

With so many visitors to deal with, she had taken to using the trolley which had been Georgina Weir's pride and joy; as she wheeled it into the parlour she noted Margaret's sudden interest. The woman had been mentally pricing and recording every single item in the house since Sander's death. Aidan Grieve was still working with his papers, seemingly quite unaware of Lawrence's impatience. His fair hair had been carefully slicked down with pomade and Morag, pouring out tea, found herself wondering idly if that was because it had a tendency to spring up if left to its own devices.

Margaret accepted a cup of tea and carried it with her as she continued to prowl about the room, looking from the rear like a crow in her long black coat with its fur collar and cuffs, and her black hat shaped for all the world like a stove-pipe. It was a winter coat, and too warm for the time of year. Now and then she dabbed at her forehead and cheeks with a linen handkerchief, but

61

she had refused to take the coat off even at the funeral tea the day before.

'Thank you.' The lawyer accepted his tea with a smile and sipped at it appreciatively, then said, 'Ah . . .' as the doorbell rang.

'I'll deal with it.' Lawrence made for the parlour door, but fortunately Morag was nearer, and faster.

'I'll see to it.' The neighbours had been very kind and she didn't want her uncle, in his present uncertain temper, to insult some well-meaning soul who happened to call with condolences at the wrong moment.

But it wasn't a neighbour, it was Cal Fergusson, wearing the same neat, dark suit and tie he had worn the day before when he and all the other Weir employees had attended the funeral.

Of all the times to call, Morag thought, dismayed. Aloud, she said, 'If you don't mind coming back some other day, Cal, I've got people in just now . . .'

He consulted the sheet of paper in his hand. 'Is Mr Aidan Grieve one of them?'

'Yes, he's here to deal with the reading of my father's will.'

Cal's eyebrows shot up. 'He didn't say that in his letter, he just asked me to meet him here this afternoon.'

They stared at each other in confusion, then she stepped back, opening the door wider. 'You'd best come in, then.'

He took a moment in the porch to shake rainwater from his hat before shrugging out of his coat and hanging it up himself. Then, smoothing down his hair and straightening his tie, he gave her a slight nod. 'We'd best find out what this is about,' he said.

6

When Cal walked into the parlour John Laird's jaw dropped and Margaret stared, while Lawrence demanded flatly, 'What's he doing here?'

The lawyer got up and came round the small table which had been set up for him, hand outstretched. 'Mr Fergusson? I'm Aidan Grieve, Mr Weir's lawyer. You know Miss Weir . . .'

'Never mind the fancy introductions, I asked what was he doing here?' Lawrence interrupted, and Grieve gave him an icy glance.

'I asked Mr Fergusson to attend the reading of the will. This is Mrs Lawrence Weir,' he went on, 'and I gather that you know Mr Weir and Mr Laird.'

Margaret, her eyes fixed questioningly on her husband, ignored the introduction. For his part, Cal nodded at each person present. Then the lawyer returned to the table and said, 'If you would care to be seated, ladies and gentlemen?'

Lawrence, with another sidelong hostile glance at Cal, settled his wife in an armchair and drew up a stiff-backed chair for himself, while Morag sat down to one side, out of the way, and John Laird took a seat at the back of the room well away from the family members. After a moment's hesitation, Cal Fergusson

63

moved to a chair against a side wall.

'I hope that this won't take long?' Lawrence asked harshly, pulling out his silver hunter and glancing at it. 'Our children have seen little enough of us this week, and the maidservant can't be trusted to look after the house unsupervised.'

'I'm sure Aggie does well enough, Lawrence.'

'I don't think so, my dear. Servants need to be supervised at all times.'

'If I may start,' Aidan Grieve said with a hint of irritation creeping into his voice, 'then we shall be finished quite quickly. It is a very straightforward will.'

Morag smoothed the skirt of the plain black knitted suit she usually wore at the teashop. Margaret and Lawrence had raised their eyebrows at it, and at the dark blue coat she had worn over it for the funeral, but she didn't have much in the way of savings and had been reluctant, given the uncertainty of her future, to spend money on a special funeral outfit. There was a small sum in Sander's desk, but she had been determined that it should remain untouched, proof to Lawrence when he took over that she had taken nothing that didn't truly belong to her.

The reading started briskly enough. Sander Weir had left a few small amounts to various organisations, plus the sum of £200 to John Laird in recognition of a lifetime of loyalty to the company.

'Well deserved,' Margaret said firmly and her husband nodded, while the old man tried hard to smother the delighted smirk that rushed to his lips. Then Margaret gave a little murmur of approval and gratitude to hear that Sander had left £200 to each of his brother's children. But her husband remained motionless, his eyes fixed impatiently on the young lawyer.

Aidan Grieve read on steadily, 'I leave my dwelling

house, where she has lived for most of her life, to Morag Isabel Weir—'

Lawrence jerked abruptly in his chair. 'What?'

The lawyer glanced up at him. 'Your brother stressed to my uncle the importance of ensuring that Miss Weir continued to have somewhere to live,' he explained, and from where she sat slightly to the side and behind him, Morag saw dark red colour surge up the back of Lawrence's neck.

'That's nonsense – Sander knew full well that Morag would always have a home with me and my wife!'

'Nevertheless, Mr Weir, that is in his will. As I understand it, your brother expressed the view that you would fully agree with the importance of providing for your own flesh and blood.'

Lawrence stood up abruptly, almost knocking his chair over, and paced angrily to the window, his hands jammed in his pockets. 'Lawrence . . . your good jacket,' Margaret protested. 'You'll stretch the material!'

'Read on,' her husband commanded, wrenching his hands free.

'When everyone is seated, Mr Weir.'

'Lawrence . . .' Margaret reached out a hand towards him and he returned slowly to his seat, still flushed with anger. Morag sat still, stunned by what she had just heard. But the shocks were not yet over.

'To my brother, Lawrence Weir, the sum of £1,000 pounds, my gold hunter watch, my onyx cuff-links and tiepin . . .' The pleasantly modulated voice, ideal for a lawyer, droned on, listing a number of items, while Lawrence squirmed in his chair but managed to keep his impatience under control. 'To Morag Isabel Weir, an annual payment of £1,000 until her twenty-fifth birthday, when the balance of my estate after the

65

settlement of any debts and obligations will be paid to her in its entirety.'

'But—' Lawrence sat upright, then subsided as the young man raised cold eyes to his face.

'As to the Weir Shipping Company,' the lawyer continued after a short, reproving pause, 'of which I am sole owner; my brother, Lawrence Weir, is to hold 25 per cent of the shares. I leave 20 per cent of the shares to Calum Fergusson, in acknowledgement of his loyalty towards me and my respect for his grandfather.'

A chair creaked noisily at the back of the room, and Lawrence shifted suddenly in his chair and began to speak. His wife's gloved hand shot out and clamped itself on his arm, and he subsided as the lawyer raised his voice and read on. Glancing to the side, Morag saw that Cal's face was blank with astonishment.

'Morag Isabel Weir, in recognition of all she has done for my late wife and myself in our declining years, to receive the remaining 55 per cent of the shares in Weir Shipping, with my blessing.'

This time Lawrence Weir exploded from his chair, almost falling over the table as he leaned towards the young man seated on the other side. 'This is a nonsense! The business was to go to me!'

Aidan Grieve gamely resisted the temptation to lean back, away from the angry face only inches away from his own. 'In a previous will, sir, I believe that you are quite right, but this will was made three months ago and is perfectly valid.'

'I'll not have it,' Lawrence raged. 'He can't leave everything to a chit of a girl who knows nothing but work in a fancy teashop!' He swung round on Morag, still rooted to her chair with shock. 'You knew about this all along! You influenced my brother during his final illness and persuaded him to write a new will in your favour when he was at his most vulnerable. And I've no doubt' – now his attention was directed at Cal and he pointed a shaking finger at the young man – 'that you connived with her. I know fine and well that you came to this house several times lately. And now we know why!'

'Cal only came to help me with—'

'Oh, he helped you, all right – and himself!'

Now it was Cal's turn to come out of his chair, his face hardening. 'I must ask you to retract that, Mr Weir, and to apologise to your niece.'

'Any apologies are due to me, not to you two!' Flecks of spittle dotted Lawrence's lips. 'You connived together to work on my sick brother—'

'Mr Weir, I protest!' It was Aidan Grieve's turn to get to his feet. 'I can assure you that my uncle would not have presided over the making of this will if he had had any fears that undue pressure had been put upon his client!'

'Perhaps your uncle was part of—'

'I feel it only right to warn you to watch what you say, sir,' the young man said icily. 'There are witnesses present.'

'Aye, witnesses to a miscarriage of justice! You hear me, John Laird? I'll be calling on you to stand up in a court of law to tell of the mock my brother's made of me, even in death!'

'I – I . . .' the poor old man stammered, his eyes swivelling from one face to another.

'Uncle Lawrence, this is not the time or the place to . . .'

'She's right. Come away, Lawrence.' Margaret Weir tugged at her husband's sleeve, with no thought now to stretching the good cloth of his jacket. 'Come home and we'll talk about it tomorrow.'

'We'll talk about it here and now!' He pulled free of her, his eyes on Morag again. 'This is your revenge, isn't it? All those years you've been waiting for it, and now the time's come to vent your spite on me.' He gave a harsh laugh. 'By God, talk about hell having no fury like a woman scorned!'

'I knew nothing about it!'

'I'm quite certain of that,' the lawyer put in, and Lawrence swung back to him.

'For God's sake, boy, there has to be trickery in it somewhere. Why would a man in his right mind leave everything to a lassie who's not even his own daughter? Ah – you didn't know that, did you?' he went on triumphantly as the young man blinked.

'Is this true, Miss Weir?'

'Yes, it's true.' Looking at Lawrence, his face twisted with rage and thwarted greed, Morag felt the shock which had paralysed her in the past few minutes give way to rising anger. This was the week of Sander's funeral, a time which should have been dedicated to mourning the passing of a kind and honourable man. Instead, his long life was ending in noise and anger and recrimination.

'It's true, and there's no secret about it,' she said quietly to the startled, uncomprehending lawyer. 'You're the only person here who didn't know that Sander Weir wasn't my birth father, but I've considered myself to be his daughter ever since he took me in as a child when my own father deserted me.'

Lawrence drew in his breath sharply, while his wife said in shocked tones, 'Deserted? Morag, you can't possibly say that!'

'I can and I do.' Morag, fingernails dug deep into the palms of her hands to give her added courage, looked straight at Lawrence. 'I've never used that word to you before, but it's what you did and I don't see that you can deny it. You deserted me, and on that day I became your brother's daughter, not yours.'

For a moment he confronted her, his mouth opening and closing like a fish, then he spun on his heel and left the room without another word, dragging his wife after him by the hand. As the front door crashed shut behind them John Laird rose shakily from his chair, muttering, 'I'll just – I'll away down the road . . .'

'I'd best be going too,' Cal said when Morag came back from seeing Laird out. 'I've got the boat to see to.' He turned to Aidan Grieve, who was calmly storing papers into a shabby old leather attaché case which was at odds with his smart appearance. 'Can I . . .'

'Of course. Here's my card.'

For a moment Cal turned the card over in his big fingers, looking at Morag as though trying to think of the right words. He seemed to feel as stunned as she did. Then he said, 'I'll see myself out.'

As the door closed quietly behind him, Aidan Grieve delved into the bag and produced an envelope. 'This is for you.'

She glanced at her name, written in Sander's familiar hand, then set the letter aside. 'I must apologise for my— for . . .' She didn't quite know now how to describe the relationship between herself and Lawrence.

'Not at all,' he told her briskly. 'You'd be surprised at the things a lawyer sees and hears in the course of a normal day's work – though it would have helped if my uncle had thought to tell me more about your family circumstances.' He closed the bag and set it on the floor, then beamed at her. 'If you have the time, Miss Weir, I think this unusual occasion calls for some fresh tea.'

'There's my fa . . . some whisky if you'd prefer it.'

'I'd keep a clearer head with tea, and' – his sudden,

dazzling grin was heart-warming after the hatred she had seen in Lawrence's eyes – 'I'll need a clear head in order to fathom out how your uncle became your father and vice versa.'

They moved through to the kitchen, where the sun now streamed in through the window, and sat at the table while Morag told the young lawyer about her mother's illness and eventual death during the Great War.

'We lived in a tenement down in Bellhaven Street then, me and my parents. There was a woman who lived across the landing from us, a kind old soul; all the children in the street called her Granny Crawford. She looked after both of us during my mother's illness. Her daughter Margaret was my mother's best friend, and I always called her Aunt Margaret. When my mother died, Aunt Georgina took me to their house, just until my father came home for good. They lived in Queen Street at that time, near to the Town Hall.'

'How old were you then?'

'Six. When my father came back on furlough and went to thank Granny Crawford for what she had done for us, he met Aunt Margaret again, and the next time he came home they got married, quietly and with nobody knowing about it until it had happened.'

She vaguely remembered her father, in his soldier's uniform, walking into his brother's living-room with Aunt Margaret at his side in a smart blue skirt and a jacket with velvet lapels and a wide-brimmed hat with a large blue feather nodding round the deep crown every time she moved her head. Until then, Morag had only ever seen Margaret Crawford dressed in the ordinary, fairly colourless clothes worn by all the women living in their street. On that day, with her fine clothes and her cheeks flushed and her eyes bright, she looked like a duchess at least.

'We're wed,' Lawrence had announced flatly, defiantly; then, when his brother and sister-in-law gaped in astonished silence, 'Well . . . aren't you going to congratulate us?'

He had brought a bottle with him and the four grown-ups sat around sipping from Georgina's finest tumblers and making stilted conversation, while Morag was allowed a small glass of ginger wine. As she was only allowed ginger wine at Ne'erday, the first day of the New Year, and this was summertime, she found the whole business very confusing.

'All I could think of,' she recalled, 'was the beautiful feather on Aunt Margaret's hat. None of the birds I'd seen in picture books had such glorious feathers.'

Afterwards, when her father and his new wife had gone and long after she herself should have been asleep, she heard her aunt and uncle talking in the living-room, their voices low and urgent. Over the next few weeks there were more worried conversations, always broken off when she appeared.

Eventually life returned to normal, but the tension came back when the war ended and her father came home for good, out of his khaki uniform and back into ordinary street clothes.

'I was eight years old by then, and my aunt and uncle had just moved here after her father died and left the house to her. Aunt Georgina had always made it clear to me that I would go to live with my father and my new mother once the war was ended, but instead my father called here a lot and I was sent to my room so that the three of them could talk . . . and talk, and talk, it seemed to me. Finally Aunt Georgina told me that she and Uncle Sander had asked my father if they could keep me, because they didn't have any children and Aunt Margaret hoped to have a little girl of her own

71

quite soon. It seemed sensible, as it was explained to me
– one little girl for each brother. But Aunt Margaret had
a son, and then her daughter. By then I was calling my
aunt and uncle Mother and Father, and somehow, since
I already looked on Margaret as an aunt, it made sense
for Lawrence to become my uncle.'

'That,' said Aidan Grieve, 'is a remarkable state of
affairs.'

'Not if you drift into it as we did.'

'Did you never resent the way your real father
treated you?'

'Not then. Later, when I was old enough to think
things out for myself, I realised that I had more or less
been rejected, but I was happy here with my parents
. . . my real aunt and uncle,' she corrected herself.
'Flora and Crawford – my father's other family –
didn't even know that I was their sister, and really
none of it seemed to matter very much. That's why I
expected Uncle Lawrence to inherit everything, and so
did he. It seemed obvious to both of us that he had the
major claim.' She spread out her hands in a helpless
gesture. 'Now what am I to do?'

'Come to my office tomorrow morning at ten o'clock
and we'll discuss it,' Aidan said decisively, pushing
back his chair. 'As for now . . . I must go. Thank you
for the tea, and for the explanation.'

At the front door he hesitated, then asked, 'Do you
have a friend who could come and stay with you
tonight? I don't think you should be alone after the
shock you've received.'

'I've been invited to stay with friends in the town.'

'Good,' he said, then grinned a boyish, unlawyer-like
grin and flourished the shabby old case at her. 'My turn
to explain. My mother gave this to me when I first went
to Edinburgh University to read law, and we've been

through so much together since then that I look on it as
a sort of lucky talisman. It annoys my uncle no end.'

As he went down the steps to the garden path, she
noticed that the soft fair hairs at the nape of his neck
had managed to release themselves from the pomade
he had used and were curling endearingly above his
high white collar.

It very swiftly became clear that, now that the funeral
was over and Sander's will had dashed Lawrence's
expectations, he was no longer interested in making
sure that Morag was not left on her own in the house.
She had lied to the young lawyer about being invited to
stay with friends, fully intending to be alone that night,
but as darkness fell the house's silence began to depress
her. Eventually, she packed a small bag and made her
way to the Becketts' flat.

Mags opened the door, her face wreathed in smiles
when she saw her visitor. 'Come on in, hen . . . they're
all away out for the evening, but I was just makin' a
cup of tea and thinkin' that it would be nice tae have
company tae drink it with . . .' she began.

Morag, looking at her plain, welcoming face, began
to speak, then burst into tears.

The Beckett family began their day early. By the time
Wilma, Daisy and Archie got up their mother, who had
a cleaning job, was already out of the house. When
they had rushed out in their turn – Archie heading
for the East Harbour and the girls for the Ropeworks,
hell-bent on getting through the mill gates before the
sirens and hooters blew to mark the official beginning
of the working day – Morag cleared the table and

washed the dishes before returning to Lilybank Road to prepare for her meeting in the lawyer's office.

She and Wilma, crushed together in Wilma's narrow bed, had talked late into the night. After numerous complaints, which were ignored, poor Daisy had got up in the early hours of the morning and wandered blearily into the kitchen to climb into the box bed beside her mother. Even though she had had little sleep, Morag felt refreshed as she made her way back into the town later. Being with the Becketts, treated as one of the family, fussed over and comforted in her hour of need, she had been healed of the wounds inflicted by her father on the previous day.

Aidan came out of his office as soon as he heard that she had arrived. 'My uncle has suggested that we should go along to the house, to talk to him about your situation.' He opened the door for her. 'My car is just outside.'

7

Morag had never ridden in a car before, for Sander could easily walk to his office and despite Georgina's appeals he had refused to consider the purchase of a motor-vehicle, declaring it to be the first step on the road to decadence. 'If we all succumb to the lure of the engine we'll end up losing the use of the legs that the good Lord gave us,' he maintained, ignoring the fact that he himself possessed only one good leg. 'In any case, what would happen to the trams and trains and buses if we stopped using them?'

Morag had been happy to walk or to use the public transport available, and now she stepped into the bottle-green open car with a certain amount of apprehension. Fortunately Aidan proved to be a capable driver and, by the time they were half-way through Greenock and bowling along with the wind in their faces, she had begun to enjoy herself.

The car was clearly Aidan's pride and joy; he talked incessantly about it as he drove and Morag, who might as well have been listening to a foreign language, soon realised that the opportunity to talk was more important to him than being understood. The journey passed comfortably with him shouting above the breeze and the noise of the engine about suspension and fan-belts and spark plugs, while Morag nodded and smiled wherever it seemed appropriate.

Kenneth Dalrymple was one of the many business and professional men who had their money-making factories, mills, shipyards and offices in Port Glasgow or Greenock, while they themselves lived in comfort in Gourock away from the dust and smoke that was a necessary part of heavy industry. His large house stood in the centre of an elegant garden on the hill above the town, and Mr Dalrymple himself was waiting for his visitors on a flagged terrace at the side, seated in an armchair with a bandaged foot propped on a small stool. By his side a table bore a tea-tray.

'Forgive me if I don't get up, my dear,' he said, taking Morag's hand in his. 'A bad attack of gout – and unfortunately it struck just when you and my poor friend Sander had most need of my services.'

'Your nephew has been very helpful.'

'I'm very glad to hear it. Please sit down.' He indicated a chair close to his own, then nodded towards the table. 'I have some particularly good coffee beans. I hope you like coffee, though my housekeeper can provide tea if you would prefer it.'

Morag happily agreed to coffee, and Aidan was ordered to pour it out, 'While Miss Weir and I start discussing her future.'

'I've already decided on that. I want to give the house and the business to my . . . to my real father.'

Aidan paused in his work at the table, and uncle and nephew looked at each other thoughtfully before the older man said, 'Indeed?'

'It's only fair. He expected to inherit everything, and I didn't. After all, he is my father.'

'When it suits him,' Aidan Grieve said, adding swiftly, 'forgive me, I should not have said that.'

76

'No, you should not,' his uncle reproved him with an edge to his voice. The young man coloured and busied himself with the coffee pot.

'And he's Sander's nearest relative, when all's said and done,' Morag hurried on, embarrassed on Aidan's behalf. 'So everything should really have gone to him. All I need at the moment is a reasonable monthly income, to help me until I can make proper arrangements for my own future.'

'It seems that you and your natural father are alike – in your thoughts, at least. Lawrence called on me last night to make the very same suggestion.'

'Then that's settled,' Morag said with relief. 'Since everyone thinks that it's for the best, perhaps you could make the necessary arrangements, Mr Dalrymple.' She accepted a cup and saucer from Aidan, and shook her head at the offer of a biscuit.

Kenneth Dalrymple cleared his throat. 'As it happens, I myself am not in favour with your views, or Lawrence's. Nor, clearly, was Sander, and as the will in question is his I feel that I am still representing him,' he said mildly. 'I believe your uncle left a letter for you, Morag. Have you read it?'

'Not yet.' She had forgotten all about the envelope still lying on the dining-room table. 'What does he say in it?'

'I have no idea. The contents are entirely a matter between you and Sander. But I feel that you should read it before making any decisions.'

'Whatever the letter says, it was wrong of him to favour me over his own brother!'

'My dear, I knew Sander for the best part of thirty years and I shall miss him very much, as a friend as well as a client. And the one thing that can be said about him is that he was never wrong: he was a very shrewd man who always knew what was best. Georgina never realised it, but when Sander took over the running of her late father's business interests the quarry was in a bad way, only just limping along. Much as Sander hated having to work inland, and in an office instead of being on the river as he had before the War, he pulled his wife's business back from the brink and built it into a thriving concern. When Georgina had the good sense to agree to a move to shipping, Sander then set to and revived the ailing business he eventually bought from Samuel Fergusson. He was a fine man . . . a very fine man. The country is the poorer for his loss.'

The old man paused, his eyes on the horizon, then took a deep breath and returned to the present. 'He loved Weir Shipping, as I'm sure you'll know, and he disliked the thought of leaving it to his brother, for Lawrence knows nothing about running a shipping company.'

'Nor do I.'

'That's not quite true, if you'll forgive me for saying so. I understand that even before Sander fell ill you were assisting him with the books. He was most impressed by your grasp of business, and it was his belief that the company would be safer in your hands than in his brother's.'

'But he was always there; I only copied the figures down into another set of books so that he could read them more comfortably.' Morag felt herself beginning to panic. 'I couldn't run the business on my own!'

'You could, with Aidan's assistance – just until you feel that you have a better grasp of matters. And of course, I am always available for further consultation or assistance if necessary. The boats themselves seem to be under the control of good skippers; let them advise you as to their side of things.'

'The house is far too large for me. My father and his family should at least have the house.'

'Lawrence could not run that house on what he earns, even with a quarter-share in the business.'

'I could gift it to him, and take control of its upkeep myself.'

'The first thing you must learn if you are to succeed in business, Miss Weir, is that giving away valuable property and guaranteeing its upkeep while others live in it and treat it as their own is a certain way to lose good money.' Aidan spoke gravely, but there was a twinkle in his eye and his uncle laughed aloud.

'Well said . . . I can see that I am putting my young client into safe hands.' Then, after a pause, 'Well, my dear? Do you accept the challenge that Sander has thrown down, or are you set on denying his final wishes?'

Morag drained her coffee cup, using the moment to collect her thoughts, then set it back on its saucer and said levelly as she handed it to Aidan, 'Surely it's unfair of you, Mr Dalrymple, to try to influence me by forcing me to take responsibility for my late uncle's final wishes?'

For a moment both men gaped at her, then Kenneth nodded his balding head. 'You're quite right, and I stand corrected. I had no right to speak as I did, and I can only excuse myself by saying that I was perhaps considering my dear friend Sander's side of the matter too strongly, rather than yours. It's time to bury the dead and do all I can to assist the living.'

'If I could have a few days to think over what you've said . . . ?'

'Of course. Aidan will drive you home.'

The young lawyer whistled softly as he ushered Morag into the car, which had been parked on a wide gravel sweep at the front of the house. 'You certainly told the old man off.'

'I didn't mean it to sound as it did.' Already Morag was considering going back to apologise. 'I must have sounded very impertinent.'

'Not at all, you sounded like the sort of young woman who could run a shipping company. I believe that he was rather pleased with you.' He started the engine and then got in, glancing at her before releasing the brake. 'I know that you want to be left alone to make up your own mind, but I'd like to say just one thing before I shut up on the subject. Two things, really. Calum Fergusson came to see me first thing this morning to suggest much the same as you did – that he should relinquish his shares in the company.'

'There's no reason why he should. They were willed freely to him.'

'As yours were willed to you,' Aidan pointed out gently.

'That's different. Cal knows a great deal about the company. He's worked for it for years, and his family once owned it.'

'Even so. Not that he felt that your unc . . . your father should have his shares. He wanted to give them to you.'

'I couldn't accept them!'

'The other thing I have to tell you – strictly against my uncle's orders, so I would appreciate it if you kept this quiet – is that when Lawrence Weir came here last night to consult with my uncle, he wanted advice on how to overturn his brother's will and replace it with the previous one, which was in his favour. When my uncle refused to have anything to do with it he stormed off to consult someone else. I thought you should know that.'

80

'If he does manage to overturn the will, the matter will be settled once and for all.'

'He won't, because it's valid and watertight. But you should know what he's up to,' Aidan said. And with that, he set the car in motion and returned, happily, to the subject of engines.

My poor Morag [Sander Weir's letter began],

As you read this you must be wishing that you had put poison in my beef tea, or at least left me to fend for myself during my illness. You must certainly be wondering why I have treated you so badly in my will.

But I have my reasons, and although I admit to a certain sorrow that I will not be there in person to see my brother's face when the new will is read out, believe me, Morag, when I say that my decisions were not just taken out of malice or a desire to make your life difficult. I thought long and hard, having had plenty of time to do so recently, before making this will. You deserve your inheritance, Morag. Without it you might go on working in that teashop which my dear, misguided Georgina condemned you to years ago. You have a good brain, and more spirit than Georgina ever recognised, and someone must nudge you into using them to your own advantage. Let that someone be me.

I should have done it earlier, if not before my wife's death then most certainly afterwards, but I have to admit that I put my own comfort and need for companionship first and allowed you to remain imprisoned. Now you have the key to your own freedom in your hands.

81

You could if you wish sell the business, but I hope that you will decide to keep it and to run it, and grow with it. I have given parcels of shares to Lawrence – because it would have been too unkind to shut him out entirely – and to young Calum Fergusson, because I owed a great deal to his grandfather, who gave me work as a young man, and his poor weak father was a friend of mine when he and I crewed together on the wee boats. And I respect the man Calum has become. He can be of assistance to you, Morag; don't hesitate to lean on him when necessary. I doubt if he would ever let you down.

But the bulk of the shares are yours because you have earned them. Prosper, and enjoy your life as I have enjoyed mine, with no regrets, especially where you are concerned.

Morag read the letter several times, then put it away carefully. On the following day she went down to the harbour and found John Laird sitting in the midst of the usual muddle of paperwork, scratching away with a very old pen. The sight made her think of an elderly spider in the midst of its web.

'I thought I'd come to you, Mr Laird, and save you the bother of bringing the books to the house,' she explained as he jumped up and fussily began to clear papers from the seat of the only other chair in the room.

'Eh?' He blinked up at her, then said, 'But Mr Sander has gone. Why should I want to take the books to the house?'

'To let me see them – but as I said, I'm quite happy to come here and save you the trouble,' she explained, wondering if the old man's brain was slowing down.

'Why should you want to see them? I'm managing fine as I am.'

'I'm sure you are, and I do want everything to go on as it was before, at least for the moment.'

'It is. Mr Weir's said he's happy to leave matters in my hands.'

'Mr Weir?' Now she was convinced that the shock of recent events had affected the clerk. 'Mr Weir is dead,' she explained as gently as she could, and he looked at her as though she, and not he, was confused. Then he said testily, 'No, no, not Mr Sander – I ken fine that he's left us, poor man. I'm talking about Mr Lawrence.'

'My . . . he's been to see you?'

'Aye, to find out if I can manage on my lone for the time being, just until things are worked out with the lawyers. I told him that I could, and he was quite content to leave everything to me. So that's that settled.'

Morag folded her hands tightly in her lap and tried to keep her voice level and calm. 'Mr Laird, from now on you must answer to me, not to Lawrence Weir.'

'But he's Mr Sander's brother . . .'

'I know that, and you know that I was left the major share in the business while he was left a quarter share—'

'There ye are, then, he's got the right to tell me what to do.'

'But I have more right than he has. You were there when the will was read, Mr Laird. You know that the right lies with me, not with Mr Lawrence.'

'He's lookin' into that,' Laird said sullenly.

'So I believe. But until the matter is settled you must answer to me, not him. So – I'll have a look at the books now, if you please.'

The tip of the old man's tongue flickered along his thin, pale lips. 'They're . . . they're not brought up to date yet,' he muttered.

83

'In that case I'll come back tomorrow afternoon. Please make sure that they're ready for me,' she said and walked out, her fists clenched tightly in her pockets. She was so angry with her father that she had no recollection of the journey back to the house and only returned to her surroundings as she was opening the front door.

How dare he go down to the harbour behind her back and try to establish himself as the owner? And how dare John Laird encourage him? She dragged the pins from her hat, pulled it off and stabbed them viciously through the material before hanging it up. To think that she had wanted to hand the business over to this man who had fathered her, then left his brother and sister-in-law to raise her, and was now seeking to take everything else away from her.

'You're a fool, Morag Weir,' she told herself in the hall mirror. 'You're too soft altogether. It's time you grew up, and you can start by deciding that if "Mr Lawrence" wants the business, he'll have to fight for it!'

Much to Miss Lamont's annoyance, Morag had given up her work at the teashop after Sander's death. She had too much on her mind to concentrate on calculating the price of cups of tea and pieces of Swiss roll and counting out change, and now she had quite decided that if she should lose her inheritance to Lawrence she would move away from Port Glasgow. Even that small decision made her feel that she was taking control of her own destiny.

On the day following her confrontation with John Laird she spent the morning sorting out some of her uncle's clothing; then she returned to the harbour office, giving the somewhat battered figurehead a defiant pat on her way in.

'Whatever happens, Lady Isabella, I'll see to it that you get a nice fresh coat of paint,' she promised. 'We women have to support each other!'

Although Laird was still sullen and huffy, the books were waiting for her. She ignored him, working on her own throughout the afternoon at a corner of the battered desk, making notes in an exercise book, well aware that curiosity was driving the man mad. As the hooters and sirens sounded in the factories and shipyards she closed her book, thanked him with a sweet smile and went to meet Wilma, who had been invited to Lilybank Road for her tea.

'Oh, Morag, it's beautiful! I'd no idea that you lived in such a grand house!' Wilma said in hushed tones. She turned in a slow circle that took in the entire hall ... the stained-glass panels on the front door, the opulent embossed wallpaper, the coat-stand and the umbrella-stand made from the foot of a real elephant, the broad carpeted sweep of the staircase. 'What's in there?' She pointed at one of the panelled doors.

'The parlour. I thought we'd have our tea in here, like ladies.' Morag opened the door but Wilma, after a quick peep in at the large pieces of furniture and the heavy velvet curtains, said, 'If you don't mind, I'd as soon we had our tea in your kitchen, like we do at home.'

Morag burned with embarrassment as the two of them prepared the meal. On many occasions she had wanted to invite her friend to the house, but each time Georgina had come up with one excuse or another. Finally, when she was about 12 years old, Morag had faced her mother and demanded that Wilma be invited for tea. And Georgina had told her flatly that Wilma Beckett was not 'our sort of person', and that although she very generously allowed Morag to befriend the girl, she would never be welcome in her, Georgina's, home.

Morag could have persisted, and could if necessary have enlisted the aid of Sander – an easygoing man who, unlike his wife, judged folk for themselves and not because of their station in life. But she knew with a sense of despair that even if she got her own way, Georgina's disapproval would ruin Wilma's visits, and Morag was not prepared to let her friend be treated badly just in order to score a point over Georgina. She loved the woman and owed her a great deal, but it was at that stage in her life when she realised – and accepted the fact – that Georgina Weir, unlike her husband, was a snob. She had been born into snobbishness and raised in it, and in her case it was an incurable condition.

Morag was little better. She had learned her lesson so thoroughly that even after Georgina's death it had never occurred to her to invite her friend to Lilybank Road. Now, as they sat at the kitchen table, she said abruptly, 'Wilma, I'm sorry.'

'What for?' Wilma paused with a sandwich half-way to her mouth.

'For taking so long to ask you to this house, after all the times I've been made welcome in Ardgowan Street.'

'For any favour, is that all?' Wilma, generous to a fault, leaned over and patted Morag's hand. 'I never gave it a thought, and neither should you. Anyway, I'd have been scared to open my mouth in a place like this when I was wee.'

'No need to worry about that now. I'll show you around the place when we've finished our tea.'

It was fun, seeing the big house through Wilma's eyes. She noticed small details, such as the carving on the door panels and the plasterwork details on ceilings, that Morag had never looked at before. She was fascinated by the views from all the windows, particularly at the back of the house overlooking the Clyde.

'Are you certain that you want to sell it?' she asked when they were in the hall again. 'It seems a shame.'

'I feel as though it's my mother's house, not mine. As long as I live here I'll be her daughter and not me, a grown independent woman.'

'Then make it your house. Change the furniture about, buy some new pieces, get different curtains.'

'It's far too large for me.'

'I think it must be lovely to have so much space. If this was mine, I'd have Mam and Daisy and the others and all my friends here with me. There'd be room for everyone,' Wilma enthused; then looking at Morag, 'But I see what you mean. You could take in lodgers, though. I'd do anything to keep it if it was mine.'

'I'm not certain yet that it *is* mine,' Morag told her ruefully. 'Not until the lawyers sort things out.'

8

When Wilma had gone, Morag took out the second set of books and brought them up to date from her notebook. Tomorrow, she decided, she would start going through the contents of the small room Georgina had grandly referred to as her husband's study. In actual fact Sander had never worked in it, or even sat in it to Morag's knowledge. Instead, he had used it as a glory hole for old papers, books and ledgers. Going through them would be the perfect way to learn how the business was run.

But first she had to speak to Cal Fergusson. There had been no sign of him or his puffer, the *Pladda*, on her two visits to the harbour, and she didn't want to ask John Laird where she might find him, knowing that the man must be seething with resentment over the shares her uncle had left to the young skipper. She had found his address while going through the books, and on Saturday afternoon she went to his home, a first-floor tenement flat in John Wood Street.

The door was well varnished, the nameplate and bell-pull and door-knocker gleaming. Cal, when he came to the door, was in his shirt-sleeves with a duster in his hand. He stared, as taken aback to see her as she had been on the day he arrived for the reading of the will. 'Miss Weir?' he said and then, collecting his thoughts, 'Come in.'

'I have to apologise for calling without warning, but it's not easy for us to talk at the harbour.' She followed him along a passageway and into the kitchen, shaking her head at his offer of tea. 'I can only stay for a moment.'

The room was immaculate. The lace curtains at the window were snowy white, and the few pieces of furniture – a large dresser, a table and a set of upright chairs – had been polished until they shone. A row of painted plates on the dresser's upper shelf were free of dust, and the fireplace's wooden surround and tiles gleamed. A silver teapot and hot-water jug stood on a newspaper laid out on the table, together with a tin of paste, indicating that Cal had been interrupted in the middle of polishing the pieces when she arrived.

'These are lovely.' She went to the table to admire them while he hastily unrolled his shirt-sleeves and pulled on the jacket hanging over the back of a chair.

'They were great favourites of my mother's. She couldn't bear to let them go when we . . . when we moved here. I've not decided yet what to do with them.'

'I'm in much the same situation myself now,' Morag said with a faint smile.

'Please sit down.' He indicated one of the two tapestry wing-chairs set on either side of the fire, and turned a chair round from the table for himself when she sat down.

'I thought that I should speak to you about the shares, and it's not something we could discuss in front of Mr Laird or my father.' When he nodded silently she went on, 'Mr Grieve tells me that you have it in mind to give yours to me.'

'I would prefer it. He advised me to do nothing until I had had time to think about it – and to give you time, too.'

'I'll admit that the will came as a shock. I'm sorry you had to witness that . . . family squabble.' There was no other way to describe the scene in the dining-room at Lilybank Road.

'I'm only sorry that you had to be there yourself. Your father had no right to speak to you as he did.' His face darkened at the memory.

'He was upset. I had it in mind not to keep my shares either – or the house, or any of the money.'

'Why not? You're entitled to what you got.'

'I felt that my father was more entitled.'

'I don't agree,' Cal said, his voice tight and angry.

'I've changed my mind, although my father's doing what he can to overthrow the will.'

'I'm sure your lawyers can attend to that on your behalf.'

'Yes. My uncle made it clear in a letter that he wants me to have the shares, and to look after Weir Shipping. He said that I could rely on you for advice.'

'Did he?' Cal was startled. 'What exactly did he say?'

'That I could lean on you, and you wouldn't let me fall.'

'Oh.' There was a pause, then he said formally, 'I certainly hope that you feel able to trust me.'

'I do.' She got to her feet and held out her hand. 'So we understand each other?'

'Yes.' Cal took her hand briefly in his. His normally easy manner had changed – possibly because, she thought as she left, he had been dragged against his will into the family squabbles. Sander's will had certainly set the cat among the pigeons.

That afternoon she set to work, locating the old account books in Sander's small study and carrying them downstairs to the dining-room, where she spread them out over the large table. She had already bought a number of exercise books and pencils in readiness.

The next few days flew past unnoticed; she hurried out to the shops and hurried back, ate when she was hungry and slept when she was tired, fully involved in tracing her way through the years of the quarry as well as the shipping business and learning, slowly and painstakingly, how Sander Weir had worked.

She had quite forgotten Lawrence and the threat he posed to her, and it came as a shock when, late in the afternoon of her third day working at the books, he finally called on her.

At first, Morag was so absorbed in the task before her that she heard the doorbell as a faint echo somewhere in the back of her mind. It was only when the chimes were repeated and then, after a short pause, came in a torrent, indicating that someone had a finger firmly pressed against the bell-push, that she realised that she was being summoned.

'Oh, Lord!' She pushed aside the large book she had been studying and hobbled into the hall, stiff from hours of sitting with her feet twined round the legs of her chair. Then the sight of a familiar silhouette on the coloured glass upper panels of the front door brought her to a standstill. It was too late to take off the big work apron she had donned to protect her dress, plain as it was, from the dust of decades, or to tidy her hair. She had no option but to open the door.

It was only when she saw the look on Lawrence's face, and the fastidious way in which his eyes travelled

91

down the length of her, that she remembered the scarf tied gypsy fashion about her head.

'Uncle . . . er . . . Uncle Lawrence!' She swept off the scarf with one hand while the other groped for the apron tapes at her back. 'I wasn't expecting visitors.'

'So I see.' As usual, he stepped in as though he owned the house – which, for all she knew, he did – and handed her his hat, cane and gloves. 'I thought it high time I came to see how you are, my dear.'

Hanging up the hat, she caught a glimpse of her flushed face in the mirror and saw to her horror that streaks of dust from the old books were daubed over her cheeks and forehead. 'I've been cleaning.' Morag followed him into the parlour, glad that she had had the foresight to close the dining-room door; she had no desire to let him know that she was learning something of the business. 'Would you care for some tea?'

'Thank you.' He inclined his head graciously.

While the kettle boiled Morag wetted a corner of a dish towel and scrubbed the grime from her face, then combed her hair and made herself as presentable as she could while her mind spun through all the possibilities. Uncle Lawrence – she really must get used to thinking of him as her father now – might well have come to tell her that he was the owner of the house and business, but on the other hand . . .

Setting up the tea-tray, she wished that she had had the sense to keep in touch with Aidan Grieve, or that he had thought of contacting her. As matters stood, she was at a disadvantage. It was perhaps best, she decided as she left the kitchen, not to let Lawrence realise that, if possible.

He was standing at a window, but when she carried in the tray he hurried to take it from her and put it on a low table by one of the fireside chairs. While they both settled themselves and Morag poured tea, she tried to gauge his mood, but failed. He didn't seem to be triumphant, but on the other hand he wasn't downcast either. Perhaps he too had heard nothing, and had come to find out what she knew.

'So . . . how are you?' he asked as she handed him a cup and saucer.

'Very well, thank you.'

'We should have been keeping an eye on you, but unfortunately I was caught up in a matter of business and your . . . Margaret was confined to the house with a slight cold. Nothing serious, but she didn't want to infect you.'

'I'm not a child, Uncle Lawrence,' she reminded him gently. 'I'm perfectly capable of looking after myself.'

'Morag, don't you think that, under the circumstances, the time has come for you to give me my proper title?'

'Has it?' A sudden gust of mischief caught at her, and she frowned as though perplexed. 'But wouldn't that cause you and . . . Aunt Margaret . . . great embarrassment? Won't people gossip if they hear me speak of you as my father?'

Colour surged from beneath Lawrence's high starched collar. 'Some people may feel a little surprised at first,' he acknowledged uncomfortably, 'but they will surely have the good manners to refrain from making any comment on a matter which, after all, is none of their concern. In any case, most of the folk we know have always been aware of the true situation. And now that both Sander and Georgina have passed on I am sure that everyone will understand that by acknowledging our true relationship, I am only doing the right thing.'

'I'm sure they will, but as I said, I'm old enough now to look after myself.'

93

'In some ways, yes, of course,' he said soothingly, as though speaking to a creature of low mentality, 'but in other ways, Morag, you must appreciate that you are in need of guidance. You know nothing of the ways of the world, or commerce . . .'

It was then that she realised that he had lost his bid to overturn his brother's latest will and had come not to gloat or to take possession, but to make the most of the situation in which he now found himself. She bent her head over her cup to hide the sudden understanding in her face.

'This house, for instance,' he swept on, 'is too big for you. Margaret – your step-mother and I have discussed the matter, and we're willing to give up our own home and move in here. Then there's the business to consider . . .'

He droned on, making plans for her future, while behind a carefully maintained expression of polite interest Morag thought swiftly. She knew perfectly well that once he moved his family into the house he would become its head in a matter of days, if not hours, and she herself would revert once more to being a dutiful daughter. Events were travelling too fast for her, and she had been caught unawares and unprepared.

'I've already decided to sell the house,' she interrupted, not waiting for him to draw breath.

'Sell? But it's a fine residence, one of the best in the town!'

'It has too many memories for me. I need to move elsewhere, truly I do.'

'Oh.' He looked disappointed for a moment, then rallied. 'Well, I suppose it will fetch a good price, and then we can afford to buy a fine family house nearby. Gourock perhaps – there are some splendid properties in Gourock, and the air there is ideal for children – who's that?' he asked irritably as the doorbell chimed again.

This time Morag was delighted to see the caller waiting on the top step. 'Come in . . .'; she almost dragged Aidan Grieve into the hall. 'Why couldn't you have called earlier?'

'I thought it best to leave you to collect your thoughts and make your own plans. Besides, I had nothing to report to you until today.' He took a deep breath and beamed down at her. 'I've come to tell you that your father, Mr Lawrence Weir . . .'

'. . . is in the parlour at this very minute –' Morag stabbed a finger at the door, which she had carefully closed behind her when leaving the room '– planning my entire life. Come and support me!'

She threw open the parlour door and ushered him in, saying cheerfully, 'As it happens, my uncle . . . my father is already here. I would have taken more care of my appearance if I had known that I was going to entertain visitors this afternoon.'

Lawrence could scarcely keep the irritation from his face as he and the lawyer shook hands. 'I was discussing private family business with my daughter,' he said shortly.

'Then it's fortunate that I arrived, sir, since I represent Miss Weir's interests,' Aidan told him cheerfully, setting his battered, shabby case on a side table.

'You'll have some tea, Mr Grieve?'

'Thank you, Miss Weir, but no. I had tea with my uncle and a client before I came here.'

'My father' – Morag felt quite uncomfortable, referring to Lawrence in public as her father – 'was just suggesting that he and his family should move in here with me, and I explained that you are arranging the sale of this house.'

95

'Indeed,' Grieve agreed, without so much as a flicker of surprise marring his open young face. 'In fact, I have found an agent who's very interested in representing you in the sale. It's only a matter, now, of deciding when it goes on the market.'

'The sooner the better. I've already started sorting out my aunt's and uncle's things.'

'We'll help you with that,' Lawrence put in quickly.

'With clothes and personal possessions, of course,' Aidan was equally swift. 'But under the terms of your brother's will, my uncle's firm is advising Miss Weir until she comes of age and inherits the estate. I have already explained to her that everything to do with business, be it private or in connection with the shipping company, should be referred to me.'

'Indeed you did.' Morag beamed at him, delighted that he had chosen that exact moment to arrive.

'Then since the house is to be sold, you must move in with us, Morag,' Lawrence announced.

'But . . .'

'Just until we find something more suitable.'

'Do you have enough room?'

'Certainly. Our home may be modest compared with my brother's residence,' Lawrence said stiffly, looking around the large and well furnished drawing-room, 'but I pride myself on providing adequate and comfortable accommodation for my family. And as a member of my family you are entitled to share our home with us.' He consulted his watch, then got to his feet. 'And now I must go. Your step-mother will be pleased to hear that you are coming to live with us,' he added as he left the room.

*   *   *

96

'My step-mother,' Morag said gloomily when she returned to the parlour after showing Lawrence out, 'will not be pleased. I'm sure of that. And neither am I, but I could find no way to refuse.'

'At least he's recognising his paternal duties at last. Do you really intend to sell this house?'

'What would I want with a place this size? It must go – and thank you for helping me to convince my father that the sale was already in progress.'

'My pleasure.' Aidan, who had delved into his case, began to spread papers out on the table. 'But I regret not calling on you sooner. I decided to wait until all communication between Mr Weir's lawyer and ourselves was over and the matter settled. I had no idea that he would move so quickly once he realised that his brother's will could not be overturned. Now, there are some papers to be signed . . .'

Patiently he went through everything with her, explaining all the details fully before she added her signature. 'As to the business,' he said when he was returning the paperwork to his bag, 'you and I must go over the books with Mr Laird.'

'I've already had a look at them.' She told him about John Laird's apparent determination to take his orders from Lawrence and not from her, and he frowned.

'We'll have to keep an eye on that gentleman.'

'I believe that he understands the situation now. He does know more about the company than anyone else, now that my fath . . . my uncle has died, and although I've been looking through the old records in order to understand things more fully, I would prefer to leave it in his hands if possible.'

He nodded. 'I would still like to go over the books with you and Mr Laird. Would tomorrow afternoon be suitable, at about 2 o'clock? I'll let him know of the arrangement.'

'You'll hate it, living with your father,' Wilma prophesied flatly. 'Your step-mother'll treat you like a skivvy!'

'I'm not a Cinderella,' Morag protested. 'I've got a good tongue in my head, and a brain as well. If I'm not happy I can always leave.'

'I wouldn't mind being Cinderella for a wee while, if it meant marrying a Prince Charming,' Daisy said dreamily. She had been putting the cutlery on the table in preparation for the evening meal; now she stopped, her hands full of soup spoons, her eyes misty and a faint smile on her lips.

'God save us, she's off intae her own wee world again!' her mother said from the cooker. 'Daisy Beckett, are you goin' tae put these spoons down, or do we have tae lap up our soup like wee dogs? One of these days,' she went on as her daughter came out of her reverie and went on with her work, 'you'll dream your head clean off your shoulders!'

Daisy was unperturbed. 'D'you know any Prince Charmings, Morag?'

'There's that young lawyer,' her sister put in. 'He sounds like a nice lad. Does he have a sweetheart?'

'Wilma, I know nothing about his private life – and he's a lawyer, not a prince.'

'All the better, hen.' Mrs Beckett set down the plates of broth in front of them. 'Lawyers probably make more money.'

When Morag arrived at the harbour on the following

afternoon, Aidan Grieve's motor-car was standing outside and the lawyer himself was seated at the desk, deep in conversation with John Laird. He sprang to his feet when she came in.

'Miss Weir – if you would sit here.' He drew another chair forward for her, making a business of dusting it off with his handkerchief. 'Now, as you can see, Mr Laird has brought all the books out for us, so with your permission I will take you through them step by step.'

He proceeded to do so, and was openly impressed at her grasp of the ledgers and the origin and delivery ports of the varied cargoes the Weir boats carried. She had also, while going through the old books and the more modern set she had made out for Sander, memorised the names of the men and lads who crewed each vessel.

'I can see that you're not in great need of guidance, after all,' Aidan said an hour later.

'I learned a little while helping my uncle during his illness,' she told him modestly, though inwardly she glowed at his new-found respect for her abilities. Then to John Laird, who looked quite dismayed, she said gently, 'I don't intend to take over the running of this office, Mr Laird, while you are here to do it for me. I know that you have always had my uncle's interests at heart, and I hope that I can continue to rely on you as he did.'

He drew himself upright. 'You can be sure that I know my duty, Miss Weir, and I trust that I always shall,' he said formally, though the relief in his almost colourless eyes was unmistakable.

'You handled him very well,' Aidan murmured as they left the office together.

'Poor man, he thought that he was going to lose his place, and as far as I know that office and his work are all he has in life.'

A handful of young lads who had been admiring the car scattered as they appeared. Aidan examined it anxiously and then, finding it as flawless as he had left it, he patted it affectionately. 'What do you intend to do with the rest of your life, Miss Weir?'

'I have no idea. I need time to think about it.'

'You have all the time in the world.'

'Yes, I have,' she agreed, beaming at him. 'But first, I must pack my belongings and move into my father's house.'

'Are you certain—'

'He has invited me, and I must accept. We should get to know each other as father and daughter.'

'I'll delay going ahead with the sale of your own house for a month if you approve, just to make sure that you don't need it after all,' he said, opening the car door. 'Can I drive you home?'

'No, thank you. I believe I'll have a look round the harbour first.'

She watched him drive off in a cloud of exhaust smoke and an explosion of noise which set a carter, unloading barrels of beer at a nearby public house, cursing as he hurried to hold the head of his startled horse. Then she went to pay homage to Lady Isabella – something she hadn't liked to do in front of the young lawyer – before strolling further along the harbour.

It was busy, and she had to step over and between boxes and coils of rope and chain, and skirt great piles of sand brought in from beaches further up the coast. A number of boats were in, some loading and some unloading, the winches rumbling and screeching as they hauled their loads from uncovered hatches to carts and motor wagons above, the men on board and those ashore shouting to each other.

There were two seagoing cargo ships as well as a

number of the smaller puffers in at the harbour, the puffers looking like self-important terriers crowded round the heels of the larger vessels. Morag spotted the *Jura*, a Weir boat, with great lengths of timber, roped together, balancing precariously as they were scooped from her open hold and transferred to the harbour by means of a sling hung from the ship's derrick.

One boat finished loading and swung away from the stone wall, backing out across the harbour to let another vessel take its place. As it retreated, then turned and moved off, the black smoke which had given puffers their names began belching out of the squat smoke-stack.

'Mind, lassie!' someone shouted, and she looked up, then ducked as a metal bucket being swung from ship to shore passed just above her head. 'Ye'd no' like a ton of gravel down about yer ears,' the man warned with a gap-toothed grin, and she retreated hurriedly, glad that she had encountered him and not one of his more short-tempered colleagues who would quite possibly have cursed her out of the way. And they would have been entitled, she knew.

Watching from a respectable distance, she realised with an inner tingle of excitement that this busy harbour and these small cargo ships, essential to the commerce of the Scottish coasts, were part of her life now. Whatever she decided to do, wherever she decided to go, even though she would have little to do with the business herself, she was now Weir Shipping.

9

———◆———

'Tell your father that you've changed your mind.'

'That would hurt his feelings.'

'He didn't care about your feelings when he was trying to get that will changed in his favour,' Wilma said, exasperated. She had been tossing a pebble from one hand to the other; now she threw it into the water, where it landed with a satisfying 'plunk'. A series of perfect ripples began to spread over the surface from the point where it had fallen.

The two of them were sitting on a large boulder at the river's edge, watching the members of Newark Rowing Club in training. 'It's cheaper than going to the pictures,' Wilma had said when she suggested it, 'and it's as good a way to spend a nice summer's evening as any. Anyway, I told Danny Hastie that I'd go and see him rowing some time, so why not now?'

'You're very friendly with him all of a sudden.'

'Not really, I just said it to fuss him and make him blush – though he was nice to our Daisy that time his father swore at her and sent her home in tears. He's not a bad lad, Danny.'

As Wilma had said, it was a pleasant way to pass a summer's evening. The fine weather had coaxed a number of spectators, mainly men, to the rocky shore to cheer on the oarsmen. To the west the sun was slipping down behind the hills, and the sky was still blue above, with a series of fluffy pink-tinged clouds floating here and there. Over the hills the blue gave way to a deep bank of colour, delicately shading through aquamarine and lilac to pearl-grey and rose-pink. In the long narrow boat the eight oarsmen moved in smooth, easy unison, drops of water glittering in the last of the sunlight each time the blades were lifted from the river.

Much further out, a flock of white-sailed yachts was making the most of the evening breeze, and a pleasure steamer slid past between yachts and rowing shells on her way to the Broomielaw in Glasgow at the end of her day-long excursion, possibly having been to Campbeltown. The ladies' dresses were spots of colour all along her crowded decks, and the sound of music from the accordion band on board floated to Morag's ears. White water foamed behind the long elegant boat, and a black velvet boa made of smoke streamed out from its black-topped yellow funnel to linger over the water after the steamer had slid from beneath it. It slowly turned to grey lace as it broke up before finally vanishing into thin air.

Immediately to the left of their small bay lay the first of the line of shipyards which continued almost without a break along the shores of Port Glasgow and Greenock. In the midst of the yard stood the remains of Newark, a small fifteenth-century castle which had once been surrounded by gardens and tree-shaded walks and possibly an orchard, but was now entirely enclosed by shipbuilding paraphernalia. At that moment, the castle was almost dwarfed by a ship in the final stages of construction, up on the stocks hard by its ancient walls.

Morag made herself as comfortable as she could

on her rocky seat, and sighed with contentment. She could have stayed there indefinitely, basking in the final warmth of the sun, emptying her mind of everything and watching the Clyde pass by on its way to the sea, calm and unhurried and for ever. But Wilma was not going to leave her in peace.

'It's not as if they really want you, any of them.' She returned to the original subject. 'You said that your aunt – or your step-mother, or whatever she is – isn't any happier about it than you are.'

Following her father's visit to Lilybank Road, Morag had been invited to his small house on the Clune Brae for her tea. It had been a very uncomfortable meal for all of them. Lawrence had been over-hearty and the children – eleven-year-old Crawford and Flora, two years his junior – were obviously confused by the announcement that their cousin would from henceforth be known as their older sister. For her part, Margaret Weir clearly had no idea how to deal with the sudden addition to her family.

'It was obvious that he didn't consult her before he invited me to live with them. She was for all the world like a sparrow which had hatched out an egg and then discovered that it held a baby cuckoo. Come to think of it, that's exactly what I am,' Morag said sadly. 'A cuckoo, far too large for their nest and getting in everyone's way.'

At one point while they sat making polite conversation in what Margaret liked to call the drawing-room, Flora had tugged at her mother's sleeve and asked in a loud whisper, 'Do I have to share a room with her when she comes to live with us? I like to be with my own self in my own room, and so does Crawford!'

Morag squirmed now, remembering the embarrassment of it. Poor Flora had been reprimanded by her

father, smacked on the wrist for her cheekiness and
sent bawling to her room. It had been clear, from
Crawford's cold glare and his mother's tight lips and
rigid shoulders, that they both held Morag responsible
for the little girl's misery. She couldn't blame them . . .
she felt responsible too.

'I'll have to do something about it.'

'Indeed you will. And don't take too long, for
you can't spend the rest of your life pretending that
you're getting your own house ready to be sold. It's
time you learned to stand on your own feet,' Wilma
said briskly, her eyes on the rowers. The boat had
come to a halt some twenty yards out from the shore,
and the men were holding it motionless in the water
with the oars as they took a breather and listened to
the man in the shrouds. His voice came to them in
snatches and his hands flew about as he explained
some point to them. After some discussion amongst
themselves, the oarsmen straightened up and took a
firm two-handed grip of their oars. The blades bit into
the water again, sending the boat skimming effortlessly
across the surface.

'I wouldn't mind trying that myself. D'you think it's
as easy as it looks – rowing?'

'Things only look easy when they've had a lot of
hard work put into them first. Look at you and your
twisting machines.'

Wilma shrugged. 'There's nothing to that – just
practice.'

'You're only saying that because you know how to
do it.' Morag had suddenly noticed a solitary figure
sitting on the grass some distance behind the rocky
shore. 'There's Grace – Grace Hastie, Danny's sister.'

'Is it?' Wilma turned and stared, then said, 'Let's
go and talk to her,' and was up on her feet and

105

crunching over the pebbles before Morag could stop
her.

Grace, shading her eyes against the last strong rays
of the sun, watched their approach nervously, then gave
a tentative smile as she recognised Morag.

'All on your own? You won't mind if we sit with
you?' Wilma asked when she was introduced. She
dropped down on the grass and Morag followed suit.
'D'you come often to watch your brother training?'

'Now and again, when I can spare the time.'

'He's the foreman where I work,' Wilma explained;
then, with a hardening of the voice, 'And your da works
there as well, but not on our flat, thank—'

'How is Miss Lamont, and the others at the teashop?'
Morag asked hastily. There was no knowing what
Wilma might say to the poor girl about her father.

'They're fine. Miss Lamont's so busy worrying about
the wedding that we're all being left to look after the
teashop on our own. So it's quite peaceful just now.'

'What wedding?'

'Mrs Winters' – her sister's – step-daughter's getting
married next month and a whole lot of folk are coming
to Gourock for the wedding. Miss Lamont's helping to
find somewhere for them all to stay.'

'Mrs Winters? Would she be married to Mr Winters
at Birkmyre's?' Wilma wanted to know.

'I believe he does work there. They live in a big house
up the hill above Greenock,' Morag recalled. 'The two
sisters opened the teashop, then Miss Lamont took it
over on her own when her sister married.'

'So it's going to be a big wedding, then?'

'Oh, yes. Miss Lamont's showed us some magazine
pictures of the sort of dress the bride's wearing. It's
lovely,' Grace said warmly, 'and she's having six
bridesmaids . . .'

She and Wilma, who loved to talk about clothes, were still deep in conversation about the wedding outfits when the training session ended and the oarsmen came ashore. Danny Hastie's face, already burnished by exertion and fresh air, took on an additional layer of colour when he saw Wilma talking animatedly to his sister.

'Hello.'

'I told you I'd come and watch you rowing some time, didn't I?' She reached up towards him. 'Come on . . . be a gentleman and help me to my feet.'

Her hands disappeared into his and he lifted her as though she weighed no more than a feather. 'Thank you.' She dusted down her skirt and settled her hat – a modern version of the poke-bonnet, brimmed and with a gathered crown and broad, pleated band with a ribbon at one side – more firmly on her head. Then she slipped a hand through his arm. 'And now you can walk me part of the way home, if you like.'

As Danny blushed furiously, Cal Fergusson, coming along from the small jetty with a few other young men, broke away and made for their group. 'Hello, Grace. Good evening, Miss Weir.' He put a finger to the skip of his cap.

'I didn't know you were a member of this club.'

'I have been for years. I was watching from the jetty this evening.'

The three of them, Cal in the middle, followed Wilma and Danny through the shipyard towards the road.

'I would have thought that you'd have enough of boats without going back into them when you're off duty,' said Morag.

'A man can never have too much of the Clyde,' he assured her, 'especially when it looks the way it does tonight.' The stiffness she had sensed when she visited

107

his home had vanished, and she was glad to see that he was his normal self again.

The sun was almost down now, and the hills stood out black and solid against the rosy glow behind them. The blue had all gone from the sky, which was a mixture of turquoise, lilac and rose-brushed smoky grey.

'It makes you wish you were a painter,' Grace said, and Cal dipped his head in agreement.

'Aye, it does that.'

Once through the shipyard they caught up with Danny and Wilma, then straggled unhurriedly along Castle Road to the point where the Hasties had to cross over and make their way home via Robert Street.

'I'll see you at work tomorrow, Danny,' Wilma told him lightly, then as he and his sister were left behind she linked her arm in Cal's and smiled up at him. 'Now it's your turn to squire me.'

He wasn't as easily flustered as Danny Hastie. 'And my pleasure,' he assured her, and offered his other arm to Morag. 'Miss Weir?'

'Grace is a very pretty girl,' Wilma said as they strolled on, taking the main shore road past the shipyards. 'How can an old bastard like Hastie have such a nice daughter?'

'Wilma! If your mother was here . . .'

'I'd not have said it. You should hear what some of the women call him.'

Cal insisted on walking them both home. He and Morag, having left Wilma in Ardgowan Street, had reached Lilybank Road when he said, 'I've looked out those old account books I mentioned to you, the ones from the wood-carving business.'

'I'd like to see them. Could I call on you tomorrow evening?'

'I'll bring them here.' They had reached the house

and he opened the gate for her, then tipped his cap. 'Till tomorrow,' he said, and went swinging off down the road without a backward glance.

The old account books were slim, but large. 'I don't know why folk always needed to use such big volumes,' Cal said as he followed Morag into the dining-room.

'I think it gave them a feeling of importance. I've been going over my uncle's old records, and they were like that as well.'

He glanced, surprised, at the pile of books at one end of the table.

'You've been reading through all these?'

'You think I should be content to sit back and embroider handkerchiefs while other folk run the company for me?' she asked sharply, and to her surprise he laughed instead of looking abashed.

'You're quite right, and I apologise for my clumsiness. It's just that I didn't realise that you were taking such trouble to do things the right way, so soon.' He stopped, pondered and then asked, a frown knotting his dark eyebrows, 'Does that sound daft, or do you get my proper meaning?'

'Yes, I do, and I suppose I'm being over-sensitive because of the trouble I've had over the will. But now that I know the business is mine, I want to prove to everyone that I'm worthy of it.'

He looked at her quizzically. 'You've nothing to prove. More folk were on your side than you realise.'

'So the dispute was common knowledge?'

'You can't keep many secrets in a place like the Port. So you intend to take over as a working owner?'

'Not entirely. Mr Laird knows well enough what he's doing and I'm happy to leave him to run the office, but

I do intend to keep an eye on things, so I need to know something of the working of a shipping company. Now – about these wood-carvers . . .'

The book bindings were scuffed and scored and the pages brittle, shedding tiny flakes of ancient paper when they were disturbed. 'They had been pushed into a cupboard in the house we once lived in, underneath a great pile of unwanted rubbish. The family should have taken better care of them,' Cal said, vexed. 'There must have been papers too – invoices, bills, mebbe even letters – but they're all gone.'

Dry and factual though it was, the order book slowly drew them both back into another age, when clippers and schooners and windjammers had roamed the seas with no other engine but the wind filling the sails and making them belly out far above the decks. The captain's and passengers' cabins of these ships had been handsomely finished off with wooden mouldings and panels, and carved frames on the paintings and mirrors. And on many bowsprits figureheads of warriors and beautiful women led the way forward, be it boldly into a storm or safely towards land at the end of the long journey.

Cal had already glanced over the books. 'It was a small family business,' he explained. 'You can tell that by the way they seemed to share a lot of the work with other companies. And it was run by a family called Tollin.'

When they turned their attention to the account book, Morag located the record of weekly wages in the end pages.

'How did you know to look there?' Cal wanted to know, impressed.

'It's what my uncle did when he was running the quarry. I've been reading these books too, just to get the feel of how he went about things.' Morag nodded at the pile from Sander's study, then turned back to the open pages before her. 'But wood-carving is much more interesting than quarry work.' She pointed to an entry. 'There's your name: George Fergusson, master carver.'

'My great-great-grandfather. His son, Matthew, was apprenticed to them straight from school. It was Matthew who worked on Lady Isabella.'

The evening rushed by while they slowly brought the past to life through the accounts and order books, their heads close together. The Tollins had had a small but successful business in Greenock in the nineteenth century, passing from father to son. In the early 1860s it appeared that the male line of the family had ended, since the business was then being run by Alicia Tollin. The meticulously recorded orders, accounts, payments and receipts were inscribed in a small, clear script, and the bottom of each page bore her initials, AT.

'You can see from the wages records that Matthew, my great-grandfather, worked for the Tollins before and during the period when Alicia ran the business. But this is puzzling . . .' Cal carefully turned over a leaf and tapped a finger at a point, half-way down one page, where the neat feminine handwriting disappeared to be replaced by a larger, stronger fist. 'In 1869, only a few years after they moved from Greenock to Port Glasgow, Alicia Tollin disappears and Matthew Fergusson, her master carver, seems to take over the business.'

It was true. From then on, the pages were initialled MF instead of AT.

'Perhaps Matthew bought Alicia Tollin out.'

'He can't have, because the name of the company changed just after that to Fergusson Tollin. Why would

111

he keep her name in if she had sold the business to him?'

'She may have married, and become a sleeping partner.'

Cal frowned. 'I haven't found any record of payments to a partner, or a shareholder.'

'Have you heard before about this Alicia Tollin?'

'No, and my mother didn't seem to have heard of her either when I asked her about it. As far as she was concerned, the business was my grandfather's, then my father's. It was my grandfather William, Matthew's son, who eventually gave up wood-carving and turned to shipping. The demand for ships' carvers would have died out with the introduction of steam, and iron ships. And with so many islands to service in this area, it made sense to turn to the puffer business.'

'We still haven't found out whose initials are set beside the footprints down at the office door. Perhaps Alicia Tollin married AM,' Morag suggested.

Cal leaned back from the table and eased his back, stretching his arms up into the air. 'Perhaps, but we'll have to leave that mystery until another day. It's getting late and, since you're eager to become involved in the business, there's something I want to talk to you about before I go.'

She offered him tea, and without waiting for an invitation he followed her into the kitchen and fetched cups from the shelf while she filled the kettle.

They drank their tea at the scrubbed wooden table, while in the back garden the shadows crept further and further out from beneath the bushes and the river below stilled beneath a calm night sky. It was the second time recently, Morag thought, that she had entertained a young man to tea in the kitchen. If people really did turn in their graves then poor Georgina, who had raised her foster-daughter to observe all the proprieties, must be doing just that.

'Pat Forsyth, the captain of the *Sanda*, is retiring in a few weeks.' Cal helped himself to another biscuit, as relaxed as though he was in his own home. She marvelled again at that knack he had of always seeming to be comfortable within himself, wherever he was. 'So they'll . . . you'll be looking for another captain. I'm putting in a word for young Archie Beckett. He's been the *Sanda*'s mate for two years now and he's a good seaman. Pat thinks so too.'

'Then surely the job's his. Doesn't a mate usually get promoted when a captain retires, if he's fit for the job?'

'It's the usual way, but old—' He stopped suddenly and dipped his biscuit into his tea. 'Mr Laird's looking for someone from outside to take over the puffer this time. He thinks Archie's unreliable.'

'But you don't.'

'He's a bit too full of fun at times, and he's well known for having an eye for the women, but that's got nothing to do with his work. Mr Laird doesn't agree with me there. To be honest, he doesn't like Archie, but to my mind that's not a good reason for denying the lad his chance to get on. I'm speaking out of turn, I know, but since you say that you want to be involved in the business I thought it worth asking if you'd put in a word for Archie – if you feel that he deserves it, that is.'

'If you and Captain Forsyth recommend him, that's fine by me. I'll have a word with Mr Laird, but I'll have to watch how I go for I don't want to undermine his authority.'

He said nothing but something – a slight lift of the eyebrow, or a movement of the corner of his mouth –

appeared and then was gone before she had a chance to read its meaning.

'Don't forget your ledgers,' she said as they went through the hall to the front door.

'If it's all right with you, I'd as soon leave them here for the time being. We've not finished reading through them.'

As before, he left without turning to see if she was still standing in the doorway. She waited until he had disappeared into the darkness before going back inside, and put his family records by the other books, happy to know that he would be back.

10

The teashop was busy when Morag and Wilma went in, but they found a table for two in the corner and gave their order to a harassed waitress, whose tired mechanical smile broadened to a genuine grin when she recognised Morag.

'You're lookin' well, hen.' She lowered her voice. 'You did the right thing, gettin' out of this place. She's like a hen on a hot griddle these days.' She jerked her head in the direction of the cashier's cubicle, where Miss Lamont herself was attending to customers. 'There's no pleasin' her.' Then, aware of her employer's eyes turning in her direction, she scribbled furiously on the small pad in her hand and said in an entirely different voice, put on for customers, 'Two fruit scones with butter and a pot of tea for two. Certainly, moddom,' and flounced off with a swift wink.

'I see what you mean about the glass coffin,' Wilma said. 'How did you manage to stand it for all those years?'

'Sshh, she'll hear you,' Morag said in a panic as Miss Lamont caught sight of them and inclined her head graciously in her former cashier's direction. She began to wish that she had never given in to Wilma's

115

suggestion that they should round off their Saturday-afternoon stroll along the coast to Gourock with a visit to the teashop.

'There's Grace Hastie.' Wilma pointed to the other side of the room, where Grace was negotiating a heavy tray between tables towards a family party. 'She even manages to look pretty in that terrible apron and cap, doesn't she? It's a pity she isn't serving at our table; I'd like to get to know her better.'

The tea arrived, amber in colour and served in delicate china cups. Matching plates bore two small fruit scones. Wilma's amazement at the offerings put before them would have been amusing if Morag hadn't been so concerned about being embarrassed in front of her former employer and colleagues. 'That's not tea, that's hot water that's had a fright,' she declared. 'And these wee things are never scones. What do they do – measure out two currants and one raisin to an eggcupful of dough? Imagine charging folk good money for this!'

All Morag wished for was to finish the tea and scones quickly, pay for them and get Wilma out of the shop, but before their cups were emptied Miss Lamont relinquished the cash register to one of the senior waitresses and started making her way among the tables, stopping here and there to greet a regular customer. To Morag's horror, each step brought her nearer to them, and it began to become clear that their table was her intended destination.

'She's coming over here! Now you mind your tongue, Wilma Beckett! Don't dare to say anything that'll make me ashamed of you or I'll . . . I'll run you down to the pier when we leave here and throw you into the water!'

'What would I say?' Wilma wanted to know, the

picture of injured innocence. 'In any case, you don't work for her any more, you're here as a customer – and so am I.' Then Miss Lamont was upon them, greeting Morag effusively, shaking Wilma by the hand when they were introduced, then drawing out a chair for herself and signalling to their waitress to bring fresh tea and another cup.

'As you saw for yourself, Morag, I'm driven to be my own cashier for half the week. The girl who shared the duties with you refuses to consider taking on the post full-time, and you have no idea how difficult it is to find an honest young woman with a good head on her shoulders these days. I don't suppose you would consider coming back, perhaps on a temporary footing?'

Morag, aware of Wilma's eyes boring into her, explained that there was no possibility of it.

Miss Lamont sighed. 'I thought not, but still . . . and then of course, there's the wedding. You'll have heard that my sister's step-daughter is marrying next month – a very nice young man, an architect from Edinburgh.' She fluttered on, describing the lavish wedding plans and the problems her poor sister was having in finding accommodation for the bridegroom's many guests. Morag listened with half an ear, more concerned about Wilma's behaviour than her former employer's family problems.

For her part, Wilma hung on every word, her face such a mixture of expressions that it was fortunate, Morag thought, that Miss Lamont was speaking directly to her and ignoring her companion. Then Wilma suddenly became the focus of attention of both of them when she said, 'Morag's got lots of room for guests, haven't you, Morag?'

'What?' her listeners said together.

117

'Living on her own in that big house, she could take in these two sisters you're talking about. Couldn't you, Morag?'

'Oh, my dear, would you? It would be a great kindness . . . an act of sheer Christianity. Poor Mavis is at her wits' end.' Miss Lamont's face was radiant. 'Only for a few days – they certainly won't be any trouble to you. I understand that they are both very genteel ladies, which is why Mavis has been having such a problem trying to find suitable accommodation for them.'

'I do believe,' Morag said through her teeth as they left the teashop, 'that I really will take you down to the pier and throw you in.'

'You should be thanking me, not threatening me. I've got you out of having to go and stay with your new father and his family on the Clune Brae, haven't I? And we didn't have to pay for that dishwater tea and those tiny things she calls scones.' Wilma gave a sigh of contentment and looked out over the Clyde, busy with pleasure steamers. 'We'll have to arrange a trip on the water soon, Morag.'

'How can I find time to go for a sail on the river when I've got the house to get ready for these two genteel ladies?'

'I'll help, and so will Mam and Daisy. It'll not take long to get that house set up. And they'll only be staying for a few days. We can go before then anyway; the wedding's not for another month yet. Over to Rothesay, mebbe – I'm looking forward to it already.'

Lady Isabella was a colourful figure once again in her freshly painted blue gown and dark green shawl. Her lips red, her cheeks becomingly flushed, she looked out over the harbour with calm blue eyes, her former glory restored as much as it could be. All she needed was a fine sailing ship at her back and the waves below.

'And you would have them if it was at all possible,' Morag told her, stroking a wooden arm. 'Wish me luck . . .'

In the office, she let ten silent minutes go by before she said casually, 'I understand that Captain Forsyth's about to give up his duties on the *Sanda*.'

'Aye, he's put in many a year's work, and Mr Weir thought very highly of him. But the rheumatics are giving him a hard time and loupin' on and off the boat's more than he can manage now, specially when she's beached and there's a ladder to climb.' John Laird looked at her over the top of his spectacles. 'If it's a wee show of appreciation you're thinking of, Miss Weir, I believe that it would be very appropriate and well received.'

'I'd certainly like us to do that. Perhaps you'll advise me as to the proper amount, Mr Laird, when the time comes.' Morag bent her head over the invoices before her and let a further few minutes pass before she spoke again. 'We'll be looking for a new captain for the boat, then?'

'Aye . . . I've been working on it. There are a few men in the Port who might be worth an approach, and one or two in Greenock too.'

'Is it not usual for the mate to be considered?'

There was a pause, then he said slowly, 'You're quite right, but that depends on who the mate is. In *Sanda*'s case he's too young and too inexperienced.'

'Archie Beckett, I believe?'

'That's right. A wild tyke, not what we'd want as skipper tae a Weir boat.'

'How long has he been the mate, Mr Laird?'

119

'Oh . . .' The man stared at the opposite wall, making a great show of calculating time, then said, 'About four years, I believe.'

'So he's got a lot of experience with that boat.'

'Aye, but only as the mate, doin' as he's told.'

'Surely that should stand him in good stead?'

Laird was getting agitated; Morag could tell it by the way his nose crimsoned and his chest began to swell. He was like a bantam cock preparing for a fight; she almost expected him to start ducking his head jerkily and scraping his feet along the floor.

'Forsyth doesnae think he's ready for the job, and he should know. And I doubt if Mr Weir would have considered him fit to take over his own boat.'

'Mr Weir's no longer in charge,' she reminded him gently, for the umpteenth time, and he came back with his usual answer also for the umpteenth time.

'Aye, but if you'll forgive me saying so, Miss Weir, you've not got the experience your fath . . . your uncle had.'

'I'm learning as fast as I can,' she told him tartly. 'I happen to know that Captain Fergusson thinks well of Archie – and he holds some shares in Weir Shipping now, so his opinion counts.'

The old man was silent for a moment, then with a sly sidelong glance at her he asked, 'Is young Beckett's sister no' a good friend of yours?'

Despite herself, Morag felt the colour rise to her face. 'Yes, she is, but that's got nothing to do with it. She hasn't asked me to intervene.'

'I never thought she had,' said John Laird smoothly and bent over his own work again, a slight smirk on his lips.

Morag could see what Cal Fergusson meant. If the clerk got his way, Archie would never be captain

120

of the *Sanda* or any other Weir boat. She said no more, but made a point, when the *Sanda* was next in dock, of calling at Captain Forsyth's small flat in Bellhaven Street.

Mrs Forsyth's mouth fell open when her visitor introduced herself; then she turned and fled into the flat, leaving Morag stranded on the landing.

'Eddie . . . Eddie!' her voice chimed from an inner room. 'For God's sake, man, put your shirt on! It's Miss Weir come to call, and you sittin' there like a tink in your semmit!'

A deep voice, clogged with sleep as though its owner had been roughly awakened, rumbled briefly.

'There – there, man, hanging over the fireguard tae air! Can ye no' see what's right in front of yer nose? Hurry up, for I've left her standing out on the landing on her own. And your slippers!' Mrs Forsyth added sharply, then reappeared in the doorway, red-faced and minus her apron.

'Excuse me, Miss Weir, I just . . . come in, come in,' she ordered, as though Morag had already been invited and was hovering reluctantly. 'Don't stand there, lassie. You'll forgive us if we're not all set up for visitors, but we werenae expectin' anyone.'

There was some confusion in the tiny square hall, for Mrs Forsyth first of all tried to usher Morag past her, then changed her mind and attempted to manoeuvre around her guest in order to put her own head round her kitchen door to make sure that her husband was respectable. Finally the matter was resolved and the two of them arrived in the room with Mrs Forsyth announcing unnecessarily, 'Look who's come to see us, Eddie. It's Miss Weir herself!'

121

The captain, a small but burly man, had managed
to put one foot into its slipper while stuffing the last
remnant of his shirt-tail down inside his trousers. 'Come
in, Miss Weir. This is a pleasant surprise.'

He at least refused to be thrown by his employer's
unexpected appearance in his home. He shook her hand
heartily, then ushered her to a chair before casually
sliding the braces that dangled round his hips back
over his shoulders again, snapping them into place
with his thumbs. Just as Sander had always done,
Morag thought, taking to Captain Forsyth at once.

'Ye'll have a cup of tea, Miss Weir?' Mrs Forsyth
moved to stand by her husband, one foot sliding an
empty slipper over against his ankle. He looked down,
surprised, then sat to put it on.

'I'm only here for a moment . . .'

'Of course ye'll have a cup.' The woman busied
herself at the jawbox – the small sink beneath the
window. 'I hope ye'll excuse the mess, Miss Weir.'

The only thing out of place was the captain's newspaper, lying abandoned by his chair. As Morag looked
round at the neat room with its gleaming grate, chenille
curtains drawn across the recess where the double
bed stood, shining china plates and ornaments on
the mantelpiece and dresser, she was suddenly over-
whelmed by memories. 'You have a lovely home,
Mrs Forsyth,' she said sincerely round the lump in
her throat. 'I used to live in this street myself, on the
first floor of the next close with my parents.'

'Never!'

'Until I was six years old. We lived across from
Mrs Crawford – Granny Crawford, all the children
called her.'

'I mind her well! A grand neighbour.' Mrs Forsyth's
nervousness ebbed away in a flood of reminiscences

about the people who had once lived in the street. Her husband had finally to remind her, over the teacups, that their visitor probably had a reason for calling.

'I'm told that you're giving up your work, Captain Forsyth.'

'Aye . . . I'll miss the boat, and the life, but—' He slapped a gnarled hand against one hip. 'It's gettin' harder each time tae manage up and down tae the wheelhouse. Time tae let a younger man take her over.'

Morag nodded. She had noticed the way he eased himself now and again in his chair, favouring his rheumatic hip. 'I wanted to ask who you would recommend to take over. I believe that Archie Beckett's your mate.'

'That's right.' He chuckled. 'He's a right lad, is Archie. I've had tae pull him out of many a pickle since he joined my crew, but he's a good seaman. I've got no complaints about him in that direction.'

'Do you think he's ready to take command of the *Sanda*?'

'Oh aye,' he said at once. 'I've said tae Mr Laird.'

'You've already recommended Archie?'

'I have. He's young, and he's a bit wild in some ways, but he can read the sea and the weather, and he'd never do anythin' tae risk the boat or the crew or the cargo. If ye ask me, a bit of responsibility would settle that laddie better than anythin' else.'

'That,' said Morag, 'is what I thought myself.'

John Laird flushed with anger when she told him that she wanted Archie to be offered the *Sanda*. 'Miss Weir, I must protest! It is surely my job to run this office.'

'It is, and I have no quarrel with the way you do it,

123

Mr Laird. But surely my uncle would have been the one to appoint the skippers?'

'Yes,' he admitted, adding swiftly, 'but Mr Weir had a working knowledge of the boats.'

'A knowledge that you and I both lack,' she reminded him, allowing an edge to creep into her voice. If she wasn't careful, the man would over-rule her on every point. A stand had to be made, and the time had come to make it. 'I've consulted Captain Forsyth and Cal Fergusson, and they both feel that Archie's ready for the responsibility.'

His face tightened, so much so that he could scarcely get the words between his thin lips when he said, 'If you would prefer to take the word of a man like Fergusson . . .'

'He knows the boats better than you and me, and he's a shareholder. And I did say that Captain Forsyth himself is happy to entrust the *Sanda* to Archie. I've decided that we'll give him his chance; it's only fair. I'd appreciate it if you would tell the men tomorrow,' she said, and walked out of the office.

'If you let me down, Archie Beckett,' she told him that night in his mother's kitchen, 'I'll not only turn you off right there and then, I'll . . . I'll kick you into the harbour as well!'

'She's an awful one for threatening to throw folk in the water,' Wilma remarked. Her brother's eyes were shining, and his white teeth gleamed in a grin that almost split his face in two.

'I promise, Morag, on Mam's life – I'll be the best skipper you ever had!' He took her hand in his, then said, 'Ach, tae hell with it!' and swept her into his arms to kiss her soundly. She emerged from the embrace tingling and glowing from her lips to her toes.

'I'm not certain that kissin' your employer's the right way to behave, our Archie,' his mother said reprovingly, though her own face was one huge smile.

'I'm not complaining,' Morag said faintly, her head still spinning. Now she knew why Archie was such a success with the girls. 'Mind, now, Archie, not a word to anyone, and you've to pretend when Mr Laird tells you tomorrow that you knew nothing about it until then. It's his place, not mine. I just wanted to make sure that you'd take the position seriously.'

'I will! I'll do all of that!'

'We'll have a party,' Mrs Beckett announced. 'On Saturday, to celebrate.'

'Me and Morag were going to go for a sail on Saturday after work, Mam.'

'You can still have your sail. Daisy and the rest of them can help me to get things ready. You'll be there, Morag?'

'Of course.'

'I'm that grateful, lass,' the woman said from the bottom of her heart.

'He earned the right. I didn't do anything.'

Mags Beckett gave her a long, thoughtful look. 'Oh, I think you did. And it'll not be forgotten.'

Lawrence Weir didn't waste any time on niceties when he arrived in Lilybank Road on the following evening. 'Laird tells me you've made him give young Beckett the post of skipper of the *Sanda* when Forsyth retires.'

'So you've been down at the harbour.'

'I call on most days, to see if Laird needs advice on any matter.'

This was news to her but she held her tongue, refusing to be side-tracked. She had been expecting his visit and had rehearsed for it. 'It's traditional for the mate to take over when the captain leaves.'

'But according to Laird, the man's not fit to take the responsibility.'

'And according to Captain Forsyth and Cal Fergusson, he is. He deserves to have his chance, surely?'

'My dear, is it wise for you to interfere in the running of Weir Shipping?' His tone had altered. Now his voice was kindly, paternal . . . and condescending. 'After all, you know nothing about it.'

'I'm trying to learn. I'm trying to think of what my uncle would have wanted.'

At mention of Sander, his face tightened just as John Laird's had when she spoke of Cal. He drummed his fingers on the table for a moment, then said in the same reasonable, measured tone, 'I have to remind you, my dear, that I hold a quarter of the shares.'

'And I hold more than half. And Cal Fergusson holds twenty per cent – and he feels, like Captain Forsyth, that Archie deserves the promotion.' She was shaking inside, but she wouldn't let him know it.

Although his mouth curved in a thin, conciliatory smile, his eyes were furious. 'As your father, Morag, I surely deserve the courtesy of consultation before you make final decisions.'

'But you know no more of the business than I do, Father. Even less, for I checked over the books with my uncle every week in the six months or so before his death,' she reminded him. 'And two people who know more about the boats than either of us recommended Archie Beckett. I take it that Mr Laird announced his promotion today as I asked?'

'Yes, he did, but he and I both—'

'Then it's decided.'

'And if Beckett proves to be a disaster?'

'The blame will be mine, not yours or Mr Laird's. I accept that. And you're right,' she added, furious with herself for having given him a chance to find fault, 'I should have called a meeting and given you the opportunity to speak your mind. I'll remember that in future.'

'There's scarcely much point in that, if you and Cal Fergusson have already made up your minds,' he said tartly, but Morag had made her apology and she remained silent, determined not to be drawn into an argument.

There was a long pause, during which he rose and paced the parlour floor. Morag poured tea she didn't want and waited, sipping at her cup. Finally he said, 'About you coming to live with us – Margaret and I thought that next Saturday would suit.'

'I can't, not for at least another month. I've agreed to take in lodgers.'

'You've what?' he exploded.

'Only for a few days. There's to be a big wedding – Miss Lamont's step-niece is the bride. The family were in need of accommodation for two lady guests, so I offered them a room here.'

'What on earth possessed you to invite strangers into the house?'

'They are ladies, Father, friends of Mr and Mrs Winters of the Ropeworks. Anyway, I thought it would be . . . interesting to meet new people.'

'Interesting!' He fell into the chair opposite hers. 'Is there any more tea? So you'll not be selling the house just yet, then?'

'Not until after they've gone,' Morag said demurely, and offered up silent thanks to Wilma for having saved her from Clune Brae for a whole month.

127

11

On three separate occasions that day yarn being twisted
on one or other of the two huge machines under Wilma
Beckett's supervision had snapped, and each time she
had had to halt the guilty machine in order to effect
a repair.

Normally her temper would have been frayed by now,
but today nothing could dampen her spirits. Everything
in her life was rose-coloured. Archie, the favourite of
her three brothers, was to get his own puffer once
Captain Forsyth had retired; she and Morag had planned
a trip over to the town of Millport on the island known
as Great Cumbrae on the following afternoon, and in
the evening there was to be a party. It was Friday, and
the best weekend ever was just ahead of her.

Although the machinists normally stood at their
work, they were allowed to sit down when the machines
were running smoothly and there was little to do but
supervise them. Like most of the women, Wilma had
managed to get hold of one of the huge wooden
bobbins used in the spinning department. Empty, they
made excellent stools. Now, with the yarn mended and
her two machines working smoothly, she dragged her
bobbin into place and settled down comfortably, her
mind full of the next day's pleasures.

The Becketts were noted for their parties. Everyone in the street came, whatever their age. Those too old or infirm to manage the stairs on their own could be certain of a 'carry' on the linked arms of stronger and younger neighbours, and a seat when they got to the flat. The folk who didn't need seats were happy to stand, or sit on the floor or on the stone stairs outside, for the flats were all small and parties always overflowed upstairs and downstairs, taking up all the landings and the closes and sometimes, weather permitting, the pavement itself.

It was to be hoped that the good weather remained over Saturday, although she and Morag would go on the river whether there was rain or shine. But it would be pleasant, for their first trip of the year, to have a soft breeze and some sunshine to make the water sparkle like diamonds. There was a café in Millport famed for its ice-cream; if the day was warm they would sit at an outside table, and afterwards they would hire bicycles and take a run round the small island.

While Wilma's mind roamed free, her eyes kept checking the machines automatically. Something caught her attention and she clucked her tongue in annoyance, noting black flecks appear, disappear and then reappear as the bobbins whirled. Sometimes pieces of yarn tore loose and got caught up in the machinery, where they became soaked in oil. If they weren't spotted and eventually removed they got twisted into the bobbins, spoiling them. Every Friday afternoon the machines were stopped early so that the women could clean them thoroughly before going home, but if a machine had become too dirty to wait until then it had to be halted, which meant that the machinist lost valuable time.

Wilma chewed her lip. There must still be a good hour to stopping time. Even as she watched, more flecks danced past her vision so swiftly that she could scarcely see them, mocking her and playing their own maddening game of hide-and-seek.

She cast a glance up and down the row of machines. Danny Hastie was nowhere to be seen, and none of the overseers or engineers was in sight either. Wilma was experienced enough to know that, with care, a skilled operator could remove the dirty shreds from the back of a machine without having to stop it. She was as skilled as any of them, and she had cleared a moving machine often enough. Enough time had been lost that day as it was, she thought, getting up from her seat . . .

From the other end of the flat, where he was checking a load of completed bobbins, Danny Hastie's keen ears heard the first screams shrilling above the thunderous roar of the machines. While the men and women in the vicinity were still turning to look, just beginning to wonder what was amiss, he was already on his way down the long room with a speed that came from years of running for pleasure.

Rounding a machine and moving into the next alley, he saw the women's scarved heads all begin to turn towards one area. Some of them had shut down their own machines and were moving away from them towards the far end of the row. There was more than one throat screaming now – a chorus was beginning to rise as row after row of the machines stopped their own clamour. Danny's blood ran cold.

Exploding through the gathering women, scattering them heedlessly to left and right, he saw the unattended machine at the end of the row, still working, one row of bobbins snatching twine from the other as fast as they could pull it. Nobody would move away from their machine without switching it off first, unless . . .

Reaching it, he slammed the flat of one hand down hard on the switch. Even as the machine stopped he was rounding it to see Wilma Beckett down on the floor, crouched on her knees. The side of her face seemed to be nestled against the machine, and for a moment it seemed to Danny that she was trying to embrace it, then he realised with sick horror that one of her arms was inside, among the cogs and belts, and she was attempting with the other to prise herself free.

'No!' he screamed at her. 'Leave it!' As he threw himself down beside her, one arm out to take her weight and ease the strain on the trapped limb, she looked up at him, her eyes wide and dark, devoid for once of laughter.

'Danny, what's amiss with this thing?' She asked the question quite calmly, and he realised that the shock of what had just happened had numbed her mind to the agony she should have been suffering.

'It's all right, Wilma, it's just . . .' He felt his voice shake and tried hard to bring it under control. 'Your sleeve got caught. Just keep still while I get it out again, there's a good lass.'

There had been the faintest hope that it might have been only the sleeve of her boiler-suit which was trapped, and not the vulnerable flesh and bone and tissue within it, but one glance showed that the matter was far more serious than that. Her hand and lower arm were caught fast, and a crimson stain was spreading steadily up the rough material, going past her elbow and heading towards her shoulder. Blood began to drip and pool on the floor just below the machine.

'I'll get into terrible trouble . . .' Wilma said weakly.

'You'll not, you'll not. I'll see that it's put right for you,' he gabbled frantically. Anything to keep her attention from the truth of her situation.

By now all the machines had been shut down and the flat was eerily silent. Even the screaming had stopped; the women converging on Wilma's machine, faces ashen and eyes shocked, had reverted to low, keening moans. One or two reeled back, fighting to get out of the circle and away from the sight and smell of blood.

'Someone give me a hand here!' Danny yelled up at the white faces surrounding them. 'For God's sake get help – and tell them to send for the ambulance!'

One of the older women, more sensible than the rest, pushed through the crowd and dropped to her knees beside them, taking the weight of Wilma's body from him and talking to the girl reassuringly.

'Good lass, Elsie,' Danny said with relief. Freed, he pulled off his jacket and wrapped it about Wilma as best he could, drawing it over her head at one side to hide the bloody, trapped arm from her should she try to turn her head. Even as he did so she tried to look round at the machine, then sit upright.

'Let me up, Elsie, I've got to get back to work . . .'

'No' for a while, lassie,' Elsie told her with grim gentleness, stroking her hair.

'You're fine where you are, pet.' Danny wrenched off his shirt, cursing the strong yarn that his conscientious sister had used to sew the buttons on tightly, then managed to tear a strip of the material free with his teeth. 'Just be still for a minute longer, then we'll get you home in no time at all,' he ordered, tying the strip tightly round her arm between shoulder and elbow as a tourniquet.

She blinked up at him, then her eyes widened. A faint version of the mischievous smile that so often haunted his dreams at night flickered over her face. 'You look grand without your shirt, Danny Hastie,' she said.

He managed to summon up a smile from somewhere,

praying that help would come before the realisation of what was happening began to dawn. He didn't think that he could bear to see that.

Behind him someone moaned, then he heard vomit splattering over the floorboards. 'If you cannae help, then get out of the fucking way!' he hissed between gritted teeth, then turned back to Wilma, trying to put his body between her and the watchers.

'I never heard you swear before, either.' Her eyes were beginning to cloud over. 'It's a good thing my Mam isn't here. Mind what she did to your father when he swore at our Dai – sy . . .'

And at last she fainted, just as Danny heard the thud of booted feet racing down the room to the rescue.

12

Wilma's face was as white as the pillow behind her head when Morag first saw her in Broadstone Hospital, but her spirit was as strong as ever.

'We'll have to miss out on that trip to Millport,' she whispered, 'but I was thinking I'd as soon go to Rothesay anyway. There's more life in Rothesay!'

'More life?' choked her mother, who had scarcely left her side since she had been brought to the ward from the operating theatre. 'It'll be a while before you're ready for that!'

'Oh, Mam!'

'We'll go wherever you want,' Morag promised. 'Just as soon as you get out of here.'

'And that'll not be for a while, so you do what the nurses tell you and don't make it worse for yourself. You near lost your arm, d'you realise that, our Wilma?'

'Just nearly, Mam. I've still got it.' Wilma twisted her head round to inspect the great mass of bandages propped on a pile of pillows by her side. 'Would you look at that? It's like sharing a bed with a corpse.'

'Wilma Beckett!'

'Well! It's got no conversation at all.' Her voice had strengthened already, Morag noticed. Sparring with her

134

mother did her good. 'And there's these ladies you're looking after for Miss Lamont, Morag. You won't be able to go gallivanting off with me if they're staying with you when I get out of here.'

'I'm going to tell her to find somewhere else for them,' Morag said, distracted with worry about her friend.

'And have to go to live on the Clune Brae with your father? You will not!'

'Well then, we'll . . . we'll take them with us. Whatever you want, as long as you get your sail to Rothesay.'

Wilma brightened. 'That's a good idea. They'd like that, surely.' Then her gaze slid beyond Morag's shoulder. 'Would you look at what the cat brought in!'

'Shush!' her mother hissed, embarrassed. 'He'll hear ye! It's a pity they couldnae have found a bit of bandage to put on your tongue while they were fixing your arm! Come away in, son.' She clambered to her feet and waved at Danny Hastie, who was hovering by the ward door. He came up to the bed, crimson to the tips of his ears.

'How are you, Wilma?'

'Me and my pal here are coming along fine.' She indicated the bandaged mass on the other pillow and Morag, catching the haunted look in his eyes as he glanced at it, knew that he was reliving the accident.

'I brought you some flowers.' He laid a paper-wrapped bunch of flowers gently on the top cover and Mags Beckett swooped on them, clucking and fussing.

'That's nice. Isn't that nice, Wilma? I'll just go and find a vase for them, else they'll die in the heat of this place.'

'If I don't get out of here soon, either me or one of the

135

nurses'll attack her, then she'll end up in the next bed,' Wilma whispered when the three of them were alone.

'She's been worried about you, it's only natural.'

'I suppose so, but that doesnae make it any easier.'

'How's your arm?' Danny nodded at the bandages.

'Sore. It's like having the toothache all over. But at least I've still got it. I'll need to find the money for a new boiler-suit, though.' As it turned out, although the sleeve had been chewed to shreds by the cogs, Wilma's arm had escaped the worst of their ruthless metal teeth. The bone was unbroken, and although the arm itself was badly torn and bruised it had not been damaged beyond repair.

'I'm told it was you that shut the machine off, Danny.'

He tried to make a joke of it. 'There was no point in letting it run when the machinist wasn't there.'

'We're so grateful to you, son!' Mrs Beckett had returned with the flowers in a vase of water.

'Och, it was nothing.'

'So I'm nothing, am I?'

'I didn't – I meant that . . .' He began to colour, twisting his hands between his knees, staring fixedly at the bedhead.

'Don't be so cheeky, Wilma!'

'He doesn't mind me teasing him. Do you, Danny?'

'No,' he said wretchedly.

'In fact, I'm sure he'll come and visit me again, just for some more teasing. Won't you, Danny?'

'D'you want me to visit you again, then?'

'Of course.'

Morag saw the young man's face light up, then fall again when Wilma added carelessly, 'It gets so boring in here, I'd welcome a visit from Old Nick himself.'

The bell marking the end of visiting hour rang just

as her mother was once again rebuking her, and the three of them made their way from the ward together, Mags Beckett repeating her thanks over and over again as they went.

'I'm the foreman, Mrs Beckett, it's my job to know what to do if anything goes wrong with one of the machines,' Danny Hastie explained in an agony of embarrassment.

'That's not the point, son. It's the thought of what might have happened to my Wilma if you hadn't moved so fast. Two of the lassies from the twisting flat came to see me, and they told me all that you did for her. If anything had happened to her . . .' Mrs Beckett's voice wavered and her face suddenly began to crumple and dissolve. 'I couldnae bear to lose one of my bairns,' she said, and began to weep in earnest. 'I'm sorry—' She was crying so hard that her voice sounded bubbly, as though she was speaking from under water. 'It's the fright and the worry, and tryin' tae hide from her how upset I've been . . .'

Between them, Morag and Danny supported her to a chair in the foyer and waited – Morag with her arm about the older woman, Danny hovering round them both, occasionally patting Mrs Beckett's shoulder, until she managed to compose herself. Then, one on either side, treating her as tenderly as though she was a toddler taking its first steps, they walked with her to Ardgowan Street.

Danny shook his head when he was invited in. 'I'm expected home, I said I'd not be late.'

'Another time, mebbe, when our Wilma's back home. Thanks, son,' Mags began again. 'Tell your ma she should be proud of you.'

Danny shuffled his feet uncomfortably on the flagstones. 'My mother's dead, Mrs Beckett.'

'Aye, of course she is, the poor soul! There's me gettin' all confused again.' The tears, so near the surface now, welled up again. 'God rest her, I'm sure she knows anyway what a good laddie you are.'

He backed off along the pavement, pushing away her repeated gratitude with panicky movements of his large hands. It was a relief to him when the two women finally disappeared into the close mouth and he was free to walk home alone, hands deep in his pockets, shoulders hunched and eyes on the pavement.

He felt as though he too, in a way, had been caught up in moving machinery. He was still haunted, especially in the long hours of the night, with the memory of Wilma huddled by her machine, its wheels still turning and its belts still rolling as it tried to take her. The yearning to visit her in hospital and to see for himself that she had survived had proved to be more than he could withstand. Embarrassed though he had been by her constant teasing in front of her friend and her mother, it was worth it just to be near her. And he could put up with her banter, because that was just Wilma's way, and it was also welcome proof that she was on the mend.

It was Mrs Beckett herself who had been the last straw. Although she bore no physical resemblance in any way to his own mother, her warmth and caring, the way she had hurried to put his flowers into water and had scolded her daughter for being cheeky, then thanked him over and over again for what he had done for the girl and finally wept in public at the thought of losing any of her children, reminded him sharply, painfully, of the daily misery of his own home life.

He had refused her hospitality because he knew full well that if he had gone into her home and been exposed any longer to her warmth and kindness, he would probably have burst into tears himself.

In any case, he thought with a hot flood of self-disgust surging through his body, he had made enough of a fool of himself in front of Wilma's friend, the frighteningly cool type of girl who said little but probably saw everything. She must think that he was a complete oaf, blushing and stammering as he had. But that was the way Wilma affected him.

He wished with all his heart that he could tease Wilma back, challenge her and show her that he was worth noticing. Perhaps he could . . . if he ever got her alone, just the two of them. In front of others, he felt as though his brain as well as his tongue was tied in knots.

'You're useless, Danny Hastie,' he told himself bitterly. 'Useless!' Why would she ever want to be on her own with him anyway? But at least he had her permission to visit her again in the hospital. And visit her he would. With luck, he might even find a time when there was nobody else at her bedside.

His father and Grace were both at home. 'How's that poor girl?' Grace asked as soon as he went in.

'She's coming along. She's going to be all right.'

'Oh, Danny, I'm so glad!' She put a hand briefly on his arm as they passed each other, Danny on the way to hang up his coat in his small room, Grace going to the kitchen to start the evening meal.

When it had all ended, when Wilma had been freed from the machinery and taken off in the ambulance and Danny had finally been able to go home, Grace had been there alone. She had listened while he poured out the story, and had comforted him and given him a nip of whisky from the bottle their father kept hidden in his bedroom. Then Grace had held his forehead when his stomach rebelled and violently rejected the strong spirit.

Grace knew now that he loved Wilma Beckett, and he knew that his secret was safe with her.

'What lassie's this?' Bill Hastie wanted to know. 'Not the one that got herself caught up in the machinery?'

'Aye.'

'You've been tae see her in the hospital?'

'Aye.' Danny recalled the silkiness of Wilma's black hair against the white hospital pillows, her unusual, pale-skinned heart-wrenching fragility.

'I hope ye told her she was sacked.'

'What?'

'Have ye gone deaf? Sacked, I said! She tried tae clean a machine while it was still runnin', didn't she? That's an immediate sackin' offence, and you know it. So does she.'

'Dad, the lassie's in hospital. She's going to be there for a while yet – she's lucky to have kept her arm.'

'If she's goin' tae be laid up for a while, that's all the more reason tae put an end tae her. You can go back in and tell her before the week's out.'

'I will not!'

'You will . . . or I'll dae it for ye!'

'You,' said Danny icily, 'will keep away from the lassie and mind your own business.'

His father came up out of his chair like a cork from a bottle, the newspaper he had been reading thrown aside. 'What did ye say?'

'I said mind your own business. The twisting flat's my concern, not yours.'

'If you won't do yer job properly, I'll have tae dae it for ye. It's taken me years tae get where I am in that mill. My name's known with respect on every floor

140

and in every office, and I'll not let you or anyone else blacken it!'

'I'm not blackening your precious name, I'm just telling you that as far as I'm concerned Wilma Beckett's job will be waiting for her when she's fit to come back.'

'And I'm tellin' you she's tae be sacked! Beckett, is it? That'll teach her mother tae come tae the mill, abusin' me in front of everybody,' Hastie said with satisfaction. 'If you won't do it I'll tell them in the office what she did, and they'll sack her fast enough. And you intae the bargain . . . and ye neednae think I'll intercede for ye, either.'

A distressed whimper came from the kitchen door, where Grace stood with hands at her mouth watching the two of them. Instead of backing off, as he had always done in the past, Danny moved forward to stand toe to toe with his father. He was the taller of the two by almost a head, but Bill Hastie was as hard as iron and – in spite of his running and his rowing and his youth – Danny reckoned that if it came to a fist-fight his father might still be able to best him. But at that moment, tormented by worry for Wilma and still gnawed by self-disgust, he would have welcomed the chance to lash out with his fists and to be hit in return. Perhaps a good dose of physical pain would ease his personal suffering.

'Wilma Beckett did not try to clean her machine while it was running.'

'She did! You know full well that she did!'

'The machine was faulty. She hit the switch and it cut out, so she thought it was safe. Then it cut in again just as she started to work on it. I know what I'm talking about, for I had a look at it afterwards. I'm putting in a report on it tomorrow.'

141

His father's breath was hot on his face. The eyes staring up into his bulged with rage. 'You rigged that machine after the accident tae save her job!'

'Prove it,' Danny invited coldly. He was the better engineer of the two and they both knew it. They both knew, too, that the other machinists would back anything he said.

'I could report you instead of her, then you'd be the one turned intae the street. Would ye risk that for one lassie?'

'I'd probably welcome it.'

'Danny, don't!'

'It's all right, Grace, let him do what he wants. I'd be better out of this place anyway.'

'What good would you be anywhere else? You only got the job because of me!'

'Mebbe so, but I got my promotion on my own, and we both know it.'

'Call yourself a son?' Spittle drooled from the older man's mouth and his colour deepened. Danny wondered if he was going to have an apoplectic fit, and discovered that he didn't really care. 'You're useless, d'you know that? Useless!'

'So you keep telling me,' Danny agreed and turned away, waiting for the prod in the back, or even the blow, that would turn their quarrel into an open fist-fight. But it didn't come. Instead, there was a whirl of disturbed air behind him as his father snatched up his jacket, then the door slammed. Seconds later the outer door also crashed shut, and they heard Bill Hastie's boots clattering noisily down the stone stairs.

Grace made a little whimpering sound, and when Danny turned in her direction he was appalled to see her crouched against the door-frame, sheer terror in her eyes.

'Grace?' Alarmed, he went to her and took her in his arms.

'I thought he was going to kill you!' she whispered.

'Don't be daft, I'd not let him do that,' he said into her soft, fair hair. She was trembling all over.

'Don't torment him like that again, Danny. Promise me you won't!'

'I can't. I've had enough of his bullying. He was going to see Wilma thrown out of work, after what she's just been through!'

'But what if he puts you out of the house? I couldn't bear that!'

'It won't happen. I'll stay here as long as you do.' That promise, at least, he could make. It was the least he could do for her. But he wished that he could do more. He wished that he could bring love back into her life, or at least give her a mother like Wilma's mother.

Cal arrived at the door one evening, unannounced, just after Morag had returned from visiting Wilma in hospital. His eyes were bright, and he hugged an inlaid wooden box to his chest. 'I've just found something, and I wanted to show it to you at once.'

His excitement was infectious. In the dining-room she watched as he laid the box carefully on the table and opened it. 'I didn't even remember that this was in the house; it was at the bottom of an old trunk belonging to my father. There are some bits and pieces of paper, but nothing important. This is what I wanted you to see.' He drew out a photograph. 'It's a bit dark, but you can make it out.'

The picture was very old, and dim, but she could see that it had been taken in a workshop. There were three figures: a bearded man and a young boy, both swathed in canvas aprons and with peaked caps on their heads, and a young woman in a dark dress with a high white collar. They were posing beside a figurehead that was familiar to Morag.

'Lady Isabella!'

Cal nodded, grinning broadly. 'That must have been taken just as she was being completed. You can make out some of the detail on her if you look closely. This . . .' he rested a fingertip on the woman's face, 'must be Alicia Tollin, and the older, bearded man's certainly Matthew Fergusson. The boy might be his son William, my grandfather. Now – look at this!'

Delving into the box again, this time he brought out a tiny bundle wrapped in cloth. He laid it in the palm of one large, callused hand and unfolded the material to reveal a perfect miniature figurehead, no more than an inch and a half long.

'Oh, Cal!' Morag held out her own hand and he transferred the little carving into it as gently as though he was handing her a new-born baby.

'I've heard that they often did miniatures of the figures first, the way shipbuilders sometimes do models of their ships, but I'd never seen one before.'

'It's so perfect!' The figure was traditional, a woman holding the edges of a shawl together over her breast, her other hand down by her side, her hair drawn smoothly back from a centre parting then falling in ringlets about her cheeks. Even in miniature, every detail was exact.

When she finally relinquished it, Cal wrapped it carefully and tucked it into a corner of the box, then lifted out a pile of papers and laid them to one side. 'We can go through these at a later date. I just want you to see this other photograph. It's the same three people,

144

several years later; it was probably taken when the firm moved to East Harbour from Greenock.'

This time the man, the boy and the woman were standing before a building clearly recognisable as the harbour office. Thanks to the outdoor setting, they were much easier to see. The young boy to one side of the picture grinned at the camera, clearly proud to be having his likeness taken.

'I can see the family resemblance clearly.' Morag's attention moved to the couple standing in the middle of the picture, before the office door. Matthew Fergusson was considerably taller than the comely young woman by his side, even though her dark hair, which had been pulled severely back from her face in the other photograph, was now piled on top of her head to give her a few added inches in height. Her face was a perfect oval, with bright, heavy-lidded eyes, a straight, definite nose and a mouth that looked as though the slightest thing could curve it into a smile. Her pose was relaxed and self-confident, and she was smiling while her companion was solemn. She was plainly dressed in a plaid blouse with full sleeves, deep cuffs and a high white collar. Instead of a bow at the neck of the blouse she wore a mannish tie, and her dark, plain skirt stopped just above her ankles to reveal a pair of small, sturdy boots.

Although the outfit was practical, indicating a working woman, a love of feminine things could be seen in the stylish cut of the skirt and in the wide belt, fastened with a huge filigree clasp, that showed off a remarkably small waist.

'Isn't it grand?' Morag asked, her eyes on the photograph.

Isn't it grand, she meant, to be able to see people from the past, people whose existence she and Cal

145

had only just discovered, people who were long gone yet still, through the dry account books and the faded, cracked photographs they had left behind, part of the modern world?

She didn't need to explain any of that to Cal. 'Yes,' he said simply, and they stood smiling at each other.

13

When the photographs and miniature had been packed
away carefully in the box they drank home-made lemonade in the twilight coolness of the back garden, Cal
sitting on the doorstep while Morag used a kitchen
chair he had carried out for her. The river below was
quieter than by day, though a number of yachts taking
advantage of the evening breeze were dotted about its
surface like large white moths.

'How's your friend?'

'She's coming along fine, though she'll have to do
special exercises for a long time to get back the proper
use of her arm. She was very fortunate not to lose it
altogether.' She smiled at him. 'The family's so pleased
that Archie's to take over from Captain Forsyth on the
Sanda.'

'I meant to thank you for putting in a word for
him.'

'It needed more than a word.' She told him about
John Laird's opposition, and her visit to Captain
Forsyth's home.

'Mr Laird's set in his ways, and Archie's altogether
too brash for him.' A smile flickered round his lips.
'There's times when his sense of humour gets the
better of him, and John Laird has no sense of humour

at all. But Archie's a good seaman, you can be sure of that.'

'I just hope he behaves himself, after what I went through for him.'

'I'll make sure of it.'

'Tell me about the puffers,' she suggested, and he began to talk about taking the *Pladda* inland, through the locks on the Crinan Canal or up along the craggy West Coast, sometimes beaching her on lonely shores, far from a proper pier, to load and unload cargoes.

'Does she not topple over?'

'Of course not. These puffers are made for that sort of work. We prop her upright, and the folk bring their carts out on to the sands to take the goods off or load them on. Then when the next tide comes, we put the wee boat out with a line and haul her round as soon as the water gets under her and lifts her clear.' He sighed. 'Och, you should try waking in the early morning in a place like that, with the sea as flat as if someone had poured oil over it, and a mist over everything, and the water beginning to lap round her hull.'

'I wish I could.'

'Why not? You should come out in the *Pladda* some time and see what it's like for yourself.'

'Could I?' She was startled by the idea.

'They're your boats, you can do anything you want.'

The next question was out before she had time to wonder if it was wise. 'Is it difficult, Cal, to be working for someone who owns a business that should have been yours?'

He was leaning against the closed back door, elbows on knees and his hands loosely linked. He studied them in silence for so long that Morag began to feel nervous, then he shook his dark head.

'I never think of it. I'm sure you've heard enough

148

of the story to realise that, the way my father was squandering money, there would never have been an inheritance for me in any case. I'm just glad that Mr Weir was there to take control of the business. If he hadn't, it would have been bought out by the likes of the Arkbridges in Greenock. And if that had happened, the *Pladda* and the other boats would just have become part of someone else's fleet.'

Cal looked up, gave her a smile. 'Mr Weir dealt fairly with my father, and he gave me work as soon as I left the school. I was grateful to him, and I like working for Weir Shipping.'

Morag recalled Janet Weir's bitter mouth and the way her cold, accusing eyes had surveyed her whenever they happened to meet. 'Your mother didn't share your way of thinking.'

'My mother didn't always see things the way they really were. Women can be like that when they love a man as much as she loved him. My father was a rich man in that respect; though, sadly, he didn't realise it.'

A church clock chimed in the town and he got up suddenly. 'I must go, I'm keeping you from your bed.'

The Misses Ogilvie from Edinburgh were delighted with their accommodation.

'So much more pleasant than a commercial hotel.' The elder of the two surveyed the spacious hall, the wide sweep of the staircase and the stained-glass window on the half-landing with approval. 'And more relaxing than staying with the family, or friends of the family. You're not, are you?' she asked, fixing Morag with brown eyes as she began to peel off her gloves. 'A close friend of the family, I mean?'

'I'm not even an acquaintance. I'm just helping them out.'

'Good.' Miss Ogilvie finished with the gloves and removed the turban which had been jammed down tightly over short brown hair liberally sprinkled with grey. 'It's so tedious, having to make conversation and continually guard against saying something derogatory about someone who may well turn out to be a dear friend of your hostess – or even worse, her mother. We can relax here, Ann,' she informed her sister, running her fingers through her hair vigorously so that it stood up in little clumps all over her head.

'But you won't get the service you would receive in an hotel, I'm afraid,' Morag said nervously.

'Even better. We can fend very well for ourselves. We're used to it, and we would far rather. Talking of fending, I hope you don't mind us having a cup of tea after we unpack, my dear. We'll take it in your kitchen, so that you can show us where everything's kept and trot out any essential house rules we must obey.'

They were pleased with the accommodation, the elder woman choosing the front room and leaving the smaller back room which had been Sander's to her sister. 'Ann will enjoy looking on the river. She likes views. Don't usually notice them myself.'

Within fifteen minutes they had joined Morag in the kitchen, where they lost no time in insisting on first-name terms.

The elder of the two was called, unexpectedly, Camellia. 'A totally unsuitable name for someone like me, I know; my Mama, God rest her, was a plain woman but a romantic. I inherited her looks but not, I'm glad to say, her nature. It has been suggested that I call myself Millie, but I see nothing wrong with keeping the name I was first given. People tend to think it very striking and attractive. Now Ann here is pretty enough to suit my name down to the ground, but her mother – my step-mama – is quite the opposite to mine, being a beautiful woman with a practical soul.'

The fact that they were half-sisters explained why they were unlike each other in looks as well as in nature. Camellia, who Morag soon discovered was the older of the two by almost fourteen years, had a very positive manner and uncompromising features rescued from plainness by thickly lashed dark brown eyes. She favoured pleated skirts and brightly patterned hip-length belted jumpers.

Ann, not much older than Morag herself, was both pretty and feminine, with hazel eyes and a sleek bob that made her dark hair look as though it had been painted on her neat head. She liked to wear dresses with flared skirts, silk stockings, and leather court shoes with pointed toes and high heels.

It transpired that they were distant cousins of the bride and were representing their parents, who couldn't make the journey because Mr Ogilvie was in poor health.

'It's rather pleasant to have a few days off,' Camellia confided as the second cup of tea was poured. 'Ann is on holiday, it being August and she being a school-teacher, but I myself have had to take time off from work in order to be here.' She sighed. 'I would like to be able to say that I was the one blessed with the brains, if not the looks, in the family, but unfortunately my two brothers and Ann all have the better of me in that department too.'

'Pay no attention,' Ann Ogilvie said calmly. 'Camellia likes to fool people into thinking that she is a nobody, but it's quite untrue. She's a very successful business-woman with her own employment agency and a mind that could cut through a diamond.'

Camellia Ogilvie had a lively mind and was not afraid to ask questions. As soon as she found out about the shipping office, she insisted on going to the harbour with Morag to see the office and, if possible, some of the boats.

'Ann will do the necessary socialising. She's so much better at it than I am, so it's best to leave her to it.'

'And it saves me some embarrassment,' Ann added. 'You must have noticed, Morag, how inquisitive my sister is.'

'If folk have something to hide they can say so,' Camellia protested. 'If not, then why shouldn't they be open about themselves?'

'That,' Ann told her, 'is not the way polite society sees it.'

'Then polite society is blind. I would far rather find out more about interesting matters than discuss the servant problem or the latest fashion.'

Camellia was greatly taken by the figurehead and the footprints and the scrawled initials, and fascinated when Morag told her about the old account books and the photographs Cal had found. 'How wonderful, to have a business with a history. Do you think I might see these items?'

'I don't think Cal would mind.'

Captain Forsyth was in the office, having just brought in the *Sanda* and unloaded its cargo. He fell under Camellia's spell at once and before Morag knew what was happening she and her house guest were on board the puffer, clambering down an almost vertical ladder from the wheelhouse into the main cabin, a minute apartment scarcely larger than a decent-sized cupboard. Most of the floor space was taken up by the table, which had fixed benches running along two sides of it. Somehow, room had also been found for a cooking stove and cupboards and shelves.

'Isn't it cramped?' Camellia said. 'How can three men and a lad possibly manage here for days on end?'

'We're not at sea all the time, ma'am,' the Captain explained. 'We mainly move in short journeys from port to port. In any case, we don't spend much time down below. There's plenty to do on deck, and in the engine room.'

He showed them his own minute cabin with just room for the bunk, as narrow as the others, and a small sea chest; then he took them forward of the hatch cover to the low-ceilinged three-bunk crew cabin wedged beneath the raised foredeck that held the loading machinery.

'The bunks are like coffins.' Morag peered at one, not much more than a narrow shelf, with not enough room between it and the upper bunk for the occupant to sit upright. 'How can folk bear to sleep in there?'

'When you're bone-weary from hard work, Miss Weir, you'll sleep anywhere. Not that there's all that much time for rest on any voyage.'

'But surely there should be more space for the crew's comfort?'

'This vessel's a carrier, miss. All that matters is the cargo — finding enough space for it, stowing it away properly and making sure it gets safely from one place to another. The crew are of little account; it's a sight easier to find crewmen than cargo, or boats.' Forsyth slapped the side of a bunk and looked around, pride in his small craft shining from his face. 'And *Sanda*'s one of the best. Built to last, and as sturdy and trustworthy as any man can want. I'll miss her sadly when I move ashore, that I will!'

'It's grand to meet a man who takes a pride in what he does and isn't for ever complaining and finding fault,' Camellia said as they walked home from the harbour.

That evening both sisters exclaimed over the miniature figurehead and studied the photographs with interest.

'What became of Alicia?' Ann asked.

'Nobody seems to know.'

'Easy enough to find out. I'm sure the local newspaper office will have old copies you can look through. I'll do it if you like,' Camellia offered. 'I did some work on our own family tree once. It's fascinating, trying to trace ancestors. You don't think your friend would mind?'

'He'd like to know how his grandfather ended up owning the business.'

'You must invite him to the house while we're here. I'd like to meet him.'

'He's taken the *Pladda* to Ardrishaig, then up through the Crinan Canal to Mull. He might not be back for a few days.'

'We could extend our stay for a little while beyond the wedding, couldn't we, Ann? If you don't object to having house guests for a few extra days, my dear.'

'Not at all, but what about your place of work? Won't they be expecting you back soon?'

'I shall contact them and arrange something. Do you have a telephone? Then I shall telephone from the Winters' house tomorrow,' she said when Morag shook her head. 'You should consider having a machine installed, dear, both here and in your office. They are of great use to a businesswoman like yourself.'

'I'm not really a businesswoman. Mr Laird looks after the shipping company very well without any assistance from me.'

'Nevertheless, if the firm belongs to you, you should take a proper interest in it. And I certainly don't think that you should feel guilty about taking your father's inheritance away from him,' added Camellia, who had heard the entire story. 'Your uncle was a sensible creature, from all accounts, and a man like that knows his own mind. If he decided to entrust his business to you after raising you as his daughter for all those years, then you should accept gracefully, for his sake.' She wagged a solemn finger.

'And you'd be wise to learn something of the way the company is run, and keep an eye on the books just in case some unexpected complication flares up and you need to show that you know what you're taking about. The first rule of business is: never entirely trust anyone other than yourself where money is concerned. But having done that, I would say that if your office manager and the boat captains know their business, you should leave them to get on with it.'

'Unlike Camellia,' Ann put in with a twinkle in her eye. 'She rules her employees with a rod of iron. She terrifies them all.'

'That's because I don't have anyone else to do it for me. And of course I wield an iron rod, it's the sensible thing to do when one has to deal directly with people,' her sister retorted. 'I must make sure that they are aware of the rules and that they can stick to them. My clients depend on me to provide them with hard-working, reliable staff.'

'What sort of staff do you supply?'

155

'Oh, all sorts. Domestics, office workers, nannies. Supply and demand, my dear. Where I find a demand, I make a point of supplying it.'

'She makes light of it, the way she makes light of everything she does, but it's one of the most popular and most successful agencies in Edinburgh,' Ann told Morag next morning while they were alone in the house. 'Camellia can be totally relied upon to find honest, hard-working staff for any occasion. And she makes a point of finding work for women who need it badly, though she would never admit to that. I've known her to rescue a woman from the absolute depths of despair, feed and clothe and house her – and her children, for a lot of her staff are abandoned or ill-treated wives – then train her up for a post that will call for her particular skills. Camellia says that everyone is good at something, and she's usually proved right. It's amazing to see what pride a poor downtrodden soul can start taking in herself if she can be convinced that she can wash clothes or black grates better than most.'

She laughed, then added hurriedly as the front door opened and they heard Camellia's rather heavy step in the hall, 'But don't tell her what I said. She likes to be thought of as a hard taskmaster.'

Camellia swept into the room with the self-satisfied glow of someone who has just completed a good day's work. 'It was quite simple,' she announced. 'All there in the old newspapers. Alicia Tollin, poor soul, died of complications following an operation to remove her appendix at the age of 29. And she left the Tollin family business to Matthew Fergusson, her master wood-carver.'

The day of the wedding was also the day Wilma came

home from hospital. After helping the Ogilvies to get ready, and seeing them off to the church in the motor-car sent for them, Morag rushed to Ardgowan Street to find her friend holding court in the kitchen to the neighbours flocking to welcome her home. As fast as two or three left, others took their places.

It was some time before the crowd of well-wishers began to thin out and Mags, suddenly aware of the shadows beneath her daughter's eyes, ordered her to her bed.

'You go with her, Morag, and help her.'

Wilma would have none of it. 'I've just spent weeks in a night-gown, I'm not ever going to put one on during the day again.' Deftly, despite her bandaged arm, she stood her pillow on end to form a support and tossed the pillow from Daisy's bed on to the other end of hers. 'You down there, me up here,' she ordered and when they were settled, both lying propped up on the bed and facing each other, 'Now tell me about your ladies' wedding clothes.'

Morag had known that this would come and had tried, while helping her guests to get ready, to memorise every detail. 'Well, Camellia – Miss Ogilvie – has on a green silk dress with a squiggly black pattern all over it and quite a wide plain neckline,' she tried to describe it with a hand moving in a low curve from shoulder to shoulder, 'in a sort of pleated muslin. Short sleeves falling in three tiers, and there were three tiers in the skirt too, from the hipline. She had silk stockings – Ann insisted – and lovely green shoes with pointed toes. And over the dress she has a long black velvet cape trimmed with green ribbon. Apparently it's an evening cape she's had for years and scarcely worn, so Ann had it re-trimmed to match her frock.'

'Hat?'

'A green felt cloche without a brim, and with two black pom-poms on one side.'

'Mmm.' Wilma stared into space, trying to visualise the outfit in its entirety, then said, 'And the pretty one?'

'You know, Wilma, I'm not so sure she is the pretty one after all. Camellia can be very striking, quite beautiful in her own way, when you get to know her.'

'The other one, then,' Wilma said impatiently.

Ann had chosen a tubular dress of lilac satin overlaid with lace, a dramatic gown cut straight across from shoulder to shoulder at the front and dipping in a V-shape at the back. Her gathered lace sash was caught on the left hip with a bunch of satin flowers, the ends falling in a lacy waterfall to just below the hemline.

'I wish I could have seen them,' Wilma said wistfully, then her face brightened. 'We could watch them coming out of the church. There's still time to get there.'

'But you've just come out of hospital! You can't go out and about so soon!'

'It was my arm that got hurt, not my legs.' Wilma was already on her feet, two spots of excited colour in her cheeks. 'Anyway, I want to see the bride and the other guests. Come on, Morag, it'll be fun!'

Instead of trying to change her daughter's mind Mags announced that she, too, would like to see the bridal party and their guests. The few neighbours still gossiping in the kitchen took up the idea and five minutes later they all flowed from the close mouth like a swarm of bees from a hive, Wilma in the lead.

By the time they reached the church there was quite a crowd outside, craning their necks for a glimpse of the wedding party. 'Let this lassie past,' Mags ordered

158

them in a booming voice, one arm about her daughter. 'She's just out of the hospital.'

At sight of the sling supporting Wilma's bandaged arm, people jostled good-naturedly aside to make room for her and her party close to the church doors. They opened just then and the bride, in a cloud of embroidered lace and satin and orange blossom, floated out on her new husband's arm. Behind her came six bridesmaids in pink, with flowers in their hair.

An excited ripple ran through the crowd, almost entirely made up of women, at the sight. Then, as the wedding party proceeded across the pavement towards the cars awaiting them and the rest of the guests emerged from the shadowy interior, the soft murmur rose to a buzz as the wedding clothes were scrutinised and discussed.

'Poor soul, she must be sweatin' under that lot on a day like this,' someone commented as Miss Lamont emerged, blinking in the sunlight, in a long brown woollen jacket and skirt quite unsuited to the time of year. Just behind her came Camellia and Ann Ogilvie, both beaming at the onlookers as though they were having a wonderful day and wanted to share it with everyone.

'There they are!' Morag pointed, then waved as Ann spotted her in the crowd and brandished a gloved hand in her direction. Wilma craned forward to get a better look.

'Oh, that dress is lovely! I've never had anything in that shade of lilac,' she said enviously. 'I wonder what she's got on underneath?'

She insisted on staying until the final guest had departed and the church doors were closed, though by that time she was as white as a sheet and only managed to walk back to Ardgowan Street with the assistance of

159

her mother propping her up on one side, while Morag
supported her on the other.

'I told you that you shouldn't go,' Morag scolded as
they helped her into her room and on to the bed. 'It was
too much for you!'

'It was worth it, just to see all those folk, and not one
of them in a nurse's uniform,' Wilma said contentedly,
her eyelids already drooping and closing.

14

─────────◆─────────

True to her word, Camellia Ogilvie arranged for herself and her sister to stay on in Port Glasgow for a few days after the wedding, and at her request Morag invited Cal Fergusson to the house for supper when he brought *Pladda* back from her extended voyage.

He arrived looking quite unlike himself in a navy-blue suit and white shirt – his brown hair, normally ruffled by wind and weather, smoothed back and looking darker than usual with its gold glints subdued by a liberal application of pomade. During the meal he told Camellia all about his life as a puffer captain, and even when her questions began to concern his personal life he answered most of them candidly and cheerfully, though skilfully parrying one or two. Morag noted the gleam of appreciation in Camellia's fine eyes each time he politely slid out of a difficult situation.

She herself learned a good deal about Cal's past – the large and comfortable family home where he had been born and raised in a wealthy area of Gourock, the maidservants, the good school in Glasgow.

'I was being groomed to follow my father into the family business, of course, but things turned out differently. After he died my mother and I had to find somewhere else to live, and I left the Glasgow school and moved to a local one which I liked just as much.'

'Young people can be very resilient,' Camellia nodded. 'But it must have been very hard for your poor mother to see everything she and her husband had slipping away. Your life was still before you, but she faced an uncertain future at an age when she had no doubt anticipated comfort and ease.'

A shadow passed over his face. 'She did take it hard, but we managed very well. She still harboured hopes of me going to University when I left school, but it wasn't what I wanted at all. When Mr Weir offered me work on the puffers I was very happy to accept. And,' he smiled across the table at Morag, 'I've not regretted it.'

'So you ended up in the family business after all.'

'I did indeed,' Cal agreed cheerfully. 'Though not in the way my parents had planned for me.'

'Do you resent being an employee when you might have been the employer?'

'Camellia!' Ann protested. 'You're going too far!'

'Not at all.' Cal gave an easy shrug of the shoulders. 'Morag recently asked the same question. As I told her, I don't resent anything. Life's like a river, it twists and turns and often it takes an unexpected route. I like that.'

'Quite right,' Camellia approved. 'There's no sense in looking back all the time at what might have been. And now,' she pushed back her chair, 'I would very much like to have a proper look at those old papers you left with Morag, if you'll allow it. Morag, my dear, we'll just carry the dishes to the kitchen and Ann and I will see to them later.'

It was the first time Morag and Cal had taken a close look at the papers in the box; they consisted mainly of invoices, receipts and scribbled notes about various contracts, all of which Camellia studied closely. There was also a small bundle tied up with string, lying right at the bottom.

'Morag will have told you about Alicia's tragically early death, Mr Fergusson?'

Cal nodded. 'But I still can't understand how my great-grandfather came to own the business.'

'Perhaps there were no other relatives to inherit,' Ann suggested.

'Not at all, there was a male cousin who lived in Stirling. The house and all its contents were left to him; it said so in the newspaper. He came to Port Glasgow to organise the funeral and deal with the clearing and sale of the house. In my opinion,' Camellia said in her matter-of-fact voice, 'Alicia left the company to Matthew because she saw that as the right and fair thing to do. Had they been married he would have inherited it in any case, as her husband.'

'But there was no question of Matthew and Alicia marrying,' Morag protested, and Cal nodded agreement.

'He already had a wife and a family.'

'Exactly. He was . . . what?' Camellia made a quick estimation. 'Ten years her senior? When Matthew began work as her father's apprentice, Alicia was a little girl. When she took over the business on her father's death she was a young woman and, although Matthew was married by then, he was still in the prime of life. They were thrown together for the first time, as employer and employee.'

She looked at the disbelieving faces round the table, then picked up the bundle of papers she had been studying and held out the top one. 'This is a Christmas card from Alicia "To Matthew and Emily". And here,'

163

she selected several small sheets of paper, 'are notes from her to Matthew.'

Ann picked one up and studied it. 'I would scarcely say that a reminder about trusses and frames to be ready for a certain date constitutes a love letter.'

'There are different ways of showing love,' her sister told her crushingly. 'And I'm not suggesting that Alicia was trying to convey her feelings when she wrote this. I am merely pointing out that Matthew revealed his own feelings by keeping these little notes. Every piece of paper in this separate bundle has both their names on it. And here . . .' She pounced again and came up with a card portraying a river scene with a flock of white-sailed yachts in the centre.

'His wife's name isn't on this one. It must have been a special occasion. His birthday, perhaps, or mebbe it marked the end of a big contract. Whatever the occasion, this one was for him alone. "To Matthew, with my gratitude,"' she read aloud. '"Your friend always, Alicia."'

She handed the card to Morag who studied it with renewed interest, running the piece of pasteboard between her fingers and thinking of the man and the woman, both gone now, who had held it so many years before her own birth.

'I wonder,' Camellia mused, 'if there was a local scandal at the time over his inheritance. Probably, but I'm sure that Matthew Fergusson was strong enough to deal with the whispers and the stares. I would expect no less of the man worthy of a woman of Alicia's calibre.'

'Even if Alicia did fall in love with Matthew, there's no reason to presume that her feelings were reciprocated. Camellia, you are becoming more like your romantic mother with every year that passes.'

'Not at all, Ann, just observant.' Camellia placed the

164

photograph in the middle of the table, where they could all see it. 'Look for yourselves. Can't you see the way the two of them are standing apart from the third person in the photograph, and turned towards each other? It's as though there was an invisible cord tying the two of them together.'

'I can't really see that,' Cal began, only to be interrupted as though he had never tried to speak.

'Being a sensible businesswoman, Alicia Tollin made her will, even though she was a young woman with no thought of dying before her allotted time,' Camellia swept on. 'And she left her most precious possession, the business, to the man she most trusted and respected and, I am sure, loved. Just as your uncle, Morag, left his business to the person he most cared for.'

She began to gather up the papers strewn over the table. 'As to the mysterious initials in the concrete beside the footprints, there was no AM. They stand for Alicia and Matthew.'

'I've told Charlie Winters that you're the ideal person to accommodate any special visitors the mills might have,' Camellia said briskly on the morning of her departure.

'Me? But I don't know if I want to go on taking in paying guests!'

'Of course you do. You have the room, and you're a very good hostess.' She wrenched on her gloves, Morag noticed, rather than drawing them over her hands as other people did. 'Consider it carefully, my dear. I saw the way your father and step-mama were studying this place on the night you invited them here to meet us. If you want to go on living here – which makes sense since it's a very fine house – and you want to prevent your family from moving in with you, then making

165

your rooms available for the occasional guest is the ideal solution.'

'Do leave the poor girl alone and stop bullying her, Camellia,' Anne said from the mirror, where she was setting her hat straight. The sisters' luggage stood by the door, and a cab was due to arrive at any moment to take them to the station. 'We've probably put her right off having paying guests. She may not want to do it ever again.'

'Nonsense, of course she does, now that she's practised on us.' Having dealt with her gloves, Camellia pulled the turban she had worn on her arrival over her head without troubling to use the mirror. 'There's the money, too, a very useful source of income independent of the business. You could put it in a special bank account, or perhaps invest it. Ask that nice young lawyer of yours for advice, I'm sure he'll be only too happy to be of assistance. There's the cab,' she added as someone knocked at the door.

'We'll be there in a moment, driver,' she said briskly when she had supervised the removal of the luggage. 'Now then, Morag, don't stand on the doorstep waving like an imbecile. I do hate farewells – such a waste of valuable time'

'It's not really goodbye anyway.' Ann hugged Morag, enveloping her in a cloud of lily-of-the-valley cologne. 'You must allow us to come back some day. And you must visit us in Edinburgh.'

'Do hurry up, Ann, that poor man'll take root on the pavement if we don't go.' Camellia bustled her sister out of the door, then shook Morag's hand. 'Thank you for everything, my dear, and remember to keep Alicia in the forefront of your mind at all times. If she could run a business in an age when it wasn't really the thing for a well-brought-up young lady to do, then you most certainly can. Trust in Cal Fergusson; I like that young man, he's got a sensible head and strong shoulders. I imagine that he has something of his great-grandfather Matthew in him.'

'Camellia, I am not Alicia Tollin and Cal isn't Matthew, so don't let your imagination run away with you.' Even as she spoke, Morag noticed how like Ann Ogilvie she sounded. Probably everyone who had dealings with Camellia's quicksilver mind began to sound like that.

'I most certainly hope not. Matthew was married, and poor Alicia died – while you, I trust, will live to become a very prosperous and very old woman.' Camellia checked her hands to make sure that her gloves were on and caught up her bag. 'But time has an interesting way of circling instead of moving forward in a straight line. I've always thought that that is why people talk about "time and again". The past sometimes repeats itself, in order to let people put things right.'

'Camellia—'

'Must go. Do keep in touch!' The door closed decisively, and Morag was left in the empty hall. Outside a door slammed and an engine coughed into life, then throbbed off into the distance, and silence.

'We are most indebted to you, Miss Weir, for helping us out.' Although Mrs Winters was younger, plumper and prettier than her sister, she retained Miss Lamont's air of nervousness and indecision. Morag marvelled at how two women so lacking in confidence could have made the Gourock teashop the success it was. 'Camellia is somewhat particular as to her surroundings, and by the time she and Ann notified us of their intention to attend the wedding . . .'

167

'. . . there were no suitable hotels with vacant rooms in the area, and even our friends had already volunteered all their spare rooms,' her husband chimed in. 'Camellia tells me, Miss Weir, that you may be willing to let us approach you again, should any of the people who visit the mills require accommodation.'

'Only those who are bringing their wives with them, of course,' Mrs Winters said. 'We would never expect you to entertain a man on his own.'

'I am sure that Miss Weir is already aware of that, my dear. And not many of them do bring their wives, so we wouldn't be calling on you very often . . .'

'. . . but it would be a great comfort to know that we could, if necessary.' The Winters seemed to have a habit of ending each other's sentences. It was as well, Morag thought, that they were both sitting on her parlour sofa – making it easier for her, in a chair opposite, to look from one to the other as she was forced to do frequently.

'And the company can afford to be generous,' Mr Winters ended, nodding significantly at the envelope he had placed discreetly on the small table close to her chair.

In the twenty-four hours following the Ogilvies' departure, Morag had already made up her mind. She had thought herself quite content, living alone as she had since Sander's death; but recently she had discovered the pleasure of coming back home to the sound of voices or, if the place was empty, catching the faint scent of Ann's lily-of-the-valley cologne, and finding a pair of gloves on the hall table or a shawl tossed over a chair in the parlour, waiting for their owners to claim them. She wanted company, and she wanted to keep the house, but she didn't want her father and his wife and family to move in. The occasional paying guest was the answer.

*   *   *

Within an hour of the Winters' departure, Wilma arrived in a state of high excitement.

'You'll never guess,' she began as soon as Morag opened the door. 'Birkmyre's have paid me compensation for my accident, and here was me wondering if I was going to be dismissed for trying to clean a machine while it was still running! Seventy-six pounds, Morag! Imagine . . . seventy-six pounds!' She whirled her friend around the hall.

'Watch out for your arm, you'll hurt it!'

'Och, it suddenly feels all better,' Wilma said blithely. 'It's amazing what a bit of good news can do to mend folk.' She used her good hand to pull Morag into the kitchen. 'Come and make me a cup of tea,' she ordered, 'and I'll tell you what I'm going to spend it on.'

'You've decided that already?'

'Mam said I could, since I'd been the one to go through the pain. And I already knew what I wanted.' Her eyes were like stars. 'How would you like to come to Rothesay with me next month, for a whole week?'

'A holiday?' Morag almost spilled boiling water over her hand. 'Just the two of us?'

'Just us. Mrs McNeish in the next close to us knows a good boarding-house right on the front, where we could try for accommodation. She says they'll probably have room, since the Fair holidays will all be over and folk back at work and school. Say you'll come, Morag!'

'What about the hospital?' Wilma was still attending Broadstone Hospital once a week.

'I've already asked them, when I was there this morning. They said the arm's mending well, and it'd be all right to go away as long as I kept doing the

169

exercises. I told them that I'd be with a bossy friend who'd make sure I did. Say yes, Morag!'

'On one condition. Let me pay for the holiday.'

'But I've got this compensation . . .'

'I know, but I've just been paid for having the Ogilvies to stay and I want to spend the money on something special. I've agreed to take in other guests now and again, so I'll be getting more money when that happens. So it makes sense for us to use my money and keep yours for something else. Anyway,' she added triumphantly as Wilma chewed indecisively on her lower lip, 'it was your idea for me to take in the Ogilvies, so their payment should be shared.'

'If that's what you want – but if we're using your money you'll have to let me buy you something when we're there, instead.'

'D'you know what I'd really like? Fish and chips in a newspaper, so that we can eat them on the pier while we're looking at the sea and the boats and the moon.'

'And we'll go dancing, and go to the pictures, and have a shot on the putting green and take a wee boat out on Rothesay Bay . . .'

As Wilma listed the pleasures to come, Morag felt a tingle of excited anticipation creep over her. She had only ever been on holiday with Georgina and Sander, when she was a schoolgirl, to Helensburgh and Dunoon and once to Edinburgh, sedate holidays with no cinemas and no fish and chips and no sense of freedom. This one would be different.

Wilma ran out of breath and ideas, and for a moment the two friends beamed at each other across the table. 'Who'd ever have thought that you and me would be arguing about which of us should pay for a holiday?' Wilma asked, then, reaching out and clutching Morag's hand. 'Oh, Morag, isn't it grand to be rich?'

15

It was Cal's idea that the two girls should travel to Rothesay on board the *Pladda* instead of taking the steamer.

'Why pay one and ninepence each when you can travel for nothing aboard your own boat? I'm taking a boxed cargo over and there'll be nothing stored above deck, so there's room for you both.'

Wilma was enchanted by the prospect, and they turned up with their luggage at the allotted time to find that the puffer had almost completed loading huge tea-chests from a lorry and would be sailing within the half-hour. Cal broke off from his work to suggest that they wait in the office.

'And you'd be wise to . . . avail yourselves of the privy there before we sail,' he added, his voice husky with embarrassment and his eyes fixed on some point between Morag and Wilma. 'We've got nothing fancy like that aboard the wee boats.'

'What do you do, then?' The question was out before Morag could stop it. She regretted it as soon as she saw the colour rise from beneath the neck of his thick jersey.

'We wait,' the young skipper said abruptly. 'The boat's never at sea for all that long at the one time anyway.'

171

'Bucket then chuck it, our Archie says,' Wilma chirruped, and the colour flooding over Cal from throat to hairline deepened. He muttered something about having to keep an eye on the loading, and almost tripped over a bollard in his haste to turn away from them.

'You didn't have to say that,' Morag chided her friend as the two of them made for the office.

'I only said what they did when they were caught short at sea. It was you that started it, asking the man personal questions,' Wilma said, unrepentant. 'Anyway, what's wrong with talking about it? It's perfectly natural. Even the king has to go to the privy sometimes.'

'You would have been much more comfortable on a passenger steamer,' John Laird said disapprovingly as he served them tea in chipped mugs. 'It's not seemly for young ladies such as yourselves to arrive at Rothesay on board a puffer.'

'It'll suit us fine.' Wilma blew on her tea, then sipped it gingerly. 'And it's a nice change from the steamers.' Morag stood by the window, watching the large tea-chests being swung up into the air, then over the side of the dock to be lowered into the large open hatch that took up almost all of *Pladda*'s middle section. The tide was rising, and the small cargo boat was lifting with it. When they arrived, only her wheelhouse and her high bow had been above the harbour wall; now, Morag could almost see the open hatch. The boat was being loaded from the dock; on this occasion its own steam winch and derrick, used for loading and unloading in small ports or when it was beached with no other loading gear to use but its own, were not needed.

'How is business coming along, Mr Laird?'

'It's fine, just fine,' he said coldly. He always

sounded offended when she asked questions, as though he suspected that she was accusing him of misconduct. At first it had troubled her, but having found that it was the very fact that she asked questions at all that offended him, no matter how carefully she tried to phrase them, she had given up trying to be tactful.

It was her belief that John Laird hoped that his sharpness would eventually put a stop to her visits to the harbour, and she was not going to let that happen. Although she left the running of Weir Shipping solely to him, she made a point of visiting the office once a week and going over the books with him. Gradually, she was beginning to understand the movement of cargoes, the approximate costs, the wages bill and the expected time taken to cover the many journeys the five Weir boats made all around the Firth of Clyde and through the Crinan Canal.

The loading was completed. The lorry, its bed empty now, drove off, and the dockers moved away. Cal left his three-man crew to fasten the big hatch cover into place while he came across to the office with the easy swing to his walk that Morag would now have recognised in the dark.

'Ready?' he asked when he and Laird had completed the paperwork.

'Just before you go, Miss Weir . . .' The clerk fished in a desk drawer. 'If I could have your signature on these?'

'What are they?' Morag was impatient to be off on her new adventure. Behind her, Wilma sighed loudly.

'Orders for provisions and supplies. A paint order for the work needing to be done on the boats before the winter comes – and we need lamp oil, and rope, not to mention the coal.'

She scrawled her name hurriedly and Cal, picking

173

up their small cases, began to lead his passengers downstairs.

'You'll take good care of these young ladies?' John Laird made it sound more like an order than a question.

'No, I had it in mind to make them work their passage and then throw them overboard as soon as we got into Rothesay Bay.' Cal tossed the words over his shoulder and Wilma giggled, while the old man flushed angrily.

'Cheeky wee nyaff!' he muttered, but if Cal heard him he paid no heed.

'It's as well the weather's good,' he said as the three of them walked across the harbour. 'It's cramped below and you'd be better sitting up top, unless you're worried about getting your hair in a mess.'

They both assured him that they had no such worries and Morag, remembering the tiny, stuffy cabin on the *Sanda*, was grateful for the light wind and the dry skies overhead.

The engineer was already below preparing for their departure and Big Malky, the mate, handed them aboard while Cal stowed the cases away below and then came up and took the wheel to guide the *Pladda* out into the river. Big Malky and his son Wee Malky, the ship's lad, cast off and coiled the mooring ropes.

The two girls perched comfortably on the hatch coaming, which took up almost all of the mid-deck, swinging their legs over into the narrow passageway that ran round it on three sides. On the fourth, forward side, steps led up to the raised bow where the loading machinery stood. The derrick, like a huge lowered mast, had been folded back along the length of the hatch, ready to be raised when needed for loading or unloading.

Wilma drew her feet up, tucking her flared skirt modestly around her legs so that she could rest her chin on her knees. 'This is the best way to travel,' she said rapturously. 'Our own boat – it's next to having a yacht, isn't it? D'you think we could come home again on this puffer?'

'We'll see what Cal says.' A steamer would have been more comfortable but Wilma was quite right, it was grand to have their own transport, Morag thought as they travelled down the coast past Gourock, the engine throbbing sturdily below decks, the little puffs of steam which gave the small cargo boats their nickname jetting from the stack. Now that they were out on the river the wind was stronger. The plumes of steam from the stack and the tendrils of blue smoke curling from Cal's pipe through the open wheelhouse window were snatched away to be fragmented, then absorbed, by the wind.

They passed the opening on the right to the Gareloch, then turned from the second, larger opening into Loch Long, moving from the River Clyde into the Firth of Clyde. As they passed between the village of Inverkip on the Gourock shore and the popular holiday town of Dunoon on the opposite shore, another puffer going by on its way up-river blew its steam whistle in greeting. Cal stuck his capped head out of the wheelhouse and waved his pipe in acknowledgement, while Wilma tore off the scarf she had tied about her head and brandished it. After a bemused moment a cap was waved in answering salute from the other wheelhouse.

'They'll think Cal's brought his sweetheart aboard.'

Wilma laughed and shrugged. 'They'll think he's a very lucky man, then.'

An appetising smell floated from below, and not long afterwards Wee Malky brought them mugs of strong tea and slices of fried Lorne sausage between thick wedges of bread. Although Morag's stomach would have rebelled on shore at the strength of the tea and the size of the 'piece', the sea air had sharpened her appetite and she enjoyed every mouthful and morsel.

Ahead of them now lay the Cumbraes, two islands close together. The nearest was Great Cumbrae, where the holiday town of Millport was situated, with Little Cumbrae snugged in close behind it like a small child keeping close to its mother's skirts. The Firth divided into two channels round the Cumbraes, one running along the mainland, the other passing between the Cumbraes and Arran, the largest island in the Firth. Before the Cumbraes, however, lay Bute, the second largest island and *Pladda*'s destination.

As the boat steamed into Rothesay Bay, a wide and graceful stretch of water famed in rhyme and song for its beauty, Wilma reached for Morag's hand and squeezed it hard. 'Imagine spending a whole week here!'

The elegant town of Rothesay, with its Winter Gardens on the foreshore and its church spires and old castle, was built along the shore of the bay. To each side, luxurious homes nestled in large gardens, and the hills rising gently behind the town offered rich farmland and lush woodland.

Although the traditional Glasgow Fair holiday in July and the Paisley Fair holiday in August were well over, there were still holidaymakers and day-trippers around in this pleasant September, and several steamers lay alongside. One was on its way out of the bay and, although Cal took the puffer well to the starboard of her, the girls were awed by the size of the ship as it slid past.

'It doesn't seem that big when you're on it, does

it?' Wilma said in wonder as the steamer moved away, booming a warning from its siren to the people bobbing about the bay in small rowing-boats.

The *Pladda* used a side harbour, slipping in past wooden pilings to moor right by the main street in an area where small cargo carriers could unload on to lorries and carts. When the engine had slowed and stilled Johnno, the engineer, made his appearance, giving the passengers a brief nod and wiping sweat from his brow with a rag that was far from clean and only served to redistribute the smears of oil over his face.

'You could fry enough food to feed a regiment with the oil on that man's clothes,' Wilma whispered, wrinkling her nose fastidiously.

The boat was far below the street level, and Cal clambered up the wall ladder then took the cases from the mate and waited on the harbour to help the girls reach the top, while the mate stood underneath. First Morag, then Wilma managed to gain the street without mishap, and Cal called to the boy, who swarmed up as easily as though he was walking along a pavement to join them.

'I've to see to the unloading, but Wee Malky here'll carry your cases to the boarding-house.'

Wee Malky's face, or what could be seen of it under a skipped cap several sizes too large for him, fell, but he knew better than to argue with his superior. 'Aye, Captain,' he said glumly and, snatching up both cases, he set off at such a determined trot that Morag and Wilma had to break into a lope to catch up and keep up with him. He was a strong lad, but small as yet, so he had to hold the cases high to prevent them from scuffing along the pavement. Attempts to persuade him to let them help by carrying at least one piece of luggage met with determined opposition.

'The Captain said I was tae carry yer luggage,' he said and powered on, though noticeably slowing.

'Thank God for that,' Wilma said breathlessly to Morag as they changed from a lope to a walk. 'We must have looked as if he was stealing the luggage and we were trying to catch him.'

'Stop!' Morag suddenly rapped out, and the little procession skidded to a halt.

'Did ye forget somethin'?' Wee Malky set down the cases and tipped his head far back in order to look up under the skip of his cap. His exasperated tone said that this was just like women.

She nodded at the shop they had almost passed. 'I'm having an ice-cream. The salt air on the river's made me thirsty.'

'Me too,' Wilma said at once. 'You'll have one yourself, Malky?'

'The Captain said—'

'Never mind the Captain; I own the *Pladda* and I'm saying that we're all having an ice-cream. Wait there.' Morag marched into the shop. When she emerged a few moments later, balancing three cones generously topped with soft white cream finished off with a swirl and a peak, Wee Malky was leaning against the wall with hands in pockets, catching his breath, while Wilma peered into the window of a nearby draper's shop.

'They've got a sale on,' she said excitedly as soon as Morag appeared.

'Never mind that just now, we're going over the road to sit among the flowers and the palm trees while we eat our ice-creams,' Morag said with determination, and set off across the road, leaving her companions no option but to follow.

'D'you really own the *Pladda*?' the boy asked a few minutes later, raising a cream-smeared mouth from his

cone. He had refused to sit on a bench with them, but
had consented to rest on the grass.

'I do.'

'But you don't run her.'

'I don't know how, so I leave it to those that do.
D'you like working for me?'

'My faither and me work for the Captain.'

'D'you like working for him, then?'

'Oh aye,' said Wee Malky with enthusiasm. Suddenly his tongue, possibly affected by the cold sweet
cream, loosened, and he launched into story after story
of the *Pladda* and her crew, and the adventures they
got up to.

'You seem to have more excitement than anyone on
one of those big sea-going cargo ships.' Wilma nudged
Morag's knee with her own.

'Aye, we do. I'm going tae be a captain mysel'. My
faither says bein' a mate suits him fine, but not me.'
The last delicious piece of cone disappeared into the
boy's mouth and he got to his feet, wiping cream from
his chin and then licking it off his grubby hand before
re-settling the cap firmly over his ears and the bridge
of his nose.

'We'd best get on, they'll be needing me back at
the harbour,' he said, and snatched up the cases before
setting off with renewed vigour.

'Mebbe it was a mistake to refresh him,' Wilma
whispered as they hurried in his wake. 'He's churning
along there like a wee paddle-steamer . . . but with our
suitcases instead of paddle boxes at the sides.'

The boarding-house wasn't far from the Winter Gardens, and right on the front. Their bedroom was quite
generous in size, and well furnished, with a sea view
from the window. Wee Malky's jaw dropped at the
sight of such opulence and Morag suspected that his

179

eyes, hidden by the cap, were rounded. He beamed when she gave him a generous tip, then scooted off downstairs, pausing at the door to say hurriedly, 'Mind an' have a nice holiday then.'

'Don't you worry,' Wilma called after him. 'We will!'

It was certainly the best holiday either of them had ever had. The weather held, apart from a few showers, and they walked and cycled, went round the putting green several times and invested six whole shillings on two tickets for a round-Bute bus trip. They had more ice-cream while they sat in the Winter Gardens listening to the band playing in the handsome bandstand, and they visited both cinemas in the town, first of all to sigh over Jack Buchanan's style and elegance at the Palace Cinema, then to the Theatre de Luxe where they thrilled to a war story about a tormented girl forced to choose between duty and her love for George O'Brien, the hero.

Wilma, true to her word, bought fish suppers for them both, and they ate them on the seafront while they watched the water reflecting the moon and the lights of the fishing boats on their way out for a night's work. One wet afternoon they enjoyed the Rothesay Entertainers' musical comedy show at the Winter Gardens, and they even invested in bathing suits, blue for Wilma and black for Morag, and launched themselves, squealing at the chilly water, into the salt-water open-air lido.

Many years before, Wilma's older brothers had taught them to swim at Gourock by tossing them into the sea and standing waist deep, arms folded, watching their panic-stricken struggles to the shore and safety.

'Best way to learn,' Morag remembered Robbie saying as she stumbled ashore, choking and with water pouring from her nose and mouth. Both girls had learned, but Morag hadn't swum since and she found it best to keep to the shallow end, bending her knees and doing the breast-stroke with her arms to make it look as though she was actually swimming. Wilma, always the more adventurous of the two, went into deeper water and managed, splashily, to complete a width or two. She had stripped the bandage from her arm, declaring that she was not going to spend her holiday looking like an invalid.

'It's nothing like it used to be,' she said casually when Morag shuddered at her first sight of the scars and the marks of the stitches livid against her olive skin. 'And the marks'll fade. All it needs now is some fresh air and a bit of exercise.'

Although the limb was still weak it was able to support her in the water, and Morag had difficulty in persuading her not to overdo things. When Wilma finally consented to come out of the pool and dry herself, Morag noticed a couple of young men who were larking about at the deep end throw glances in their direction.

'Your red hair looks wonderful against that black suit,' Wilma said.

'Carroty, you mean. That's what the boys called me in school, remember?'

'They were just wee idiots. They called me fat, and look at me now.' Wilma looked down complacently at her curvaceous body, seen to its best advantage in the wet suit. 'Your hair's much nicer than you realise. You should get it bobbed – you could have it done here in Rothesay.'

'I'm not sure,' Morag said evasively. Georgina had loved to brush her hair, and had never allowed her to have it cut short. Even though she could please herself now, Morag was still nervous about breaking free altogether from childhood regulations.

181

'You'd have to if you worked in the mills. That's why I had mine done, and I've been on at our Daisy to gets hers cut too. I've heard of lassies that got pulled into machines by their hair and got half their scalps torn off.'

'And I heard of a lassie with short hair who got her sleeve caught and almost got her arm torn off.'

'I know, I know. I was a daft fool, and I'll never do that again. You've got a nice long neck,' Wilma changed the subject hurriedly, 'and such good skin. You'd suit a bob.'

The young men Morag had noticed at the lido were at the putting green on the following afternoon, and in the Madeira Palais de Dance on Saturday evening. Almost at once they came over and requested the pleasure of a dance, and when the evening ended they escorted Morag and Wilma back to the boarding-house, where they discreetly managed to change from a foursome to two couples. In the bedroom after-wards the girls exchanged notes amid a flurry of giggles.

'Clive was quite a gentleman, really. I hope Robert was too.'

'Oh yes.' Morag had been quite nervous, but so had Robert, so a chaste kiss and a cuddle had satisfied them both. 'He wanted to go out with me again.'

'What did you say?'

'I said I'd see what you were doing,' Morag con-fessed. She might be the owner of five puffers, and she might live in a large house, but she knew nothing of the art of courting.

'Good. Clive asked too, but I said we wanted to just have this holiday on our own. You don't mind, do you?'

'No,' Morag said contentedly. It would be much

easier to enjoy herself without having passionate young men to deal with.

The four of them met again on the following day during a boat trip round the island on the paddle-steamer *Duchess of Rothesay*, but after that Wilma made it clear, in a friendly but firm way that left Morag green with envy, that there was to be no hope of a holiday romance. On the day after that, Clive and Robert were spotted in the town with two other girls on their arms.

Wilma's compensation money was burning a hole in her pocket, and she dragged Morag back to the draper's where they had bought their bathing costumes. 'There's a sale on. You should always take advantage of a sale,' she insisted. 'Besides, I've got presents to buy for Mam and our Daisy and the rest of them.'

She bought cambric petticoats for Daisy and her older sister and two sisters-in-law, as well as one for herself, then invested in a pair of gloves for her mother. After that, heady with the thrill of having money to spend, she had bought herself two pairs of cambric knickers before her eyes fell on some art silk underwear.

'The cambric's more practical, and fivepence half-penny cheaper,' Morag pointed out.

'I know that,' her friend retorted, pulling out her purse again. 'But silk feels nicer next to my skin. And in any case, I'm on my holidays. I can do whatever I want on my holidays! What about you?'

With a sense of shock, Morag realised that she had nobody to buy gifts for. Her step-mother would probably think she was showing off if she spent money on a present for her, or for her father. She compromised by buying rock for the two children and handkerchiefs for Mrs Beckett and Daisy. Then, egged on by Wilma, she bought herself a cotton frock in a floral pattern, a slip and a pair of knickers . . . cambric, for she steadfastly refused to invest in the art silk.

After leaving their parcels at the boarding-house they walked along the coast to the village of Port Bannatyne, where they spent a pleasant hour or so paddling in the water and searching for small crabs, and fronds of seaweed with air bladders which could sometimes, after considerable effort, be 'popped' with a small but satisfying explosion.

'Look!' Wilma said suddenly, and Morag turned to see the clear imprint of their bare feet following them in a wandering line over the damp sand. Even as they watched, a small wave hurried in and swept the sand clean, as though their prints had never been there.

'Just like chalk being wiped off a blackboard,' Wilma said, fascinated, and squatted down to write their names on the sand with a piece of shell. 'D'you remember the way we used to take off our socks and shoes and make footprints in the melted tar on a hot day when we were wee?'

'I took off my socks and shoes. You were lucky, you didn't have to wear any; you got to play in your bare feet.' Pools of tar left to dry and harden in the gutter after the road-menders had gone by melted in the heat of a summer day and made a wonderful playground for street children. Morag could still recall the summer heat on her head and shoulders, and the smell of the melted tar. There had been an exquisite pleasure in pushing a bare foot into the warm sticky stuff, and feeling it squish between her toes.

She could vividly remember, too, the sting of Georgina's palm on her calves when she went home with her socks ruined by the tar and her feet still sticky and clogged between the toes. It had taken ounces of good butter to get all the tar off, but even while the red imprint of Georgina's fingers still stood out on her legs Morag felt that it had been worth it.

Wilma tried to make her mark on the sand above the water-line, where her footprints wouldn't be washed away, but the sand was too soft there and as soon as she took her foot away thousands of grains spilled in, just as the waves had down by the shore, to obliterate the dents made by her small round heel, the fleshy section behind her toes and her neat little toes themselves.

'It's difficult to leave anything of yourself here, to show you've been,' she said, frustrated, and Morag thought of the two recorded footprints, Alicia Tollin's and Matthew Fergusson's. They had made sure that their prints remained after them.

Perhaps Camellia was right, and they were trying in their own way to record a secret love.

She wished, as she and Wilma walked again on the sand, then watched their prints disappear under creamy ripples of water, that she had someone who cared enough about her to want to announce his love to those who came after.

16

'Are you sure this is a good idea?' Morag asked doubtfully.

'Of course I am, there's nothing to it. Is there?' Wilma appealed to the lad waiting to help them along the wheeled wooden pontoon and into the rowing-boat bobbing in the water at the far end. He gave her a cheerful, gap-toothed grin.

'Nothin' to it,' he agreed. 'Just dip the oars in, then pull them through like this, then lift them out.' He demonstrated, swishing imaginary oars through the air with ease.

'I don't know . . .'

'It's this, or the aeroplane trip at Ettrick Bay.'

'I told you, I'm not doing that!' Morag had been horrified when Wilma, spotting the posters, had suggested a flight in a small plane over the island.

'Well, then. You've rowed a wee boat before, Morag.'

'Only on a pond, and that was a good while back.'

'It's like bicycling, you never forget,' Wilma told her firmly, while the lad chimed in with, 'And if you get into trouble, I'll come out and tow you in.'

'There you are, then. Go on,' Wilma ordered him, then clambered up the steps on to the pontoon at his

186

back. Morag had no option but to follow the two of them – keenly conscious, as she made her way cautiously along the temporary gangway, of the water moving below the open slats she walked on.

The boat seemed very small, and it rocked quite alarmingly when the boy handed them both in. Morag settled herself on the bench facing Wilma, who was seated in the stern, and grasped both oars firmly while the boy released the rope.

'Just keep clear of the pier where the steamers are,' he said as he gave the dinghy a hearty shove which sent them away from the pontoon and out towards the open bay.

It was harder to row than Morag remembered. The water was surprisingly resistant, and it took all her strength to pull back on the oars while the blades were submerged, but gradually she got the idea and the rhythm and they began to move slowly and somewhat jerkily into deeper water and among the other hired boats. Mindful of her personal need to stay close to the shore, she managed to turn the dinghy so that it moved parallel to the pier while keeping well clear of the steamers moored there.

'I told you you could do it,' Wilma encouraged. 'Isn't this lovely?' She peered over the side, holding on to her new wide-brimmed straw hat. It had been bought especially for the occasion, and its long green ribbons fluttered jauntily in the breeze. 'Oh, look, you can see the bottom! Look at that wee crab!'

'I can't look and row at the same time,' Morag told her, breathlessly and somewhat irritably.

'Stop rowing, then. We're not near any of the big boats, it's quite safe.'

Morag carefully shipped the oars and they hung over opposite sides so as not to rock the boat, enchanted with the submarine world they could faintly make out below. After a few moments Morag, feeling more comfortable with the oars, rowed a little further out while Wilma trailed her hand in the water. Then they stopped again to peer into the depths.

'I wonder if we'll see a wreck, with fish swimming in and out of it.'

'We're too close to shore for that.' Morag paddled her hand in the water, letting its movement tickle her fingers. The sun was pleasantly warm and there was just enough of a breeze to prevent the heat from becoming too oppressive. The gentle bouncing of the dinghy on the waves was as soothing as being rocked to sleep in the safety of a mother's arms, and the cool, soft touch of the water on her fingers and her palm . . .

A sudden blast of sound tore through her reverie and she jumped so violently that she almost toppled from her seat and into the water. The noise came again, like the fabric of the universe being ripped asunder. Wilma, sitting opposite, was screaming; Morag knew that, because her friend's mouth was open as wide as it could go, and she could actually see Wilma's tongue vibrating within the moist pink cavern. But she couldn't hear the scream because her ears were ringing, deafened by the terrible blaring noise which had come from nowhere.

Wilma's eyes were fixed on something beyond Morag's shoulder. Twisting round to see what it was, she discovered that the wide stretch of Rothesay Bay and the other dinghies that dotted it on this fine day had disappeared. There was nothing to be seen now but an enormous black wall which rose from a stretch of foaming water and filled the horizon from end to end. Tipping her head back to look up its sheer cliff, and up . . . and up . . . Morag saw that where it ended high above there were tiny railings and people peering down on her.

It was then that her numbed mind began to function again, and she realised that the wall was in fact the bows of a passenger steamer, coming closer by the second towards the tiny boat which held herself and Wilma.

'Oh, my God!' For a further brief stretch of time she was motionless, mesmerised by the way in which the water which had lapped gently at her fingers foamed around the great black hull as though hungry for prey. Then she grabbed at the oars, whimpering in frustration as they jiggled awkwardly in the rowlocks.

'Row, Morag!' This time she heard Wilma's voice, shrill with panic. 'Row!' Hard on the heels of the final word came another blast of sound from the steamer's siren.

Finally Morag got a good grip on the oars. Aware that their bow was turned towards the oncoming monster, she managed in a floundering way to turn the dinghy before digging both oars deep into the water. Unfortunately, only one blade went below the surface while the other merely skimmed it, throwing her off-balance. She managed to right herself, and this time both blades bit into the waves. They seemed to take for ever to reappear. With an energy born of desperation and terror, she swung them back until her shoulders cracked and then dug them in again.

Now that she had turned the dinghy she was facing the oncoming steamer, a sight more likely to paralyse her with fear than galvanise her into action. She closed her eyes against it, gritted her teeth and managed to get in three good strong strokes which sent the tiny, fragile shell moving through the water. Morag was encouraged to redouble her efforts, but just as a tongue can never refrain from probing the exposed nerve of a broken tooth, so her eyes popped open of their own volition.

The sight of the approaching steamer, moving fast and still bearing down on them, caused her to misjudge her next stroke. This time both oars merely skimmed the water's surface, and again she was almost sent backwards off her seat.

A sudden gust of wind blew Wilma's hat off and she lunged forward as it caught for a moment on one of the rowlocks.

'Sit down!' Morag screamed at her. 'You'll have us over!'

The hat flopped clear and into the water. As a wave took it Wilma teetered, off-balance in the shifting, tossing boat. Both girls screamed as she spun round on one foot, then miraculously she fell away from the edge of the boat to land beside Morag, though almost in her lap. As she did so, she knocked one of the oars from Morag's grasp.

The hat began to skim across the water, waving its ribbons at its frustrated owner, as the oar started to slide overboard. Wilma caught it just in time, and hauled it back into position.

'I'll help you.'

'You'll hurt your arm!'

'It's not going to be any use to me if I'm dead, is it?' Wilma screeched above another blast from the steamer. She glared up at it. 'We know you're there, we can see you!' she yelled, frantically settling the oar into place. 'I can help. I've watched Danny rowing. In, through, out—'

'Not that way, the other way! You'll have us going round in circles!'

'Oh, God,' Wilma panted, reversing her stroke. 'Oh, Morag! I wish Danny was here! Oh, Mammy!'

*   *   *

Throughout the trip from Gourock Danny Hastie had been positioned on the top deck of the *Duchess of Fife*, standing as far forward as possible and clutching at the rails in an absurd effort, born of sheer desperation, to urge the paddle-steamer on towards Rothesay. In one way he wanted to reach the place at once and get his business over with, but in another he didn't ever want to touch land again.

He was one of the first passengers to notice the little rowing-boat drift into the steamer's path, its female occupants too interested in the water to see what was happening. Danny threw himself round to shout to the bridge just as the first warning blast from the siren thundered out.

Turning back to the rail, leaning far over, he saw one of the women snatch up the oars and start rowing. He watched anxiously, willing her on towards safety, her imminent danger momentarily wiping his mind clear of the reason for his journey.

Then as people began to gather at the rails beside him, pointing out the boat to each other, the dinghy turned and he got a better look at its occupants. A huge invisible hand gripped and squeezed his stomach as he saw that the girl at the oars had long auburn hair tied back with a blue ribbon, while her companion, in a sleeveless summer frock, had a large bandage on one bare arm.

Just then Wilma's hat blew off, revealing her sleek black bobbed head. As she rose up in her seat, reaching for the hat, Danny gripped the rail so tightly that his knuckles popped. Straining his eyes, he felt weak with relief when, instead of flopping into the water, she landed beside Morag. While the two of them wrestled with the oars, the distance between the dinghy and the *Duchess*'s high, sharp stem continued

191

to decrease with every turn of the steamer's powerful paddles.

'They'll never do it,' a man further along the rail said flatly. 'If the bows don't cut them in half they'll collide with the paddle-box and be pushed under.'

'Of course they will!' Danny snarled at him, and several people turned to stare at him as a sailor ran past on the way to snatch at a lifebelt hanging nearby. Bells clanged as the men on the bridge frantically signalled the engine-room, where gleaming, oil-slick pistons still drove the steamer's 329 tons forward.

They had to succeed, Danny thought desperately. There was enough suffering already, without Wilma being lost as well. As the siren boomed out again, he tore his eyes from the dinghy and threw himself round to face the bridge.

'Turn away!' he screamed at the white faces bobbing behind the glass windows, though he well knew that they would already be doing everything possible to avert tragedy. Just then he felt a slight lurch beneath his feet, while overhead the stream of smoke from the single buff funnel took on a distinct curve. Both were sure signs that the *Duchess* was changing course, her crew managing slowly, slowly, to start turning the boat away from the minute dinghy now almost beneath her bows. He looked down again, pushing someone away impatiently and straining over the rail to see the little boat.

It was so close to the steamer now that it was beginning to disappear from his sight beneath the *Duchess*'s curving hull. For a moment he contemplated running down to the lower deck and jumping into the water in an attempt to reach it. But that would be madness. Instead of helping Wilma, he would almost certainly kill himself.

So he stayed where he was, oblivious to the pain in

his fingers, telling himself over and over again that it couldn't happen. Wilma couldn't escape death in the mill, just to be taken away from him a matter of weeks later!

It seemed to Morag that everything was moving very slowly. She and Wilma were at last working in unison and the dinghy was crawling through the water, though since she was tiring, and Wilma's arm was weak, each stroke barely nudged it forward. The only thing that moved fast was the steamer, so close now that as the water boiled round its sharp bows she glimpsed the red paint beneath its waterline. The thud of its huge ironwood paddles filled her head.

'Pull, Morag, pull!'

'I *am* pulling!' Morag snapped back. Her shoulders were on fire, and she was beginning to pass beyond fear into acceptance. All she really wanted now was to let go of her oar and slap Wilma very hard. It had been her daft idea to come out in this boat, and if they died it would be her fault.

But first things first, she decided as she laboured. She would get back to shore and out of this boat by hook or by crook, and then she would slap Wilma Beckett. And she would have a word to say to the captain of that stupid steamer too, for bringing his boat into their wee bit of the bay when he had such a large stretch of water to choose from.

The surge of sheer rage which ran through her just at the moment when she had begun to decide that there was little point in trying any more, brought renewed strength with it. She set her teeth, swung her arms back, plunged her oar into the water, dragged it through and out and swung her arms back again.

193

She took time to shoot a furious glance at the offending steamer, and suddenly realised that she was no longer looking straight at the sharp, straight stem but at a different section of black hull. Even as she watched, a paddle-box began to swing into view. It was edge-on at first, then slowly the entire box, with its painted crest, came into view.

'Wilma, look! It's turning!' Then, as Wilma slowed in her rowing to look up, 'Keep going! We've got to get away from the paddle!'

Somehow they summoned up the energy for one last effort and, although they were almost exhausted, it was enough. As they moved shoreward the steamer turned the other way, back towards the mouth of the bay, sliding past them with very little room to spare. For a final moment it loomed over them like a massive sea-monster, then it was gone and the boiling foam churned up by the paddles reached them. They clung to their oars, squealing in unison as they were tossed and rolled about.

The foam subsided, leaving them in flat, pale green water flecked with patches of lace from the remnants of the foam. And when Morag lifted her head, she saw to her surprise that they were quite close to the promenade where several people had been standing watching the drama unfold.

'Oh, Morag! Let's get back in quick,' said Wilma in an unusually subdued voice. 'And get rid of this damned boat before that captain comes looking for us!'

By the time they got back to the section of beach they had started out from, the *Duchess of Fife* had completed an extra circuit of the bay and was edging in to the pier. Hand in hand, they ran for the safety of their boarding-house on shaky legs . . .

'Is your arm all right?' Morag asked anxiously.

'It seems to be. It must be stronger than I thought. My poor hat!' Wilma lamented.

'Never mind the hat! You nearly didn't have a head to put it on.'

'I'll tell you one thing,' Wilma said with feeling, 'I'm glad I bought those extra knickers. The fright I got out on that bay damned near ruined the ones I have on.'

They covered the last part of the journey home in a silly, giggly mood which had them clutching at each other and reeling over the pavement. But they sobered up at once when Mrs Cameron, their landlady, met them in the hall and announced that a visitor was waiting for them in the dining-room.

As Mrs Cameron disappeared along the passageway towards her kitchen they looked at each other in horror, then eyed the polished wooden panels of the dining-room door.

'He surely never got off the boat that fast,' Wilma said in a weak whisper. 'Does the captain not have to stay on board till everyone's gone?'

'Only when the ship's sinking. We'll just have to face him. We can explain about your arm and everything. Mebbe he'll understand,' Morag said without much conviction. Without giving herself any further time to panic, she threw open the door and marched into the room with Wilma at her back.

They were so sure that they were about to be confronted by an angry man in naval uniform and a shiny-peaked cap that the sight of Danny Hastie in his best suit threw them completely for a moment. Then Wilma surged past Morag, almost throwing herself into his arms in her relief.

'It's only you, Danny! What are you doing here? Are you on holiday too?'

'I've just arrived.' He was twisting his cap round and round in his fingers.

'You were never on that paddle-steamer!' Wilma clapped her hands to her mouth, then spread her fingers to say through them, 'Did you see us? We thought we'd been sent for!'

Morag thought that Danny's face looked very white. Because Mrs Cameron's house opened directly on to the pavement, thick lace curtains covered the ground-floor windows to deter inquisitive passers-by. She wondered if the dining-room's permanent twilight was responsible for his apparent pallor.

'Wilma!' He cut into her babble, his own voice hard and sharp and angry. 'Listen to me! I've come to tell . . . tell you . . .' An involuntary spasm of the throat choked him into silence.

'Tell me what?' Wilma was suddenly very still. 'What, Danny? Has something happened to Mam?'

'She asked me to come. It's your Daisy, she's . . .' He choked again, then said on a note of utter despair, 'She's dead, Wilma.'

'Don't be daft, how can she be dead? She's only fifteen!'

'It's true.'

'It's not!' she contradicted him sharply; then, 'How?'

'One of the bobbins in the spinning department came off its mounting and caught her on the head. She . . .' Again his throat spasmed and his fingers almost tore the tweed cap in two. 'She didnae know a thing about it, Wilma.'

The room was so quiet that a fly buzzing irritably at the closed window sounded like a hundred people all talking at the tops of their voices. Yet when Wilma

196

spoke, her voice could scarcely be heard. 'But she's not seen her present yet. It's not true. Not Daisy. Not wee Daisy . . .'

From where she stood by the open door, Morag saw her friend's shoulders heave as the first sob began to tear its way through her body. She saw Danny drop the cap and start forward just as Wilma turned blindly away from him towards Morag.

The rejection and the helplessness in Danny Hastie's face was terrible to see. 'Wilma, I'm sorry,' he said and then, as though he couldn't stop himself, 'I'm sorry, I'm sorry, I'm sorry, I'm sorry . . .'

Mrs Cameron had no vacant rooms, but under the circumstances she allowed Danny to spend the night on her parlour sofa. Not that there was any sleep to be had for the three young people beneath her roof. Wilma talked all night, recalling every moment of Daisy's life from birth, castigating herself bitterly for all the times she had spoken sharply to the girl or refused to take her on a trip to Gourock or a walk up the hills.

Although Morag bought cabin tickets on the morning steamer to enable the three of them to sit in comfort in the saloon, Wilma, silent now, stayed on deck the whole way, staring down at the tumbling water which had almost claimed her life the day before.

When they finally reached Ardgowan Street she insisted on taking her case from Danny and going in on her own.

'At least let me carry it up the stairs for you.'

'I'll manage fine. I just want to go home alone,' she said politely but firmly, and vanished into the close, leaving the two of them on the pavement.

Danny looked totally lost. 'Will you let me carry your case, then?' he asked Morag, who agreed, partly because she was so sorry for the man and partly because she wanted to know more about what had happened to Daisy.

'There's nothing more to tell. It was in the spinning room,' he said as they trudged along the pavement. 'One of the women asked her to mind her machines while she went to the privy . . . for a smoke, as like as not. She'd no sooner gone than a bobbin came off one of the machines. The wee lass wouldn't even have known what happened, let alone have time to get out of the way. These bobbins are made of wood, and they're large enough to sit on. It near took her head off. Are you all right?' he added with sudden concern as Morag's world turned grey and she gave a murmur of surprise.

'I'm fine,' she said automatically, then stumbled. She would have fallen to the paving-stones if he hadn't caught her with an arm about her shoulders. Her muscles and joints were in agony after her frantic rowing the day before, and she had to bite back a yell of pain as Danny propped her against a house wall.

'Rest here for a minute. D'you want me to knock on a door and ask if you can have a seat and a drink of water?'

'No, I'll be all right in a minute.' She took a deep breath, then smiled up into his anxious face as the greyness cleared and the world steadied. 'I'm feeling better already.' She had never noticed before what nice eyes he had, clear and honest and kindly.

'You're very fond of Wilma, aren't you?' she asked as they started walking again.

'I love her. I've loved her from the minute she stepped inside Birkmyre's door,' he said simply, and gave her a wry grin when she gaped up at him, astonished by his forthright reply. 'You're her best friend, so I might as well be honest with you.'

'You might as well be honest with her.'

'Can you really see the likes of Wilma Beckett caring what the likes of me think? She'd laugh if I told her what I just told you.'

'Mebbe not.'

'Don't be daft,' he said bluntly. 'She's beautiful, and she can have any man she wants. And she needs more excitement than I can ever give her. I'm not the sort she'd look at twice, but I keep hoping that one day she'll get tired of excitement. And then, mebbe, she'll notice me.'

They had reached Lilybank Road, and he followed her along the path and into the hall, where he put the case down. 'Look after her,' he said, and made for the door.

'Come in for a minute.'

He shook his head. 'I'd best get back to work. I took the time off without permission, and now I have to make it right with my father.'

'Will you get into trouble?'

He shrugged. 'I'm always in trouble with him. I'm used to it and, anyway, I wanted to be the one to tell her. You'll not let on about what I said, will you?'

'That's your place, not mine,' Morag told him; then, as he reached the gate, 'Danny—'

When he looked back at her she said from the doorway, 'Perhaps what Wilma needs is someone who'll fight for her – someone who'll tell her what she wants instead of waiting for her to find out for herself.'

'You think so?' He didn't sound convinced.

'It's worth trying. It would be such a shame if she lost you.'

199

'It's me that's more likely to lose her,' he said, and closed the gate carefully behind him before setting out along the road to face the music at the mill.

17

'There's something you should know,' Cal said bluntly as soon as Morag opened the door.

'If it's to do with work, surely Mr Laird can see to it.' She was tired to the very centre of her being, and not in the mood to see anyone. Daisy Beckett had been buried on the previous day and Morag was devoting all her energies to the girl's family, devastated by the tragedy which had torn the youngest member from their midst.

Mags Beckett, usually so resilient, had become a silent shadow of herself, and so had Wilma. Archie, unable to stand being in the house, hadn't been seen there since the funeral, although Morag knew that he had been at work, with nothing to say to anyone for once.

She herself had been at Ardgowan Street until late on the night before, helping to deal with the neighbours who had poured into the small flat in a steady flow to offer their condolences and bring food to help to sustain the family in their time of grief – not that Mrs Beckett and Wilma could eat a morsel.

She had come home after midnight and fallen into bed exhausted, only to lie awake unable to sleep, watching her bedroom ceiling gradually reveal itself as the sky lightened outside. When the birds were resting from their dawn chorus she had finally fallen into a deep sleep, and then wakened late. She knew full well, as she drooped in the doorway, that her hair was untidy, her face pale and her eyes shadowed with sorrow and exhaustion, but she didn't care. She just wanted Cal to go away.

He wouldn't. 'That's your problem – Mr Laird *has* been seeing to it,' he said tersely. 'I've said nothing, for it wasn't my place to interfere, but things are going too far now and it's time you did something about it.'

'Cal, you'll have to leave it just now. Come and see me next week.' She stepped back and began to close the door, but to her astonishment and shock he surged forward and pushed it open again, stepping into the hallway almost on to her toes so that she was forced to step back out of his way.

'Next week might be too late!' He caught hold of her shoulders. 'Listen to me, will you?'

'Cal!' She wrenched herself free, stumbling back along the hall. 'Have you taken leave of your senses? Get out – get out at once!'

'Not until I've had my say!'

'Have you no decency at all? Wilma's sister's been killed . . . they only buried her yesterday, and I've got my hands full trying to help them.'

'I know.' He took a deep breath and made an effort to control his impatience. 'I know about it, and I'm sorry about the poor lass. But,' his voice began to harden again, 'you're a ship-owner now, Morag Weir, and like it or not your business has to come before anything else, even friends. Now . . .' He pushed her towards the stairs. 'Go and wash your face with cold water to waken yourself properly. Then we've got things to talk about.'

She was shaking with anger as she washed her face and brushed her hair. He had gone too far. Just because they had become friends over the past few weeks, he was presuming an intimacy which went far beyond anything she herself had intended. Anger pushed her exhaustion back, and she felt quite energetic when she marched downstairs to deal with him.

He was sitting at the kitchen table, a mug in his hands and steam curling from another opposite. Morag opened her mouth to speak as soon as she went in, but he cut across her. 'There's no sense in saying anything until you know why I've come bursting in on you as I did. Drink some tea while I tell you what's been going on.'

The tea was hot, and very strong. She put the mug down, wrinkling her nose. 'It's terrible!'

'It's the way we make it on the boats. Here . . .' He had found the sugar and now he ladled spoonfuls of it into her mug, added more milk and stirred it, splashing tea over her well-scrubbed kitchen table. 'If you want something more ladylike you'll have to make it yourself.'

'I've no intention of making tea. Once I've sent you packing I'm going back to Ardgowan Street, where I'm needed.'

'Listen to me, Morag . . .' He leaned over the table, his voice and his eyes urgent. 'I believe that John Laird's out to do you down. It's been going on for a while, and it's getting worse.'

She had been about to take a cautious sip of the tea, but instead she put the mug down suddenly. 'You can't mean it!'

'I had to wait until I was certain enough to tell you. And now I am. You've heard of the Arkbridge company?'

'Of course I have.' Everyone knew of the largest puffer fleet on that coast, and Sander and Georgina had on occasion entertained Leonard Arkbridge and his wife to dinner.

'Mr Arkbridge and his sons have been coming about the East Harbour more often than usual since your uncle's death. I've seen them myself, talking with John Laird on several occasions. And some of your boats have been carrying cargo for Arkbridge's.'

'That's not unusual, surely? The puffer owners sometimes help each other out.'

'Aye, if they have the room on their boats. But never at their own expense before. The *Jura*'s carried a split cargo on more than one occasion recently . . . The last time was the other day, when she had a half-load of timbers for one of our own customers and a half-load of farm machinery for someone we've not dealt with before – one of Arkbridge's clients. And the *Ailsa Craig* had to carry the other half of the timber load, with a lot of wasted space in her hold. So two Weir boats were used to carry cargo that one could have held. Why is Laird accepting contracts from Arkbridge when your boats already have all the cargoes they can handle?'

'Have you asked Mr Laird about this?'

Cal gave a mirthless laugh. 'That would go down well!'

'You're a shareholder.'

'A minor shareholder . . . and that's one of the reasons he'd not talk to me or let me look at the books. He resents your uncle leaving those shares to me. And I can't say that I blame the man for that,' he added with a frown, but she ignored the comment.

'So you want me to tackle him.'

'If I'm right, and he's cheating you, he'd scarcely tell you about it. You need to get hold of the books.

204

I've been keeping my own records of the things I've been hearing and noticing, and I believe that matters have reached a dangerous stage.'

'I already have my own set of books.'

His eyebrows shot up. 'In this house?'

As she led the way into the dining-room, Morag explained about the extra set she had started for Sander. 'I've just continued the habit, for it saves me having to bother Mr Laird.'

As soon as she took the ledger book from the sideboard, Cal relieved her of it without ceremony. Opening it on the table, he ran a finger down each page until he found what he was looking for.

'There . . . last week, that's the cargo I was telling you about. And this' – he stabbed at her neat figuring with his finger – 'is not the truth.'

'But I copied this from the ledger in the office. I go down every week and bring my own set up to date.'

Cal's face was grim. 'That can only mean that he keeps a false set of books for your benefit. You'll have to do something about it, Morag, and as soon as possible, or the man'll have you bankrupt before you know it. Tell that lawyer of yours for a start, then you must go to the office with him and try to find the real books.'

Still suffering from lack of sleep, she put a hand to her muddled head and concentrated on the problem. 'Tomorrow afternoon – if I can arrange to have Aidan here at 2 o'clock, can you come too? He should hear the story from you.'

He nodded. 'Then you must go to the office.'

Her instinct was to see Aidan Grieve at once, but she had promised to go to Ardgowan Street that morning. The Becketts must come first. Her mind was in turmoil as she walked to Ardgowan Street. John Laird had been a loyal employee of Weir's for as long as she could remember. It was inconceivable that he would deceive her, but at the same time she had no reason to doubt Cal.

Wilma was at the hospital having her arm examined and Mags was alone in the house, sitting by the fire, the hands which had never before been idle curled on her lap. Morag, not wanting to disturb her, busied herself at the sink peeling potatoes for the evening meal.

Suddenly Mags began to talk about Daisy, and once she had started the words poured out as though floodgates had been opened somewhere within her. Morag said nothing, but finished what she was doing and went on to do something else, letting the words surge and flow around her until they finally trailed away into silence.

'Come and sit down here, and have a rest,' Mags said after a while. 'Ye're a good lass,' she said when Morag did as she was told. She fished a handkerchief from within the sleeve of her cardigan and wiped her eyes, which looked red-raw and swollen from endless weeping. 'It's hard sometimes tae talk tae the rest of them, for I just get them as upset as myself. And the neighbours keep tryin' tae console me, when that's not what I need.'

She sniffed and wiped her nose, then looked ruefully at the sodden handkerchief. 'Fetch me a clean rag from that drawer, will you, pet? Something soft that'll not hurt my sore face. I'll never try tae console anyone again,' she went on, taking the clean soft rag and mopping at her eyes with it. 'Not now that I mind what it feels like tae suffer loss. It's been that long since my man went that I'd forgotten the sharpness of it. I need tae say my lassie's name, and bring back all the memories of her. I'm feared that if I don't

they'll go away from me and take her with them.'
She leaned forward, her swollen face earnest. 'I have
tae hold on to her.'

'Of course you do.' Morag patted her hand. 'I'll sit
here with you for as long as you want.'

'No, no . . .' The older woman squared her shoulders
and lifted her chin. 'I've had my say, and my weep,
and our Wilma'll be back from the hospital soon. But
if ye'd go and get in some messages for me, hen, I'd
be grateful.' She managed a watery smile. 'I'm no fit
sight tae go intae the town just now. This face'd scare
away the dogs.'

Armed with a shopping list and a basket, Morag went
into the town, where her first call was at the lawyer's
office. Aidan's face lit up when she was ushered into
his small office, then darkened when he found out why
she was there.

'If Cal Fergusson's right, we'll have to take steps to
protect your interests as soon as possible. I'll certainly
come along to the house tomorrow afternoon.'

'Do you think I should inform my father, and perhaps
ask him along too?' she wanted to know. 'He's a
shareholder as well.'

'I'd keep things among the three of us for the
moment,' he advised, 'until we've had a chance to
find out exactly what is going on.'

'So . . .' he said on the following afternoon as the three
of them sat round the table in Morag's dining-room,
'you believe, Cal, that Mr Laird is using the Weir
boats to carry cargo for the Arkbridge company and
withholding the payments for himself?'

'I do. When seamen are waiting in some wee
port for a cargo to arrive or sitting out a bout of

207

bad weather, there's nowhere to go but the public house. And as often as not there's little to talk about but cargoes and ports of call. I began to pick up words here and there that made no sense, then I started to listen harder and put all the wee comments together. And the Weir boats,' Cal looked across the table at Morag, 'just don't seem to be carrying the cargoes they once carried. I've been hearing of some cargoes turned down by Laird because, he claimed, the boats were too busy to take them. I've a suspicion that they were busy with Arkbridge work.'

'Why would a big company like that need help from the likes of Weir's?'

'Arkbridge recently got a fine contract, coaling some of the big cargo carriers lying in at the Tail of the Bank. And he's got two boats undergoing repairs in the yards just now. His best boat went aground over by the Dunoon shore and took a lot of damage, and another was in a collision going through the Crinan Canal. The coaling contract came at a time when he was short-handed. But it's not just that – his men seem to think that he's planning to add to his fleet, and I've a suspicion that he's interested in taking over the Weir boats.'

Aidan tapped his pencil on the table. 'I've heard nothing of that.'

'Neither have I, and if Mr Arkbridge does come to see me he'll discover that I have no intention of selling,' Morag said crisply.

Cal gave her a long, level look. 'Are you sure that decision'll be yours to make?'

'Of course it is!'

'If Weir Shipping fell on hard times . . . if money was lost, you might be glad of the chance to sell out.

And a big powerful owner such as Arkbridge could buy a company in distress for a song.'

'That's not going to happen to us. Our boats are busy.'

'With Arkbridge cargoes! We're in danger of losing our usual customers to them. Then we'll end up carrying the same cargoes for the same folk – with Arkbridge collecting the payments!'

Cal let his words sink in, then went on, 'How often do you read every piece of paper that John Laird asks you to sign, Morag?'

'I always do.'

He leaned across the table, his grey eyes cold as stone holding hers. 'I mind one occasion when I was waiting to take you and your friend over to Bute on the *Pladda*, when you signed some papers without giving them a look.'

His contempt was withering and she found herself floundering for excuses. 'You were in a hurry to get your cargo away.'

'But you should always read everything you're shown! You could have signed the whole business over to Arkbridge that day, for all you knew.'

Aidan jumped to her defence as she flushed beneath Cal's accusing gaze. 'I'm sure that Miss Weir's interests are safeguarded,' he told the seaman coldly.

'By whom? Have you forgotten that her own father fought tooth and nail to overturn the will that gave the business to her? And he and Laird are cronies.'

'You think my father knows what's going on?' asked Morag, startled.

Cal started to reply, then stopped and shrugged. 'I've no proof, but he's been down at the harbour a fair bit recently. More often,' he added, 'than you.'

Exasperated, she slammed down both hands flat on

the table surface. 'I've been away! And my friend's lost her sister, and nearly lost her own arm in an accident too!'

'As I've already said, if you own a business you must put it first! If you're just going to play at being an owner, you might as well let Arkbridge have it, then at least me and the other skippers will know where we stand!'

'That is not fair!'

'Quarrelling like children,' Aidan cut in icily, 'is not the way to resolve this issue. Be quiet, the pair of you!' He let a moment's angry silence pass, then went on, 'It seems to me that we must go down to the harbour now, as Cal has already suggested, and look at the books. My car is outside.'

'And guaranteed to attract attention.' Cal got to his feet and pulled his jacket straight with angry tugging motions. 'We'll walk.'

18

***

They found the books which Morag had copied her set from without any trouble, then began to search for the second set which Cal was certain lay hidden.

'In his home, perhaps,' Aidan suggested. 'If so, we could have a problem.'

Cal shook his head. 'He couldn't carry them home every night without being seen. They're here somewhere.'

'If they exist,' Morag said and he shot a cool glance at her, their quarrel in the house still rankling.

'Oh, I'm sure they exist.' He was ploughing through a pile of papers from the untidy desk and he stared down at one, then gave a disgusted exclamation. 'Look at this! It's the bill for a load of gravel I brought back from Loch Fyne, and it says that *Pladda* sailed there light.' He waved the paper at them. 'She carried machinery from Greenock, for Arkbridge probably. I doubt if you'll find any record of that contract, or the payment.'

As he had said, there was no invoice and no payment recorded. It was as though the cargo had never existed.

'We've got something on him now,' Aidan said with satisfaction, but Cal wasn't content.

'There has to be more than that. There has to be another set of books!'

He refused to give up and, when the ledgers were found at the bottom of a cupboard in the store-room downstairs, it was obvious that John Laird, as Cal had said, was up to something. For what was left of the afternoon, the three of them sat at the desk; Morag with the set of ledgers she had worked from, Aidan with the hidden set and Cal with the invoices, orders and bills. By the time they were finished they were in no doubt that since Sander Weir's death Weir Shipping had been systematically cheated out of a considerable amount of money.

'John Laird feathering his own nest before he gives up work,' Cal said grimly.

Aidan consulted his scribbled notes, muttering under his breath as he swiftly added up rows of figures.

'Working from the approximate cost of those hidden cargoes, I would say that Mr Laird must be looking forward to a very comfortable retirement. Unless . . .' He looked across at Cal, then at Morag, before saying gently, 'He might not be alone in this.'

'If you mean my father, Aidan, I don't believe he would do such a thing.'

'It's true what Cal said – he did try to get the business away from you.'

'No! I'll not have you suspecting him! Either of you,' she added, glaring at Cal.

He shrugged, while Aidan said, 'You're quite right, it's Laird we have to deal with.' He tapped the ledger lying before him. 'We've got sufficient proof to send him to court, and probably to prison too.'

'Prison? We can't let that happen!'

'Morag, he's been stealing large sums of money from you, and destroying your company into the bargain.'

'But he's an old man. He'd not last long in a prison cell.'

'And you'll not last long as a boat-owner if you let your heart rule your head.' Cal's voice was sharp with irritation.

'I won't be responsible for putting an old man in prison. When it comes down to it, he gave my uncle loyal service for years – and probably your father too, Cal, before then.'

'It's a pity that he couldn't have respected your uncle's memory enough to be loyal to you, too.'

'Be that as it may, I'll not agree to handing him over to the police.'

'I have to advise you to think again, Morag,' Aidan told her. 'You have a better chance of getting some of the money back, at least, if you let the courts deal with him.'

'No.'

'Then he must be faced on Monday with his misdeeds, and dismissed on the spot,' Aidan told her.

'And you have to be the one to do it, Morag,' Cal added relentlessly.

'I know. And I will.' She had no option. She knew that both men were right, but she was convinced that John Laird would not survive a prison sentence, or even the public shame of being revealed as a thief. And she couldn't bear to have that on her conscience. As it was, she thought miserably, watching Cal stride away from them with scarcely a word when they left the office building, she had lost his respect, and that in itself was misery enough.

She and Aidan, who had left his car in Lilybank Road, walked back there in silence, Morag's thoughts occupied with the suggestion that her father had connived with John Laird. She remembered what Sander had said during his final illness about the way his brother's early ambition and his hopes of marrying Georgina were thwarted.

'It's soured him,' Sander had said from his big chair by the window in the back bedroom. 'He's resented me for it ever since.' Then he had said, 'It's strange how daft folk always seem to think that it's others that are daft, not them at all.'

It must have been about then that he had decided to leave everything to her, and not to her father. There was no doubt that Lawrence resented that – just as John Laird resented her, on the grounds that she was a woman who knew nothing of shipping. But Lawrence was the only family she had left. The stark truth was that even if he was guilty, as Cal clearly thought and Aidan suspected, she didn't want to know – because that would mean that she was quite alone in the world.

'Are you all right?' Aidan asked when they reached the car.

'Yes. I'll see you on Monday, at the office?'

'Don't worry, I'll be there with you, Morag. I'm truly sorry that you've had to go through this, but Fergusson's right when he says that you must face Laird yourself on Monday.'

'I know. I'll not be able to sleep all weekend for thinking of it,' she confessed.

'I tell you what, why don't I take you out to dinner tonight? Somewhere pleasant. That should take your mind off it for a while, anyway.'

'I'm not in the mood to be much of a companion.'

'You don't have to be.' He grinned down at her. 'I'll tell you the story of my life, and all you have to do is listen. Don't refuse me,' he added as she opened her mouth. 'You may not feel like going out, but it will do you good. I'll be back in two hours' time.'

They drove along the coast to Largs, where they dined in a comfortable hotel on the shore. The linen was stiff and snowy white, the cutlery shone, the waiters were deferential yet at the same time superior, and Morag felt that she was completely out of her depth. Aidan, however, was quite relaxed, ordering for her, handling the waiters skilfully and talking throughout the meal about his childhood in Edinburgh and his time as a law student. He had a lively sense of humour and, although at the beginning of the evening Morag had been convinced that she would never feel light-hearted or cheerful again, he – and perhaps the three glasses of wine she drank – lifted her spirits wonderfully.

Later, they walked along the front and out on to the pier, where they stood and looked out across the dark water.

'There's an autumn nip in the air,' Aidan said after a pause. 'Summer's over.'

Morag nodded. Directly ahead of them, unseen in the dark, lay Bute. Only two weeks earlier, she and Wilma had been on that island without a care in the world. And Daisy had been alive. Only two short weeks . . .

She shivered, and Aidan put an arm about her shoulders.

'Cold?'

'No, just . . . wondering what's going to happen next.'

'This, for one,' Aidan said, turning her to face him. He kissed her, tentatively at first and then, as she made no move to draw away, more firmly, gathering her into his arms and against his body.

It was almost the first time Morag had ever been kissed, for it wasn't the Scottish way to hug or kiss folk and neither Georgina nor Sander had been physically affectionate, either to her or to each other in front of her. And it was the first time a man had kissed her, other than a few light, shy caresses from the young man she had met briefly in Rothesay.

But this was entirely different, and Morag was quite astonished by the sudden and immense pleasure she experienced in her first close contact with a man. Her abysmal ignorance of courting meant that she had no way of knowing if she was responding correctly, but when she put her own arms around Aidan's back and let her mouth soften beneath his, his embrace tightened and he murmured against her mouth before claiming it again. She was trembling . . . or perhaps it was him, for they were now so closely entwined that she was no longer sure whether she was sensing her own emotions or his.

He took his mouth from hers and moved it over her face in a delicious dance of soft, teasing little kisses that paid homage to her forehead, her eyes, her nose and cheeks and even her chin before returning to her lips, which eagerly awaited his. She lost all sense of time and had no idea how long they stood there, locked together as one person. Finally, reluctantly, Aidan straightened and relaxed his hold on her.

'Have I presumed too much?' His voice was husky and strangely unsure.

'Oh, no . . . not at all,' she added hastily, afraid that she sounded too eager.

'I should take you home.'

'Yes.' She would rather have stayed where she was, being kissed again, but she didn't like to say so.

They drove back in a companionable silence. When they reached Lilybank Road, Aidan helped her from the car and walked with her to the door, but declined an invitation to go in.

'I don't want the neighbours gossiping about my client and maligning her good name,' he said with a laugh in his voice.

'I don't truly mind. Have I said the wrong thing?' she asked swiftly when he laughed out loud. 'I don't know about . . . the right things to say and to do.'

He took her hand and kissed the palm. Warmth immediately sparked from the spot his lips touched and flared all through her, causing her to give a slight gasp.

'You're a very sweet, special person, Morag Weir,' he said softly. 'Don't ever change.' Then he kissed her on the lips, lightly this time. 'But I am, after all, your lawyer, and my uncle would never forgive me if I forgot that. Will you go out with me again some time?'

'I'd like to.'

'Good. Now – in you go. D'you want me to call tomorrow?'

She did, with all her heart, but she shook her head. 'I'm seeing Wilma tomorrow. I'll meet you on Monday morning at the harbour.'

'I'll call here for you at 7 o'clock. We should be in the office before Mr Laird arrives. Sleep well, Morag,' he said, and waited until she had gone into the house and switched on the light before walking back down the short path.

She waited behind the closed front door until she heard his motor-car driving away, then peered into the hall mirror. The face that peered back at her was much prettier than the one she was used to. Her normally solemn brown eyes were huge and had a sparkle to them, and for once there was a rosy glow to her cheeks. Now that it had been soundly kissed, her mouth looked

217

fuller and softer, and even her red hair had taken on a new sheen. Tendrils had escaped from the pins to curl down on each side of her face, adding to her new overall prettiness.

Morag wandered restlessly about the house for a while, unable to settle. Mr Winters had contacted her during the week to ask if she would give accommodation to a mill visitor and his wife at the beginning of October, and she had agreed, too involved with the Becketts' problems to think much about anything else. Now, recalling her promise, she looked at each room she went into more critically. If she was going to take in paying guests on a regular basis she must make the bedrooms look smarter, buy new matching ewers and basins and towels. Perhaps it would be a good idea to enlist Wilma's help. There was so much to be done – and John Laird to be faced on Monday morning, she suddenly remembered, and all at once she felt tired.

She went to bed, determined that she would put Laird out of her mind and lie awake all night thinking only of Aidan. But almost as soon as he took her into his arms and claimed her mouth with his own, she fell into a deep, dreamless sleep.

Wilma was thrilled to be asked to help with the house. They toured every room, discussing new curtains and bed-linen and, in some cases, new furnishings.

'Nothing too elaborate,' Morag said anxiously, and Wilma shook her head emphatically.

'Of course not, you'd not want to have anything fussy in a bonny house like this, it'd spoil the look of it. But it's surprising the difference a picture on the wall, or a footstool, can make to a room.' An enthusiasm which had been missing for the past two weeks had crept back into her voice and her face. 'There are some good second-hand shops around.'

Although she had lived all her life in a cramped tenement flat, her love of magazines and fashion papers had developed a hitherto unused flair for interior decorating. 'One day, when I'm married, with a place of my own,' she had often told Morag, 'I'm going to make it look like a palace!'

'There's something different about you,' she said when the tour was over and Morag had made several notes in the exercise book she carried with her.

'No, there's not.'

'There is. A sort of—' She stopped and studied her friend, head to one side, before asking abruptly, 'Where were you last night?'

Morag didn't have time to think of any answer other than the truth. 'Aidan Grieve took me to Largs for dinner.'

'Ah-hah!'

'It was in the way of business!'

'I've discussed business that way myself,' Wilma observed, 'but never with a lawyer. Do they kiss different from shipyard workers?'

'How would I know that? I've never kissed a man before!'

'Before last night,' Wilma pounced triumphantly. 'I knew I was right!' Then, as Morag clapped her hands to her face in a futile effort to push back the heat in her skin, 'Did you like it?'

'I did! Oh, Wilma, I shouldn't be talking like that, and things the way they are with you and your mother.'

'Of course you should, that's what life's like. We're managing, and with every day that passes we'll manage that wee bit better. There's nothing else for it. This is the first day Mam's gone out, even if it is just to see Mrs McNeish in the next close. Come on . . . we'll go out for a walk and you can tell me all about it.'

'It's raining. And I'll tell you nothing!'

'Everyone born in this part of the country's got waterproof skin.' Wilma caught up her coat and tied a scarf about her sleek dark hair. 'And of course you'll tell me everything. I'm your best pal, aren't I?'

Cal arrived late in the afternoon. 'I came earlier,' he said as he followed her into the kitchen which had, for Morag, become the heart of the house. 'I thought you must be with your friend.'

'We went out for a walk.' After their angry exchange the day before, she wasn't quite sure how to deal with him.

'How are they?'

'They're managing.'

'That's all they can do, for the time being,' he said, echoing Wilma's philosophy. He dropped into a chair at the table and added, with a direct glance, 'How are you?'

'I'm fine, why wouldn't I be?'

His eyebrows lifted. 'I came to apologise for being so short with you yesterday, but it seems that you didn't notice after all.'

Morag wasn't sure which was worse – Cal's anger, or Cal's amusement. 'I was as much to blame. I suppose I was worried about having to face John Laird.'

'It has to be done, Morag,' he said gently, 'and it must be done by you.'

'I know. Then I have to decide how the business is to be managed in the future.'

'By you, obviously.'

'Me? What do I know about it? All I've ever done is work in a teashop.'

'You know the books, and how they're kept . . . supposed to be kept,' he corrected himself. 'And you've studied the way your uncle ran the business, and his previous business too. You've got the ability.'

'Do you think so?' She was surprised, and flattered too. She knew that Cal's approval wasn't given lightly and a little glow of pleasure warmed her, although his next words were somewhat dampening.

'As much ability as it needs to run that wee office, for the skippers can all keep you right.'

'So anyone could do the job?'

If he noticed the sudden tart note in her voice, he gave no indication of it. 'More or less, but the one factor you can never be sure of in a stranger is honesty. Is there any sense in bringing in another manager who might decide, just as Laird did, that an owner who doesn't work in the office herself will make an easy target? The only way to build Weir's up again and keep it safe is to run it yourself.'

'But I've promised Mr Winters at Birkmyre's that I'd supply accommodation for some of their guests. I've got two people arriving next week . . . I can't possibly be in the house for them and down at the harbour every day as well!'

'Tell him you've changed your mind, or else hire a housekeeper,' he said irritably. 'You can afford one, and it would be easier to find someone capable of cooking and cleaning and looking after your house than an office manager. There's Grace Hastie, for one. Danny tells me that the lassie hates working in that teashop. I'm sure she'd make a grand housekeeper.'

'I know nothing about the boats, or the sort of cargoes we carry!'

221

'I've told you, me and the others can keep you straight there. You'll learn, Morag!' He ran his fingers through his hair. 'Will you for pity's sake stop throwing problems at me?'

'Mebbe I will – when you stop ordering me about! Who employs who here?'

His face turned brick-red and he jumped to his feet. 'I beg your pardon, Miss Weir, for presuming,' he said stiffly. 'Good day to you.'

'Cal!' She caught up with him in the hall. 'I'm sorry, I shouldn't have said that.'

'No, you shouldn't,' he agreed, his hand clenched on the door handle.

'It was you who found out about what John Laird was up to. I know that you've only got the firm's interests at heart.'

He turned back towards her, his anger ebbing. 'And yours, though you don't seem to realise that. You can do it; I know that, and Sander Weir knew it or he would never have entrusted Weir Shipping to you. It was his brother he didn't trust—' He checked himself abruptly, then said, 'I'm sorry, I shouldn't have said that. You and your father are so different that it's hard to remember you're blood kin. But Sander was right in his judgement.'

He took her shoulders in his big hands, his face intent and his eyes holding hers. 'You can do anything you want to, Morag Weir. Mind that. All you need is the determination and the courage. I know that you think I'm bullying you, and mebbe I am, but you can't own or run a business properly by leaving it to others. You have to take the responsibility yourself. I'll help you, if you'll trust me.'

'Of course I trust you, more than anyone else. And you're right, I must run the office myself.' Morag

222

smiled tentatively, and was relieved to see a slight softening of the corners of his mouth in response. Suddenly, quite against her own will, she wondered what that mouth would feel like against hers. As soon as the thought registered she thrust it away, embarrassed. Aidan Grieve must have cast some magic spell on her.

'Morag? Are you all right?' Cal was staring down at her, puzzled. The mind-picture she had had of being kissed by him melted away, and she returned to the present.

'I was just wondering . . . do you really think that my father was working with Laird?' All at once she felt that she should know, even if the answer was not what she wanted to hear.

'I've no proof, and it was wrong of me to miscall the man. I was just upset over what's being done to you, and to Weir Shipping. I'd best be off. I didn't mean to stay overlong anyway.' His hands dropped away from her. 'Don't worry about tomorrow,' he told her. 'You'll be fine. I know it.'

As he strode along Lilybank Road, Cal Fergusson wished that he could have been honest with Morag. Of course her father had been plotting with Laird, and Cal had sufficient proof to face him and make him admit to it. But Morag had a remarkably open and expressive face, and her yearning to hear that the man who had abandoned her as a child was innocent of further deceit had been so obvious that he had not had the heart to tell her the truth. All he could, and would, do was to try to protect her – and Weir Shipping, of course – in the future.

There had been another look on her face just before

she mentioned her father. A sudden luminous glow that had made him want to . . .

To forget that the woman was his employer, he told himself sternly. And it was just as well that the look had been fleeting.

Otherwise, he might have made a right fool of himself.

19

Morag knew that she would never, no matter how long she lived, forget the expression in John Laird's eyes when he came slowly up the stairs and let himself into the office to find her sitting at the desk with the secret ledger open before her.

After that one startled look, his face seemed to close down and his eyes slid away from her to where Aidan sat in a corner. 'So,' he said flatly, 'ye've been meddlin', have ye?'

She had had no way of knowing whether he would react with rage, protestations of innocence or a flood of regrets, so she had been unable to prepare any speeches. 'Just decide what your own attitude is going to be,' Aidan had advised during the nerve-racking half-hour spent waiting for the old man to arrive. 'What he says is of no matter, it's what you say that counts. And . . .' he had taken her hands in his and squeezed them reassuringly, his only physical contact since kissing her good-night on Saturday '. . . remember that I'll be here if I'm needed – though it would be best if you could deal with things on your own.'

She was able to do that by holding Cal in her mind and trying to behave in a way that would meet his approval. Taking a deep breath and lacing her fingers

EVELYN HOOD

together on top of the open ledger, she recalled reading somewhere that a circle was the strongest shape there was; there was truth in that, for clasping her hands and forming her own circle made her feel less vulnerable.

'It's not me who's been meddling, Mr Laird. It's you, and with my money.'

'There's no need to say anything more. I'll go.'

'There's plenty to say,' Morag told him sharply as he turned towards the door. 'I have to know why you've done this to me. I'm quite sure that you never tried to cheat my uncle, so why me?'

'Mr Weir was a good employer and, forbye, he knew the business inside out,' the old man said gruffly. 'He should never have left it to a lassie who knows nothing of office work, or of the boats. It should have been Mr Lawrence's, everyone's saying that.'

'And what does my father know of office work and boats?' Morag challenged.

'He could have learned. He's a man, and he deserved to be given his place in that will. I don't know what Mr Sander was thinkin' of!' Indignation over what he saw as a genuine grievance was beginning to give Laird some strength. 'You've not even tried to take charge of this place.'

'I tried to give you your place, and you chose to reward me with deceit.'

'But ye didn't consult with me, did ye?' Now that he was found out, Laird made no attempt to hide his contempt. 'Keepin' in with that Calum Fergusson because he speaks nice tae ye, and giving a young waster like Archie Beckett his own boat because you're pals with his sister! That's not the way to run a business!'

Aidan came forward, his face tight with anger. 'That's enough, Laird. Collect your things and—'

'No, Aidan.' Morag held up a hand to stop him.

226

'I'll deal with this.' Although he didn't know it, the old man's contempt, following on Cal's comments the evening before, had brought it home to her that they were both right and she had been wrong. Sander had trusted her with the most important thing in his life, his shipping company, and until now she hadn't taken her responsibilities seriously enough.

'Cal Fergusson is a shareholder under the terms of my uncle's will,' she told Laird coolly as Aidan subsided. 'And he's a skipper. Naturally I've listened to his opinions.'

'He only got those shares because you persuaded Mr Weir tae give them to him when the man was in no fit state to resist ye.'

'Did I indeed? And who told you that, Mr Laird?' She felt sick. She knew full well who must have been speaking to him; that was something else that she had tried, wrongly, to hide from. When Laird said nothing but lowered his eyes and fidgeted with his gnarled fingers, she pressed on, punishing herself as much as him. 'Not going to tell me? Mebbe you want me to guess?'

He had said the wrong thing, and he knew it. Suddenly his bravado and his contempt were gone, deflated like a child's toy balloon. 'Everyone knows it,' he mumbled.

'Then everyone's wrong and I'd thank you to remind them, the next time they say it, that there's a place in the courts for folk that spread malicious gossip. As to the allegations you have made about Cal Fergusson and Archie Beckett,' she swept on, 'at least they haven't taken advantage of me as you have.'

He lifted his head, one last spark of fight returning to his faded eyes. 'Give them time, Missy!' he spat out. 'They will!' Then he shuffled over to the desk. 'If ye don't mind movin' aside, Miss Weir . . .' He gave her her title with contempt, as though it was a curse. 'I'll just collect my own possessions before I go.'

She stood up and moved away as he came round the desk and opened the drawer that, she knew, held nothing but a pipe, a tobacco pouch, a box of matches, a penknife and a pencil stub.

'There's the matter of the money you took, Mr Laird.' Aidan rose to his feet. 'My client wants it back.'

'Aye, well, she can want but she'll not get, for it's all gone.'

'Indeed? You must have been living well to spend all that we estimate you to have taken. Perhaps you weren't the only one to dip into the till. Perhaps you have a partner?'

Where she stood, Morag was close enough to the old man to see his hand, fumbling to pick up the shabby tobacco pouch, suddenly freeze.

'Well, Mr Laird?' Aidan persisted. 'If there's someone else involved in this sorry business, I must have his name. It might even help you. For all we know, he might have led you astray.'

A long moment passed before Laird moved again, scrabbling up the pouch and pushing it deep into his coat pocket. 'Nob'dy!' His voice was loud. 'There's nob'dy!'

'Are you quite sure? It might help your own case if you told us everything.'

'So it's to be the polis, is it? And the court, and mebbe the jail for me if you get your own way?'

'We'd . . .' Morag began, then fell silent as Aidan made a sharp movement of the hand behind Laird's back. She had had her moment, and now the ground was his.

'What else do you expect? You've deliberately stolen money from your place of work, betrayed your employer's trust. You don't deny it – indeed, you can't deny it, for we have enough evidence to prove your guilt. The courts don't look leniently on folk such as you.'

The old man said nothing but, as he retreated back to the other side of the desk and faced them both defiantly, Morag saw his chin tremble slightly. The sight of that small weakness almost unnerved her.

They could get no more out of him, and after a fruitless five minutes Aidan shrugged and retreated to his chair, leaving Morag in charge once more.

'I'm sorry, for my uncle's sake as much as yours and mine, that it's come to this.' She held out her hand. 'I'll have my keys, if you please.'

Laird ignored the outstretched fingers, choosing instead to drop the keys with a noisy clatter on to the desk. Then, with a final sneer at the two young people, he turned and left the office for the last time.

As his feet went shuffling down towards the outer door Morag collapsed into the desk chair, shaking.

'Not satisfactory,' Aidan said, frowning. 'Not satisfactory at all. He's getting away with the money and, if there was a partner, he's getting off scot-free. The police might well get the truth out of him if we call them in. We should, you know.'

'No, let it be.' Morag got up and went to the small window. It was filthy; rubbing a clear space in it, she made a mental note to clean it, and the entire office, as soon as possible.

'Do you have any idea how much money you've lost?' Aidan asked at her back, his voice edgy with irritation.

'At least we've put a stop to it.' Peering through the smudged space she had cleared she saw John Laird, a stooped, pathetic figure, trudging away towards the street, his life's work suddenly at an end.

'At least Laird will be sweating for a while, wondering when the police are going to knock at his door. That's always something, I suppose,' Aidan said disconsolately, then cheered up slightly. 'But you did a grand job, Morag. You handled things very well.'

'I was terrified.'

'You didn't show it.' He came to her and would have put a reassuring arm about her shoulders if she hadn't jerked away from him.

'Don't!' she said sharply, then at once, 'I'm sorry, Aidan, I just . . . I don't want to be touched at the moment.'

'I understand,' he said, although the tone of his voice and the look in his eyes said that he did not. The truth of the matter was that his timing had been all wrong. If he had comforted her as soon as Laird had gone, she would have clung to him gratefully. Instead, he had berated her for not being harder on the old man.

He left not long afterwards and Morag sat on in the office, turning the pages of the order book, familiarising herself with the daily routine . . .

Between them, John Laird and Cal Fergusson had shown her where her duty lay. She would have to hire a housekeeper to look after the house, for she herself was going to be very busy from now on.

Lawrence came to the office the next afternoon, early closing at the shop.

'So here you are. I tried the house, but there was no reply.' He took off his hat, shook the raindrops from it and then hesitated for a moment, holding hat and umbrella awkwardly as though not certain what to do with them. It was all that Morag could do to keep from hurrying round the desk to take them from him, but she made herself stay where she was, pen in hand, and after a moment he spotted the coat-stand in the corner. Having stowed away his umbrella and hung up his hat and coat, he dropped into the chair on the other side of the desk.

'Well, this is a pretty state of affairs. I hear that you've dismissed John Laird.'

'Did he tell you so?'

'Er . . . no, I believe that I heard someone talking about it in the shop,' Lawrence said vaguely.

'Then no doubt you heard that he was caught pilfering.'

'Laird? The man's as honest as the day's long. He'd never put his hand in the cashbox!'

'He didn't, he was contracting out the Weir boats to someone else and pocketing the payment instead of putting it through the books.'

'Are you quite certain of this?'

'Quite.'

'Are you going to charge him?'

'I'm . . . not certain yet,' Morag said cautiously. 'I've still to find out just how much he's taken.'

'Surely you'd not be so vindictive! He's an old man, and he served Sander well for many years—'

'And took only a matter of four months to start cheating me!'

'He's old, forgetful mebbe, rather than dishonest.'

'More than forgetful, Father. There's a great deal of money missing, yet he says he has nothing left. Aidan thinks,' she said, frowning down at the invoice in her hand, 'that he must have had a partner who put him up to it.'

Her father shifted suddenly in his chair. 'Never!

What does that boy know about anything? You should put your affairs into his uncle's hands, Morag. Kenneth Dalrymple should never have let his nephew take over the Weir account. He should have had more sense. I'll speak to him personally, if you like.'

'That won't be necessary, Father. Aidan seems to me to have a proper sense of things himself.'

'Hmmph,' Lawrence said dismissively. 'Two young folk who know nothing of the ways of the world! You need an older man to advise you – someone you can rely on.'

'I did rely on an older man,' she pointed out, nettled by his condescending attitude, 'and he robbed me.'

'If you take my advice, Morag, you'll let well alone where Laird's concerned. What's done's done, and if the man was tempted because there was no proper hand on the tiller it's not entirely his fault. The question now is, what do we do about this place?'

'As you can see, I'm putting my hand to the tiller, Father.'

His eyebrows shot up. 'You? But that's preposterous! You know nothing but working as a cashier in a teashop.'

'I'm prepared to learn. The skippers can deal with the boats, and I'll take advice on that side of things from them.'

'But shipping's a man's world, it's not for women at all. You can't possibly run this place!'

'I can do anything I want,' Morag said, and wondered why her own father couldn't have as much faith in her as Cal Fergusson had.

'Why don't I take over as your office manager? After all, I own a quarter of the business, and we're the same flesh and blood. You could be certain that I'd look after both our interests.'

232

'But you don't know any more than I do about office work, Father.'

'I can learn.'

'And so can I. Lots of women work in offices.'

'But not in positions of authority.'

'It's very kind of you to worry about me, Father, but it's all been decided.' She indicated the books spread over the desk. 'As you can see, I've started already.' To prove her point, she made an alteration on the page before her, then studied the rest of the figures intently in the hope that he would take the hint and leave.

Instead, he got to his feet and paced the length of the small room a few times before saying abruptly, 'Have you considered selling Weir Shipping, Morag?'

'Why should we sell?'

'Why not? You'd get the place off your hands, and the money would come in useful. You're a young woman with your whole life still before you. You don't want to stay here for ever; you could travel, go wherever you please and do whatever you please. And if you sell while it's still a going concern, we could both do nicely out of it.'

'You'd advise it, then?'

'Yes, I would,' he said at once, then added swiftly, 'in your interests as much as mine.'

'I'll ask Aidan,' Morag said, and Lawrence had no option but to go out into the rain again without a proper answer.

Aidan and Cal arrived together, half an hour later.

'We met at the door, and I thought it only right that Cal heard my news,' Aidan said. 'I had a word with George Arkbridge – we play golf together sometimes. It appears that Arkbridge Shipping approached Laird, as your office manager, and asked him to carry cargo for them on Weir ships. The Arkbridges had no idea that he was pocketing their payments. From what I can gather they handed over a tidy sum, and none of it went into your accounts.'

'I can't understand why he took such a chance. He must have known that he would be found out.'

'Remember that he expected to leave in October,' Cal said. 'He probably had it in mind to get right out of the area. He could have been well away by the time you or your new office manager discovered what had happened.'

Aidan cleared his throat. 'There's something else. I've discovered that Arkbridge's want to extend their fleet because of the new coaling contract. They arranged for Weir's to sub-contract to them as a way of finding out how well your boats performed before making an offer to buy you out. As far as they were concerned, it was all above board.'

'How could it have been, when I knew nothing about it?'

The two men exchanged glances; then, at a faint but firm nod from Cal, Aidan said, 'According to George, they dealt with your representatives.'

'Who were . . . ?'

'John Laird, of course, and—'

'My father.'

'I'm sorry, Morag.'

She shrugged. 'I think I knew it all along. John Laird couldn't have dealt with Arkbridge's on his own.'

'George claims that Arkbridge's company acted in good faith, and they were assured that your father had the authority to negotiate on your behalf.'

'But he only holds 25 per cent of the shares!'

Aidan looked at Cal, who said reluctantly, 'He's been

trying ever since your inheritance was confirmed to buy my shares, Morag. That would have given him 45 per cent – not that he ever had any hope of getting them.'

'Why didn't you tell me?' She glared at him. 'What is the point of telling me that I must take charge and be responsible for myself and for Weir Shipping, when you keep the truth from me?'

He had the grace to look sheepish. 'I'm sorry. When all's said and done, the man's your father and I just couldn't bring myself . . . I'm sorry, Morag,' he said again. 'I wish you hadn't had to find out.'

'That's why you didn't want him to attend our meeting on Saturday, Aidan?'

'I . . . felt it might be best to keep everything confidential among the three of us,' he said carefully.

'He was here a short while ago, pressing me to consider selling.'

Cal made an explosive sound while Aidan merely said, 'Ah,' with a wealth of meaning.

'Or let him take over as office manager.'

'Good God! I hope you refused?'

'I said that I would have to consult you, Aidan. And he said that he would prefer me to be represented by your uncle.'

'My uncle and both the Weir brothers have been friends for most of their lives, but you can be sure that Uncle Kenneth would certainly not stand for any interference in a client's affairs.'

'Can I buy out my father's shares?'

'What with?' Aidan raised an eyebrow. 'Thanks to John Laird, the business is in a shaky position. You have no surplus money. Your father will have to remain a shareholder for the time being, but we must keep a careful eye on him.'

Morag looked from one man to the other, cringing

inwardly at the pity she saw in both faces. It seemed so obvious, now, that Lawrence had been John Laird's partner. She doubted if he would have been able to make an offer for Cal's shares unless he had had some extra money to hand. Money stolen by deceit from Weir Shipping – from his own daughter.

'Perhaps,' she said wryly, trying to summon a smile, 'I've just found out that blood isn't thicker than water after all.'

Morag had never been to Bouverie Street before, and she was impressed by the row of high, handsome tenements with wide pends set at intervals between the closes to give access to the rear courtyards. They were far superior to the older buildings in Ardgowan Street, where the Becketts lived, and Bellhaven Street, where she herself had been born. The buildings there were very old, with outside back staircases and tiny rear yards where weeds grew through cracked and broken stone flags. In some cases, the weeds even flourished in the guttering and mildewed walls of the outside privies and wash-houses.

Grace peered round the edge of the door nervously, her eyes widening when she recognised her visitor. 'Miss Weir!'

'I thought you'd be back from the teashop by now. Can I come in for a minute?'

The living-room was so immaculate that it seemed a shame to sit on the armchair with its perfect, puffed cushions. It was more like a museum than a home – perfect, but not a place where folk lived.

'Would you like some tea?' Grace asked automatically.

'I've just had some,' Morag lied, noticing the girl's

fleeting, anxious glance at the clock on the mantelpiece. It would soon be time for the Ropeworks to close for the day, which meant that her father would be home shortly for his evening meal. From what she had heard of the man from Wilma, Morag knew that he was a martinet in his own home, the type who would expect his food to be on the table as soon as he stepped over the lintel.

She got down to business with no more time-wasting. 'I came to ask if you'd be interested in leaving the teashop and working for me instead.'

Grace forgot all about the time. 'Work for you? Doing what?'

Swiftly, Morag explained about her arrangement to take in occasional paying guests for the Ropeworks, and the decision to be her own office manager at the East Harbour. 'I don't want to let Mr Winters down, but it's not possible for me to be in two places at once. I need someone reliable to see to the housework, the shopping and the cooking for me, and be there for the guests during the day. It would be unfriendly to leave them on their own, particularly the ladies, while their menfolk are at the mill on business.'

'And you think that I could do that?'

Morag indicated the spotless room they sat in – or, rather, that she sat in, for Grace was hovering on her feet as though unable, or perhaps not generally allowed, to sit down frequently in her own living-room. 'I've no doubt at all that you could. And anyone who feeds two working men day in and day out certainly knows how to cook.'

'Nothing fancy, though,' Grace said anxiously.

'I can't cook fancy food either, and any guests who expect it can move to an hotel. You mebbe don't care for the idea of cleaning in my house, though, when you've got this flat to see to as well.'

'Oh, no! It would be different, working in someone else's house. More of a pleasure than a duty.'

'So you'll do it?'

'I'd like to, but surely you'll only need someone now and again when you have paying guests?'

Morag had already thought of that. 'If I'm going to be spending most of my time at the harbour, I could really do with someone in the house every day, even when I'm on my own. Then I wouldn't have to do all my housework in the evenings. I thought that we could come to some arrangement that allowed you sufficient time to see to this place, and tend to your brother and your father, as well as helping me. As to salary . . .'

As the former cashier, Morag knew that the girl was not very well paid at the teashop, which meant that she was in a position to offer more without putting herself seriously out of pocket.

Grace's eyes widened at the sum mentioned and she accepted there and then, though she added, 'Of course, I'll have to speak to my father . . .'

'Tell him that I'd be happy to explain it all to him if he wants.'

'I'm sure that won't be necessary.' At mention of Bill Hastie, his daughter's eyes returned again to the clock and Morag knew that it was time to take her leave.

'If you do come to work for me, I'd like it to be as soon as possible,' she said at the door. 'And there's just one other thing – if you're willing, that is. The office at the harbour is in a terrible state, and I must clean it out before I can start work in it.'

'I'd not mind giving you a hand,' Grace said at once, her eyes shining.

Morag was on the final downward flight when footsteps echoed in the close below and Danny Hastie started up towards her, stopping dead when he recognised her.

'Miss Weir? Is anything the matter?'

'No, I just wanted a word with your sister. I'll leave her to tell you about it herself.' She came down a few steps, then asked quietly, 'Have you spoken to Wilma yet?'

'Soon. I wanted to leave time for . . . after Daisy's death.'

'That was thoughtful of you, but I think she'd appreciate a shoulder to lean on now.'

He nodded, then said awkwardly, 'I've been thinking a lot about what you said, and you're quite right. I'll get nowhere if I don't try.'

'I'm glad to hear that.' She smiled at him, thinking again what a nice man he was. 'I tell you what – when the holiday season starts next year, why don't you take her to Largs and hire a wee boat, and teach her to row properly? Then next time she and I go out on the water she can take the oars, and I can feel safer when the steamers are about.'

20

As the *Pladda* left the comparative shelter of Little
Cumbrae's rocky mass and moved into the open Firth,
the powerful south-easterly wind met her head on. The
shock of the impact made the wheel buck hard, and
Morag would have lost control of it if Cal Fergusson,
standing at her back, hadn't reached both arms round
her to catch the spokes and hold them steady.

'What happened?' she asked as the *Pladda* responded
to a familiar touch and settled down to butt against the
oncoming waves.

'We've just moved into the path of the wind, and it's
stronger than we are. We'll not make much headway
now, for puffers don't have the strength or the bulk to
fight a heavy sea. We'll just hold firm until it abates.
If we try to turn towards Arran just now, the wind'll
blow us on to the Little Cumbrae. We're fine where
we are for the time being.'

As she ducked out from beneath his arm, Morag
peered through the side wheelhouse window. The most
westerly tip of Little Cumbrae's stony shore should
have been sliding smoothly past and dropping astern
of them, but instead it was motionless to starboard.
Although she was nudging into the oncoming waves
and her engines could be heard roaring below-decks

with the effort of striving to move her forward, the little cargo ship had been stopped dead in her tracks by the force of the wind sweeping in from the Irish Sea.

'The wheel's too strong for you now,' Cal said. 'You go down below.'

The thought of sitting in the small, stuffy cabin didn't appeal. 'I'd as soon go forward.'

'Mind yourself, then,' he said, as she stepped out of the wheelhouse door. The wind immediately took her breath away and she had to pause for a long moment to steady herself before making her way forward, clinging to handholds as she went, to the sheltered spot where the raised foredeck kept off the worst of the wind.

Above, grey skies massed with rolling cloud lowered and, as the boat rolled, spray – or perhaps it was squally rain – was thrown in great handfuls into Morag's face. She lifted her face to the weather, unseasonable for April, and pulled off her sou'wester to let her hair blow in the wind.

She was cold and wet, but she had never felt so free or so happy. Terrified though she had been at the prospect of running the shipping business by herself, she now loved it and awoke each morning looking forward to the challenges the day would bring. Between them Cal and Aidan had nurtured and encouraged her self-confidence – something which her father, continually seething on the sidelines, had never attempted.

And thanks to Grace Hastie, who had turned out to be a godsend, she was free to concentrate on the business. Over the six or seven months since coming to work at Lilybank Road, Grace had changed almost beyond recognition from a nervous shadow to a confident young woman, aware of her own abilities and talents. She coped tactfully and cheerfully with the Ropeworks' paying guests, and when Morag was asked

by other local businessmen to provide similar accommodation for visiting clients and their wives, Grace
readily agreed.

'I hate being left with nothing to do,' she said. 'And I
never knew before how much I like meeting people.'

The only person who wasn't happy about Grace's
new-found independence was her father.

'He's not able to bully her any more,' Wilma reported
gleefully to Morag, 'and he can't understand what's
happened to her. But Danny's delighted, because the
way Grace used to be, he worried all the time about
how she was going to manage when he was gone and
she was left on her own with that old devil.'

Wilma had returned to work just before Christmas,
her arm as good as new, and much to her surprise she
had discovered a new and more positive side to Danny
Hastie. They had started walking out together at the
turn of the year, and just a week ago they had become
engaged to be married.

'I can't understand it myself,' Wilma admitted,
blushing, when she broke the news to Morag. 'Me
. . . and a quiet soul like Danny Hastie! I just enjoyed
going to see him rowing, and going to Leith and places
with the rowing club for a bit of a laugh. And he was
fine for a walk now and again, and mebbe a visit to the
pictures. But I swear that I never thought of marrying
him. Then when he said out of the blue that we should
get wed, I couldn't for the life of me come up with a
reason why not!'

'You must love him, or you'd not have accepted.'

'That's the strange thing about it,' Wilma confessed.
'I do, yet I didn't even know it was happening. He's
just . . . just so caring. And he's much more masterful
than you'd think. In fact, he's just what I want in
a man.'

'He must have hidden depths,' Morag had said solemnly and Wilma, radiant with happiness, had agreed.

'You should be down below, in the dry.' Cal came to stand with his back against the raised deck. Turning to squint at the wheelhouse, she saw through the water-patterned glass that Big Malky had taken the wheel.

'I'm fine where I am. Are we going to get to Arran today?'

'Of course we are.' His words were snatched away by the wind, and she just caught the gist of them as they whirled briefly round her head before rushing off to become part of the wild April day. 'It'll just take time, and patience.'

Morag knuckled rain and spray from her eyes. She knew from previous trips that by then they should have seen Arran with its distinctive mountain range, known as The Sleeping Warrior because of its outline. But there was nothing but grey tumbling sea and curtains of water.

'What happens if we don't make it?'

'We'll just turn back to Great Cumbrae and stay there for the night.' Cal had fumbled his precious pipe out of his pocket and now, to her surprise, he reached into his jacket and brought out a box of matches.

'You're never going to try to light that pipe, are you?'

'Ach, I've smoked it in worse than this.' He moved to sit on the hatch by her side and she watched, fascinated and amused, as he struck match after match, crouching forward to get as much shelter from the raised deck as he could and protecting the pipe with his free hand. Finally, irritated by the number of failed attempts, she pulled off her warm gloves and stuffed them in the pocket of the long waterproof coat she had bought for her trips on the puffers, then offered the

243

additional shelter of her own cupped hands about his.

It worked. Cheek to cheek with him, she saw the tiny spark as the tamped tobacco in the bowl caught. She knew a moment of suspense, of doubting that the spark would hold; then the glow began to spread, turning the pipe bowl and its contents into a miniature forest fire. Cal drew on the stem to encourage the tiny flame, and Morag suddenly realised that her own lips were pursed to suck in little draughts of air, just as she had done as a small girl watching Sander work at lighting his pipe.

Then her nose caught the now-familiar aroma of the tobacco Cal always used and he sat upright, moving away from her, as he said triumphantly, 'I told you I could do it!'

Just then the boat bucked as a particularly large wave roared down on it. Cal automatically reached out an arm to coil it about Morag's shoulders, but she had begun to get used to the puffers and, as she saw the wall of water advancing, she swung one leg across the narrow passageway around the hatch, jamming a booted foot against the bulwarks so that she was wedged securely, while her hands gripped the rim of the hatch cover. The *Pladda* was thrown to one side for a moment, then righted herself as soon as the wave had passed.

Cal cursed mildly as he saw that the burst of spray from the wave had extinguished his carefully nourished pipe. He put it into his pocket, then took hold of Morag's arm. 'Come on,' he told her firmly when the boat was on an even keel again, and pulled her to her feet, then eased her before him along the passage and up the few wooden steps to the bridge deck, and into the wheelhouse.

'Down you go, now.'

'I'm fine on the deck.' Morag tried to protest, but he would have none of it.

'It's too risky now we're on the open Firth. If we let you fall overboard, who'll see to the office and the orders and our wages packets?' he said brusquely, clearly anxious to take over the wheel again and concentrate on getting his boat safely to its destination.

On the boats, the captain was always master. Morag held her tongue and began to clamber down the narrow, vertical ladder, clinging tightly as the *Pladda* bucked and rolled.

Down in the cabin Wee Malky was darning the sleeve of a jersey, seemingly oblivious to the boat's erratic corkscrewing movement which was more apparent below than on the open deck.

'It's a wee thing wild,' he said mildly when she appeared, then went back to his work.

Morag would have offered to do the darning for him, but knew that that would offend him. At least, she thought as she perched on the opposite bench and watched his grubby, surprisingly deft fingers ply the needle, he wasn't scrambling up the ladder and out on to the heaving deck to get away from her, as had happened on her first few voyages on the *Pladda*.

Since dismissing John Laird and taking the running of Weir Shipping into her own hands, she had made a point of going out at least once on each of the five puffers to see for herself what the life was like.

Pladda was her favourite,. The captains on *Jura*, *Coll* and *Ailsa Craig* were all older men, clearly uneasy about having a woman – particularly a woman who owned the company that employed them – on board. On *Sanda* the problem was just the opposite, for Archie

Beckett, now the boat's master and handling the job capably, tended to treat Morag as his sister's friend, to be teased and flirted with but never taken seriously.

Cal, on the other hand, knew how to treat her as a friend or, when the occasion demanded it, as an employer, although not shy to remind her – as he had just done – that he and not she was in charge of his boat. In spite of their occasional differences of opinion, she had discovered that she could talk easily to him, and he had been of invaluable assistance during the long winter months spent struggling to understand the way Weir Shipping was run.

It was fortunate that she had taken over at a time when winter was approaching and there was less work for the little fleet, since it gave her time to catch up. While the boats, one at a time, were being taken out of service to be checked over, repaired, repainted and readied for the spring, Cal had spent hours at Lilybank Road going over the books with her. He had even tested her, listing imaginary cargoes on imaginary runs and making her work out which boat should carry which cargo, what cargoes could be found for the return trip, how much the overall journey would cost, including harbour dues, and how much the customer should be charged. It had felt like being back in school, but this time there had been purpose to her studies and her reward was the glow of pride which filled her each time he nodded approval.

Something caught her attention now. She cocked her head and saw that Wee Malky, at the other side of the cabin, had done the same. Their eyes met.

'The seas have calmed down,' Morag said tentatively, 'and we've turned towards Arran.'

He nodded. 'Aye, we're makin' headway now. I'd best go up. I'll be needed,' he said, eager to be on deck with the men. As his well-scuffed boots disappeared up the ladder, Morag picked up the jersey with an eye to finishing the mending for him. The job was almost complete and the darning far neater than anything she had ever been able to achieve, even with Georgina as a teacher.

Sighing, she put the jersey down again and went to make sandwiches for the crew.

As they tied up at Brodick harbour Johnno appeared from below, wiping his hands and his hot face, as usual, with a dirty rag.

'I'm no' happy about thon boiler,' he told Cal. 'She still needs nursin' along.'

'And you're the man to do it, Johnno.'

'I'm no' a miracle worker, though,' the man said gloomily.

'What's wrong with the boiler?' Morag wanted to know.

'It's dyin' on its feet, that's what's wrong with it.'

'It's not that bad, Johnno.'

'Who's the engineer here, you or me?'

'You, Johnno.'

'And the engineer's saying,' the man fixed Morag with a red-rimmed eye, 'that we need somethin' done about that boiler.'

'How much will it cost?' Morag wanted to know as Johnno went to help Wee Malky with one of the mooring lines.

'Nothing. It's fine; it's being a wee bit temperamental,' Cal hurried on as she began to ask more questions. 'It'll do until the boat goes in for her overhaul in the winter.'

'Are you certain?'

'Of course I'm certain. Now . . . either get back down below or go on to the pier, for there's no room on deck while we're unloading,' he ordered, and she hurried ashore, knowing from experience that if she went down to the cabin the noise of the winches emptying the hold, and the thunder of feet on the deck, would drive her mad. In any case, she longed to stretch her legs after being cooped up since mid-morning.

The greening fields and budding trees had a freshly washed look now that the storm had blown itself out. Morag picked her way round the carts and vans and lorries which had gathered as soon as the *Pladda* had been sighted on its way into harbour. The islands were all dependent on the sturdy little puffers for the goods they couldn't produce for themselves, and the drivers were there to collect the unloading cargo and convey it to houses, farms and shops all over Arran.

She strolled along the waterfront, watching some early holidaymakers throwing stones for their large, enthusiastic dog which hurled itself into the water after every stone, returning each time with something in its mouth – though how it could tell one stone from another on the seabed, she didn't know. Then she wandered further afield, admiring the small houses along the edge of the bay, most with their paths between gate and door edged with clumps of crocuses and snowdrops and their flower-beds glowing in the late-afternoon twilight with yellow daffodils and bunches of scarlet tulips.

When she arrived back just as the last of the cargo was unloading, Cal introduced her to Mr Pinkerton, the farmer who had offered her a bed for the night.

'The timber we're taking back's ready and waiting.' He nodded to a great stack further along the pier. 'But we'll leave it till the early morning light, then we can load the rest once the timber's in place.'

The timber would fill only half the hold, so Morag had arranged to ship back a motley cargo of bits and pieces; not much, but enough to fill the space left in the hold when the wood was all aboard.

Cal handed her up on to the loaded cart and looked up at her, his hand resting on the wheel. 'I'll see you later, for Mrs Pinkerton's invited me for my supper.'

'Everyone's welcome,' the farmer said cheerfully. 'The wife keeps a good table, and she can always find more plates if needed.' But it seemed that Big Malky's sister lived on the island, and he and his son and Johnno were going to visit her.

The Pinkertons' farm lay half a mile inland, along the main road for a few hundred yards then over a lane which must, Morag thought, be pleasant on a hot summer's day, for ancient trees grew on both sides, their leafless branches forming an arch overhead. Mrs Pinkerton welcomed her guest as though she was a member of the family returned home after a long time away.

'I've put you in this room, it's small but it's comfortable. There's hot water in the jug and clean towels, and plenty of time to get yourself ready,' she said, then hurried back to her kitchen which was fragrant with the smell of cooking.

Morag, suddenly aware how untidy and weary she felt after hours at sea, stripped and enjoyed a luxurious wash in hot water, with soap that smelled of roses. After dressing in a long plain jumper patterned in brown and cream, and a brown pleated skirt, she turned her attention to her hair which was a mass of tangles from the wet, salty wind.

Not long after taking over the office from John Laird, she had given in to Wilma's nagging and reluctantly gone to have her hair cut short. She had endured the ordeal with her eyes closed tightly, wincing inwardly with each crunch of the scissors as they took off another lock of her long hair. When it was over and she was finally persuaded to look at herself in the mirror, she had squealed, horrified, 'I look like a man!'

'Of course you don't,' Wilma said briskly. 'It's very stylish and you suit it.'

Morag couldn't tear her eyes away from her reflection, even though she hated it. Without its usual frame of thick hair, her face seemed much larger and more obvious than it had ever been. 'I'm all face . . . and all neck!' she wailed. 'I should never have allowed you to have your own way, Wilma Beckett!'

'You'll like it when you get used to it,' her friend told her, unruffled.

'How can anyone get used to that? I want it the way it was!'

'Here you are,' Wilma said unfeelingly, scooping up a handful of red tresses from the floor, 'though I don't see how you're going to stick it back in place.'

'I won't be able to go out until it grows back again,' Morag had mourned, her hands clasped at the back of her neck. She was used to feeling hair there, but now there was only the nape which felt very fragile and vulnerable.

'You can tie a scarf over your head, though you'd be a fool if you did. She's always been a coward,' Wilma told the hairdresser, who was beginning to look nervous at her customer's panicky reaction. 'She was just like this the time we went rowing in Rothesay Bay.'

'And look what happened then! Your daft idea almost killed the two of us!'

'We're still here, aren't we? And you'll get to like it,' Wilma said again, patiently.

The maddening thing about Wilma was that she was

usually right. Once the initial shock eased Morag had discovered that her new hairstyle, cut close in to the nape of her neck and shaped to fall in soft waves at the sides and over her forehead, really did suit her. Her hair could now be washed and dried in half the time it had taken before, and the short style was ideal for her new life since it gave her an efficient air and was easy to manage when she went out on the boats.

Her father and step-mother disapproved. Lawrence thought that it looked 'fast', and Margaret said flatly that it simply didn't suit her, and what a pity that she hadn't had the sense to keep her lovely long hair. Aidan, on the other hand, admired it greatly and had taken her out to dinner to celebrate her new look.

There was only one disappointment. Morag would have liked her hair to lie neatly to the line of her head, like Wilma's, but once cut it had developed a tendency to curl. When first washed, and brushed hard, it lay quite nicely, but sooner or later the curls bounced back.

They appeared now as she brushed the tangles out one by one, and by the time she had finished her face was framed with feathery fronds which reflected the light from the oil lamp on the table and became tawny flames.

'I used to have hair that colour,' Mrs Pinkerton said when Morag went into the kitchen. 'A lovely rich glow it had, just like yours. My man used to say when we were courting that it was the colour of conkers.' She laughed, and for a moment the young pretty woman she had once been shone through the soft lined skin and faded blue eyes and double chin. 'You'll mind the conkers that laddies play with?'

'Oh, yes.' Morag recalled her schooldays, when the boys used sticks to bring down the prickly green fruits of the chestnut trees, then stripped off the outer husks to reveal the hard chestnuts, a deep, burnished red colour. The boys pierced the nuts and threaded string through them.

'Mind you, it wasnae just the lads that used to play, for I was a champion myself,' her hostess prattled on. 'That was the first time my man noticed me, when I beat him at conkers!' The youthful smile burst through again. 'It was the only way to make him notice me, and I'd had to practice awful hard. But once I had his eye, I made sure I never lost it again. Now,' she handed Morag a handful of cutlery, 'you set the table, for he'll be in from the byre directly and Calum'll be up from the boat, both of them more than ready for their dinners.'

Her use of Cal's full name intrigued Morag. 'D'you know him well?'

'He used to come here for his holidays every year with his parents when he was a lad. He loved the farm, but he loved the sea just as much.' Mrs Pinkerton smiled fondly. 'He'd be back and forth all day, morning till night, between one and the other. But it was the sea that won – I thought it would, though there was a time when my man hoped it'd be the land. We were never blessed with bairns of our own, and he'd some idea in his head that young Calum might be the one to follow him in this place. Though I'm not certain that the lad's mother would have approved, for she was set on him inheriting the family shipping business, of course.'

She tasted the contents of the soup pot and nodded her approval. 'It was a pity about what happened – his father dying and all. There was a time after that when his mother wanted to take him off to live somewhere else, like Glasgow, but Calum was dead set against it. He even came over here on one of the steamers to ask if he could live with us instead and let her go away on her own. Not that we could have agreed to parting him from his mother, though we'd both have had him to live with us willingly. In any case, it never happened, and I know that Calum's well content with the life he has now. He comes to see us every time he calls at the island. He's a fine man . . . though don't let him know I said that,' she added as the door opened and the rumble of men's voices was heard in the small hallway. 'It never does to let a man know that he's being praised.'

'By God,' Mr Pinkerton said approvingly as he came into the kitchen, 'it's grand tae see such a bonny young lass in my kitchen again – two bonny lasses, I should say,' he added swiftly as his wife raised her eyebrows at him. He grinned, and nudged Cal. 'Am I not right, Calum?'

'You are that.' Cal had changed into a high-necked jersey and his hair, still damp from being washed, was smoother than usual. As Morag passed him to put a bowl of thick vegetable broth on the table, she could smell the carbolic soap that was used on board the *Pladda*.

'Sit in, now,' Mrs Pinkerton ordered, putting a large plate bearing a great pile of thickly sliced bread on the table before turning her attention to the soup pot.

As they started on their soup, Morag glanced across the table at Cal, thinking of the boy who had been torn between farming and the sea, and had been so determined not to go away from the Clyde that he had considered letting his mother leave without him. It must have been a difficult time for him.

Since the night when Aidan had kissed her on the pier at Largs, the two of them had gone out together on a regular basis. Occasionally they went dancing, but more often they enjoyed a meal or a run in his smart motor-car. Sometimes they visited his uncle, or friends of his. She enjoyed his company and his gentle love-making; but although he had made it clear that he was more than willing to make a deeper commitment to her, Morag had refused to consider it. Having finally gained control of her own life, she had no desire at that moment to make any further changes to it.

But sitting opposite Cal, watching his capable hands as he broke pieces from a thick white slice of home-baked bread, and his mouth as he spoke; noticing how, when he was contented, his grey eyes took on a smoky blue look, and the way the gold flecks came to his brown hair as it began to dry and curl, she wished . . .

Mr Pinkerton's hearty laugh tore her from her day-dream – which was just as well, she thought. She and Cal were like chalk and cheese; they could never be anything other than employer and employee.

But even so, thinking in the comfort of her bed that night of him in his tiny cabin down at the harbour, part of her mind still wished.

21

'Cal's at the door. He says . . .' Grace, hovering in the kitchen doorway, gave a yelp of surprise as Cal, appearing behind her, lifted her off her feet and set her aside.

'There's trouble,' he said bluntly.

The late September day was mild but drizzly, and the back door was open to let out some of the heat generated by the large copper pot simmering on the stove. The kitchen was filled with the sweet, almost perfumed scent of brambles being turned into jelly, and both women's hands were stained purple from the large black berries they had gathered together from the hedgerows on the braes above the Clyde.

Morag, busy with a bowl of berries, stared up at her visitor in dismay. 'Has something happened to one of the boats?'

'No, it's Archie Beckett.'

She felt her blood run cold. It had taken Mrs Beckett a long time to recover from the shock of Daisy's death. The news of Wilma's engagement had helped, but the woman would never be able to deal with the loss of another member of her family. 'Oh God, Cal, what's happened to him?'

'It's not what's happened, it's what's going to happen.

You know he's been to Islay to deliver a load of furniture?'

'Of course I know. I arranged it.' An old lady had died in Paisley and her great-granddaughter, who lived on the Inner Hebridean island of Islay and was about to marry, had been invited to visit her house and take any furniture she chose for her new marital home. She had opted for everything, and *Sanda* had been commissioned to transport both furniture and bride to the island.

'What's happened? Archie should surely have got back from there by now.'

'Oh, he's arrived all right, but he didn't unload his full cargo at Islay,' Cal said grimly. 'He's brought part of it back with him – the bride.'

Morag stared. 'She travelled all the way home, then came back again? Why would she do that?'

'It seems that she and Archie met recently during one of *Sanda*'s trips to the island, and they got the chance to know each other even better on this last voyage. And you know what young Archie's like with a pretty lassie . . . I don't know what you thought you were about, letting her go on his boat,' Cal added. 'By the time he'd got her and her furniture to Port Ellen she'd lost all notion of marrying the man she was promised to, so the bold Archie turned about and got out of the port as soon as the furniture was on the pier, with her still on board, daft fool that he is. Now he says he's going to marry her himself.'

'Where is he?'

'I've told them both to wait in the office. What d'you think this is going to do for Weir Shipping?' Cal asked angrily as Morag deserted the brambles and ran to wash her hands at the sink. 'We'll lose the Islay trade for sure, for they'll all be on the side of the poor man that's been

256

jilted two days before his wedding. And he'll probably come down here to take it out of Archie's hide.'

Grace, who had been listening wide-eyed to the story, pushed a towel into Morag's hands and she had begun to dry them before she discovered that she hadn't washed all the juice away. 'Here, put that in with the dirty clothes, mebbe the stains'll wash out.' She thrust the towel, now generously daubed with purple, at Grace and began to roll her sleeves down. 'I'll have to leave you to finish the jelly yourself. Can you manage?'

'Of course I can.'

'I don't know what I'd do without you,' Morag said breathlessly, pulling her apron off as she hurried into the hall and dropping it on the small table that stood by the stairs. Cal opened the door as she snatched her jacket from its peg and helped her into the garment as they were going down the steps.

As he had said, the sweethearts were waiting in the office and whiling away the time happily enough. As Morag burst into the room with Cal at her heels they broke away from each other, the girl turning her back modestly to tug and fuss at her clothing and pat her hair back into place.

Morag, torn from a busy day at home and aware of the repercussions her ardent young captain's actions might bring down on her head, was in no mood to mince her words. 'Archie Beckett, have you gone mad?'

His hair was tousled, his face flushed and his eyes glowing. He looked totally unrepentant as he put his hands in his pockets and grinned at her. 'Only mad with love, Morag.'

'It's Miss Weir to you when you're in this office,' Cal rapped at him. 'You're the skipper of one of the Weir boats and this is your employer, and don't you forget it!'

257

Archie shot to attention, although nothing could dim his glow. 'Aye, sorry. Only mad with love, Miss Weir,' he said with no sarcasm intended. 'Mhairi . . .'

He held out his hand and the girl turned at once to put her fingers trustingly in his. 'This,' said Archie, bursting with pride, 'is Miss Mhairi McIntyre from Islay. My intended.'

It was clear to see why he had been attracted to the girl. She was beautiful, with corn-coloured hair and perfect features set in an oval face. The hand she held out to Morag was small but roughened, indicating that Mhairi McIntyre was a working lass.

'How do you do?' she asked politely, her green, thick-lashed eyes wide with apprehension.

'How do you—' Morag suddenly noticed that her own extended hand was splashed with vivid purple stains. 'I'm sorry, I was in the middle of making bramble jelly,' she apologised and sensed, rather than saw, Archie's sudden interest. Every year when she made raspberry jam from fruit grown in the garden and bramble jelly from the hedgerow, she gave some pots to the Becketts. Archie, she remembered, had a particularly sweet tooth.

She quelled him now with one steely glance and marched round the desk to her usual chair, where she felt more in control of the situation.

'I believe that your intended is already promised to someone else, Archie?'

'She was, and that's the thing,' he said earnestly. 'Mhairi's supposed to be getting married in just three days' time, so I couldnae leave her once we'd realised how much we love each other. I had tae bring her back with me, for God knows what the folk on Islay would say if she tried tae stop the wedding now.'

'It's not just God who'll know quite soon, for I

258

assume they'll come to tell her. And you, and me. I'm responsible for you,' Morag told the girl. 'I guaranteed to get you safely home on one of my boats, and that's not happened.'

'You did get her safely home,' Archie protested. 'At least, I did.'

'Aye, and then you brought her right back again,' Cal interrupted, unable to hold his tongue any longer. 'You should at least have gone ashore and spoken to her father and the man who expects to marry her.'

'Me and my three crew against all the men that'd have supported him?' Archie asked, astonished. 'And one of the crew just a lad not long out of the school and with a mother that still worries about him when he's away from her? You'd have expected us tae face the great lot of them? Anyway, I'd the boat tae think of. I had tae get the *Sanda* back here safely.'

'Archie, you can't go kidnapping brides!' Morag thumped a purple fist on the desk. 'You're not Young Lochinvar, you're a puffer captain from Port Glasgow!'

'Who's Young Lochinvar?' Archie wanted to know, mystified.

'Someone with no more sense than yourself,' Cal told him shortly. 'But at least he didn't drag Mor . . . Miss Weir into the mess he made!'

Archie scowled. 'I'm able and willing tae fight my own battles, when they're fair and square!'

'You may not be the best judge of that. What about the man this lassie's thrown aside for you? D'you think he'll take this lying down?'

'Wait!' Mhairi spoke with the perfect diction of one whose first language was Gaelic, and although her voice was soft and she seemed to sing the words rather than speak them, it carried enough authority to make them listen. 'I'm very sorry for the trouble we've caused to you, Miss Weir, and for the bother I've got Archie into—'

'You've not—'

'Hear me out now, Archie,' she said firmly, and he subsided. 'As I said, I'm sorry, but I love him and I'm content that he loves me, for all that he's always had an eye for the lassies. You have, Archie,' she went on as he opened his mouth to speak, 'and no sense in denying it, for you're known up and down the West Coast for it. But that's over now, and I'm certain in my own mind that I no longer want to wed Hamish, even if Archie was to tell me he'd changed his mind and didn't want me any more.'

Archie, mindful of the fact that he was forbidden to speak, put an arm about her and held her close to indicate that he had no intention of changing his mind.

'Let me telephone my father and explain everything to him. I'll tell him that I'm safe, and that the wedding must be called off.'

'You'll be able to reach your father?'

'He runs the public house on the harbour,' Archie broke in. 'That's where Mhairi and me met. She works there.'

'I can telephone him, then? And you'll stay here with me while I do it, Archie,' Mhairi said when Morag nodded and vacated her seat at the desk, 'for he'll no doubt be wanting a word with you.'

'Mhairi's the only daughter in the family, and the apple of her father's eye,' Cal said as he and Morag waited outside the office. 'The man's quick-tempered as well. Archie could be in a deal of trouble.'

The rain had come on in earnest now and they sheltered in the doorway, watching the drops run over Lady Isabella's freshly painted figure and bounce on the flagstones. Over at the edge of the harbour they could see the top of *Sanda*'s high foredeck, with the winch gear on it.

'Unless he and Mhairi can persuade her father to accept the situation.'

'If they can't, Archie'll have done for Weir Shipping where Islay's concerned. How could he have been so irresponsible?' Cal fumed.

'I can see how it happened. She's very beautiful. Any hot-blooded young man might lose his head over her.'

'Oh, she looks well enough, but that's not sufficient reason to do what he did,' Cal raged. Then, after a silence, 'Young Lochinvar, indeed!' A smile tugged at the corners of his mouth. 'You've got a fancy turn of mind, Morag Weir – comparing a reprobate like Archie Beckett with a romantic figure like that.'

'What Archie's done may be irresponsible, but he's every bit as romantic as the man in the poem.'

'Women!' he scoffed, but the smile had become a grin.

The rain drizzled on down, filling the two footsteps set in cement with water. 'Don't you believe in love, Cal?'

'Not when it gets in the way of work.'

Another ten minutes passed before Archie and Mhairi came down the wooden staircase hand in hand, beaming with relief, to report that the girl's father, though angry, had agreed to let the girl stay in Mags Beckett's care for a few days until he and his wife travelled to Port Glasgow. In the meantime, the wedding would be cancelled.

'Now,' Archie said, 'to tell my Ma. But you've no need to worry about her,' he assured the girl, catching her up in his arms and hugging her. 'For she'll love you as much as I do.'

'I just hope that my father doesn't get to hear of

this,' Morag said when the two of them had gone off with Archie's waterproof coat spread over their heads as protection against the rain. 'He's always so eager to find fault with the way I run this business.'

'I don't see why he should blame you. Archie's stupidity isn't your fault. I'll see you home,' Cal offered. 'I'll fetch that old umbrella from the office.'

The rain had settled in for the day. By the time they got back to the house Grace was preparing to go home, so Cal offered her an umbrella escort too.

'Young Lochinvar . . .' Morag murmured as the girl scurried to fetch her coat.

'Women!' he countered.

Mags Beckett insisted on Mhairi sharing Wilma's room, using the bed that had been Daisy's.

'There'll be no carrying-on under my roof,' she told Morag firmly. 'If our Archie wants the lassie for his own, he'll have tae wed her first. And I hope he does, for she's bonny by nature as well as in looks, and she seems tae have the measure of him too. Archie needs a woman who can stand up tae him.' Her face softened. 'Just like his father – a wild rogue, he was, but as handsome as the devil and able to charm the birds from the trees. Now that our Wilma's tae marry with Danny, I'd like tae see Archie settled as well. Then I can end my days safe in the knowledge that they've all found their way in life.'

'You're not nearly old enough to start thinking about the end of your life, Mrs Beckett.'

'Times, hen, this lot's got me so's I feel like an old crone. And anyway' – a flicker of sadness ran across the woman's normally cheerful face – 'I've learned the hard way that we never know when we're goin' tae be taken.'

Morag offered Mhairi's parents accommodation at Lilybank Road when they arrived from Islay to confront their runaway daughter and meet the man who had stolen her from her fiancé.

'It's kind of you,' said Mrs McIntyre, an older version of her beautiful daughter. 'Especially after the trouble our Mhairi's put you to.'

'It's me who should be apologising to you, for Archie's in my employ.'

'Ach, the lassie's always been self-willed, not in the least like her brothers. It's her father's doing,' the woman confided in her soft lilting voice. 'With her being the youngest, and the only lassie, he dotes on her. She's been allowed her own way too often.'

'If it's any consolation to you, I believe that Archie really does love her and he'll be a good husband to her.'

'Aye, he seems a decent enough lad, for all that he was a bit hasty,' the woman admitted. 'And his mother couldn't be kinder to us, or to Mhairi.'

The McIntyres spent long hours closeted in the parlour with their wayward daughter and with Archie who, at Cal's suggestion, had been taken off sailing duties until the Islay matter was settled. Winter was on the way and, even though they were still carrying cargoes for the Arkbridge company when possible, the other four boats were able to handle the work between them. *Sanda* had been moved into dry dock for some general maintenance and repair work, and would take over from *Pladda* when her turn came to be checked over.

There was no doubt that even though Mr McIntyre was protective towards his precious daughter, he and his wife were impressed by Mags Beckett and her hard-working, cheerful brood. Even Archie, to his great relief, finally won the man's grudging approval, and it was agreed that the engagement would be allowed on condition that the young lovers waited for at least six months before marrying.

'It's far too long,' Archie protested when a family council consisting of the two McIntyres and Mags gave their verdict.

'It's a drop in the ocean compared with the time you'll spend as man and wife,' his future father-in-law told him tersely. 'And if you cannot wait for my daughter for six months, then you're not the right man for her.'

'I can wait twice as long if I must! Though I'd prefer not to.'

'You,' his mother told him, 'will do as you're told. You've caused enough trouble as it is, and there'll be no more. Forbye, you've still tae find somewhere for you both tae live when you are wed, for you're no' movin' in with me. And that'll take all of six months.'

Archie looked suitably humbled, though he earned himself a maternal cuff on the ear when the McIntyre family was out of earshot by remarking that it was a pity that he had unloaded Mhairi's wedding furniture at Islay before decamping with her, for it would have come in useful.

With Mrs Winters' help, domestic work was found for Mhairi in one of the big houses and Mags, determined to keep her promise to look after Mhairi, found accommodation for Archie with a retired widower in Ardgowan Street who appreciated the chance to make some extra money.

'He's a right respectable man, and it's the only way to make certain that our Archie'll not get the chance to anticipate marriage,' she said primly to Morag. 'For all his promises, I know fine and well that he would if he got the chance. I've told ye he's the spit of his father, and I was six months gone with my eldest by the time I got *him* tae the minister.'

'It'll be hard on him, paying rent and saving to get married.'

'Not at all. There's Mhairi earning too, and it'll do him good tae find out somethin' about the cost of runnin' a house. Marriage isn't all about four bare legs in a bed.'

On the evening before the McIntyres returned home, Morag held a party at Lilybank Road for the two families which was a far cry from any gathering the house had ever seen before. The Becketts, who attended en masse, babies and all, knew how to enjoy themselves; Mr McIntyre turned out to be a fine singer and an accordionist of considerable talent, while his wife, for all her grey hairs and advancing years, was still a nimble dancer.

The crews of all five Weir boats were invited, together with their families, and the party swiftly developed into a good Highland ceilidh. Danny was there, and so was Grace – almost as beautiful, when she was animated, as Mhairi.

'I wish we could find a man for Grace,' Wilma said as she and Morag hurriedly made a fresh batch of sandwiches. The dining-room table had been almost groaning under the weight of the food prepared for the party, but drinking, dancing and singing proved to be a hungry business.

'If there's someone for Grace, they'll find each other. Don't you start match-making,' Morag warned.

'That's fine advice coming from you! Did you think Danny wouldn't tell me about you pushing him into going after me?'

'I didn't push him,' Morag protested, wondering why men hadn't the sense to keep their mouths shut. 'I just encouraged him a bit.'

'And I'm glad you did. That's why I think someone should do it for Grace,' Wilma persisted just as the bell high on the wall jangled. 'Who's that? I thought everyone was already here.'

She whisked out of the kitchen and Morag followed her in time to see Archie, glass in hand, throw the front door open, roaring, 'Come in, come in! Come and drink our health, whoever you are!'

He stepped back, tripped over his own feet and staggered sideways in an attempt to stay upright. His arms semaphored frantically and Cal, who had just come out of the parlour, deftly caught his half-full glass as it left his fingers.

Morag reached the door, her welcoming smile freezing and then dying at sight of her father and step-mother in the porch, their faces blank with astonishment.

A sudden burst of accordion music and the shrill whooping of folk enjoying a rousing eightsome reel poured from the parlour, while a hearty burst of laughter echoed through the open door of the dining-room.

'Come in . . .' Morag began, then her voice died away as, without a word, Lawrence Weir turned and hustled his wife along the path and out of the gate.

22

'Would the end of the week do? The *Ailsa Craig* could handle your cargo then,' Morag was saying into the telephone when she heard someone coming in at the lower door and mounting the stairs. Her stomach clenched, then fluttered. Ever since the ceilidh party three nights earlier she had been waiting apprehensively for a visit from her father, and steeling herself for the fury that she knew would descend on her when he did arrive.

'I need to have the gravel uplifted on Wednesday,' Mr Arkbridge said tinnily into her ear. 'If you can't help me . . .'

The fluttering had eased because she had recognised the step on the stairs as Cal's. 'With the *Pladda* going in for repair and the other four boats already committed . . .' she was saying when he came into the office. He raised an enquiring eyebrow, and she excused herself and covered the telephone mouthpiece for a moment.

'It's Mr Arkbridge, with a load of gravel to be collected from Loch Fyne the day after tomorrow and brought to Greenock.'

'I'll take it.'

'But *Pladda*'s due into the repair yard in two days' time. I've just been explaining—'

'If the cargo's ready and waiting we can manage to get back for that. We leave here first thing tomorrow, load right away when we arrive, then sail with the first light. You can't afford to turn the work down,' he added impatiently as she hesitated.

He was right. Weir Shipping had still not made up all the money John Laird had stolen, and any extra income was welcome. After taking charge of the office Morag had agreed, with the support of her father and Cal, the two other shareholders, to continue carrying cargoes for Arkbridge Shipping when required. There was one condition – that all Weir contracts were honoured first.

'Are you sure that *Pladda*'s boiler can hold out?' she asked as she hung up the receiver after confirming that Weir's could handle the order. The ageing boiler had been causing intermittent problems throughout the summer.

'For one last trip? Of course. Johnno's the best engineer in the Weir fleet, and Arkbridge pays well. You try to find me an outgoing cargo, and I'll go and tell the rest of them that we're off tomorrow morning.' He hesitated at the door. 'Any word from your father?'

'Nothing. Mebbe I should go and see him.'

'Why? You've done nothing wrong. If you go to him, he'll see it as an admission of guilt.'

'I can't help feeling guilty,' she admitted. 'He has that effect on me.'

He gave her a cool, grey look. 'Don't be daft,' he said and went off down the stairs, whistling at the thought of another trip.

The news that *Pladda* had gone aground on her way back from Loch Fyne was brought to Morag by the skipper of a collier which had just come into harbour.

'She's drifted ontae the Gantocks. I couldnae stop tae help her, for I was takin' in water and I had tae get back as fast as I could.' The man wiped rain-water from his weathered face. 'The rain's fallin' like sheets on a washin'-line out there, and the wind's gustin'. I just caught a wee sight of her before the rain closed in again, but I know her well.'

Cold fear struck at Morag. The Gantocks, a reef on the opposite bank of the Firth, was a known hazard to shipping. 'Is she holed?'

'Sure tae be. She's caught forrard. If the wind changes tae the south, hen, she'll be driven further ontae the rocks and then she'll go down, sure as anythin'. Best call a tug out,' the man advised.

After making the call, Morag pulled on her coat and wrapped a scarf about her head before running downstairs to the harbour. It had rained all night, and since early morning the weather had deteriorated. As the collier skipper had said, the rain was coming down in sheets of water and being blown across the harbour by a gusty, stormy wind. What little could be seen of the river was being whipped into a white-clawed fury, and not far out a thick, wet grey mist obscured everything.

As always happened when a boat was in danger, word had spread like wildfire. By the time Morag went out the men had begun gathering in small groups to discuss the *Pladda*'s fate.

'There's not much chance for her now, not in this squally weather,' one old man was predicting as she hurried past. 'I've seen plenty of boats smashed tae bits on those rocks. When the reefs get them, they're finished.'

Someone else, recognising Morag, shushed him.

Sanda was unloading and Archie jumped ashore and came hurrying to meet her, water sluicing from his oilskins, his young face grave for once. 'You've called out the tugs?'

'Yes. What are their chances, Archie?'

'Och, they'll be fine,' he said stoutly. 'The tugs'll get to them quickly, and from what I can make out they're not badly holed. They'll be—' He stopped, then said, 'To hell with that cargo! I'm going out to them.'

She ran to keep up with him as he headed for the *Sanda*. 'What can you do to help?'

'Mebbe not much, but at least I'll be there if I'm needed.'

'I'm coming with you.'

He stopped in his tracks and peered down at her. 'There's no sense in you going!'

'Mebbe not . . .' she threw his own words back at him. 'But I'm going anyway. *Pladda*'s my boat, and so's *Sanda* if it comes to that, so I'm going!'

'You'll have to put on something sensible. I'm not waiting for you,' he called after her as she ran back to the office. 'We're away as soon as the unloading gear's cleared and the hatches are closed!'

'Please . . . ,' Morag prayed silently as she sped up the stairs to the office, where she kept the set of oilskins and strong boots she used when she travelled on one of the puffers, '. . . not *Pladda*.' And she knew, as she hauled her boots on and then fastened the long, clumsy oilskin with trembling fingers, that what she really meant was, 'Not Cal!'

By the time she got back to the harbour edge the dockers had stopped work on *Sanda*, the hatch covers were back on, smoke puffed from her stack and Archie was at the wheel, while the mate saw to the mooring lines. Even though she was hampered by the long oilskin and the heavy boots that would take her straight to the bottom if she should fall in, she managed to make the leap from the solid stone harbour wall to the deck, which was already swinging away. The mate caught her arm and dragged her across the low bulwarks, and *Sanda* was off, heading into the grey world of the river.

'It's as well she was only half unloaded,' Archie said as Morag squeezed into the wheelhouse, followed by the mate. 'The cargo that's left'll help to hold her in the water. I'd not like to travel lightship in this weather.'

'As long as what's left doesnae shift,' the mate added. 'It's got a lot of room tae move down there.'

'It'll not move,' Archie snapped at him as he swung the *Sanda* round to face the harbour entrance.

As soon as they were clear of the shelter, the wind struck and the puffer began to dance about like a nervous carthorse. Archie's feet held the deck as though he was rooted there, while his hands gentled the wheel one minute and then held it back the next as it tried to follow the sea's command and tear itself free of his control. Despite her worry over Cal and the *Pladda*, Morag was impressed by his calm confidence. Cal and old Captain Forsyth had been right to recommend Archie's promotion. On land he might be irresponsible and easy-going, but at sea, in charge of his boat, he was a different man.

By the time they had struggled round the coast and across the Firth to where the Gantocks lay just off the popular holiday town of Dunoon, the wind had lessened and the rain was no longer sluicing across the wheelhouse windows so hard that they could scarcely see anything.

'We're in luck, for once. Mebbe that's a good

271

omen.' Archie handed the wheel over to the care of the mate and picked up the telescope he had bought at a second-hand shop and always took on board with him.

Morag followed him from the wheelhouse. Although the wind had dropped and the rain eased the weather was still rough, and the boat heaved and tossed beneath their feet.

'There's the tug . . .' Archie pointed, and through the cold misty drizzle Morag made out the distinctive high wheelhouse off to one side.

'Can you see the *Pladda*?'

'Not yet, we'll have to go forrard. Stay close behind me, and hold on all the time,' he instructed, and she used his oilskinned back as a shelter as they went down the steps and along the narrow passageway by the side of the raised hatch.

Ordering her to wait in the comparative shelter by the hatch he went up on to the foredeck, making his way around the steam winch gear to the mast, where he held on to the guy ropes with one hand while the other operated the telescope. Peering over the edge of the foredeck, Morag saw him scanning the horizon then pushing the telescope inside his oilskins and cupping his hands to his mouth.

She could hear him shouting and caught muffled answers, but she couldn't make out the words. It seemed an age before he finally rejoined her.

'What's happening?'

'I saw *Pladda*. She's wedged fast, and holed.'

'Is . . . is everyone all right?'

'Aye, it seems so.' He had pushed off his sou'wester so that it hung down his back by its ties, and a mixture of rainwater and spray trickled down from his curly black hair. He pushed the drops away impatiently. 'We'll get

272

back to the wheelhouse, there's no sense in standing out here.'

Back in shelter, he explained the situation swiftly to the mate. 'There are two tugs there, putting lines aboard her. The crew are dumping as much of the cargo as they can to lighten the boat. The tugs can't start pulling her off until high tide, for fear of ripping her belly out altogether, so that gives Cal some time to work with.'

The mate shook his head. 'They're takin' a chance, uncoverin' the hatches,' he said lugubriously. 'One big sea could fill her and be the end of her.'

'They've got no other choice, man.' Again Archie pushed back his wet hair, showering Morag. 'If she starts to slide, the lines'll at least hold her for a wee while and give the crew the chance to cut the dinghy free and get into it. We're not needed just now, but we'll stand by. They'll be taking the boat to Dunoon once she floats loose, so we can follow them in and take the crew home.'

They had a long, harrowing wait. As the weather continued to ease Archie took his boat as close to the Gantocks as he dared, and Morag got her first sight of the *Pladda* as the heavy sky slowly cleared. The tide had turned, and the only indication of the reef's presence now was the way the water foamed here and there, showing that the waves were breaking on submerged rock. The puffer was lying over slightly to one side and her mast, instead of being vertical, lay at an awkward, unnatural angle. She looked as though on her way home she had decided to stop and lie down for a rest. Her hold was open, and her crew's oilskinned figures worked feverishly about her deck.

'It looks as though they've no steam to work the

winch,' Archie explained. 'They're having to bring out the gravel bucket by bucket, hand to hand.'

'Will she last until high tide?'

'Surely. The damage doesnae seem to be too serious, and these wee boats are hard to finish.' He put a reassuring hand on her arm. 'Don't fret yourself, she'll be fine. And her crew, as well.'

The late-afternoon lights were going on in the streets and houses of Dunoon, only a short distance across the water, when the tide was finally judged high enough for the rescue work to begin. During the long hours of waiting Cal and his crew had jettisoned some of the puffer's cargo and moved what was left to the side furthest from the hole in her bows, in the hope that once freed and floating she would list to one side, keeping the damage above the water's surface. Her hatch covers had been fastened down again and she was secured to both tugs by lines – one from the bows, one from the stern. By then the seas had quietened to a slow, heavy swell.

'Not perfect, but better.' Archie pushed the words through unmoving lips, his eyes not moving from the trapped boat. Morag knew how he felt; her own jaw was aching from tension and she was afraid to take her eyes from the *Pladda* in case, the next time she looked, there was only air where the boat had been.

When the tugs first took the strain, nothing seemed to be happening. The trapped puffer, now only a dark shadow against the sky, was motionless. From where she stood Morag could just catch sight now and then of *Pladda*'s oil lamps fore and aft, flickering like puny candle flames in a mighty cathedral. She strained her eyes until they watered, willing the boat to move.

'She's shifting,' Archie said beside her. 'She's moving . . .'

Morag's fingernails dug into her palms. The danger was at its most acute now. If the sea flooded in through the hole in the puffer's bows, she might go down quite suddenly. She knew from what Archie had told her that Wee Malky was crouched in the stern with an axe, ready to cut the dinghy loose to give the crew a chance of survival if the boat should go down.

'She's floating!' the mate yelped.

'Archie?'

'Aye, she's free of the rocks, and she's managing.' Beneath the telescope, his face was one big grin. He handed the instrument to her and, when her eyes got used to it, she managed to make out the *Pladda* lying well over to starboard. Her deck was at a frightening angle but she was undeniably afloat, lifting and falling on the swell.

The boat wallowed slowly, like a tired whale, in the wake of the tug towing her into Dunoon. The second tug had cast off its line as soon as the *Pladda* was free of the rocks, and had moved close in to help to support her if need be.

'Jamesie, get some more cocoa on the go,' Archie ordered the cabin boy as *Sanda* followed the slow procession. 'We could all do with it.'

'We've not got much left,' the lad protested.

'Then we'll have it finished by the time we reach home. I'm sure that the gaffer won't mind paying for extra rations for once,' Archie said with a sideways grin at Morag. 'You might say that, tonight, it's medicinal.'

When *Pladda* had been edged into shallow water and safely moored to the harbour wall, her crew came aboard *Sanda* for the journey back to Port Glasgow.

They were all filthy from head to foot after the hours spent emptying the hold, and so weary that they could scarcely move. Only Wee Malky, proud as a peacock now that he had been involved in a near-tragic accident at sea, had retained some of his enthusiasm for life.

'That damned boiler!' the engineer raged bitterly. 'Could it no' have held out until we were home?'

'You did all you could, Johnno, and more.' Cal put a torn, bleeding hand on the man's shoulder. 'If we'd not had you aboard we might never have made it as far as the Gantocks.'

'What happened?'

'The boiler gave up, and left us drifting and helpless.' Archie and his mate were in the wheelhouse, and the rest of them had crowded into the *Sanda*'s tiny cabin. Cal rested his head against the wall at his back, his face gaunt with exhaustion.

'The boiler gave up entirely just as we passed Toward Point, and the current took us on to the rocks. If the tide had been higher the puffer's shallow draught might have let us float across the reef and off at the other side. But as luck would have it, we scraped over this spur.' Cal winced at the memory. 'It sounded as though it was tearing the boat's hull apart, but it was just a scrape. Then a big wave came from nowhere and lifted us up, then slammed us down again . . .' He threw out his dirty hands in a gesture of helplessness. 'The weight of the gravel in the hold sent the rock right through her timbers.'

'We were stuck there like a winkle on a pin!' Johnno glared at Morag. 'Have I not been saying ever since that time you came tae Brodick with us that the boiler needed attention?'

'I didn't realise that it was as bad as that,' she said

defensively. 'I'd arranged for *Pladda* to go into the yard today.'

'It was my fault, Johnno,' Cal told the man. 'I said we'd be fine for one more trip, and I was wrong. We'll go back over to Dunoon tomorrow morning, you and me, and arrange for temporary repairs so that we can get her over to the yard as soon as possible.'

'We were so close to getting away with it!' he raged the next morning, pacing the office floor. 'If the boiler had held out another half-hour or so we might have made the harbour, or been close enough for someone to tow us in. And we'd have saved the cargo!'

Morag sat at her desk and watched him. He was cleaner than she had seen him the night before, but just as gaunt. Clearly, he had not slept well.

'At least you're all right.'

He spun round and glared at her. 'Will you never learn how to behave like a boat owner? It's the puffer and the cargo that count, not the crew. If the lot of us had been drowned, you could have replaced us more easily than you'll replace the money you've lost because Arkbridge's gravel's scattered all over the bed of the Clyde now.'

'I could never replace the crew. None of them,' Morag said quietly, but he paid no heed.

'Arkbridge'll get his money back, for he'll be well insured. But the cost of having temporary repairs done to the boat in Dunoon so that she can be towed back . . . and the towing charges themselves, and the repairs. Do you know how much a new boiler costs?'

'I know that we need one, and we'll just have to find the money from somewhere.'

'Why did Arkbridge have to ask us to take on a cargo

this week of all weeks?' Cal stormed. 'Why didn't I listen to Johnno? He's the engineer, for God's sake! I'm only the skipper!'

'Cal . . .'

'If you were a proper owner, you'd turn me off here and now.'

'I can't turn you off. You're a shareholder.'

'So I am!' He spun round towards the desk, his grey eyes alight. 'I could sell my shares to raise the money to repair the boat!'

'You could not!'

'But—'

'I can't afford to buy them from you, and Mr Arkbridge would be sure to put in an offer. D'you want him to gain part ownership of Weir's?' She watched the hope die from his face. 'We'll manage, Cal. The first thing to do is to get *Pladda* back to this side of the river, and into the shipyard. Then it's my job to work out how to pay for her repairs.'

When Cal had gone off to Dunoon with Johnno to assess the damage and arrange for temporary work to be carried out on the puffer, she put aside her pen and went downstairs and out on to the stone platform at the door. The weather, contrary as always, had improved. The storms which had made *Pladda*'s rescue so difficult the day before had given way to sunshine and clear skies as blue and serene as the eyes with which Lady Isabella surveyed the harbour.

Morag, who had had little sleep herself the night before, stroked the figurehead's cheek and wondered if Alicia Tollin had fallen in love while watching Lady Isabella come into being beneath Matthew Fergusson's skilled hands. Had she fallen in love gradually, through friendship and understanding, or had it been a sudden, burning passion? And how long had it been before she and Matthew spoke to each other of their feelings?

If, indeed, they ever had . . . Perhaps they been silenced by the immovable barrier of Matthew's marriage. Perhaps he never knew of her feelings until she left him the business. And perhaps she never knew of his.

It was a sad thought.

23

The kitchen at Ardgowan Street was crowded, as usual, but this time none of the menfolk were present, for tonight was for the women.

Danny Hastie had been given tenancy of a small flat in Bouverie Street, a few closes away from his father's house, and he and Wilma had set the date for their wedding. She had asked both Morag and Grace to be her bridesmaids, and had found a capable seamstress willing to make dresses for the three of them.

Wilma had been gathering fashion magazines for weeks and now the time had come for the three of them to choose their bridal outfits, assisted by Mags, Mhairi and both Wilma's sisters-in-law, each with her children.

The young couple had agreed to follow the old Scottish tradition of marrying on Hogmanay, the final day of the year, so that they could start the new year and their new life at the same time. Because of the time of year Wilma had set aside the idea of a traditional gown, settling instead for fine woollen dresses or costumes for herself and her two attendants.

'With lots of warm underwear,' she said, turning pages busily. 'It's strange how you always dream about wearing a long dress and a veil, and getting wed in a big church full of flowers and top-hats and everything. Then when it comes down to it none of that seems to matter any more.'

'It's love that does it, hen,' her mother told her. 'Nature's way of cheatin' women. It's just the same way with havin' bairns. When the first one comes you swear you'll never go through that again, then a year later there you are, screamin' your head off, and the midwife scurryin' up the stairs with her wee bag. And in between the screams you're beginnin' tae realise that it'll be the same every year.'

Her two daughters-in-law nodded nostalgic agreement, but Wilma said firmly, 'It won't be like that for me and Danny. We'll have things different.'

'And me and Archie,' Mhairi backed her up. All three married women in the room looked at each other and nodded, this time agreeing to some comment heard by nobody but themselves.

Choosing wedding clothes proved to be a long and difficult process. Each of them had her own ideas, and it didn't help when the toddlers discovered the joys of tearing up Wilma's precious fashion magazines and then handing the resultant shreds to the babies, who immediately tried to eat them. But progress was made, and by the time the men came noisily up the stairs – looking for sustenance and ready, when they had eaten, to take their families home – Wilma had settled on a low-waisted long-sleeved dress which would be worn beneath a still-smart fur jacket that had belonged to Georgina. It was decided that Grace and Morag were to have straight-cut dresses, also long-sleeved, with bolero jackets.

'We'll not be out in the cold for long,' Morag pointed out. Her suggestion that there should be two wedding receptions, the first at Lilybank after the church service and the second in Ardgowan Street for the neighbours, had been agreed on.

When the three of them had arranged to go to Glasgow on the following Saturday to buy material and choose hats, Wilma announced that she was walking both Grace and Morag home. Mhairi was walking Archie home, so they all went down the stairs together and parted company at the close mouth.

'Now she'll walk the fifty yards to his close, and they'll have a cuddle,' Wilma said as her brother and his sweetheart, closely linked, disappeared into the night. 'Then he'll walk her back, and they'll go on like that until Mam sends one of the lads down to walk the two of them home and put an end to it. They make such fools of themselves,' she added witheringly.

'And what's your reason for coming out with us?' Morag wanted to know, and Wilma laughed.

'I just wanted to get away from all that noise for a wee while.' She moved to walk between them, linking arms. Morag was reminded of the times she had longed to walk like that with friends, arm-in-arm and stretched across the width of the pavement. It was every bit as enjoyable as she had imagined. They were approaching the chip shop, and the smell wafting from its open door was mouth-watering.

'Let's buy chips,' she suggested on an impulse. Wilma agreed at once, but Grace was dubious.

'I'm not really hungry. Your mother makes such lovely scones, Wilma.'

'Chip-shop chips,' her future sister-in-law told her firmly, 'have nothing to do with being hungry. Come on!' She swept into the shop with Morag hot on her heels, leaving Grace with no option but to follow them.

*   *   *

'Danny frets about her,' Wilma said as they left Grace, who had done full justice to her bag of chips, at Bouverie Street. 'He's worried that when he's not there to look after her, the old man'll bully the poor girl and turn her into a skivvy.'

'He wouldn't lift his hand to her, would he?'

'Not as far as I know, but men can often be violent just by shouting and that one's a natural bully. Not that he'll ever get the chance to bully me, or Grace or my Danny, while I'm around to stop it!' she added pugnaciously. Then, on an anxious note, 'You don't mind her being my bridesmaid too, do you?'

'Of course not, why should I?'

'I always meant you to be my bridesmaid, and our Daisy of course. But now that she's not here, I thought it would be right to ask Grace.'

'I like her. She's a wonderful housekeeper.'

'Danny says she's been a lot more confident since she started working for you. If she could just find a nice man of her own . . .'

It was like old times, Morag thought. The two of them walking through the dark evening, with Wilma's voice rattling away.

'Seemingly Grace was nearly engaged at one time to a friend of Danny's, but Bill Hastie made all sorts of trouble for them. The lad went away, and Grace's heart was broken. Danny's blamed himself ever since for not having stood up to his father at the time. Talking about folk settling down, you and Aidan Grieve have been walking out together for a long time.'

'Only for companionship.'

'D'you care for him?'

'I'm too busy to bother with romance just now.'

'When you've got the time, d'you think it might be him?' Wilma persisted.

'No.'

'Why not?'

'Because he's . . .' Morag hesitated, then said slowly, 'He's not exciting enough.'

'You're not getting any younger, you know. You don't want to end up on the shelf.'

'Why not? It suits Camellia Ogilvie. She's thinking of coming over for a week or so before Christmas,' Morag said, happy to change the subject.

They had reached Chapelton Street, where they usually parted to go their separate ways. Wilma lingered, peering into the darkness, as though reluctant to go home.

'Would you like to come to Lilybank Road for a wee while?'

'No, no. They'll probably have taken the bairns home,' Wilma said. 'There's times when all that noise wears me out. I sometimes wonder why I'm rushing into marriage when I know fine that it'll only mean me ending up with a houseful of noisy bairns of my own.'

'There's still time to change your mind.'

'Oh, no! Now that I've found Danny, I'm not going to let anyone else have him but me. Isn't life strange, Morag? Not fifteen months ago I wouldn't even have thought of going out with that man, and now I want him so badly that I'd walk down the aisle in an old sack if I had to, just to get him.'

'You won't need to wear an old sack. You're going to look lovely in that dress you've chosen.'

Wilma's face lit up at the thought of it. 'I just hope Danny likes it!'

'Danny,' Morag assured her, 'would think you looked beautiful in an old sack.'

Boots clattered along the pavement towards them,

and Morag peered in the direction of the sound. 'It's your Danny.'

'Is it? I thought he was at a rowing-club meeting tonight.'

Danny came to a halt beside them. 'Sorry I'm late,' he said breathlessly. 'The talking went on longer than I thought. Can we walk you home, Morag?'

'No, I'm fine. You just see Wilma back to her house. That's why you're here, isn't it?' Morag said. 'If you hurry, you might catch up with Archie and Mhairi, making fools of themselves.'

As they parted, Wilma had the grace to look embarrassed.

Pladda's new boiler was going to take all the money Morag could scrape together.

'We'll have to hope for a mild winter, and use the other four boats as often as we can,' Cal said grimly. 'With five crews, we can work the boats hard.'

They were both at the office desk, poring over the order books and trying to find ways to cut costs.

'We'll manage.' Morag spoke with an optimism she didn't really feel. 'With any luck, Arkbridge's will give us more—'

Hobnailed boots thundered up the staircase and a shrill voice screamed Cal's name.

'What now?' He began to get to his feet as the door was thrown open with such force that it rebounded off the wall, swung back and came perilously close to hitting Wee Malky as he came hurtling in through the aperture.

'There's men on the harbour,' he bawled, sidestepping deftly so that the door swept past his back with less than an inch to spare, 'layin' intae Archie Beckett!'

'What men?'

The boy danced up and down with impatience. 'Come on! They're goin' tae kill him, and mebbe my faither tae if ye don't stop them!' he screeched, then almost fell over backwards as Cal swept round the desk, his chair toppling as he kicked it aside.

As man and boy disappeared out of the door Morag dropped her pen, heedless of the huge ink blot that splashed from the loaded nib on to the neatly written columns of weights, pounds, shillings and pence, and ran after them.

She reached the office entrance in time to see Cal charging across the flagstones towards a knot of struggling men swaying back and forth across the harbour, dangerously close to the edge. A group of onlookers – dockers, puffer crews, lorry drivers and the others, mainly elderly men retired from their work on or by the water, who were to be found lingering on the harbour at any time of the day – was already gathering to cheer on the combatants.

Cal threw himself into the mêlée and without any hesitation Wee Malky, close on his heels, followed suit. The lad reappeared almost immediately, soaring into the air as though he had been spat out. He landed on his back, then rolled immediately on to his hands and knees. As soon as he was back on his feet again he attempted another lunge, but fortunately one of the bystanders stepped forward to clamp a big hand on the collar of his jacket and hold him back.

'Let me go!' Morag heard the lad yell as he pummelled furiously at the air. 'They'll kill my faither!'

'They'll kill you an' all, son,' his captor said, holding on. 'Yer faither'll manage fine without ye.'

The fight looked, and sounded, vicious, and Morag realised almost at once that this was no scrap among hot-blooded friends but a serious fight with the combatants hellbent on hurting each other. The thud of bare fists landing on faces and bodies, the roars and gasps and grunts of men either venting their rage or responding to a well-landed, painful blow, were sickening to hear. Sparks flew from hobnailed boots scrabbling for purchase on the flagstones and now and again a face, white against the bright blood trickling from nose or mouth, flashed into view then disappeared again.

'Stop them!' she appealed to the crowd, but nobody had any intention of doing such a thing. A fight was one of the best forms of entertainment in their book and she could tell by the blood-lust in some of their faces that, to them, this one looked as though it was going to be well worth seeing.

Archie seemed to be in the thick of it; several men Morag didn't recognise were concentrating on him, while Cal and Big Malky and the mate and engineer from *Sanda* tried to reach him.

His boat, just in from a trip to Millport, had commenced making preparations for unloading before the trouble arose. Her deck winch was rigged and half of her hatch cover had been removed. Her cabin boy was jumping up and down on the other half, punching at the air, screeching at the top of his voice as he cheered his fellow crewmen on, seemingly oblivious to the fact that he was in imminent danger of bouncing too close to the open hatch and falling in.

'What in the name of God is going on here?'

Morag turned to see Lawrence Weir by her side, staring at the mêlée with open disgust and revulsion.

'It's . . . some men seem to be after Archie.' She cursed at the ill-luck which had caused him to appear at the wrong time yet again.

'You mean that these are Weir employees?'

'Some of them. Cal's sorting it out,' she said in a feeble attempt to minimise the brawl taking place before their eyes.

Just then Cal came hurtling out from the mad tangle of arms and legs and bodies, much as Wee Malky had earlier. He sprawled on his side for a moment, winded, then wheezed, coughed, spat out a bright red mass and began to struggle to his feet. Several men in the crowd helpfully dragged him upright and pushed him back into the fight, slapping him on the back and roaring encouragement as he disappeared, fists flailing. His face was bloody, and one sleeve had almost been ripped from his jacket.

'I'd not call that disgraceful display sorting things out!' Lawrence's face was a mask of disapproval, and his fingers caught at his daughter's arm. 'I'd call it sheer hooliganism – and Fergusson's as bad as the rest! Come away, Morag, this is no place for you or me!'

'I can't leave them like this!'

'Will you do as you're told for once!'

Just then Archie went down under a vicious onslaught. Peering through the mêlée of shifting, struggling legs, Morag saw that he had curled up into a ball with arms wrapped over his head to protect it as heavy boots thudded into his back and ribs. The force of the blows sent waves of nausea through her.

'Make them stop!' She pulled away from her father and flew at an older man, a former seaman she knew well by sight. 'Please, make them stop. They'll kill each other!'

'Lassie, it's more than my own life's worth tae get intae that. Let them fight it out, there's nothin' else for it.'

'You heard what he said, Morag. Leave them to their fighting.' Lawrence grabbed her arm again and this time he managed to swing her round, away from the group struggling by the harbour's edge. And there was Mhairi, who always came to meet Archie at the harbour if she could, hurrying towards them.

'What's happening?'

'Just a bunch of hooligans enjoying themselves,' Lawrence told her shortly. 'You'd better come with us, my dear, this is no place for—'

'Archie?' As Mhairi, ignoring Lawrence's outstretched hand, ran towards the struggling mass, a burly man with a shock of red hair tore free of the others and rushed to intercept her. He caught hold of her arm and began to pull her along the harbour to where a fishing boat was moored at the end – out of sight, Morag now realised, of any puffer coming into port.

Mhairi resisted, kicking at him and hitting out with the clutch bag she carried. 'Let go of me, Hamish! Let go, I said!'

'Oh, my God!' Lawrence yelped. 'Morag, will you come away at once!'

Bellowing, Archie Beckett erupted from the tangle of limbs and bodies and began to run towards his beloved and her abductor, scattering droplets of bright blood on the flagstones as he went. Several others immediately went in pursuit of him, followed by Cal and the rest of the Weir men.

Because Archie was limping badly, he was caught before he had reached Mhairi and the struggle began again, only this time several yards further down the harbour. The onlookers, their ranks swelling with every minute that passed, hurried to regroup nearer the action. Mhairi made a massive effort to break away from her captor and reach Archie, but the red-headed man held on, enduring the kicks and blows she rained on him.

Behind Morag, a whistle shrilled and voices yelled

289

out. A blue-clad figure rushed past, then another and another. The police had arrived, and the fight was over.

Most of the Weir employees spent that night in the local prison cells, together with the four Islay men who had sailed down to wreak vengeance on Archie Beckett for stealing one of their women.

After a sleepless night, dominated by the terrible sound of blows and kicks landing on human flesh and bones, and the memory of the bruised and bleeding figures led away by the police, Morag attended the police court on the following morning. Astonishingly, no lasting damage had been done to any of the men, who made a sorry, battered sight in the dock. Islanders and locals alike pleaded guilty and were made to endure a robust scolding from the magistrate, followed by a crisp order to keep the peace from then on. After that, they were all fined.

When Morag had paid all the fines, Hamish and his friends set sail back to Islay after shaking hands with the men they had been trying to kill only hours before. Honour had been satisfied, and the red-headed fisherman had accepted that Mhairi's heart was now set on Archie and a future in Port Glasgow.

The Weir employees then had to suffer a further tongue-lashing, this time from their irate employer. When Morag finally allowed them to go home to clean themselves up, she ordered Archie, the cause of the trouble, and Cal – who had, without being officially promoted, become the men's supervisor – to stay behind.

'It's hard to believe that there were only four of them,' she said icily. 'They were outnumbered, for there were five Port Glasgow men.'

'Aye, well, the islanders had drink in them and that made them more dangerous,' Archie mumbled through a painful jaw. 'Anyway, we were given no time tae count heads and arrange a fairer fight just tae please you.'

'You mind your tongue!' Cal admonished him sharply. He too mumbled, although in his case it wasn't his jaw that pained him but a swollen lip and a huge bruise that spread over the lower left area of his face. Someone had stuck a strip of plaster over a cut just below his hairline. Both men were a sorry sight, their faces swollen here and there and covered with black, yellow, blue and purple bruising. Morag might have felt sorry for them if she hadn't been so angry.

'It wasnae my fault, but!' Archie protested. 'I just brought the wee boat into harbour and started gettin' ready tae unload, mindin' my own business. And the next thing I knew I'd been dragged ashore, and I was down on the ground being kicked tae bits. By four men, and me on my lone!' he added, squinting at Morag from his one good eye to make sure that she understood the point he was making.

'Heaven only knows what my father's going to say now,' she fretted when Archie had gone. 'He'll blame me.'

'How can he? You weren't to know that the Islay men were going to arrive. And the fight was all because of Archie.' One of Cal's eyes was closed and the knuckles on his right hand, she noticed, were split and swollen. He moved carefully, and she guessed that his body was a mass of bruises.

'I employ him. And I promoted him against my father's wishes.'

'You're too quick to take the blame,' he told her. 'It's more my fault than yours that it got bad enough

291

for the police to get involved. I was supposed to be trying to put a stop to it.'

'I didn't see much evidence of that, Cal Fergusson.'

'I'll admit that there's something exhilarating about a good fight.' He began to grin, then winced and clapped a hand to his painful mouth. 'It's been a while since I had one,' he mumbled through the undamaged side. 'There's one good thing, though. The Islay men have settled their score with Archie, so our boats can go back to the island.'

'Not the *Sanda*, though.'

'Her as well. I told you, the score's all settled.'

'I'll never be able to understand the way men's brains work! If they work at all,' said Morag, thoroughly exasperated.

There was little use in trying to reprimand Archie for the fight, Morag thought that evening in his mother's house, for everyone else insisted on treating him like a hero. Tonight he was sitting in the best armchair, with Mhairi perched uncomfortably on the arm fussing over him.

'It was a cowardly thing that Hamish did, and I'm right ashamed of him!' the girl said, stroking her sweetheart's hair gently.

'I cannae blame the man. I'd do the same if someone took you from me,' Archie said magnanimously, then yelped as Mhairi gave him a loving hug. His mother shook her head.

'What would ye do with him, Morag lass? Fighting one minute and charming the heart out of a woman the next.'

'It's romantic, right enough. I've never had a man fighting over me,' Wilma said wistfully.

'Don't you go trying to provoke Danny into a fight,' Morag warned her. 'It's not romantic at all, it's barbaric!'

Archie gave her an endearingly lopsided smile. In Ardgowan Street, she was no longer his employer but merely his sister's best friend.

'It's no' barbaric at all if you're a man, Morag,' he pointed out pityingly. 'It's a way of life.'

24

'Are you alone?' Lawrence Weir asked as soon as his daughter answered the door.

'No . . . parties?' Margaret's eyes searched the hall apprehensively.

'I'm expecting Cal Fergusson in half an hour or so on a matter of business.' Morag stepped back and opened the door wide. As they came into the hall, their grim faces made her uneasy. It was all very well for Cal to tell her that she had no reason to feel guilty; she wished that he was there to support her.

'We apologise for having arrived unannounced, Morag,' Lawrence said stiffly as he helped his wife off with her coat, 'but there are important matters to be discussed, and they can't wait any longer. I had hoped that you would have come to speak to us by now, instead of waiting for us to visit you.'

He held out Margaret's coat, then his own hat and cane. Morag put them on the hat-stand, trying not to be reminded of the days when, in his eyes, she had been merely Sander's housekeeper.

'Why should you think that?' She led the way to the parlour. 'You'll have a cup of tea?'

They both refused, and Margaret seated herself by the fire while her husband remained on his feet. 'I had hoped for an explanation of that disgraceful scene on the harbour – and a discussion over what's to be done about it.'

'There was nothing to discuss. The matter was settled and the fines paid. Fortunately, nobody was seriously hurt, and now the Islay fishermen are home and the others back at work.'

'Exactly!' Margaret pounced. 'The others are all still working for Weir's, including Archie Beckett. You've not dismissed him yet.'

'Why should I dismiss him?'

'Because he was the ringleader,' Lawrence said, as though speaking to a particularly stupid child. 'Weir's cannot be seen to be employing a trouble-maker like him. I don't know what Sander would say if he knew.'

'He'd say that it would be wrong to dismiss a good, hard-working skipper. Archie's not a trouble-maker; he simply fell foul of the man his girl-friend was going to marry.'

'There you are, then.' Margaret nodded at her husband. 'He stole someone else's future wife. You can't deny it, for the story's all over Port Glasgow. Your father's heard about it I don't know how many times in the shop.'

'And it was all over the local papers! Weir employees in court! How can I hold up my head in the town with my name spread all over the newspapers?'

'It's my name too, Father, and I have no difficulty in holding up my head. Court cases appear every week in the local paper. Folk read them, then forget about them at once. If it's the ladies who frequent the shop you're worried about,' Morag added, unwisely, 'you can be sure that they've forgotten the stain on your name already, since most of them are only silly, empty-headed gossips. They'll have found something else to turn over by now, like cats round a dustbin.'

'Well!' Margaret said on an outraged gust of breath, while her husband turned puce.

'Insulting my customers will not cover up your problems, Morag. Didn't I advise you not to give Beckett control of the *Sanda*? Didn't I? And John Laird was against the whole idea too.'

'John Laird—' Morag began, but her father talked her down.

'His mistakes are over and done with, and he's not the issue under discussion here. It's Archie Beckett we're talking about! You promoted that young rascal beyond his station against all the sound advice you were offered. You gave him an inflated idea of his own importance. And now see what's come of it!'

'Archie's neither a criminal nor a hooligan.'

'He's a bad influence, and an example must be made of him if you don't want the rest of them to go to the dogs as well! The last time your step-mother and I called at this house it was Archie Beckett who opened the door to us, wasn't it? Drunk as a lord! And there was a rowdy party going on!'

Margaret had brought out a little lace handkerchief from her bag. She pressed it against her nose, then said, 'We were both shocked, Morag.'

'Indeed we were. Goodness only knows what your neighbours must have been thinking!'

'The neighbours haven't complained, nor have I given them any reason to. And the party was not rowdy. I was entertaining friends.'

'Friends! You never used to have friends like these!'

Margaret made a determined effort to change tack. 'It's difficult for a woman to run a man's business, Morag,' she sympathised. 'Sander should never have burdened you with it. It's not your fault if the men got out of hand.'

'They did not get out of hand,' Morag protested. A dull headache was beginning to niggle behind her eyes. 'A group of fishermen from Islay came to settle a personal grievance with Archie, and they just happened to find him down at the harbour.'

'Are you trying to tell me that it was the fishermen that started it all?' Lawrence asked in disbelief. 'When everyone knows that puffer men are enlisted from the riff-raff to be found on every harbour—'

'That is not true!' Morag's temper snapped. 'They're decent hard-working men who take their lives in their hands every time they go out on the water!'

Lawrence gave a short, sneering laugh. 'You're far too soft, just like Sander. You take after him more than me.'

'That's scarcely surprising, since he was the one who raised me,' Morag retorted, earning another furious gasp from her step-mother.

'Don't upset yourself, Margaret,' Lawrence ordered his wife. 'Morag, as a shareholder in Weir Shipping, I'm telling you that I want Archie Beckett dismissed first thing tomorrow morning!'

'And as the major shareholder, Father, I'm telling you that I'll do no such thing.'

'Very well, you leave me no alternative but to sell my shares.'

'What?' This was the last thing she had expected.

'You have brought Weir Shipping into disrepute, and I want nothing more to do with it. I wash my hands of the business.' Lawrence Weir plucked his wife from her chair. 'Come along, Margaret. Good night, Morag.'

'Father . . .' She followed them out into the hall, where he was already bundling Margaret into her coat.

'You still have time, Morag, to agree to my suggestion.'

'And dismiss Archie? I'll not do that, but surely—'

'Then there is nothing more to say. Under the terms of my brother's will, you have the right to buy the shares from me at an agreed price within ten days. If you cannot, or will not, buy them, then I am free to sell to the highest bidder. You can tell your young lawyer friend' – there was angry emphasis on the last word – 'that I shall expect to hear from him tomorrow morning. The matter is one of urgency. Good night.'

He snatched up his hat and cane and threw open the front door. Cal Fergusson, standing on the top step and about to ring the doorbell, blinked in the sudden dazzle of electric light spilling through the open door, then was forced to move nimbly aside as the Weirs left without a look or a word.

'What's happened?' Cal wanted to know as the gate clashed shut at Lawrence's back and he and his wife stormed off along the road.

'Just my father being difficult.' Morag tried a short laugh, but failed.

'There's more to it than that,' he insisted as he followed her into the kitchen. 'What has he said to upset you?'

She sat down heavily in a chair at the table, suddenly too tired to remain on her feet.

'He's selling his shares in Weir Shipping.'

'Selling up?' Without asking permission, he filled the kettle and lit the gas stove; then he turned, leaning the small of his back against the sink, to look down at her. The marks of the fight were beginning to fade; his eye had almost fully opened again, the cut on his forehead was merely a red line and the bruises a delicate pattern of lilac and pale yellow. 'I can't believe he'd do that!'

'It's a punishment for refusing to dismiss Archie.'

'Because of the fight? It's short-sighted of him, for Weir's is going to do well once we get past this bad patch.'

'Short-sighted or not, he means it . . . Under the terms of my uncle's will, we have the right to buy his shares at a reasonable price.' An uncomfortable lump was forming in her throat, making it difficult to speak, but she swallowed it down and soldiered on. 'But if we don't, or can't, make an acceptable offer within ten days he can sell them on the open market.'

'And Arkbridge will be able to buy them. You can't allow that to happen!'

'I don't see how I can stop it. What little surplus money we have has gone into paying for *Pladda*'s new boi . . . boil . . .'

The lump returned, dissolving into a warm softness even as it rose up behind her eyes, which started prickling. She put her hands to her face in an attempt to force back the tears, hating herself for her weakness. But they came anyway, spilling through her fingers and running down the backs of her hands. She got up abruptly and began to blunder towards the door, but Cal intercepted her.

'Don't, Morag. Please don't,' she heard him say above her head. But the concern in his voice was too much. Everything slid beyond her control, leaving her with no other option but to lean against his jacket, which smelled of fresh salt air, and let the tears flow.

His arms closed about her, rocking her slightly in a

way that reminded her of the few treasured occasions when Georgina had taken her on her knee as a little girl. The sensation was immensely comforting.

There was little she could do to stop the tears. They flowed as though some natural spring deep inside her had suddenly been uncapped. It had been instilled in her throughout childhood, first by her mother and then by Georgina, that little girls never cried. It was a belief she had held on to but now, for the first time, she wept for the loss of her mother, and her father, and Georgina and Sander.

Finally, the tears slowed and stopped. Cal, still holding her with one arm, produced a handkerchief from his pocket and mopped her face gently.

'Better?'

She nodded, summoning a watery smile. 'I thought I was never going to dry up.'

'You'd a lot of grief and worry to get rid of. I keep telling you that you expect too much of yourself at times, Morag Weir,' he scolded gently.

'And look what you get in return for your kindness. I've soaked your jacket. And my face must be all swollen.' It felt twice its usual size, her eyes and cheeks stinging.

'The jacket'll dry. And you look . . .' Cal began, then stopped and bent to her.

As his mouth took and held hers, something as deep down as the spring from which the tears had come opened like a flower bursting from dark cold earth. Of their own volition, Morag's hands slid up over his chest to clasp around his neck.

His own embrace tightened in response until she was on tiptoe, being held close, yet hungering to move closer, then closer still.

When the kiss finally ended and he said her name, she

shook her head impatiently. Words could only destroy what they were sharing.

He buried his face in her hair, then his lips began to trace a path over her temple, the lobe of one ear, down the line of her jaw and over the corner of her mouth to her throat. His hair was thick and soft against her face, and he murmured inarticulate pleasure as her fingertips found and caressed the nape of his neck. Something – she realised later that it was the kitchen sink, of all things! – pressed into her spine and acted as a support, allowing her to lean back, drawing him with her.

When he lifted his head and she felt his gaze on her face, she pulled him close again in an attempt to hold fast to this unknown but wonderful world they had entered, and to her relief he responded, one hand drawing her head down to nestle in the hollow of his throat. His skin there was surprisingly smooth and silky against her mouth when she kissed it, and it left a salty tang on the tip of her tongue. The intensity of the sensation brought a new, even stronger yearning pulsing through her, and when he tipped her face up again and claimed her lips with his she responded fiercely, opening her mouth to him.

They clung, kissed, moved against and with each other. Their interlocked figures, reflected in the darkened window, swayed in a dance newly choreographed just for them. Her fingertips traced the scar below his tumbling brown hair and her mouth slid over the slight puffiness beneath his wounded eye, then followed the outlines of his bruises. She lifted one hand to her lips and kissed the healing grazes on his knuckles, one by one.

Then suddenly it was over. Cal's arms fell away from her, and he stepped back.

'I'm . . . I'm sorry.'

Morag looked up at him, dazed. He was moving away from her, smoothing down his hair. His breathing, and hers, sounded loud and ragged in the quiet room. When he said, 'I'm sorry,' again, his voice was shaking. 'I'd no right . . .'

'Cal . . .' She didn't know what she had done to offend him.

'I took advantage of you when you were upset. It was a . . . a terrible mistake.' He turned away from her, pulling his jacket straight. She saw him through a mist, and thought for a dreadful minute that she was about to faint. Then she realised that the neglected kettle had been boiling for some time, filling the kitchen with steam.

Turning off the gas and checking to make sure that the kettle hadn't boiled itself dry gave her an excuse to turn her back on him for a moment. Passion was driven out by embarrassment. 'It was a mistake,' he had said. Only a mistake.

It took all the strength she could muster to face him and say, 'It was my fault as much as yours. We'll say no more about it.'

When she had seen him to the front door, she returned to the kitchen and washed her face with cold water at the sink, rubbing hard to remove his kisses. Then she rinsed her mouth, trying not to remember how, only moments before, his tongue had teased hers into unbearably sweet intimacy.

A mistake . . . She dried her face, then dried it again. Finally, she gave up and let the shamed tears lie on her cheeks. It seemed to be her night for crying.

Instead of turning towards his home when he left Lilybank Road, Cal Fergusson went the other way, walking uphill fast with fists jammed tightly into his jacket pockets. The street-lamps ended, then the last of the few houses on the fringe of the town fell away behind him and he was out into darkness, putting one foot before the other, wishing that he could just keep walking until Port Glasgow and everything and everybody in it disappeared behind him for ever.

But the thing that he was really trying to walk away from refused to be left behind, and he knew that it would follow him and stay with him wherever he might go. As he left the road and struck out across grass he groaned aloud, tormented by the memory of Morag's body in his arms, her mouth soft and silky against his hand as she kissed his bruised fingers.

Over and over again, he damned her fool of a father for upsetting her as he had – and for choosing to do it just as Cal was about to arrive on the scene. And he damned himself, too. He should have mopped her face when the tears were over and made her that cup of tea. Then he should have helped her to think of a way to buy the shares. And then he should have wished her a good night and gone home.

Aidan Grieve would no doubt have done all the right things, he thought bitterly. Aidan never seemed to put a foot wrong, whereas Cal Fergusson jumped right in, almost eager to make a fool of himself and ruin the friendship that he and Morag had built up between them. Hadn't her uncle advised her to lean on him for help and advice? Hadn't the man said that Cal Fergusson would not let her fall? He had been proud, when she told him, to know that the old man had thought so well of him. He had been determined not to betray Sander's memory, or Sander's niece.

But what in God's name, he asked himself, would Sander Weir think of him now?

He gave another anguished groan as he reached the top of the hill. On one side lay dark moorland; on the other, the town's street lights and house lights spilled down to the river, calm and dark beneath a clouded sky. The night was clear enough for him to see the great shipyard cranes along its bank etched against the water like faint scribbles from a child's pencil.

Cal sat down on a rock, elbows on knees and fists locked together, and envied the Clyde. It knew where it belonged, where it came from and where it was going. It allowed itself to be used, but never to be dominated. If at any time it should take a notion to go where it had never been before it would do so, steadily and with purpose. Whereas he . . .

His mother came into his mind, not the elegant, gracious and remote woman she had been before his father lost all their money, but old and bitter as he had known her best. As a child he had been looked after by a nursemaid because his parents were both too busy with their lives, and with each other, to have much time for him. Later, when he was all that Janet Fergusson had, the graciousness had gone. Her voice was a harsh whine, her face hard. She had been eaten up with hatred for Sander Weir and his family, and Cal's attempts to explain that Sander had not stolen the company but rescued it were brushed aside.

When Sander offered him work, he had accepted because it was what he wanted to do. His mother had been furious at first; then, to his dismay, she had begun to talk of ways in which he could worm his way into Sander Weir's confidence and regain the company.

'Sander Weir's a fool, everyone knows that,' she had said over and over again, her thin, once beringed fingers twisting at the long filmy scarves she always wore. 'And that girl's not even Sander's. He and his wife only took her in because his brother didn't want her. But he thinks well of you, Calum.' Her eyes always glowed at this point, and her fingers began to tie the scarf into knots. 'If the man comes to rely on you, then perhaps . . .'

He had steadfastly ignored her continual plotting, and had thought it a mercy that she was dead by the time Morag inherited the company. Otherwise, he knew, she would have seen marriage between himself and Morag as the answer to her plans for him. Marriage with Morag Weir had therefore become the last thing Cal wanted, but despite himself he had come to love her over the past fifteen months, not for what she had but for what she was.

It had started with admiration at the way she had looked after the ailing, widowed man she had looked on as her father, trotting uncomplainingly between the house and the harbour office at his bidding, weighed down with heavy ledgers. And then he had admired the way in which, despite her apparent meekness, she had found the courage to defy her acquisitive father when he tried to wrest the shipping business from her.

Then had come the shared pleasure of uncovering the story of Matthew Fergusson and Alicia Tollin, and the less pleasant business of John Laird's deceit. Watching Morag not only take charge of the office but show an interest in the puffers and their crews to the point of going out on the boats herself, Cal's admiration had grown.

He hadn't even realised that it had ripened into love until one afternoon when Aidan Grieve had called at the harbour in his smart car to take her off on some outing. Seeing them together – seeing the young lawyer kissing Morag lightly on the cheek, handing her possessively into his car, saying something that made her laugh –

had almost set him afire with envy. Shaken, he had forced himself to deny the truth. In his view, he and Morag Weir would never be right for each other.

But the sight of her face upturned to his that evening, her brown eyes with the sparkling tears making them look like moorland pools in sunlight, had been too much. The girl nobody had wanted was now the woman he wanted more than anything else in the world. And like a fool he had given in to his own desires, betraying them both and putting Morag in particular into an impossible situation.

'She responded,' a small voice whispered in his head. 'She didn't try to fight you off.' But that was because she was vulnerable. Like him, she had nobody; Lawrence Weir didn't count, and never had. She had been upset and worried, and in a state where she would have responded to any man who had wished to take advantage of her . . .

He yelled his anger and self-disgust aloud to the night, and some nocturnal winged hunter called out in response, a lost and lonely sound which suited Cal's own feelings.

The clock in a church tower chimed and he got up, stiff now with cold, and began slowly and reluctantly to descend the hill.

Morag had said that they would say no more about what had happened, and that was the only thing to do. Weir Shipping was in trouble, and they would have to go on working together in the company's best interests.

Later, when business had improved, he would leave Port Glasgow and start anew somewhere else.

25

'I know that business is bad all through the country and that people are being laid off from the shipyards,' Morag said despondently, 'but there's more to it than that.'

'You're wrong,' Aidan told her. 'Weir's is small, but it's a well-known firm. The bank managers told you that, time and time again. If they had the money to lend, they'd be happy to entrust it to you.'

'They'd find it if my uncle was still running the company, or even if my father was in charge. Mebbe I should start wearing a suit instead of a skirt, and smoking cigars!'

He began to laugh, and she glared at him. 'I'm serious, Aidan! They're reluctant to lend me money because they don't think a woman should run a shipping company. They don't trust me.'

'Even if you do manage to borrow enough to buy those shares from your father, you'd have nothing left and a loan to repay. You'd be in a very precarious position.'

'Only until we start building up the revenue again.' It was almost the first thing Cal Fergusson had said since the meeting began. 'We can do it.'

'I'm not sure that Morag can afford to take that

EVELYN HOOD

chance,' Aidan told him crisply. 'Morag, as your lawyer
it's only right that I ask you to consider selling out.'
Cal came upright in his chair, but it was Morag who
said, sharply, 'No!'
'You've done well.' The three of them were sitting
round Morag's desk; now the lawyer leaned forward,
propping his elbows on the old scarred surface. 'Far
better than anyone expected. You've proved that you
have the ability to do whatever you put your mind to.
Perhaps now's the time to put yourself first, instead of
fretting over the business any longer.' Aidan looked
from one set face to the other, well aware that he was
treading on dangerous ground. 'My uncle and I have
talked the matter over, and he agrees with me that you
should consider selling while the business is a going
concern. Between the proceeds and your income from
your uncle's estate, you'd be comfortably off. You'd
even have enough capital to start a new business, if
that's what you want.'
'Something better suited to me, like a sweet-shop or
a coffee house?' she asked, and he flushed at the cool
edge to her voice.
'There's nothing wrong with catering to the needs of
the public.'
'I'm already doing that, Aidan, and I like what I
do.'
'When you mention selling,' Cal asked, 'd'you have
a buyer in mind?'
Aidan shifted in his chair. 'We've already had an
indication of interest . . .'
'From Arkbridge,' Morag said flatly.
'They've only made an informal approach, but I
believe that they would be willing to put in a good
offer if you let it be known that you're interested.'
'Cal?' After the unfortunate episode – as she insisted

308

on calling it in her own mind – in her kitchen a week earlier, she and Cal had found it difficult to talk to each other, or even to look each other in the eye. But with each day that passed it was becoming easier. Morag knew that she needed him – purely as a business partner, of course – and that the sooner they got back on a proper footing the better for Weir's.

Even so, her eyes didn't quite meet his as she turned to him, and he avoided meeting hers when he said, 'I'm opposed to selling out. We can weather this. *Pladda* will be out of the dry dock next week, and if we're willing to ship whatever cargoes we can get to wherever they're needed, we'll manage. Once we've got through the winter, everything will start to go our way.'

Morag nodded, and wished that Aidan had given her that answer.

'How long will my father wait, Aidan?'

'He must give us another four days, but I'm certain that he'll not wait any longer than he must before going elsewhere.'

There was work to be done, and the meeting had reached its useful end. 'I suggest that we all make the most of the next four days,' Morag said. 'Something might turn up.'

'I wish,' Aidan said civilly as the two men went downstairs together, 'that you wouldn't encourage Morag to believe that everything will come right for her, Cal. It's only going to make the final decision all the harder.'

'So you don't believe that she will save the company?' Cal ducked his head slightly as he led the way through the door and out on to the harbour.

'I'm practical enough to recognise that she has no

chance. And to realise that the longer she waits and hopes, the less money she'll get – you'll both get – when she does sell.' Aidan shifted his shabby briefcase from one hand to the other. 'You must realise that yourself.'

'Why don't you buy the shares?'

'Me?'

'You probably have the money – you and your uncle between you, perhaps. Or don't you care for Morag enough to help her out?'

Aidan flushed. 'My feelings for Miss Weir are my business! And as her lawyer, it would be improper for me to invest in her company.'

'But not illegal, surely? It must be possible for you or your uncle to do it somehow. Talk to Mr Dalrymple about it,' Cal urged. 'Ask him what he thinks.'

'I'll . . . consider it.'

'Like hell you will,' Cal murmured softly as he watched the man walk, straight-backed, to his car. Aidan Grieve wasn't going to risk a penny of his money, or his uncle's. And in any case, he wanted Morag to let Weir's go. No doubt he hoped that she would then have more time to devote to him.

Cal gave Lady Isabella a friendly pat on the arm, and thrust his hands in his pockets as he walked across the harbour to where the *Jura* was loading. He missed the river, and couldn't wait to feel the *Pladda*'s deck beneath his feet again. It had been difficult, spending most of his time in the office in close proximity to Morag, now that his stupidity had destroyed their friendship.

George Arkbridge telephoned Morag only an hour after

her meeting with Aidan and Cal, and asked if he might call on her at Lilybank Road that evening.

'Just the two of us. An informal visit, my dear, for an informal discussion.'

Intrigued, she agreed. When she had hung up the receiver, she thought hard for some time before turning to a blank page at the back of the ledger on the desk. She spent a few more minutes deep in thought, then finally began to make notes.

Mr Arkbridge arrived promptly, bearing a bunch of roses.

'In mid-November?' Morag asked, astonished, as he placed the fragrant blossoms in her arms.

'Grown in my own greenhouses. My wife likes to have flowers in the house all the year round, and our gardener is a very clever man. I've got no talents that way myself. No green fingers.'

'Your talent lies in growing money, Mr Arkbridge,' she said, and he gave the booming laugh she remembered from the days when he and his wife were occasionally entertained at Lilybank Road. Georgina had complained, after those evenings, that George Arkbridge's laugh had given her a headache.

'Very good, my dear,' he said. 'I must remember to tell my wife.'

When she returned to the parlour after putting the roses into water, she found him studying the room with approval. 'You've made some changes here. Very nice indeed.'

Over a period of time she and Wilma and Grace had re-curtained the entire house, replaced some of Georgina's heavy, dark furniture with more modern pieces and had the rooms freshly painted and papered.

311

EVELYN HOOD

They had also replaced the oil paintings – which had been on the walls even when Georgina was a little girl – with water-colours in pastel shades.

'Thank you. You'll have some refreshment?'

He glanced at the massive cabinet which still stood against one wall. 'Sander, I seem to mind, kept a very good whisky . . .'

There was still some left. She poured him a generous dram and took a glass of ginger wine for herself; then she prompted, after he had drunk her very good health, 'You wanted an informal discussion?'

'Yes, I did.' He ran his tongue appreciatively round his lips and lifted his glass to the light to admire the whisky's amber richness before leaning back in his chair. 'I was very sorry to hear of the trouble between yourself and your father, my dear. As a family man, I know how important blood bonds are.'

'So you're here because you've heard that my father wants to sell his shares in Weir Shipping.'

He blinked, and gave her a pained look. Clearly, in his world businessmen took their time to get down to the nub of the matter. 'Partly. I was sorry, too, to hear of the problems you've been having with your fleet.'

'*Pladda* will be back in harness next week. I regret the loss of your cargo, but there was nothing we could do to save it.'

He waved the apology aside. 'Don't you worry your pretty little head about that. It was well insured. It's your difficulties I've come to discuss. And the main problem,' he leaned forward in his chair, ready at last to get down to business, 'is that your fleet is too small.'

'We don't have a Weir Shipping Company to call on when we need extra tonnage,' she agreed dryly and he blinked again, startled, then barked out an amused laugh.

312

'Well put! I like your sense of humour. But that's my point exactly. We've been sub-contracting your boats because even though I have a decent-sized fleet, I've more work on my hands than my boats can handle at times. Now I like the Weir boats, and I like their crews. Hard-working and reliable, men and vessels alike. But the problem there is that I never know when you'll be free to carry cargo for me. So,' he finally got to the nub of the matter, 'I've thought of a way round that, while helping you out at the same time.'

He reached into an inner pocket, hesitated, glanced at the recently papered, light-coloured walls and withdrew his hand, empty. Morag, guessing that he had been about to light a cigar, held her tongue. If he had wanted to smoke during their discussion, he should have invited her to his home or his office.

'You were saying, Mr Arkbridge . . . ?'

'Yes.' He cleared his throat and eased himself in his chair. 'Lawrence Weir wants to offload his shares in Weir Shipping, and you can't afford to buy them at the moment because of having to pay for a new boiler for one of your boats. No sense in tiptoeing round the truth, for it's common knowledge that young Grieve has been round the banks trying to raise money, and not getting very far.'

'It's hard to keep a secret in Port Glasgow.' Arkbridge had drained his glass and was looking at it in mild puzzlement, as though wondering where the whisky had gone. Although she had denied him his cigar, Morag was happy to replenish his glass. It gave her the chance to get up and move about the room, pulling her growing anger under control. His condescending attitude was choking her more than the cigar smoke would have done.

'Not so hard, but you have to know how to go about

313

safeguarding your secrets. Thank you, m'dear.' He accepted his drink and waited until she had resumed her seat. 'Now then. I could wait for another week, then pay Lawrence what he wants and become a shareholder in Weir Shipping. But that's the easy way and, as I always counted Sander as one of my closest friends, I'd not want to become involved in any differences his flesh and blood may be experiencing amongst themselves. Instead, I'm willing to give you – not lend, mind, but give – whatever you need to buy your father's shares, and a good sum over and above as a sort of fee for acting as my agent in the matter.'

He sat back in his chair, delighted with himself. 'Then you sign the shares over to me. That way your father's happy and you have your money. I'll set up my eldest lad Patrick as shareholder in your company. He's got a good head on his shoulders, has Patrick; you'll find him an asset. Weir Shipping will carry Arkbridge cargoes, but you'll still be in charge of your own boats and your own office. Here . . .'

He reached into an inside pocket again, and this time he brought out a fat envelope. 'I've written it all out for you. You take twenty-four hours to think it over, and discuss it with young Grieve and your other shareholder. I think they'll tell you that it's a very fair offer, well worth accepting, and I can have the money in your hands within an hour of hearing your decision.'

'Thank you.' Morag accepted the envelope and put it into a drawer of the writing desk. She removed a similar envelope from the drawer and handed it to her visitor. 'And this is yours.'

'What's in it?'

'My proposal.' She sat down again. 'You lend me the money to buy my father's shares, but instead of signing them over to you I retain them for a year. At the end of that time I repay your loan with generous interest or, if I'm unable to do that, I give you the shares, which as you know come to 25 per cent of the business. I also give you 30 per cent of my own shares, free of charge. This means that in a year's time you either gain a very good return on your loan, or you become the major shareholder in Weir Shipping.'

George Arkbridge had been blinking furiously as he tried to take it all in.

'When you've had time to read through my proposal, Mr Arkbridge, I think that you will find it very fair. If I fail to repay your loan, you will end up with 55 per cent of the Weir shares. As Cal Fergusson already owns 20 per cent, and I will hold 25 per cent, the company will in effect be yours.' She smoothed her skirt over her knees. 'In addition, during the year after buying the shares from my father I will guarantee to make two boats available to carry cargo for you whenever you want – at the usual charges, of course. Even if it means turning down other contracts.'

'By God!' Arkbridge said, and he downed half a glass of Sander's excellent whisky in one draught. 'Who thought that one up? Young Grieve?'

'He knows nothing about it. This is between you and me, as you said when you arranged the meeting.'

'It's your idea? You realise,' he said when she nodded, 'that I only need to wait for a few days more and then pay Lawrence whatever he wants for his shares?'

'Yes, I do realise it. But you're too shrewd to do that, surely? That way, you'd have only a quarter of the shares. My plan would guarantee you the use of two cargo carriers, and either a handsome return on your loan or a major interest in the business at the end of a year.'

315

'I'll consider it.' He set down his empty glass and got up, stuffing the envelope into his pocket.

'And I,' Morag said sweetly, 'will consider your proposition, Mr Arkbridge.'

'Are you quite mad?' Cal wanted to know on the following morning. 'You're handing everything over to Arkbridge on a plate!'

Aidan would have leapt angrily to her defence, but Morag held up a hand to stop him. 'We might be doing that if we agreed to his idea, but my proposition means that we keep control of the company.'

'For a year!'

'We'll have that loan repaid at the end of it, and the interest as well. We can do it, Cal!'

'What if another boiler goes? What if one of the boats founders?'

'You can't run a business on pessimism. If I start letting myself think along those lines, I might as well give up and just sell to Arkbridge here and now.'

'You might as well,' he agreed coldly, 'for the man'll get the better of you long before the year's out!'

She had never seen him so angry. His entire body was tense with rage and his grey eyes flashed fire, reminding her of an opal ring which still lay in Georgina's leather jewel case. As a child, Morag had loved to hold the ring to the light and watch hidden colours sparkle up at her unexpectedly from the stone's milky depths.

'Aidan will draw up a watertight agreement—'

'Watertight!' Cal scoffed. 'For God's sake, Morag! Arkbridge was in business while you were learning your alphabet in the infant class. One way or another, he'll have Weir's well before the end of your year's grace!'

Morag deliberately turned away from him. 'Aidan?'

Cal had reacted so abruptly to her news that the lawyer had not had a chance to speak. Now, he cleared his throat. 'I prefer Mr Arkbridge's option,' he said, and she looked at him in dismay. She had counted on his support, at least.

'Why?'

'Because your idea means that in a year's time—'

'You can be sure it will take less than that!' Cal interrupted, but they both ignored him.

'—you will either have to hand over a considerable sum of money, or you will lose control of Weir Shipping. Surely it would be better to let the man have 25 per cent of the shares now and leave it at that?'

'And all the Weir boats would carry Arkbridge cargoes,' she reminded him. 'He'd more or less own us, even with a small percentage.'

'Does that matter?'

'Of course it matters!' Cal burst out. 'In everyone's eyes, we'd be Arkbridge boats – Arkbridge's lackeys. There has to be another way!'

Aidan bristled. 'I've already explored every avenue.'

'Morag, if you agree to Arkbridge's proposition – or even if he agrees to yours – Weir's will be swallowed up. Is that what you want?'

'You're exaggerating,' Aidan told him icily.

'I know what I'm talking about! That's the mistake my—' he stopped suddenly.

'The mistake your father made,' Morag finished the sentence for him. 'The mistake that leaves me sitting behind this desk instead of you. I'm hardly going to do that.'

All at once the hidden flashes of colour disappeared and his eyes became the same grey as an unfriendly sea on a bitter winter day. His face closed to her. 'Oh, what's the use of talking to the pair of you!' he said explosively and stormed out of the office.

Morag ran round the desk to the door. 'Cal, wait!'

The outer door slammed shut.

'I shouldn't have said that,' she said, stricken.

'If you ask me,' Aidan said, 'you'd be far better with George Arkbridge as a shareholder than Fergusson. The man's far too mercurial.'

'He's a good skipper, and the business did belong to his family. My uncle was right to leave shares to him.'

'My dear girl, there's no room for sentiment in commerce, and I for one am tired of trying to hold meetings with him raging up and down the room and refusing to discuss things rationally.'

'Mebbe I need Cal's mercurial temperament,' Morag said with an attempt at a smile. 'He keeps me in mind of the other side of the argument. And he does care about Weir's.'

'If he really cared, he would try to come up with sensible ways of helping you out of your present troubles.' Aidan began to pack papers into his case. 'Instead, he loses his temper and then storms out of the room like a spoiled brat. It's at times like this that I can see why his family lost control of the business in the first place.'

'That's not fair, Aidan. Cal's father drank and gambled, and he does neither. He puts me in mind more of his great-grandfather Matthew, the man who brought the firm into the family in the first place.'

'I wouldn't know about that,' said Aidan, who had shown total disinterest when she had tried to tell him the story of the figurehead, and Matthew, and Alicia Tollin. 'Are you free tonight?'

'Camellia's telephoning to let me know when she's

arriving. I'll have to stay in – alone,' she added as he started to speak. 'I have things to do.'

'You're always busy these days. You should take a holiday; you look as though you need one. I could take time off and we could go together to Edinburgh,' Aidan suggested, brightening up at the prospect. 'You could stay with my parents; they want to meet you.'

'Perhaps, later.' He had suggested a visit to Edinburgh on several occasions, but she had managed to turn him down gently, so far.

'Christmas will be here in a few weeks. We could go then. Dancing, shopping with my mother, parties; you would enjoy it. Promise me you'll seriously consider it,' he said, and kissed her before finally leaving her in peace.

When he had gone Morag sighed. Now she had more than Weir's and Cal to worry about.

26

Over the next two days Cal wasn't to be seen on the harbour or in the office. Morag was relieved rather than concerned by his absence, which gave them both time to calm down. She assumed that he was at the shipyard, overseeing the final stages of the repair work on the *Pladda*. She herself was busy arranging as many cargoes as she could for the puffers.

When he eventually walked in, he dropped a thick envelope down on the desk before her. 'There it is. The money to buy your father's shares.'

'What?' Morag picked up the envelope and looked inside; it was crammed with bank notes. 'Where did you get these?'

He was still withdrawn, still angry, and he looked as though he had had little sleep since storming out of the board meeting. 'Don't worry,' he said, 'I haven't turned into a gambler, like my father.'

The words hit her like small sharp stones, and she winced.

'Cal, I'm sorry about what I said. I didn't mean—'

'It doesn't really matter. All that matters is buying those shares as soon as possible. Oh . . . and *Pladda* will be back in the harbour tomorrow morning.' He started towards the door.

'Cal! I've surely got a right to know where the money came from,' she said as he swung round on her. 'I must, if I'm going to use it.'

He shrugged. 'I sold my flat. To the bank, for the sake of speed. And I insisted on being paid in notes.'

'You sold your home?'

'It wasn't a wrench. It's never had very happy memories for me. I'll be lodging with Pat Forsyth and his wife; the arrangement suits us all very well. And now,' he put both hands palms down on the desk and leaned towards her, still angry, though she didn't know if it was with her or himself, 'stop wasting time and get those shares from your father before Arkbridge gets in first.'

'It's your money. Why don't you buy them?'

'Because,' Cal said patiently, ignoring the proffered envelope, 'you have first refusal on them until tomorrow. And even if you hadn't, do you seriously think that Lawrence Weir would sell his shares to me? Even if he was willing, he'd push the price up and make me compete with Arkbridge. And my flat wasn't worth the sort of money Arkbridge can pay. *You* have to buy them.'

'And then I'll sign them over to you, the way I was going to sign them over to Mr Arkbridge.'

'I don't want them. They're yours.'

'But . . .'

'I don't want them,' Cal said again, insistently. 'All I want is to make sure that Arkbridge doesn't get them.'

'Cal . . . ?' He stopped at the door as she scrambled from her chair and hurried round the desk. 'Thank you.' She held out her hand. 'I appreciate this more than you will ever know.'

After a moment's hesitation, he took her hand in his.

'The pleasure is mine,' he said, and for a moment the anger faded and the glimmer of a smile appeared in the grey depths of his eyes, like the flashes of colour in the opal ring. Then he let her hand go and said briskly, 'And now I'm going to make sure that they're getting the *Pladda* ready. It's high time she was back on the river.'

Aidan was strongly opposed to Morag's decision to put the shares bought from Lawrence into Cal's name.

'If he's so eager for you to have them, why not just accept that?'

'I'd not feel right. It would be like stealing.'

'Of course it wouldn't. And your life would be easier if you held most of the shares. You would have more power to make decisions.'

'Cal paid for them, and he must have them!' she told him angrily. 'And I'm not going to change my mind.'

Cal was equally annoyed. 'I told you that I didn't want them. I don't even want the parcel your father left to me.'

'You've earned the first lot and paid for the second. In any case, I want you to be a shareholder. It gives me the right to depend on you for advice.'

'You already know that you can have that whenever you want it – and even when you don't want it,' he said with the glimmer that was all she ever saw of his smile these days.

All too soon it had disappeared, and he shook his head when she held out the envelope containing his new shares. 'If you insist, you'd better keep them here or in your home,' he said shortly. 'I've not got the room for them.' And he turned on his heel and left the office.

*　　*　　*

'You look dreadful,' Camellia Ogilvie said flatly when she arrived for her long-awaited visit.

'Thank you, that makes me feel much better.'

'No point in lying; although I would, of course, if you were really ill. Then I'd tell you that you were blooming, just to keep you breathing.' Camellia, Morag was very glad to see, was completely unchanged.

'Why don't you come back to Edinburgh with me and spend Christmas with us?' she suggested during breakfast on the morning after her arrival. 'There's a very tiny spare room in our flat, and Ann would love to see you. We'd make sure that you had a good rest, if that's what you want.'

It sounded tempting, but Morag had to shake her head. 'I can't. Aidan has already asked me to go to Edinburgh to spend Christmas with him at his parents' home, and I refused him.'

'Because you're too busy?'

'Partly.'

'But mainly because you don't want to spend Christmas with him, and meeting his parents means that everything is becoming too serious.'

Morag groaned. 'I seem to have made a mess of things, Camellia. Aidan's a very nice man and a good friend – and a good lawyer. But you're right. I don't want to spend Christmas with him, and I most certainly do not want to spend the rest of my life with him.'

'I could have told you that the first time I ever set eyes on the pair of you.' Camellia buttered a piece of toast as though punishing it for some misdemeanour. 'He needs a submissive society wife, and you need a man who can challenge and stimulate you – and know when to cosset you as well.'

'I don't need a man at all,' Morag told her sharply, adding immediately, 'I'm sorry if that sounded snappish.

323

It's this wedding of Wilma's. She's so happy that she wants everyone else, especially me, to be happy too. And as Wilma sees it, that means falling madly in love and marrying. Sometimes it's hard to listen to.'

'You can't blame her. Love is what most girls want. It's what begets the next generation and keeps the world revolving. Which reminds me – is there any further information about your ships' carvers?'

'No,' Morag said regretfully. 'We've reached the end of the road where that story's concerned. Cal cleared out his flat when he moved to the Forsyths', but he didn't find anything else.'

Morag and Camellia had corresponded with each other ever since the Ogilvies' visit, and the older woman knew all about Cal purchasing Lawrence's shares.

'You must invite him to supper while I'm here. I like Cal. I'd enjoy meeting him again.'

'I doubt if he'll come. He's . . . changed.'

'What happened to make him change?'

Morag got up to pour out more tea; it was the only way she could think of to hide her face from Camellia's sharp eyes. In her letters she had held nothing back – except the night in that very kitchen when she and Cal . . .

The mental defence mechanism she had managed to set up moved smoothly into place, and the memory was swiftly blotted out.

'I think that business of the *Pladda* going on to the reefs dented his pride,' she said, settling herself at the table again. 'And he was angry with me for making him take those shares. You'd think he would be pleased to own a larger slice of the business, since it once belonged to his family. But he's not.'

'Mebbe I'll meet him at the harbour,' Camellia said.

'How are the Forsyths? I'll never forget that man's enthusiasm when he was showing us round his beloved boat. Now *there* was a love affair! I do enjoy meeting people who adore their line of work. It happens so seldom, unfortunately.'

'The Forsyths are both very well, and the captain comes down to the harbour often. He's been out on the *Sanda* once or twice with Archie. He tells me that he and his wife are pleased to have Cal lodging with them; the money comes in useful, of course, and the captain enjoys having someone to talk to about the puffer business.'

'You really must have a party while I'm here, Morag, so that I can meet them all again. Wilma of course, and her young man, and her lovely family. And that handsome brother of hers; I'm longing to meet the beautiful bride he stole from beneath her fiancé's very nose.' She laughed. 'Ann, being such a romantic, loved that story. And the Forsyths, and your fath . . . well, perhaps not your father and step-mother under the circumstances,' she corrected herself. 'But there's Aidan, and I'll invite Cal personally if you'd rather not. And I'll have a word with Aidan Grieve as well, about you coming back to Edinburgh with me. You can meet his parents while you're there, and Ann and I shall go with you for protection. He knows what a stubborn old bird I am; I shall simply tell him that I've bullied you into agreeing to stay with me for Christmas. He has a two-seater motor-car, doesn't he? So he couldn't take both of us, which is a bit of luck. We'll be able to travel to Edinburgh together, you and I, in the train.'

'I must come back here directly after Christmas, for Wilma's wedding.'

'Of course.'

'And I can't leave for another ten days. I'll have to make sure that the business can manage without me for a week, and a paying guest's coming next Monday for two days.'

'Then I'll extend my stay, so that we can travel together. I take it that you can accommodate me and your other guests?'

'Oh, yes. There's only one this time – a man.'

'No wife? A young man?' Camellia pressed as Morag shook her head.

'I have no idea. All I do know is that he's an engineer, called in to do some essential work in the mill, and they couldn't find suitable hotel accommodation for him. There may well be a wife at home. I didn't pry,' Morag said with meaning.

Camellia ignored the hint. 'It's just as well I'm here, then,' she said briskly. 'I can act as chaperone for you. Or, if he happens to be an older gentleman, you can be my chaperone.'

The guest sent by the Ropeworks arrived just as Morag, Camellia and Wilma were preparing to go out on a shopping trip to Gourock, followed by afternoon coffee at Miss Lamont's teashop. Morag and Wilma were in the kitchen and Grace was putting the final touches to the visitor's room upstairs when the doorbell rang. They all went to answer it but Camellia, writing a letter in the parlour, got there first.

'Good afternoon.'

The young man in the porch removed his hat and revealed wavy red hair. 'Good afternoon, my name is Buchan. I understand that Mr Winters of Gourock Ropeworks has booked a room here for me.'

In the space of two seconds Camellia noted that he

had a pleasant, open face, good eye contact, square shoulders and a good clear voice. She would have been happy to recommend him as an employee to any of her clients.

'Do come in,' she beamed, stepping aside and opening the door wide just as Morag and Wilma came into the hall from the kitchen and Grace reached the landing on her way downstairs.

'Thank you.' Mr Buchan picked up his suitcase – smart, leather, nicely monogrammed, Camellia noted – and stepped over the threshold. He put his case down in the hall. 'I'm a little early, but I thought it best to come straight from the station,' he began, then stopped as Grace gave a muffled cry. She halted, clutching the banister, her blue eyes widening until they almost filled her small face.

The new lodger looked up at her and said in wonderment, 'Grace?' Then, throwing his hat aside, *'Grace!'*

He passed Camellia, Morag and Wilma without a second glance and raced up the stairs two at a time. When he reached Grace he swept her into his arms, burying his face in her fair hair.

The three women in the hall looked up at the clasped figures, then at each other in blank astonishment. Camellia was the first to recover.

'Now why,' she asked Morag, 'did you not think to lay on a welcome like that for me?'

There was no trip to Gourock that afternoon. Instead they all ended up in the kitchen, where everything happened these days. Tom Buchan and Grace sat close together, mainly because each was reluctant to move even a table's width from the other.

'It was the biggest mistake I ever made in my life,

listening to you when you told me you'd not marry me,' he said fiercely.

Grace had scarcely said a word, seeming content just to sit and look at her former sweetheart as he told the three of them about their relationship three years earlier, and Bill Hastie's fierce opposition. A cup of tea lay cooling unnoticed in front of her. It seemed to Morag that the girl hadn't yet accepted that Tom was really there in the flesh. But now she put a restraining hand on his arm.

'Tom, don't talk about such things in front of folk!' she protested.

'To bl—' he began, then stopped hurriedly and amended it to, 'I mean, I don't care who's here. The more the merrier! We can do with witnesses. It means that you'll not be able to get away from me so easily this time.'

'Hear, hear!' Camellia approved and he turned back to Grace, encouraged.

'I was younger then, and daft enough to believe that you meant it when you turned me down, even though Danny tried to get me to wait. But things are different now!'

'Why didn't you come back for her when you were settled?' Wilma wanted to know.

'I wrote several times, but you never answered, Grace.'

'Knowing her father, I doubt if the letters ever reached her.'

The girl was shaking her head. 'No, not one. I thought . . . I thought . . .' Her eyes sparkled with sudden tears, and Tom took both her hands in his.

'Danny was right, I should have fought harder for you. But my pride wouldn't let me. Anyway, I was certain you'd found someone else. Look at her,' he appealed to the others, 'would you expect a woman as beautiful as that to remain unmarried for long?'

'I would if she had Bill Hastie for a father,' Wilma said. 'He did everything but imprison her in a tower – and he'd have done that if they had such things as towers in Bouverie Street.'

Tom had taken a snowy handkerchief from his jacket pocket and was dabbing gently at Grace's eyes. 'Don't cry, love,' he begged, and Morag, suddenly reminded of Cal saying something like that to her once, shifted restlessly in her chair as she called up the defence mechanism in her mind. 'It was all my fault, I should have come back for you!'

'Yes, you should,' Wilma told him sharply. 'But at least you're here now, and it's a case of better late than never. You're not married, are you?' she added, struck by a sudden thought. 'Or spoken for?'

'No, of course not. But I was certain Grace must be. I couldn't believe it when I was told I was being sent to Port Glasgow for a few days. I had it in mind to get a hold of Danny while I was in the mill, and find out from him what had happened to Grace. And the very first place I go to when I get off the train . . . there she is!' He beamed round the table at them all. 'It's a miracle!'

'The next miracle,' Wilma said flatly, 'will be getting her away from her father. And you'd better do it properly this time, or you'll have me to answer to. And Danny!'

From all accounts, Bill Hastie fought hard to prevent Grace from becoming engaged to her former lover, but Danny, Tom and Wilma – and, when she had regained her senses, Grace herself – made a formidable team, and the man had no option but to accept the fact that his daughter was going to marry Tom Buchan.

'Now you'll definitely have to have a party, Morag,' Camellia said when Tom and Grace, both radiant, brought the news to Lilybank Road. 'And it will have to be arranged quickly, before Tom returns to England.'

Even Cal accepted his invitation, though Bill Hastie declined.

'The loss is his,' Danny said shortly. 'If he won't accept that Grace and I have as much right to our lives as he's had to his, then that's his worry. He'll have only himself to blame if he's left on his own.'

'He won't be alone in any case, for we'll be just two closes away,' Wilma chimed in. 'And I've no intention of leaving him to his own company. I lost my own father when I was just wee, and now I'll have Danny's in his place.'

Her affianced blinked at her in bemused admiration. 'You're taking on a lot, if you've got a mind to tame that old curmudgeon.'

'I'm of a mind to try it, at any rate,' she retorted coolly.

Tom took Grace to Glasgow a few hours before the party began, to buy an engagement ring, 'To remind that father of hers that she's mine now,' he said as she showed it off. 'And I'll be back to claim her as soon as I've arranged somewhere for us to live.'

'You'll be looking for another housekeeper, Morag. I'll come through and find one for you,' Camellia offered.

'I'll see.' Morag wasn't certain that she wanted to go on taking in paying guests. She didn't quite know what she wanted these days. Watching Wilma and Danny, Archie and Mhairi and Grace and Tom at the party, she wondered where her own life was going.

Even the business, which had been her entire life for the past eighteen months, no longer seemed to be enough.

Camellia was right, she thought. She did need to get away from Port Glasgow for a while.

27

Aidan accepted Morag's decision to stay with Camellia in Edinburgh, rather than with his parents, with bad grace.

'It means that we can't travel there together. Or even back here, because I'm staying until after the New Year and you have to get back home for this dratted wedding,' he said gloomily on the night before she left. 'And goodness knows if we'll get any time on our own while you're there. That friend of yours is very possessive.'

'I don't see her and her sister often,' she said guiltily. 'You and I can see each other every day.'

'Yes, but only with other people around, apparently. You've changed, Morag,' he complained. 'You're always so preoccupied these days.'

'That's what Camellia thinks too. That's why she invited me to Edinburgh. I need a rest.'

'I believe that I know better than Miss Camellia Ogilvie what you need,' he said, reaching for her in the darkness. They had been to their favourite hotel in Largs for dinner, and on the way home he had turned the car off the road and on to a piece of ground overlooking the sea. Even with the windows closed against the cold December air, Morag could hear the soothing hush of waves breaking on pebbles not far away.

Aidan's mouth was warm and eager and his hair, silky beneath her hands, smelled of pine trees. She gave herself up to enjoyment, but when his hands and his lips became more urgent she found herself drawing away. 'Aidan, that's enough.'

'No, it's not,' he whispered. 'Not nearly enough.'

'It is; it has to be. Camellia will be alone in the house. I can't stay away for too long, she's my guest.'

He groaned, then pulled himself upright in his seat and ran his hands through his hair. 'Oh, very well. But you can't put me off much longer, Morag, for I'm crazy about you.'

At the house, which was dark apart from the glow of a hall lamp lighting the glass panels of the door, he opened the car door for her. 'I don't suppose I'll be invited in – in case I wake Camellia.'

'Best not.' She wasn't even sure whether Camellia, who had been invited to spend the evening with the Forsyths, was home yet, but she didn't tell Aidan that. Sometimes guests could be very useful.

Morag let herself into the house quietly, in case Camellia had already arrived home and was in bed. She started towards the stairs, then jumped as the dining-room door creaked open slightly and a spiky grey head appeared through the gap.

'Are you alone?' Camellia hissed.

'Yes.'

'Oh, good!' She emerged, wrapped from head to foot in a woollen dressing-gown. 'I had just got into bed when my stomach decided that it needed cocoa. Then I heard you at the door as I reached the bottom of the stairs, so I rushed to hide in case you were bringing Aidan in for a night-cap.' She gestured to her wrap, which looked as though it had been a favourite garment for many years. 'I didn't want the sight of me in my night attire to inflame his youthful passions. Come and keep me company.'

Without waiting for an answer she waddled off towards the kitchen, her slippers slapping against the linoleum.

Heating milk and measuring cocoa powder and sugar, she chattered on about her evening with the Forsyths. Then, putting the steaming mugs on the table and easing herself into a chair, she asked, 'What have you done to Cal Fergusson?'

'Nothing.'

Camellia gave her what Mags Beckett would have described as an old-fashioned look. 'You were right when you said that he had changed – and not for the better, either. He's lost that air he always had of being completely at ease with himself. He escorted me back here and came in for a wee while, but he was on edge all the time. I got the distinct feeling that he was eager to leave before you came back. You've surely not become such a martinet of an employer that you've terrified the man?'

'He's unhappy about owning almost half of the business,' Morag said, but Camellia dismissed the idea with a flap of the hand.

'It's not that. Well, not entirely, though that does seem to be a problem for him. I can't think why, for if things had gone differently he'd have owned the company himself, and I'm quite sure that he would have run it just as efficiently as you have.'

'More so.'

'Don't throw any red herrings across my path, Morag,' Camellia ordered briskly. 'You're at the root of his problem, and you know why. I can see it in your eyes, so there's no sense in pretending that you don't. You might as well tell me now instead of waiting until I drag it out of you.'

Morag sighed, then said reluctantly, 'If you must know, I kissed him.'

There was a slight pause, then, 'You kissed him,' Camellia repeated thoughtfully. 'You, a spinster of this parish, kissed Cal Fergusson, bachelor of this parish, and he's taken an attack of the vapours over it? He's scarcely a shy little Victorian miss!'

'I didn't just kiss him,' Morag snapped at her, goaded into saying more than she had intended. 'I threw myself at him. I embarrassed him, and myself, and spoiled everything. And I'm a fool, for Cal's friendship meant a lot to me!'

'You threw yourself at Cal,' Camellia mused. 'Somehow I can't quite see you as a femme fatale like Greta Garbo or Marlene Dietrich.'

'Don't you dare laugh at me, Camellia!'

'I'm not,' the older woman protested, though Morag, finally lifting her eyes from her entwined fingers, thought that she caught a glimpse of mirth in the depths of the eyes surveying her from the other side of the table. It was extinguished before she could be absolutely certain. 'Have you told anyone else about this? Wilma?'

'No. I've been too ashamed to talk about it, and in any case Wilma's so busy planning this wedding that we don't spend much time together now.'

'Why don't you tell me?' Camellia coaxed. 'I don't live here, so there's no danger of me telling anyone else. Not that I would in any case. And you need to talk to someone, instead of bottling it all up.'

She was right. Once Morag began to speak the words tumbled out, a flood that she couldn't have dammed if she had wanted to. None of the pleasure of that evening came back to her as she described it, but the self-loathing did, burning her face and making her hands tremble. When she had finally finished, she tried to take a nonchalant sip from her mug. The cocoa splashed over the rim when the mug was only half-way to her lips, and she set it down again, defeated.

'Leave it, it's stone cold by now anyway.' Camellia got up. 'I believe I saw some whisky in that cabinet in the parlour during your party . . .'

When she returned she splashed the whisky into two tumblers and added water from the tap. 'I know that as good Scots we shouldn't dilute a fine malt,' she said, setting down a glass before Morag, 'but since you're not a whisky drinker and we have two train journeys ahead of us tomorrow, we'd best play safe. Lift the tumbler carefully, with both hands. Now then,' she went on as Morag took a sip and coughed at the strength of the watered drink, 'the question is, who kissed who in the first place?'

'I kissed . . . or perhaps he . . .' Morag had pushed the shameful incident to the back of her mind so many times that she had become confused. 'It might have been Cal first, but I was to blame, getting so upset in front of him. He probably had no option.'

'You're very hard on yourself, Morag. Did you enjoy it at the time?'

The unexpected question jerked Morag into an honest answer. 'Yes,' she said and then, hurriedly, 'but . . .'

'Perhaps Cal enjoyed it as well. Have you thought of that?'

'If you'd seen the look on his face just before he walked out,' Morag said bitterly, 'you'd know that that's not true. He was horrified.'

'Mmmmm,' Camellia said, and fell into a reverie.

The kitchen was warm and the whisky, after a dreadful moment when it threatened to rebel and leave Morag's stomach almost as soon as it got there, had settled down and was sending out a comforting glow. Confession had been good for her. She felt at peace with herself for the first time in weeks, and she had almost drifted off into a doze when Camellia finally stirred and spoke.

'Cal's had a hard time of it one way and another. Watching his father disintegrate and turn to drink, being removed from one school and put into another – and quite possibly being taunted in the local school about his father's weaknesses. Children can be very cruel; they learn well, from their parents. Seeing his mother forced to give up her comfortable life, move to a little flat and learn to live on what must have seemed to her to be very little money – knowing that as soon as he was old enough to leave school he must somehow support the two of them . . .'

'It hasn't scarred him. We've both heard him say that he didn't let that happen.'

'I know, it's his past that's made Cal the strong, proud man he is. I feel,' Camellia said thoughtfully, 'that all this business about his great-grandfather and Alicia Tollin has had some effect on him. Matthew Fergusson gained the business through the woman he loved, and now a woman controls it again. Perhaps that's why Cal isn't happy about owning those shares. Perhaps he's being as hard on himself as you, my dear, are on yourself. He's refusing to allow history to come round full circle – which, of course, it does whenever it chooses, time and time again. Mere humans can't stop that happening, but mebbe Cal's refusing to let love for a woman win the business back—'

'Stop it, Camellia!' Morag sat bolt upright, suddenly realising where the conversation was leading. 'You're talking nonsense!'

'Am I?'

'Yes, you are, complete rubbish! When a man loves a woman he does something about it. Look at Danny, working away at Wilma, making her finally acknowledge his existence and fall in love with him. And Archie, risking his own life for Mhairi. And you were there when Tom Buchan set eyes on Grace again. Perhaps he let her go the first time, when they were both too young to defy her father, but he made certain to keep her this time. Cal Fergusson wouldn't hesitate to do the same if he cared two hoots about . . . anyone,' she hastily amended the final word.

'I told you – Cal has a lot of pride. And he can't just throw it aside, because I suspect that his pride is the only thing that's kept him going for a very large part of his life. You have to understand that, Morag, if you want to understand the man himself. Perhaps you need to make the first move. Or . . .' she stopped and gave a massive yawn, 'you could just remain a spinster of this parish, or become a lawyer's wife. The choice must always be yours.' She got up, and stretched.

'And I promise that will be my final word on the subject. Now I'm ready for my bed.'

Edinburgh was enormous, and colourful, and filled with people. It was motor-cars and buses, shops with huge plate-glass windows filled with clothes and toys and pretty winter scenes featuring Father Christmas and his elves packing exciting, mysterious boxes on to sleds drawn by wide-eyed cardboard reindeer. It was the Castle looming over Princes Street from the bluff above, and the boom of the one o'clock gun from the ramparts. It was theatres and smartly dressed people with lilting accents. It was history and elegance and architecture. It was the 'haar' – the bitter wind that swept in from the nearby North Sea to ravage the area almost all the year round.

And, most important of all, it wasn't Port Glasgow.

From the moment she stepped from the train at Waverley Station Morag sank into the city's depths, drowned in it, allowed it to soak into her very pores and enfold her and, for the short time she was there, turn her into an entirely different person. She revelled in the sense of freedom which being away from her usual environment bestowed on her.

She and Camellia and Ann spent all their time talking, shopping, sightseeing, talking again, visiting friends of the Ogilvies and talking. They went together to Aidan's parents' grand house for dinner, and were very well received by his father, an eminent surgeon, and his mother, a society hostess.

'Charming people,' Ann commented afterwards, when they were discussing the visit round the fireplace in the sisters' cosy flat.

'And very kindly disposed towards you, Morag,' said her sister.

'But not your sort of people,' Ann finished decisively.

'And what do you consider to be my sort of people?'

'Down-to-earth people who do something with their lives,' Camellia said at once, and her sister nodded.

'If you married that young man, who so clearly wants to marry you, you'd find yourself running a perfect house and joining your mother-in-law in doing good works and entertaining the right people.'

'That sounds quite attractive, compared with the life I've been leading.'

'You would become very bored almost at once,' Ann insisted. 'You need a challenge. Someone like . . .'

'What she really needs,' Camellia cut in, yawning, 'is a night's sleep. And so do I.'

'You're not you any more,' Aidan said, and Morag laughed.

'That's an improvement, surely?'

'I'm not so certain.'

'It must be. Let's dance again.' She took his hand and drew him back into the throng on the dance-floor. Better to dance than to talk.

She had taken pity on Aidan and agreed to go with him to a Christmas Eve ball. They had gone dancing together a few times in Glasgow but this, she thought as she whirled round in his arms, was so much better. Balloons were suspended from the ceiling high above, waiting to be released at midnight, and the huge ballroom was filled with the fizz and sparkle and chatter of young people celebrating a special occasion. Aidan's parents, and Camellia and Ann, were all going to midnight church services, but Aidan had persuaded Morag to remain at the back with him instead.

As the time approached, waiters and waitresses roamed the room with trays bearing glasses of champagne, and the high windows were opened to let in great draughts of icy air. Some of the young women, bare-armed, pouted and shivered and had to have their escorts' jackets wrapped about their shoulders. Morag, who had brought a wrap with her, shook her head when Aidan eagerly offered her his.

'I'm fine. Listen . . .' The sound of the bells drifted

in through the windows, and a great cheer swept the room as a rainbow of balloons and streamers floated down from the ceiling.

'Happy Christmas, Morag!' Aidan managed, with care, to put one arm about her while his free hand balanced a glass of champagne, and he kissed her.

'Happy Christmas!' They touched glasses, and drank.

'I wish you could have stayed for New Year,' he said for the umpteenth time as they drifted round the dance-floor later. 'You'd really see some celebrations then.'

'So do I.' But even as she told him what he wanted to hear, Morag wasn't sure that she meant it. Edinburgh was wonderful and she had, as Camellia said, badly needed to get away from Port Glasgow. But even while she was enjoying herself with Aidan and Camellia and Ann, part of her had begun to want to go home again.

28

The sun shone on Wilma's wedding day, and the hills on the far side of the Clyde stood out against a blue sky. There had been frost during the night and the air was clear and cold, with a keen edge to it. Like the champagne she had drunk in Edinburgh with Aidan less than a week earlier, Morag thought as she opened the kitchen door and stepped out into the garden.

Frosty patterns had decorated every window in the house when she got up, and out here the hedges bordering the back garden glittered with crystallised spider-webs. It looked as though Mother Nature had tossed a very fine lacy shawl over them, in celebration of Wilma Beckett's special day. Morag stood for a long moment admiring it all, then decided that while it was very bridal, it was also very cold. As she swiftly retreated to the cosy kitchen she decided to put on her warmest underwear beneath her fine wool bridesmaid's dress.

After pulling on a skirt and jersey, she started preparing sandwiches to take to Ardgowan Street. Packets of biscuits and tea and sugar were already waiting in a bag, for there were bound to be a lot of people calling at the Becketts' flat that day and, as the ceremony wasn't taking place until the afternoon, everyone would expect to be fed.

Miss Lamont had agreed to provide the catering for the wedding party in Lilybank Road. When she arrived in a motor-car with two of her most reliable waitresses and a considerable amount of food packed into hampers, Morag left her in charge of the preparations and donned a warm coat before hurrying to Ardgowan Street, her wedding outfit in one bag and the refreshments in another.

As she had expected, the Beckett flat was packed with people. The entire family was there, children and all, and a steady stream of neighbours came and went, bringing gifts and plates of food for the evening reception and lingering to share in the general excitement.

'It's a madhouse, that's what it is . . . a madhouse!' Mags said, battling with the enormous kettle which had refreshed Becketts and visitors for all the years since her marriage.

'Can I do anything to help you?'

'I'm fine, hen. There's plenty of helping hands here. You just make sure our Wilma gets ready in time. Grace is with her already.'

'There's hours to go yet.'

'I know, but you know Wilma. She's that easy-going; she was three days being born. We can't afford to let her take as long to get to the church.'

'I doubt if she'll keep Danny waiting,' Morag assured the harassed mother of the bride.

Wilma lounged on her bed in her dressing-gown, turning the pages of a fashion magazine. 'We're looking for some nice outfits for Grace's wedding,' she explained when Morag went in.

'Think about your own first.'

343

'There's no hurry, I'll be ready in plenty of time. Is there anything to eat? I'm starving!'

When the time came and the three of them were dressed and ready, they went into the kitchen to be greeted with excited gasps from the womenfolk waiting for them.

'Wilma, hen, you've never looked bonnier!' Mrs McNeish from the next close declared, and a dozen heads nodded affirmation. Wilma did indeed look beautiful in her ivory woollen dress, straight-necked and low-waisted, with the skirt caught over the left hip by an ivory satin rosette. In place of a bridal head-dress, she wore an ivory felt cloche hat, narrow-brimmed and with a large bunch of artificial violets pinned at one side, and as there were no fresh flowers to be had at that time of year she was carrying a Victorian posy of artificial violets with trailing lilac ribbons.

Morag and Grace carried similar, smaller posies, but without the ribbons. They were both dressed in lilac, which went well – to Morag's surprise – with her auburn hair, and their neat-fitting hats had wider, down-turned brims and were trimmed with ivory ribbon.

'You're a picture, Wilma!' Mags Beckett, in navy blue with a hat that resembled a flower-pot, drank in the sight of her daughter in all her finery. 'The three of you look so . . .' Her eyes suddenly glittered with tears, and she fumbled in her best handbag for her handkerchief.

'Now don't start crying before you even get to the church, Mam,' Wilma begged.

'It's not that, it's our Daisy. She'd have loved tae have been here tae see . . .'

'Oh, Mam!' Wilma threw her arms about her mother, the ready tears spilling down her own cheeks, and for several minutes the room was like bedlam with some neighbours throwing their arms about mother and daughter and adding their own tears, while others bustled about fetching glasses of water and suggesting remedies from smelling-salts and burning feathers under noses to 'a wee sip of brandy'.

The menfolk looked on, embarrassed, and the younger children – bewildered by the speed with which happiness had turned to sorrow – burst into tears and ran to tug skirts and demand to be lifted and comforted. Morag, appalled at the prospect of Danny's happiness being ruined by the appearance of a tipsy bride with eyes reddened by liberal applications of smelling-salts and burned feathers, frantically tried to calm everyone.

It took some time, but she and Grace finally managed to restore order and mop up the tears without the need to resort to any drastic measures. The two of them then set about smoothing powder over Mags' and Wilma's damp faces, while the children were calmed by their mothers and the men began to breathe easily again.

'Do I look terrible?' Wilma wanted to know, flying to a wall mirror as soon as Morag finished wielding the powder-puff.

'You look lovely!' It was true; the bout of crying had given the girl's eyes a wide, dewy softness which only added to her beauty.

'I'm sorry, pet.' Mags gave one last sniff and stuffed her handkerchief back into her bag. 'I just had tae have that wee moment for the lassie's memory. But from now on it's you I'll be cryin' for, Wilma.'

'Oh, Mam, don't say that! This is supposed to be the happiest day of my life, and I don't want you weeping all over it. Oh, would you look at this! Isn't it beautiful?'

Wilma went into transports of delight as Morag helped her into the sealskin jacket which had once

been Georgina Weir's pride and joy. 'It feels so . . .
rich! Look, Mam!'

The last of Mags' tears vanished as she stroked the
lush fur. 'It's lovely, hen. Danny'll think he's marryin'
royalty, so he will!'

'And it meant that I could put on my really nice
underwear instead of having to wear my woollen vest,'
Wilma said happily

As was only to be expected, the word 'underwear'
caused Archie to make some remark to his brothers
under his breath. They laughed heartily, glad that the
mood had risen again, and Archie had his ears boxed
by his mother who had sharp hearing.

Ignoring the noise, Wilma threw her arms about
Morag and hugged her tightly. 'You're such a good
friend to me! I hope,' she whispered, 'that one day
you'll be as happy as I am!'

Unlike most brides, she arrived at the church five
minutes early. 'Danny'll think I'm being over-eager,'
she fretted as Morag and Grace helped her off with
the fur jacket, which was not being worn during the
service, and tweaked at her dress, making sure that it
was hanging correctly.

'Of course he won't,' Grace assured her, holding a
small mirror steady so that Wilma could make sure that
her hat was on straight.

'It's the truth, anyway. Isn't it a blessing that short
hair's in style just now?' Wilma poked at a curl.
'Imagine having to deal with a huge lump of hair at
a time like this! Where's my posy?'

Then the organ was playing and they were walking
down the aisle towards Danny and Cal, who was the
best man, both of them so smart and well-groomed as
to be almost unrecognisable.

Although the church was cold, Wilma and Danny

346

gave off such a glow of happiness that Morag could almost feel its heat. Grace glowed too, and as the wedding service progressed Morag could see that beneath the shelter of her posy the girl was fiddling with the ring Tom Buchan had placed on her finger. She felt that she and Cal – standing rock-steady one step behind Danny, his face sombre and his hands clasped loosely before him – were like shadows beside such radiance.

When the ceremony came to its close Danny and Wilma, husband and wife, kissed in a circumspect manner before walking back down the aisle together. Morag followed, her hand on Cal's arm, then came Grace with Wilma's eldest brother Robbie who had given her away. Mags was escorted by Bill Hastie, who had been alone in a front pew throughout the ceremony. Outside, he remained slightly apart from the others, giving in with a bad grace when Mags dragged him bodily into the group posing for photographs.

As well as the Beckett family, all the members of the rowing and harriers' clubs came to the reception at Lilybank Road, together with their wives or sweethearts. The house was filled to bursting, with people crowding into the hall, parlour, dining-room and kitchen, and even sitting on the stairs. Miss Lamont and her waitresses were hard put to it to manage, but within five minutes of arriving Mags had shed her hat and coat, found an apron large enough to go round her ample waist and started working alongside them.

'You're not supposed to work today, you're the mother of the bride,' Morag protested when she and Mags met at the kitchen door.

'Ach, it's not in my nature tae sit around like a lady when there's work tae be done, hen. Now let me by before these sausage rolls go cold.'

Someone had brought a gramophone and a pile of

records and, once the food had been eaten and the happy couple's health had been drunk and Danny had replied briefly and bashfully on behalf of himself and his wife, a dozen young men pushed the parlour furniture back to the walls and rolled up the carpet to make a small dance-floor.

As partner after partner demanded a dance, Morag silently blessed Aidan for introducing her to the basic popular dance-steps. Edging about – for the lack of space made it impossible to whirl or spin, even to catchy tunes like 'I Can't Give You Anything But Love, Baby' – she was glad that the lawyer was safely in Edinburgh. He would surely have felt quite out of his depth in this noisy, perspiring, happy throng.

She wondered, as her partner of the moment crushed her to his waistcoat, stepped on her toes and yelled, 'Grand party, isn't it?' into her ear, which world she herself belonged to: Aidan's, with the sense of security and permanence that only wealth could provide, or the one she was in now?

The dance ended and she thanked her red-faced partner before making her way, thankfully, towards an empty upright chair by the wall. But before she reached it Archie waylaid her. 'My turn now. We haven't danced yet.'

'Archie, I'm exhausted.' She fanned her hot face with a hand. 'We'll dance later.'

'We'll have to dance now, while Mhairi's away powdering her nose. I'm only dancing with her when she's here,' he explained, sweeping her away from the chair as the gramophone's owner finished winding it up and the strains of the next record began to throb. As he ploughed his way through the others Morag, clutched to his broad chest with no more control over her own movements than a rag doll would have had, decided that when all was said and done, she preferred this life to any that Aidan could offer.

'You've done Wilma and Danny proud,' Cal said when he finally came to claim a dance. By then most of the younger folk had decamped to the kitchen in search of cooling drinks, and the parlour was quieter. On the gramophone a man was crooning 'Just One More Chance', allowing them to move slowly and easily. Which was just as well, for neither she nor Cal were expert dancers.

'They deserve it. It's grand to see her looking so happy.'

'And him. And Grace,' he added. 'It'll be her turn soon, then she'll be off to England with Buchan. I wonder what the old man'll do then?' He gave a swift jerk of his head to indicate Bill Hastie, sitting alone on an upright chair against the wall.

'I've a feeling that Mrs Beckett's already decided to take him under her wing.' Morag had noticed Mags Beckett making sure that her new son-in-law's father was offered a steady supply of food, and constant refills for the glass in his hand.

'You don't mean that she's got her eye on him?'

She laughed aloud at the look on his face. 'Of course not. She's just taking him under her wing, the way she does with everyone.' The way she did with me, she thought with a rush of affection for the woman. If it hadn't been for Wilma and her mother, her life might well have been empty and meaningless.

'She'll have a job,' Cal said in amusement.

'Not her. But Mr Hastie might! If Wilma and her mother decide to look after him, they'll do it whether he likes it or not. Then,' she added with some satisfaction, thinking of Grace's wan face and nervous manner on the day she visited Bouverie Street to offer the

349

girl work, 'he'll find out what it's like to be under someone's thumb.'

'He reminds me of Jacob Marley's ghost, sitting there,' Cal murmured, laughter bubbling into his voice. 'All he needs are the chains.'

They were the only two people dancing now, and in order to keep his comments from being overhead he had to whisper into her ear. His mouth brushed against her earlobe and Morag stiffened in his arms, remembering the last time that had happened. Such a wave of longing for him swept over her that she felt weak. Just then the music stopped and Cal drew away from her.

'You look hot. Would you like something to drink?'

'Lemonade, if there's any left.' She sank down on to a chair and watched him disappear into the hall. Bill Hastie's eyes – impassive, black and flat – were on her face. She summoned up a smile. 'It's hot,' she said, smoothing her hands over her flushed cheeks, wondering if the old man could see into her mind.

'Aye.' He got to his feet, put his half-full glass down and held out his hand. 'I'm away home now. Thank you for your hospitality.'

'But it's early yet, Mr Hastie. Are you not coming to the Becketts' with us to see the New Year in?'

'I'm an early riser. I retire early, whatever the time of year.' His hand was hard and callused.

At eleven o'clock the party ended, to suit those who – like Mags Beckett – preferred to be in their own homes to welcome in the New Year. Most of the guests departed and the rest walked down to Ardgowan Street, carrying what was left of the food and drink.

'What about the mess your house has been left in?' Cal wanted to know on the way.

'I'm staying with Mrs Beckett tonight, and she's coming back with me tomorrow morning to put it to rights.'

'I'll come along too,' he said. 'You'll need someone to move the furniture.'

They were turning into Ardgowan Street by the time they realised that the bride and groom had disappeared, melting discreetly into the night to start their married life alone together in their own newly decorated and furnished flat.

'Ach!' Archie was disgruntled to find that his victims had slipped through his fingers. 'We'd a grand send-off all ready for them when the right time came, too. I've a good mind tae follow them and give it tae them anyway.'

'You'll do nothing of the sort,' his mother said, scandalised. 'You leave those two young souls alone.'

'We can always keep the send-off for you when it's your turn, Archie,' Robbie suggested.

'You'd better . . . I'll be looking forward tae it. By God, it's cold!' said Archie, and with a sudden bellow he lunged along the pavement towards the rest of the women and the children who were walking sedately at the front of the procession. They scattered, screaming, as he landed in their midst and plucked Mhairi off her feet.

'Come on, woman, come home and warm me!' he roared, and went off down the street with his fiancée face-down over his shoulder, screaming with laughter as she flailed at his broad back with her fists.

'Will you stop giving me a red face, our Archie?' his mother yelled after him. Then, with a fond smile, 'He's that like his father!'

The flat was so crowded, this time with neighbours, that there was no space for dancing here, and in any case the gramophone had gone home with its owner. The cold air blowing through the windows, opened to catch the sound of the bells ringing in 1932, was more than welcome. When midnight came, there was such a concerted howl of 'Happy New Year!' that Morag half expected the plaster to come down from the cracked ceiling.

An elderly man standing nearby scooped her into his sweaty, alcoholic embrace and kissed her soundly before passing her on to the next person. She was passed through the room from one to another, men and women alike, her feet scarcely touching the floor, kissing and being kissed until she was breathless.

It was a good five minutes after midnight before she turned automatically, arms outstretched after being hugged and released for the umpteenth time, and found herself face to face with Cal. For a moment they both hesitated, then Morag took a deep breath, said, 'Happy New Year to you, Cal,' and lifted her mouth up towards his.

His hands were firm on her shoulders. 'Happy New Year, Morag,' he said, and stooped to deliver a brief, chaste kiss on her cheek.

29

Cal was waiting at the gate in Lilybank Road when Morag, Mrs Beckett and the Beckett sons and son-in-law, who had been ordered to report for duty at ten o'clock – 'And never mind moaning about it being Ne'erday; it'll stop you from drinkin' too much and that can only be a good thing,' Mags had told them all the night before – arrived, together with the Beckett wives and their children.

There were so many of them that the house was put to rights in no time at all. Once Mags was satisfied, she dismissed her brood and insisted on taking Morag back with her to Ardgowan Street for her mid-day meal.

'You too, Cal. The rest of them'll be coming tonight for their dinner, so it'll only be me and Morag just now.'

He escorted them back to Ardgowan Street but declined the invitation, saying that Mrs Forsyth expected him back for his meal.

'He's a nice laddie, that,' Mags said as they watched him go down the street with his easy, loping walk. 'A wee bit quiet, though. He needs a life of his own.'

The house was eerily silent and empty when Morag returned to it later in the afternoon. She could have

353

stayed with Mrs Beckett and been part of the evening festivities, but she had decided to catch up on some bookwork for the firm and had made up her mind to write to Camellia with a detailed description of the wedding. Instead, she closed the ledgers and pushed them away, then left the letter only half-written while she roamed the house room by room, unable to settle.

A new year, a new beginning . . . the words kept runnng through her mind. She had thought that she had her new beginning when she took over the shipping business, and started taking in paying guests, but all at once these beginnings weren't enough.

As darkness fell, she went back to the writing desk and selected a fresh sheet of paper.

Morag made a point of going to the harbour early on the following morning, but even so Cal was there before her, overseeing loading operations on the *Pladda*. He came into the office before he left to check the list with her.

'And the crew's finally arrived. Still half-asleep, but at least they're on their feet,' he said tersely. Her heart sank. She had hoped, when he let his guard down during the wedding and while he helped to get her house in order again, that the tensions between them were easing, but today he was as remote as ever. 'We'll be back by late afternoon.'

'Cal, there's something I want to show you before you go.'

'Tomorrow,' he said over his shoulder as he made for the door. 'If I don't get that lot on the water they'll either fall asleep or disappear into the nearest pub.'

'Cal!' But he was gone, and frustrated and angry

though she was there was nothing she could do about it, short of running after him and causing a scene in front of a harbour full of men.

Darkness fell and the normal time for Morag's departure from the office came and went. She was waiting for the *Pladda* to return, determined not to leave until she had told Cal about the decisions she had made the day before.

She was at the small window overlooking the harbour when the puffer's squat shadow, dimly lit by a lamp hanging from the mast, slid into place alongside the harbour wall. Wee Malky jumped ashore and took the rope his father threw him, then the others came ashore once the boat had been made fast. The dockers had long since gone home, so the unloading would have to wait until the next morning.

Morag went back to her desk and waited, trusting that Cal would come in when he saw the office light burning. After a few minutes she heard his familiar step on the stairs.

'You're staying late tonight.'

'I'd some work to catch up on,' she lied. 'Did the trip go well?'

'Aye.' He dropped some papers on the desk. 'Farm machinery delivered, and some furniture brought back.'

'No bride this time?'

The ghost of a smile flickered across his face. 'I leave that sort of nonsense to the likes of Archie Beckett. The furniture'll be unloaded and collected first thing in the morning.' He stretched, bending his arms slightly so that his clenched fists didn't knock against the low ceiling. 'I'll walk you home if you're ready to go.'

'There's just one last thing to see to.' She took an envelope from the drawer and handed to him. 'This is for you.'

He took it, frowning. 'For me? What is it?'

'A New Year's gift.' Morag went to fetch her coat from the stand.

Surprise turned to embarrassment. 'But I didn't . . . I never . . .'

'You already gave me my gift, Cal, when you bought those shares from my father.'

'Even so—'

'Are you not going to open it?' she asked and waited, holding her breath, as he tore open the envelope and scanned the few lines she had written on the single sheet of paper.

After an agonisingly long time he asked, his voice cold, 'What are you playing at, Morag?'

'I'm not playing at anything. As the letter says, I'm making you a gift of five per cent of my shares in Weir Shipping. When Aidan comes back from Edinburgh next week, I'll get him to draw up the necessary paperwork.'

'But that means—'

'That you and I will have an equal number of shares,' she agreed, beginning to button her coat with fingers that shook. 'We'll be equal partners.'

'I can't accept this!'

'You deserve it. It was you who supported me when nobody else did. You believed in me when my own father was trying to destroy me, and you saw me through the business with John Laird.' She faced him squarely. 'You've worked hard for this company, Cal. You even sold your home to save Weir Shipping. I only inherited my shares, but you've earned every one of yours. All fifty per cent of them.'

His face was dark. 'I can't accept them.' He thrust the letter at her. 'I *don't* accept them!'

Morag started pulling on a glove. 'Why not, Cal? Because your great-grandfather Matthew's looking over your shoulder like . . . like Jacob Marley's ghost?'

'Don't be ridiculous!'

'I can't think of any other reason. Matthew and Alicia belong to the past. You and I are now, and our children could be the future!' She knew as she spoke that Camellia had been right. Cal was locked in combat with ghosts from the past, while she was fighting for the future – their future. She realised that somewhere along the way she had stopped talking about a business partnership and started referring to marriage. She was saying far more than was wise, but this was surely her last chance to get through to him. She had everything to win and nothing to lose.

'I'm thinking of your best interests,' he said harshly, 'and Grieve will have to do the same. He'll never allow you to sign away any of your shares.'

'Aidan's my lawyer, not my keeper. He'll have to do as I say. If he refuses, I'll find another lawyer. I don't care what he thinks,' Morag said passionately, still wrestling with the glove. 'And before you remind me of it, I can tell you that I know very well that my father'll whisper about us, and gossip and spread malicious rumours. But I don't care about him either, because I've got nothing to hide and neither have you. I'm taking control of my own life, Cal, however much that might upset other folk. Why can't you do the same?'

'Perhaps I am. Perhaps I'm doing just that, when I say that I'll not take those shares.'

Her fingers just refused to fit into the glove properly. Exasperated beyond measure by material and man, both

357

completely inflexible, Morag tossed her gloves aside and picked up her bag.

'Dammit, Cal, if you won't accept the shares as your right, then have them as a . . . a . . . a wedding present!'

He looked at her as though she was going mad before his eyes. If the situation hadn't been so serious, she thought, if she hadn't been fighting for everything that mattered to her, she might have started to laugh.

'I'm not getting married,' he said, bewildered.

'How do you know? It's in the air these days. Though with Wilma wed and Grace promised, it looks as though the only possibility left to you would be me, and at this precise moment' – she swept to the door – 'I would probably refuse you. Put the lights out when you leave.'

It was very cold outside. Behind her, as she stopped on the cement platform, the town was lit against the darkness, but before her the harbour was a great empty sweep only dimly lit by lamp standards here and there. One, situated at the corner of the office building, shone on Lady Isabella keeping her eternal, lonely vigil.

Morag rested her face on the painted wood and closed her eyes, remembering her childhood and Sander's promise that the figurehead could grant wishes. 'Oh, Isabella,' she said miserably. 'Make Cal understand what's best for both of us! Please!'

Sugar mice and liquorice straps had been one thing, but the future was quite another. Even so, Morag wouldn't let herself give up hope entirely. The painted wood was icy cold against her face as she began to count backwards from fifty. If he hadn't come downstairs by the time she had finished, she would go home, alone.

She had reached ten and was beginning to despair

when she heard Cal hurrying down the stairs like a man who had suddenly forgotten something very important. He erupted on to the platform, halting on the first of the two steps to stare out over the empty stretch of harbour. Then he swung round to look towards the town, and saw her.

'What are you doing there?'

'Waiting for you. And freezing to death,' she added, folding her arms and tucking her hands under. She wished that she hadn't cast her gloves aside so impetuously before leaving the office.

He came across the small platform and put his hands on her shoulders. The lamp shone on his face, emphasising the furrowed lines between his brows.

'Morag Weir . . .' His voice cracked slightly on the second word, as though he wasn't sure whether to laugh or cry. 'Are you completely daft?'

His breath, and hers, crystallised into steam, two white puffs of smoke meeting and mingling in the winter night.

'Not completely,' she said, hope beginning to stir. 'Not enough to refuse you.'

The frown melted and the heart-stopping grin which had been missing for so long started to appear. At sight of it the glow she had once known with him, then lost, began to kindle again. It caught hold swiftly; all at once it was so strong that she felt as though she must be giving off rays like a lighthouse.

'But just daft enough,' she said, 'to accept.'

Bibliography

The Gourock by George Blake
The Light in the Glens – The Rise and Fall of the Puffer Trade by Len Paterson
Memories of the Clyde – the Duchess of Fife by Hart, Maclagan and Will
The Clyde Puffer by Dan McDonald
Puffer Ahoy! by George W. Burrows
British Figurehead & Ship Carvers by P.N. Thomas

7198